THE EAST WIND

ALEXANDRIA WARWICK

SIMON & SCHUSTER

London · New York · Amsterdam/Antwerp · Sydney/Melbourne · Toronto · New Delhi

First published in the Australia by Simon & Schuster Australia, 2025
First published in Great Britain by Solstice Books, an imprint of Simon & Schuster UK Ltd, 2026

Copyright © Alexandria Warwick, 2025

The right of Alexandria Warwick to be identified as author
of this work has been asserted in accordance with the
Copyright, Designs and Patents Act, 1988.

1 3 5 7 9 10 8 6 4 2

Simon & Schuster UK Ltd, 1st Floor
222 Gray's Inn Road, London WC1X 8HB

For more than 100 years, Simon & Schuster has championed authors and the stories they create. By respecting the copyright of an author's intellectual property, you enable Simon & Schuster and the author to continue publishing exceptional books for years to come. We thank you for supporting the author's copyright by purchasing an authorised edition of this book.

No amount of this book may be reproduced or stored in any format, nor may it be uploaded to any website, database, language-learning model, or other repository, retrieval, or artificial intelligence system without express permission. All rights reserved. Enquiries may be directed to Simon & Schuster, 222 Gray's Inn Road, London WC1X 8HB or RightsMailbox@simonandschuster.co.uk

Simon & Schuster Australia, Sydney
Simon & Schuster India, New Delhi

www.simonandschuster.co.uk
www.simonandschuster.com.au
www.simonandschuster.co.in

The authorised representative in the EEA is Simon & Schuster Netherlands BV,
Herculesplein 96, 3584 AA Utrecht, Netherlands. info@simonandschuster.nl

Simon & Schuster strongly believes in freedom of expression and stands against
censorship in all its forms. For more information, visit BooksBelong.com

A CIP catalogue record for this book
is available from the British Library

Hardback ISBN: 978-1-3985-3369-1
Trade Paperback ISBN: 978-1-3985-3387-5
eBook ISBN: 978-1-3985-3263-2
Audio ISBN: 978-1-3985-3264-9

This book is a work of fiction. Names, characters, places and incidents are either
a product of the author's imagination or are used fictitiously. Any resemblance to
actual people living or dead, events or locales is entirely coincidental.

Cover design and illustration © 2025 Story Wrappers LLC
Map by Robert Lazzaretti
Typeset by Midland Typesetters, Australia

Printed and Bound in the UK using 100% Renewable Electricity
at CPI Group (UK) Ltd

For Jon, love of my life

Part 1

What the Water Takes

1

From the northern tower, there comes a scream.

I pause amidst chopping herbs. The spacious, stone-walled workshop at the rear of the estate coaxes forth the crumbling sound. Moments later, a second cry follows, a hoarse shriek of harrowing pain.

A thread of unease slinks through me, and I glance toward the narrow staircase where Lady Clarisse vanished hours before. The screams should not trouble me. They are frequent, expected, wrenched from all manner of prisoner my employer has confined in the cells below the estate. But these particular sounds arise from the northern tower. And the northern tower is seldom used.

I glance down at my unfinished work as the distant chapel bell tolls the eleventh hour. Today's delivery must be made before noon. According to the bell, I am already behind.

Lover's Dream, one of the apothecary's most popular teas, begins with four parts golden ash to one part larkspore, followed by a sprinkling of sleeping grass. After combining the ingredients into the small pot of liquid boiling atop the stove, I set it aside to cool before shifting my attention to Bones of Stone: two parts oleander, one part white clay, two parts griffin saliva.

Recent illness sapped the village mason of his strength. He now requires something potent enough to grant him the ability to lift entire homes by himself. I work as quickly as I'm able to without slicing off my finger. The only thing Lady Clarisse loathes more than tardiness is incompetence.

The slap of footsteps reaches me, and I stiffen. From the corner of my eye, I watch my employer emerge from the stairwell and march gleefully toward a large metal basin tucked in the far corner. Her blood-spattered dress swings about her slender calves as she proceeds to wash the crimson from her hands.

"I assume, Min," Lady Clarisse drawls without looking at me, "that the lack of chopping indicates your work is complete?" Water gushes from the metal pump, smacks against the brick floor surrounding the basin. Blood smears the hardened clay in red.

I resume slicing the oleander stems. A sticky white substance wells from the incision. Alone, it is toxic to mortals, but when mixed with griffin saliva, it is able to restore eyesight, grant incredible strength, and enhance healing, amongst other things.

"Lover's Dream is ready for the final ingredient," I say.

Lady Clarisse huffs with irritation, yet dries her hands and moves toward the locked cupboard, which I'm forbidden from accessing due to the prized nature of the contents held inside. After unlocking the door, she pulls a glass bottle and pipette from the shelf before squeezing two pearly drops into the cooling liquid. Lover's Dream: a draught promising everlasting love. One part larkspore, four parts golden ash, a sprinkling of sleeping grass—and sea-nymph tears, procured between the hours of midnight and dawn.

Lady Clarisse is neither god nor saint, but she certainly acts like one. *Lady Clarisse's Apothecary* supplies the villagers of St. Laurent with miracles daily. But to do so, she must twist an elixir's elements until it becomes something else entirely, a form of dried, pressed, or distilled power that once belonged to those immortal beings.

For that is who occupies the cells belowground: immortals. She snags their hearts, peels the hard-as-diamond nails from their fingers, squirts the juices from their eyes. She steals their hair, flaxen and ebony and flame, makes brews from their blood, bottles their voices—whispers and confessions and pleas.

From these components, her ladyship crafts the most remarkable teas. She promises undying love, miraculous healings, impossible swiftness of the feet. But the brightest jewels are her timeless beauty teas, which repair all manner of damage to the face, including natural aging. Lady Clarisse appears just shy of her third decade, though only I know that she is well into her fifth.

As the steam clears from Lover's Dream, her ladyship narrows her eyes. "What is this?"

My attention shifts to the cooling liquid. According to *The Practice of Herbal Remedies*, the brew should be a bright shade of violet, but the color is more akin to lavender.

I wipe my palms on the front of my apron. *Breathe, Min.* "We w-were out of sleeping grass," I explain. "I substituted it f-for charred fennel—"

"What have I told you about substitutions?" she snarls.

Two, three, four heartbeats pass before I'm able to speak. "That you n-never w-w-want to see them in y-your presence."

"So why have you ruined my tea with them?"

Generally, one may substitute sleeping grass with charred fennel without issue. "*The Practice of Herbal Remedies* s-states . . ."

Her ladyship's milk-white skin curdles into a mottled shade of red. She snatches the frayed, self-bound manual from where it rests on the counter. "This?" she hisses. "This is what you are referring to?" She shakes it so hard a page tears free, and I inhale sharply, worried Nan's old book will fall to pieces. Along with a cookbook and a religious tome depicting the deities of Jinsan, this is one of the few things Nan left to me.

"Let me remind you that you work for *me* now. So whatever that old woman taught you, banish it from your thoughts." Lady Clarisse tosses the manual onto the worktable where I have set various herbs out to dry. I hurriedly shove it into my apron pocket. "The next time I see that stupid book," she seethes, "I will throw it into the fire."

I drop my gaze. "Y-yes, my lady."

She shunts me aside to mix additional ingredients into Lover's Dream, likely to fix my error. Briefly, she stirs a pot simmering on the back burner, an unidentifiable tea she has been nurturing for weeks now. "Fetch me breath-of-a-saint. And make haste."

I stumble through the back door, down the sagging steps, to the garden at the rear of the estate. A chill wind bites at my stockings, and a whiff of salt-soaked air cuts through the bright crispness of autumn. The estate clings to the cliffside like a barnacle. Eastward lies the sea, though I avoid peering in that direction if I can help it. To the west, the beech trees bordering the property have begun to rust.

The garden is all snarling bramble and climbing weeds. A short, rotting fence surrounds the plots of vegetables and herbs. I bang at the gate until the latch unsticks. Nan would be horrified to see this level of neglect. Always, the land must be tended to, otherwise the Mother of Earth will not provide. Then again, Nan is long gone, only my memories a reminder of our time together. What I wouldn't give to feel my grandmother's embrace again.

I make a note to replace the gate latch before returning to the workshop with the requested cutting. Her ladyship is busy pouring dried herbs into a small woven bag stamped with the words: *Lady Clarisse's Apothecary.*

"I will be heading into town shortly," she says, her back to me. "I expect your work to be complete by the time I return."

Not that it's any of my business, but Lady Clarisse rarely ventures into town so late in the week. "Are there additional supplies you need? I'm happy to go in your stead."

"This has nothing to do with inventory." She snatches the breath-of-a-saint from my hand, tossing it into the pot. The tea's lavender shade deepens to violet. "I'm meeting with someone about selling the estate."

A low, incessant drone begins to flood my eardrums, not unlike a swarm of bees. "You're s-selling the estate?"

"Yes." She sounds positively charmed. Giddy, almost. "I'm tired of this dump. It's too far from town, too expensive to maintain, and business suffers as a result. It's time for something new." Grabbing a small flask, she fills it with Lover's Dream, then stoppers it. "Imagine:

a shop on Market Street. No, *two* shops, a whole slew of them!" Her soft, girlish laugh tinkles the air. "I deserve this."

Color bleeds hot across my pale cheeks. It feels as though her ladyship has taken a pitchfork and rammed it straight through my chest. What is left? A heart full of holes.

I love the estate dearly. How can I not? I've lived the last sixteen years of my life amongst its wild grounds. Nan took me in—a young girl of six—when my mother failed to care for me. I've lived here ever since.

"I don't understand," I croak. "How will y-y-you—"

"What have I told you about your incoherency? Speak clearly, or do not speak at all."

I swallow down all the mangled bits and fractured words. "How—" I pause. "How w-will you find enough land to grow everything required for the business? Moving into town means higher property taxes, l-less space, and—"

My employer whirls around, regarding me with familiar disdain. "When I want your opinion, Min, I will ask for it."

I fall mute. Lady Clarisse's name may be marked upon the deed to the estate, but she does not love this place as I do. To her, the narrow stairs are a nuisance. The kitchen is cramped, outdated. She despises the wallpaper, yet has never made an effort to replace it.

The estate is not perfect, but it is home. It is here I first learned to create teas, a child standing only as tall as Nan's hip. My grandmother loved the land, loved the character of the warped floorboards and creaking beams, though both the landscape and architecture of St. Laurent differed greatly from her homeland. Following Nan's passing, Lady Clarisse was kind enough to allow me to stay on as an employee, after having bought the estate in a private sale. If it is sold, I will lose Nan's crushed ginger fragrance, which still lingers in certain rooms. I will lose, too, those memories of belonging, of *Nan*. "My lady—"

"Come here, Min."

My pulse scatters, a wild-eyed beat bruising my sternum. Head bowed, I shuffle across the room, skirting the small woodfire stove.

Selecting a flower stalk from a nearby vase, she holds it up for my perusal. "Identify."

How can she expect me to focus after informing me I will lose my home? I try to concentrate on the flower, its spherical head. "Handmaiden's basket."

She dips her chin in satisfaction. "Uses?"

"It is a natural blood thinner. When picked after the frost, the petals may be used as a temporary stimulant."

"And?"

Was there a third use? Not that I can recall. I have scoured *The Practice of Herbal Remedies* and committed its instructions to memory. There is no third use, which means this is a test.

"There is none," I state firmly. Only when she returns the bloom to the vase do my lungs loosen.

"Adequate," she says, though the curtness with which she speaks suggests otherwise. "But tell me, what do you get when you combine handmaiden's basket with three wings from the sand dusk moth?"

A decade I have worked for her ladyship, yet I am still no more than a lowly apprentice despite my twenty-two years of age. She does not trust me to handle the immortal-born ingredients, secured always under lock and key. She believes me incompetent. At this rate, I will never become a full-fledged bane weaver. "I don't know," I whisper.

"Of course you don't." Pityingly, she smiles. "I see this is too complex for you, but I suppose I should not be surprised. Some of us are destined for greatness. Others, unfortunately, are only fit for chopping herbs."

My tongue falls slack behind my teeth. She is correct. Someone needs to chop herbs—and I am adequate at the job.

Lady Clarisse shifts her focus elsewhere, much to my relief. "I'll need you to bring the prisoner in the northern tower his meal while I'm out," she states, snagging her sweater from the wall hook and shrugging it on. "Can I trust you to do this properly?"

I straighten in surprise. Each day, I bring meals to the prisoners in the cells below. Never this one. Never the northern tower. "Yes, my lady."

Satisfied, her ladyship brushes past me. She has nearly reached the front door when my foolhardy tongue decides to expose itself. "Are y-you sure this is the best w-way to go about things?"

She halts in place, spine rigid. "Excuse me?" Slowly, she turns to face me, strands of her black tresses pulling free of the low tail hanging down her back.

My fingers clamp the rough cotton of my apron. I force them to loosen, though I cannot mask their trembling. "The prisoner." I lick my lips. "It's b-b-been three months since he w-was captured. If you have b-been unable to glean whatever information you n-need from h-him, might it be possible that he doesn't kn-kn-know anything?"

The vacuity of her expression is one I know well. I have irked her, or made a nuisance of myself, or both. "And what makes you think you have the authority to question my work?"

I drop my eyes. "I apologize, m-my lady. I did not mean to imply th-that I have authority over anything." All of it, every hoarsened word, uttered in a breathless rush. "I am only concerned that th-th-these attempts will lead to d-disappointment, and I would not want your efforts to go to w-waste."

Breath held, I peer upward through my eyelashes. With pursed lips, her ladyship wanders nearer, considering what I have said.

Luckily, she is lenient this morning. "Worry not. The faster you can make what I require, the quicker I obtain what I need from the prisoner." She pats my arm with all the compassion of a venomous snake. "I know it might be difficult for you, Min, but surely even the least intelligent people can manage to harvest a sprig of mint." She shoves me toward the table, where the dented metal tray used for serving meals rests. "Now make haste. Oh, and mix two spoonfuls of Nightmare's Blood into the soup before serving it to him. The potion is finally ready."

I stare at my employer with thinly veiled shock. Nightmare's Blood?

"Is there a problem?" she demands.

"N-no, my lady." My gaze lowers to the floorboards beneath my scuffed loafers. The floor is safe, always safe. I stare until her footsteps recede, and I am alone.

Nightmare's Blood. What a vicious brew. In essence, it bleeds one's mind of clarity, casts a veil across their senses so that the line between waking and dreaming is blurred. Such vulnerability will allow her ladyship to wring whatever information she seeks from the prisoner. Three months she has tortured this man. But he has yet to break.

The thought of administering this poison chills my blood, but the power to decide does not belong to me. I cannot change what is. I must eat, sleep, make a living. I must carve out a life, same as all the rest. The last thing I want is to attract Lady Clarisse's wrath. She favors the lash, amongst other cruelties. But I see myself in this man, as I do in all the prisoners. It would be a comfort to receive kindness, however reluctantly given.

After gathering the prisoner's soup—potatoes in bone broth—I squeeze two drops of Nightmare's Blood into the meal, as instructed. The scent of crushed cherries unfurls as the liquid blackens. Two heartbeats later, it lightens to its normal hue.

Six hundred and forty-four stairs carry me up the long, spiraling throat to the northern tower. When the solid steel door at last flickers into view beneath the lone torch set into the wall bracket, I slow, halting a few steps below the landing.

The cells buried in the belly of the estate are barred in iron, with narrow holes cut into the upper walls, which allow the glow of sun and moon to pierce the gloom. The northern tower is different. It is singular, its isolated chamber offering neither window nor light. As such, the prisoner has spent three months in darkness. If he was separated from the rest, he must be powerful indeed.

Warily, I step onto the landing, whose window offers a view of the realm beyond: the sea, the cliffs, over which the tower juts. My fingers tighten around the tray of food pressed against my belly. A sound, heavily muted, comes from behind the steel door. As I strain my ears, it comes again. Metal. It sounds like a heavy chain being dragged across the stone floor.

The knots within me tangle further. My task is simple: push the tray through the slot located at the bottom of the door.

"Walk away," I whisper. Easy, to do what is expected of me.

Instead, I slip my hand into the pocket of my apron.

Only one universal antidote exists: Winter's Sunrise. It requires no less than six weeks of steeping, the water continually refilled as its three components—pumpkin seeds, sweet mint, and the hair of a demon—break down into a paste. As a precaution, I always carry a small vial with me, for exposure to poisons carries significant risk.

I am moving before my mind has the opportunity to deter me. Pulling free the stopper, I pour three drops of the antidote into the man's soup, watching as it disperses. Then I shove the tray through the slot in the door and flee down the stairs as though death itself is in pursuit.

2

"GET UP."

I'm jerked upright in bed. The world spins, caught in the blurred gloom of interrupted sleep. I blink rapidly, my narrow bedroom coming into focus. Something stings my arm. Five pointed nails, gouging deep.

Lady Clarisse looms over me, dressed in her finest. She grasps a tall candlestick, a single red bloom unfurling. Its glow daubs her smooth cheekbones in the pink of damaged flesh.

Another wrench against my arm. "Get up," she growls. "Now!"

I'm yanked from the cot. My body hits the ground, limbs asprawl. Through the pulse of panic clawing my skin, I think only two words: *She knows.*

Lady Clarisse returned to the estate late this evening. I was half asleep, but the clip of her gait as she ascended the stairs to her bedroom on the third level foretold her arrival. Did she visit the prisoner? In her attempts to gather information, did she notice the man's failure to yield, his lack of disorientation? "My lady—"

She hauls me from the room, my arm crushed in her powerful grip, my nightgown fluttering around my pale legs. Physically, she is not a large woman. Then again, I am equally slight, both in height and weight.

Down, down, down into the dim of the night-shrouded workshop.

The curtains are drawn, always drawn. Lady Clarisse is suspicious of villagers snooping, despite the estate's vast grounds.

Clamminess prickles my underarms. I cannot run. I have nowhere to go, and I would not get far. Only one option remains: I must repent. I must beg forgiveness. If I am to receive the lash, or boiling oil, or isolation, then I must accept the punishment as a consequence of my actions.

My knees fold, cracking against the floor. "My lady—"

She whirls around. "What are you doing? Get up." It is not my arm she reaches for. Rather, her fingers tangle in my long black hair. The pain drags a yelp from me. I stumble to my feet, then overbalance and go down again.

She all but drags me into the kitchen, where an oil lamp sputters. The wide bay window frames the star-studded night. Faded, floral-printed wallpaper peels in long strips from the walls, revealing the white plaster beneath.

"I'm s-s-sorry, my lady," I manage, voice strained. "It w-was a moment of w-w-w-weakness, but it will not happen again, I p-promise you—"

"What are you talking about, stupid girl?" She releases me. "I've a very important client due to arrive here within the hour. Put on a pot of tea and gather refreshments. Is the sitting room in order?"

My mouth snaps shut. So this is unrelated to last night's disobedience? "Y-yes, m-my lady. I d-d-dusted—"

Lady Clarisse's glare is potent enough to melt the skin off a lesser creature. "Why is it so difficult for you to speak without stumbling over your own tongue? Hurry up and get dressed. We must look presentable for our guest. I dare say a prince would not appreciate clutter."

I startle. "Prince?"

She turns toward the old brass mirror hanging from the wall and smooths her palms across her cheeks. "That is what I said." Then she scowls, noting a blemish near her chin. Due to the beauty teas she consumes weekly, one would never know Lady Clarisse possesses a brutal scar extending from chin to temple. Her attempts to erase this mark have led to an obsession with her appearance. She does not speak of it, and I know better than to ask.

My employer drops her arms with a sound of frustration before spotting my reflection in the mirror. "Why are you still standing there?" she bites. "Get dressed." Then she disappears into the workshop, likely to take an extra dose of beauty tea.

Beyond the window, a sickle moon digs its lower point into the canopy of trees that shades the road into town. Dawn is still hours off. What could be so important that a client would insist on meeting at an hour so late?

I return to the second floor and cloister myself in my room. Technically, it is a broom cupboard, only large enough for a cot and the small chest at its foot. When Lady Clarisse bought the estate, she claimed Nan's bedroom and forced me from mine, stating that she required the extra space to store her dresses. I will never forget what she told me upon seeing my teary-eyed confusion in being moved to these cramped quarters, my grief at Nan's passing still fresh: *Be thankful it is not the garden shed.*

After tugging on a clean blue dress and white stockings, I quickly yank a comb through my hair before hurrying downstairs to boil water for tea, slipping an apron across my front. I slice pears, brie, and a day-old baguette, arranging the food on a tarnished silver platter. Rare it is that her ladyship allows me into the kitchen. Most nights, she cooks for herself and I am tossed the leftovers. *Better than nothing.* At least, that is what I tell myself.

A knock cuts the quiet as I place the refreshments in the sitting room and return to the kitchen. Curiously, I peer around the corner toward the foyer.

The front door opens with a muffled creak. I wince. Lady Clarisse ordered me to oil the hinges, but with the approaching harvest, my workload has increased, and it slipped my mind. No doubt she will carve marks into my skin for the oversight.

"Welcome, Prince Balior. I trust your journey was uneventful?" Her ladyship is all smiles for this guest.

"I would not call it uneventful, exactly." As she steps back, a tall man dressed in a black robe and loose, ivory trousers crosses the threshold. His dark brown complexion and unusual manner of dress suggests he has traveled from a distant realm.

"But where is the, ah ... *companion* that you mentioned in your letter? Not delayed, I hope?" her ladyship asks sweetly.

"We'll get to that." As his gaze sweeps the foyer, it comes to rest on my form. I immediately retreat. "At the moment, I'm far more interested in the prisoner you have detained. You say he is a god?"

"One of the Anemoi, if I'm not mistaken."

My mouth shapes a soft *o*. Lady Clarisse has imprisoned plenty of immortals. Fair folk and demons, mostly. Never a god. How was she able to overpower him? As for these Anemoi ... I've never heard of them. In Marles, we venerate our Mother of Earth for her abundant harvests and our Master of Sea, who supplies the fishermen their daily catch.

The guest—Prince Balior—chuckles softly. "Lady Clarisse, you cannot know how glad I am to hear this." He glances at her left hand, which is bare. "Are you alone, or ...?"

Her ladyship's expression shutters, and she takes a small step back. "I called you here for business, Prince Balior. If that does not interest you, please let me know."

"Of course. I apologize, madam."

The sitting room door snicks shut, muting their conversation. They will likely be preoccupied for some time.

My thoughts drift upstairs, toward the northern tower, and my gut cramps sickeningly. One of the divine. That would explain why he is entombed in steel and stone. His power is too great to be contained by the cells belowground. Three months of suffering ... Now I am all the more curious to learn what information Lady Clarisse covets from this deity.

Back in the workshop, I hunt through one of the cabinet drawers for supplies. This might be my only opportunity to aid the prisoner. As much as I fear her ladyship's wrath, it feels wrong to harm one of the divine. Without them, our farms would cease to flourish. The sea would not provide. Why should I stop with an antidote when I can offer blessed respite, a means to numb the pain of whatever anguish Lady Clarisse has inflicted upon him?

Seeing as I do not know the extent of the prisoner's injuries, I cannot determine how strong a healing salve is needed. I do, however, know my employer. She would have carved into his skin, let the blood weep from a thousand cuts. It is not the first cruelty I've witnessed. The list is as long as it is gruesome.

Nails ripped from nailbeds.

Hot oil poured into eyes.

The crack of a split bone.

Selecting the strongest salve available, I shove it into my pocket and hasten up the tower stairs as quietly as possible. Upon reaching the landing, I mince toward the solid steel door. To my left, the single window reveals the waves that grow blacker as autumn's chill sets in. Late is the hour. The prisoner likely sleeps. Carefully, I open the slot and push the tin of salve through.

Immediately, the container is hurled back through the opening. It bounces across the ground with a sharp clatter before rolling to a stop.

As I reach down to pick up the healing balm, I'm suddenly wrenched forward. My body slams against the door, pain rupturing near my shoulder as something shoves my face against the freezing metal. I struggle against a nameless, faceless captor to no avail.

"What did you put in the soup?"

The voice is low, encased in ice. It rasps along my bare arms, drawing the hairs to shivering points.

"N-nothing." When I attempt to twist my face away from the door, the pressure increases, drawing tears to my eyes.

"Do not lie to me, mortal."

"I d-didn't put anything in the b-b-broth!" I manage, molars clenched in pain.

There is a silence, unbroken except by the rapidity of my breathing.

"Very well. If what you're saying is true, then surely you would have no objection to consuming the meal you served me?"

I scan the area wildly. There is no hand that I can see, though it certainly feels like one—five sturdy fingers wrapped around my throat. The snap of the metal slot sounds, and suddenly the bowl of soup I served the prisoner yesterday hovers before me in a sphere of wind. A pitiful mewl slips out of me. What is this sorcery?

"The less you struggle, the less pain you will experience." His next words emerge as a growl. "Drink."

I shake my head. If I were not so paralyzed by terror, it might have occurred to me to scream.

Something pinches behind my jaw. I whimper. "You're hurting m-me."

"As I said, the less you struggle, the less this will hurt."

"Her l-ladyship ordered me to poison you. I p-p-put the antidote in the s-soup to negate the effects," I choke through a tightening airway. "I s-swear it."

The pressure around my throat eases, but I remain pressed against the door, trembling. Eventually, the prisoner says, "Why would you act against your employer?"

"I'm n-not working against her," I rush to say.

The silence speaks. It tells me he does not believe a word I utter.

And yet, this god releases me. I fall forward, panting hard as I rub behind my jaw, along my neck. Not hard enough to bruise. I know what sort of pressure a bruising requires.

"If you're not working against her, as you claim," he says, "why add the antidote?"

"I don't kn-know," I whisper.

"A likely story."

Before I can defend myself—though truthfully I'm not certain *what* I would say—he goes on, the resonance of his voice managing to vibrate through solid steel.

"If this is a ruse designed to beguile me into lowering my guard, I warn you: it won't work. She cannot break me. And neither can you."

Nothing I say will prove my intentions are noble. Mainly because I understand the sentiment. If our positions were switched, I wouldn't trust him either. And yet—

"Why w-would I seek to cause you additional h-h-harm? You are already captured. I hear how her l-ladyship tortures you. If you give her what she w-w-wants, there would be no reason to keep y-you here—"

I fall silent as an eerie, ragged gasp gathers strength from inside the cell.

Laughter. I have never heard so spiteful a sound.

"Do you honestly think that witch will let me walk free once I give her the information she wants? Do you think she lets *any* of the immortals she imprisons walk free? Tell me, does she give them a hearty send-off before dumping their bodies over the cliffs?"

That's not ... Lady Clarisse sets the prisoners free. She has told me this. When I think deeper on the matter, however, I realize I've never witnessed this with my own eyes. I have simply taken her word for it.

"And anyway," he goes on, "why should I give up my secrets to that hateful woman when her apprentice is so willing to help me?"

I am suddenly aware of my position: palms plastered to the fortified metal, ear angled toward the seam in the door.

I scramble back so quickly I slam into the wall. Snatching the salve from the ground, I descend the stairs as rapidly as my feet will allow.

"Fly away, bird," the prisoner calls to my retreating back. "Fly away."

3

"Min." A piece of parchment slaps my chest. "Master Alain should have everything listed in stock, but if for some reason he doesn't, go to Pierre's on Market Street and tell him I'd like to call in a favor."

"A favor?" I accept the list from Lady Clarisse in puzzlement. Behind me, a kettle boils over the hearth, and hot porridge bubbles in a small pot on the kitchen stove. "Why—"

"No questions."

I duck my head. "Apologies, my lady."

Each week, Lady Clarisse sends me into town to collect the ingredients she requires. Though we grow the majority of our herbs at the estate, those originating in far-flung realms can be difficult to source. In these instances, we purchase from Master Alain, a local herbalist who has a reputation for acquiring rare flora.

"While you're gone," she says, turning to study her appearance in the mirror, "I'll be working on Our Lady of Mercy. It's paramount that you acquire every ingredient on the list. If you fail, the draught will be useless, and I'll be forced to start over." Her dark eyes seize mine through the looking glass, and I freeze, a hare caught in a toothed trap. "Understood?"

The threat of punishment is enough to ensure I obtain the necessary components, whatever the cost. "Yes, my lady."

Her mouth wilts with distaste as she smooths a bit of powder over her cheek. No sign of the scar. Nevertheless, it is clear her appearance does not satisfy her, as she shies from her reflection to tie sprigs of lavender with twine, oddly quiet. She slips the bunches into a glass jar and rests it on the wooden shelf over the sink. Meanwhile, I glance through the list more carefully. I don't want to miss anything. One item, however, gives me pause.

"Pardon, my lady, but I'm not familiar with this ingredient. What is *vanishing night*?"

"Ah." Her features grow pointed with pleasure as she turns. "A few months ago, I stumbled across a merchant who hailed from a realm called Under. He showed me all manner of oils and herbs, powders and poultices. Vanishing night was one of his rarer finds, a dust ground from the fangs of a darkwalker."

My attention latches onto that word: *darkwalker*. "What is that?"

"An immortal born of darkness, originating from a realm far north of the Gray. They feed on humans."

"They consume mortals?" I ask in borderline horror.

"Not their bodies. Their souls." The edges of her mouth curl upward in some horrid likeness of a smile. "Once I have the vanishing night for my brew," she whispers fervently, "I will finally learn the location of the prisoner's god-touched weapon. For months, I've tried every potion under the sun to weaken his defenses; nothing has worked. But with *this* element, I shall succeed."

I stare at her in confusion, my dismay surrounding the darkwalker already forgotten. "God-touched weapon?"

"Slow, stupid Min. Have I taught you nothing over the years?" Yet she speaks with rare affection, as though I am but a loveable, senile pet. "Only a god-touched weapon can fell a god, and if I am correct in assuming our dear prisoner is, in fact, one of the Anemoi, then he possesses a weapon powerful beyond measure."

My eyes are wide, wide, wide. "What sort of weapon?"

"An ax. Not only is this weapon a conduit to his powers, but it is perhaps my only means of obtaining what I seek: the heart's blood of a fallen god. With it, I will have no need for those lesser immortals. Why, I could create a tea that would grant immortality itself!"

Immortality. What wonders this word wrought. "That's amazing," I say, because it is what she would expect from me. "I wasn't aware that was possible."

"The naysayers doubt me. But soon I'll have the evidence to prove them wrong. You know what I have endured. What I continue to endure," she says, glaring in my direction. My stomach lurches, and I angle my face toward the floor. "With immortality, I will reclaim the power I lost. Never again will the gods take from me those I love most. Never again," she whispers with curdling fury, "will I be *weak.*"

Lady Clarisse returns to her herbs, a clear dismissal, but my feet remain entrenched in the floor. *Everlasting life.* Not once had I questioned my employer's motives, but it makes sense. The unexpected death of her husband left her ladyship with a hole in her heart. She wants to ensure that will not happen again. And I realize now that the prisoner was correct: Lady Clarisse would never let him, or any of the immortals, walk free. At the very least, disposing of them would prevent the prisoners from taking their revenge.

"What are you waiting for?" she barks. "Off with you!"

My heart trills alongside my ribs. *Mother of Earth, give me strength.* "If it's not too m-much trouble, my lady, I w-w-wanted to broach the topic of s-selling the estate."

Her thin eyebrows climb, and a lock of ebon hair falls across her sweat-glistened cheek. "Oh?" She cants her head, inspecting me as though I am a small grub. Something in need of squashing. "And why is the estate any of your business? You should be thankful I provide a roof over your head at all."

"Understood, my lady. But I w-w-was thinking. Wh-what if *I* bought the estate from y-you?"

Her dark eyes bulge. "You? Purchase the estate?" She crows a laugh. "You need *funds* to purchase property. What will you do, pull coin from out of thin air?" Shaking her head, she rinses her hands in the washbasin, dries them on a cotton rag hanging from the wall. "Not that it's any of your concern, but I already have a buyer interested."

No, I cannot accept this. "Wh-what if I offered something else besides c-coin?" Contrary to Lady Clarisse's beliefs, I've a small inheritance left to me by Nan that I refuse to touch. The funds are buried in a metal tin behind the garden shed. I'd hoped to one day use them to reinstate Nan's business, once I gained enough experience. Surely St. Laurent is large enough for two apothecaries?

"Something besides coin," she iterates, curious now. "Like what?"

"Information. From the p-prisoner." My voice strengthens. It could work. "I could f-find out where this god-touched w-weapon is."

My employer considers me with new eyes. There is no laughter, no scathing remark or questioning my intelligence. I have captured her attention at last.

Then she snorts. "Have you been listening to anything I just said? The brew will gift me what I seek."

"But—"

She lifts a hand, cutting me off. "While there's still daylight."

I bite my cheek, knowing better than to argue. Gathering my basket and coat, I hurry out the back door, down the pathway cutting through the overgrown grass until I reach the iron gate guarding the entrance to the estate. Steel clouds roll in from the east, and large waves hammer the rocks below. My body stiffens, already anticipating the water's icy touch, but I am safe here, on these cliffs that rise high. The wind, cutting and cold, tugs at my threadbare dress and apron. Gooseflesh prickles my skin, and I shiver.

I've two, maybe three, hours before the storm hits. My pace quickens as the path angles downhill toward St. Laurent, with its shining bell tower and lustrous pillars nestled like pearls against the expansive lavender fields and tidy vineyards. Dirt hardens to smooth, rust cobblestones, their uneven surface poking painfully against the worn soles of my loafers. I wince. The thin rope I've used to bind my shoes is slowly disintegrating. Lady Clarisse gives me a few pennies' worth of salary each week, whatever remains after room and board have been deducted. In a few months, I should have enough saved to purchase new shoes. I dare not risk spending my inheritance on something so minor.

Apartment buildings border the northern edge of town, arched windows stamped button-like down their fronts, the corroded copper roofs akin to sloped green hats. As I travel farther south, storefronts begin to replace the elegant structures. A small chapel has burrowed itself into a hillside. The sparkle of its windows reminds me of jewels: emerald swirled with aquamarine. Meanwhile, a chorale drifts through the open doors of the sanctuary.

Whisking around the corner, I step onto Market Street, which is wide, framed by green hedges and two-story edifices constructed of gray stone. Ivy climbs the ancient walls and iron balconies ornament the upper levels. The air, perfumed with warmed sugar and yeast, drifts from the bakers' carts that are too many to count. Truly, one may purchase a tart or loaf of bread from any corner. Farther on, a large fountain burbles at the entrance to the local park.

After purchasing a small sourdough bun, I tear into its soft center and allow my pace to slow. Each window is dressed dashingly in dried flowers and wreaths. Welcome mats grace the doorways of every bakery, florist, butcher, and grocer. A fine-looking gentleman in a tweed coat walks his dog along the strip of grass bordering the road. He tips his hat in my direction with a freckled hand, and I drop my eyes, hurrying onward. Two women bundled in sweaters sip hot tea on the small porch of a bookshop, their bronzed skin flushed in the chill of morning.

"I, for one, thought the production was phenomenal," says the first woman as she refills her porcelain cup from a teapot. "I swear I could *smell* the meat as he cooked her dinner."

"Agreed!" her curly-haired companion exclaims. "I wished he was cooking *me* dinner!" They share a cackling laugh. "What did you think of his reaction when she revealed that she was with child?"

The woman's response is lost as I enter a nondescript shop. A silver bell chimes, and the wooden floors gleam in the autumn sun. I breathe in deeply. Lemon, a sharp itch against my nostrils, paired with the mellow fragrance of tarragon. "Good morning, Master Alain."

"Ah, Min! I was wondering when you'd arrive." A beefy, brown-skinned man wearing a loose, linen shirt rounds the back counter. Walls of shelving showcase an impressive array of herbs, from the common and familiar to the rare and unique. "The usual?" he asks, accepting my list.

"Not quite," I say with a tense smile.

He frowns at her ladyship's penmanship. "Vanishing night?"

"That won't be a problem, will it?"

"No, but it is an unusual request. Difficult to acquire." He taps the list against his palm thoughtfully. "Not to worry. I have connections in Under. Occasionally, we get a few fair folk passing through, asking for it. Drifters, usually. See them once and never again."

Yes, because Lady Clarisse tosses any and all immortals into the cells below the estate. Currently, she has two fair folk imprisoned. There was a third, but after several weeks, the poor soul expired, unable to withstand the prolonged suffering.

After placing my basket on the counter, I browse the offerings while Master Alain gathers my supplies. Though I work for Lady Clarisse, I've known his lordship since I was a young girl. He and Nan were close friends, having met shortly after my grandmother arrived at St. Laurent from Jinsan, her homeland.

It is then that a curious plant draws my eye: dusky petals, velvet to the touch.

"Black iris."

I snatch my hand away. "Pardon?"

"The plant you're touching." He tugs at his beard. It is spectacularly red. "It's called black iris. Comes all the way from Ammara."

"I see." I've heard of Ammara. Realm of sand and sun. "What are its properties?"

"Well, many like to crush the roots, as it is a diuretic if mixed with Ammaran salt. Others prefer to dry the leaves and use them to scent their linens. The petals haven't much of a taste." He removes a small envelope from beneath the counter and slips it into my basket.

Interesting. I will see what further research I can uncover on this specimen.

I pay for the items and grab my basket. "Good day to you, sir."

"And to you, Min."

As I reach the door, my hand tightens around the knob. Easy—too easy, perhaps—to step beyond the shop, return to the estate, brew the next poison, remain silent as the dead. But the hole into which my dismay floods yawns wider. Something is not right.

Turning, I say to him, "Vanishing night." I hold up the small envelope. "May I ask what its properties are?"

He studies me a moment, suddenly guarded. "That depends on what ingredients you're brewing it with."

"Silk violet, liquid amber, hair of a banshee, tears of a pregnant mortal in her second trimester."

He frowns, pondering this information. I shift uncomfortably in place. "Sounds to me like a poison to drain a body of strength."

I blink at him. "Come again?"

"When the liquid is consumed," Master Alain explains, "it will move through the bloodstream like threads with small hooks, which attach to the victim's arteries and veins, siphoning all nutrients from the muscles and flesh."

I am struck mute with horror. Her ladyship's cruelty is a staple in my life. *Artistic ingenuity*, she calls it. Why do I continually underestimate her? "But the strength will return, won't it?"

"Yes, but it may be days before that occurs."

So Lady Clarisse intends to drain the prisoner of strength, thus removing the last barrier—his will—barring her from the location of his ax. The man—*god*—will survive, but only long enough for her to bury that god-touched weapon in his chest.

"Good day to you," I say, then depart the shop swiftly, my basket of supplies banging against the side of my leg.

"My lady?" After wiping the dirt from my loafers, I enter the workshop. The door leading to the basement stands open a crack. A pained shriek splinters from the obscured depths below, and I flinch. Nothing I can do. Not unless I, too, wish to be confined belowground.

As I do every week, I remove the ingredients from my basket and line them across one of the battered work tables. Our Lady of Mercy simmers in a pot on the stove. It reeks of spoiled meat. Once vanishing night is added, the poison requires another ten days to steep.

I fiddle with the powder-filled envelope uneasily. This is not how Nan conducted business. Her teas promoted healing. They never inflicted pain or granted one person power over another. Some nights, when I am feeling particularly daring, I consider the possibility of resuming her legacy: bringing healing back to St. Laurent.

And so I wonder. Might I obtain the information Lady Clarisse seeks *without* forcing a poison down the deity's throat?

What makes you think you have the authority to question my work?

My hand trembles. The envelope slips from my grasp. It hits the table, and powder clouds the air, the floor, the front of my apron. I snatch the envelope, peer inside. Less than a teaspoon remains.

Dread. Dread like nothing I have ever known hardens my stomach to stone. Her ladyship will kill me. I know this as a truth of the world, like the easterly sunrise, the flow of water downstream.

Tiptoeing toward the basement door, I press my ear to the crack. A dull roar floods my eardrums, my heartbeat a cacophonous *thump, thump, thump.*

"Again," Lady Clarisse snarls. *Crack!* A weakened cry crumbles, petering out beneath the hiss of the simmering brew. I recoil, nausea ringing my throat. I'm sweating so profusely the envelope wilts in my dampened palm.

Seconds later, the creak of wood pricks at my awareness. Footsteps, ascending the stairs.

Move, Min! She can't learn of my mistake.

My body lurches into motion. Two steps, and I reach the open window, nearly dropping the envelope in my haste to empty the remaining powder onto the overgrown hedges. A gentle wind wipes all evidence away.

Envelope clutched in hand, I spring toward the supply cabinet and select a powder of summer thyme, a harmless ingredient similar in color to vanishing night. I add five tablespoons to the empty envelope—the amount required for the draught—and shut the cabinet door seconds before Lady Clarisse stomps into the kitchen, her boots marking bloody prints on the scuffed floorboards.

"Oh." She blinks. "You're back." After peeling the soiled apron from her front, she tosses the garment into a basket in the corner before washing her hands in the washbasin. "I trust Master Alain had everything in stock?"

With her back to me, I'm able to slip the envelope amongst the ingredients unnoticed. "He d-did." *Breathe. Just breathe.* "I ... didn't w-want to disturb you."

My employer ignores me as she stirs Our Lady of Mercy, wisps of steam rising to moisten her pale face. As though sensing my attention, she glances toward me in irritation. "Well? Don't just stand there. Fetch me a glass."

As she dumps the envelope's contents into the pot, I retrieve a copper mug from the cupboard, accidentally hitting a stack of plates in my haste to comply. The sharp clatter causes her head to whip in my direction. Her dark eyes promise pain, always pain.

"S-sorry," I whisper.

"Hurry up," she snaps.

I place the mug on the table, and she ladles the poisoned tea into the hammered metal. A drop of liquid slides free of the rim.

"I th-thought the tea needed an extra ten d-days to steep?" I ask tentatively.

"Our Lady of Mercy requires ten days to reach full strength, but I need to test a sample, make sure everything is in working order."

My hands fist behind my back, fingernails cutting deep into my palms. She will force the substance down the prisoner's throat. With his wrists shackled, his ankles, he will be helpless to escape. Not that it will matter. She will soon learn the poison is defective. "My lady—"

She brushes past me, and the swish of her dress vanishes up the stairwell leading to the northern tower. My knees wobble. I collapse onto a chair and wait, heart in throat, for the sword to fall.

A furious shriek heralds doom. I lurch to my feet as her ladyship stomps downstairs. Should I flee? No, that would surely mark me as guilty.

Catching my arm, she yanks me up the stairs with impossible strength. When we reach the cell door, she flings me onto the ground.

"It didn't work," she snarls. "Tell me why the poison didn't work."

I scramble onto my back. "I d-d-don't know, I—"

"What do you mean *you don't know*? You informed me Master Alain had all the ingredients. Did you lie?"

My mind is a frozen wasteland. Nothing roots. All I know is this: she cannot learn that I replaced vanishing night with a completely different substance. "N-no! Perhaps M-Master Alain gave m-me a d-d-different powder by mistake?"

"I see." Her upper lip curls. "That is unfortunate."

Sweat drips beneath my arms, and I gulp in air. Lady Clarisse has enormous influence in this town. If she believes Master Alain to have sold her the wrong ingredient, she might think it intentional, a means to steal her coin. It would not take much to blacklist his business.

"I-I-I'll go b-b-back," I whisper. "I'll inform h-h-him of the m-mistake." By which I mean, I will purchase another five tablespoons of vanishing night with my own meager funds. New shoes will have to wait. "I'm sure he'll be h-happy to accommodate."

"Stupid girl," she snarls, and kicks my stomach. I curl inward with a pitiful cry. "Have you heard anything I've said these past weeks? Vanishing night must be added today. *Before* noon. If Our Lady of Mercy steeps longer than twenty-one days without the additive, the powder will not bind properly with the solution."

She kicks me again, again, again. My stomach throbs; my bones quake in pain. I go limp. If I do not move, then I am not a threat. If I am not a threat, she will grow bored of me and eventually depart.

"Enough!"

The low growl lashes through the steel door. Through the shadows blotting my vision, I watch Lady Clarisse straighten, lips peeling back in a silent snarl. She slams a fist against the door's metal face. "Quiet, worm!"

There is a heavy thud, and suddenly, her ladyship is plastered against the door, her startling shriek cut short.

I stare, wide-eyed, at the semi-transparent tendril that has coiled itself around her neck. She scrabbles at the noose with sharp fingernails. Her boots kick at the wall. "*Min!*" It emerges as a fraught wheeze.

I remain motionless, my feet fixed to the floor. No one outmaneuvers Lady Clarisse—no one. What sort of power does this god possess? It seems he can manipulate the air, but if that were so, why not force the door open? Why not fight back? Unless she has weakened him with other insidious brews?

"My ... pocket," she chokes, face purpling to indigo. "Toss it ... inside."

I lunge, searching her pockets. My fingers close around a small metal tin: sleeping powder. Prying open the top, I send it through the slot in the door. Seconds later, the noose vanishes, and her ladyship collapses onto the ground.

I rush to her side. "My lady, are you all right?" When I reach for her arm, she slaps my hand aside.

Sweat dots her upper lip. She wipes it away with the back of her forearm, then shoves to her feet, expression thunderous. "Min." She glowers down at me as though *I* am to blame, and within her black eyes, there is the promise of blood. "Come with me."

I wake to darkness.

I lie on the squeaky cot in my room, blankets having twisted around my bare legs. Any slight shift sends fire rupturing up my back. I muffle a cry, biting my cheek so hard copper coats my tongue. A chill rolls through me, and I shiver, though my skin is feverish to the touch.

Gingerly, I push into a seated position. Beneath my nightgown, a horrific bouquet blossoms across my skin: blue, green, mauve. Along my upper ribs, where Lady Clarisse's boot made contact, the color has rotted to a mealy gray. I do not want to look at my back. In tatters, like the rest of me.

Her ladyship wields the whip infrequently, yet always lovingly, fervently. I'd forgotten how excruciating healing is, each brush of air like a thousand lit matches against my pulped flesh. Falling back asleep will be impossible. Without something to dull the ache, I will lie here in agony until the sun chases back the dark.

It takes long minutes to slip a dress over my shredded back. Hunching forward, I carefully shove my feet into my tired loafers. Then I'm up, easing slowly down the stairs. The bottom step whines as I plant my weight on it. I wince, holding still. Nothing stirs. Good. I would not wish to disturb my employer at an hour so late.

After filling the kettle, I place it on the stove. I build the fire beneath, puffing hard through the pain. I'm not sure which hurt is worse—my back or my ribs. As I wait for the water to boil, I collect the necessary ingredients to make a healing tea that will induce restorative sleep. This, at least, soothes me. My hands fall into motions familiar and safe. Herbs cut and pressed, sliced and rolled.

The kettle screams. I remove it from the heat, steep the brew in boiling water. It is then that a note catches my eye—her ladyship's elegant script.

Gone to inspect a few potential flats in town. Will return tonight. Stir Our Lady of Mercy thrice at sunrise.

I stir the fresh batch of poison, though it will take weeks before it is complete. I have erred—badly. If she is inspecting flats in town, is it possible the estate's sale is already in motion?

Fear of losing my home draws my attention toward the stairs leading to the tower. Time is a luxury I cannot afford. However, if I can find the prisoner's ax myself, I know Lady Clarisse will give me anything I ask for in exchange—including my home.

Swiftly, I down the healing tea. The relief is immediate, a cool numbness encasing my shoulders, spine, and ribs. I pour a second cup for the prisoner. If I approach this god with kindness and understanding, if I offer him relief, might he grant me the information freely?

Lady Clarisse believes she is the only one who knows where the spare keys to the northern tower are hidden, but she is wrong. Tonight, I retrieve the key ring from one of Nan's old teapots, tuck it against my palm. Chilled metal, small yet mighty.

It is a laborious ascent up the stairs. My legs shake, and twice I'm forced to rest, my sharp, open-mouthed gasps splintering the quiet of deep night. By the time I reach the landing, I require the wall for support, sweat drenching my front. But hesitate I do not. Inserting the key into the lock, I slip inside, quiet as a wraith.

4

"So, the bird has returned."

The prisoner's coarse rasp emerges from the back corner, where the shadows breed thickest. The sound's echo folds onto itself: small, smaller, gone. All is obscured: the walls, the floor, even the shape of my own hands. This is no cell. It is a tomb.

I am a fool to have placed myself in such a vulnerable position, but ... a curious fool. Tentatively, I take a shuffling step forward, porcelain cup gripped tightly. My hand trembles. It sloshes the boiling brew across my wrist, and I expel a hiss of pain. "I m-m-made you a cup of tea."

The scuff of chains pricks at my ears. "You mean like the poison that witch forced down my throat while I lay senseless from her cursed sleeping powder?"

"No." Another step forward. It's impossible to determine how far from the prisoner I stand. "This is a h-healing tea."

"I'm sure."

Gradually, my eyes adjust to the gloom. Stone walls. Stone floor. The available light is scant, naught but a thin outline surrounding the slot used to shove food through the door. From what Lady Clarisse has told me, the prisoner is shackled to the far wall, with only enough length in his chains to reach the meager meals we serve him. The manacles were enchanted by a witch her ladyship captured many years before and forced to do her bidding. They are unbreakable. So long as I keep my distance and do not provoke the prisoner into using his mysterious powers, I am safe.

"If it w-would help," I say, "I can take a s-sip of the tea and prove there is n-n-nothing wrong with it."

Once more, quiet takes shape. It is decidedly suspicious.

Lifting the cup, I take a hearty swallow. By now, the numbness has spread to fully envelop my hurts. "Does that p-prove anything?"

"It proves you believe me gullible, soft," he bites out. "You're her employee. I can't trust you."

"Fine." I'm not sure why his judgment irks me. It is understandable, considering his captivity. Maybe I take umbrage with him lumping me together with my employer. We are not the same, she and I. Lady Clarisse relishes others' pain, she lusts for power, covets leverage. My desires are humble: food on the table, a roof over my head. A home of my own.

Gently, I set the cup on the ground. Maybe he will choose to drink if I do not hand it to him directly.

"What did she do to you?" the prisoner asks.

His voice now sounds like it is coming from my right, whereas previously it emerged from the left, though I'm not sure how that is possible. I peer hard into the blanketing darkness. Nothing. I see nothing. "Excuse me?"

"She hurt you. I heard your cries earlier."

I curve one hand over my shoulder as if to shield my wounds from his gaze. "N-nothing I d-d-did n-not deserve."

"Why do you feel you deserve such punishment?" If I'm not mistaken, he sounds peeved. "There are other employers who would treat you better. Why stay and endure this pain?"

"My l-l-lady has m-my best interests at heart. Everything she does is to m-m-make me into a better apprentice—"

He scoffs. "Don't tell me you honestly believe that."

My eyes narrow in irritation. He is quick to pass judgment, this deity. He knows nothing of my life.

"How did you come to work here?" he asks. "Where are your parents?"

"My mother doesn't w-wish to know me, and I have mostly accepted that. As for m-my father, he died shortly after I was b-born. This estate w-was my grandmother's. It is wh-where I grew up." I cross my arms over my stomach. "Now you understand why I s-stay."

"I don't. Your grandmother is dead. You've no family to keep you here. Why chain yourself to this fate? You cannot live for what is already gone."

I do not agree. The past is always present. Always.

"There are plenty of opportunities for employment in St. Laurent," he argues, "or elsewhere in Marles."

I have considered it. I have thought of how different my life might be, were I to find other employment. But Lady Clarisse would never allow it. The only reason I am permitted to continue living at the estate is because I am her apprentice. No, if I am to one day follow in Nan's footsteps, I must remain.

"My skills apply to only a v-very narrow industry," I explain to him. "There are not m-m-many opportunities."

"What about something completely different. Fishing is robust in this town, is it not? I am sure someone would be willing to take you on as a deckhand."

It is eerie, to feel the weight of another's gaze and not see it yourself. "My f-father was a fisherman, but I unfortunately did n-not grow up with an affinity for w-w-water."

"And? That can be learned, as can any skill."

"My m-mother tried to drown me as a child. I was six. I'm ... afraid of the s-sea. Well, deep water, rather."

To this, he does not deign to respond. If only his face were not cloaked behind the thickening opaqueness. Perhaps then I could distinguish the quality of this stillness, whether pity or judgment, shock or disgust.

A drawn-out scuffling catches my attention, and I stare across the veiling black, willing something to take shape. Yes, I see it now. The figure of a man, crouched, heavy chains pooling at his feet.

"I imagine that's n-n-not something that bothers y-you," I tell him. "Death?"

"No," he says. "I can't say that it does. You mortals are afraid of such little things."

Why does his disdain bother me so? After all, I am well used to it. "The w-world is a scary place, especially when one does not have d-doting parents to guide them."

"I am well aware of that," he spits out, the words soaked in resentment. What was it Lady Clarisse had referred to him as? One of the Anemoi. I wonder what that means. I wonder what powers he holds. "There's something you should know about the divine. Historically, we are amongst the worst in terms of rearing children. Consider yourself lucky you are no longer in contact with your mother."

Lucky is not exactly the word I would use. "Then wh-why the disdain?"

His scoff resounds against the stone walls. It falls into the darkness and is buried. "Do you expect me to extend compassion toward someone complicit in my torment?"

My face grows hot with a shame I am unable to hide. Most days, I shut my ears to the screams. I draw the cloth across my eyes. "Y-you can help y-y-yourself, you know. M-my lady wants information. If you tell m-me what it is she wants to know, p-p-perhaps I can convince her to let y-you go?"

He barks a laugh, shifts in his distant corner. "That witch will never let me go. No, I have endured far worse. I am a god. When all the earth is dust, I will still be here, meting out my vengeance." There is a bitterness to his response, and if I am not mistaken, a subtle urgency. In what ways has he attempted to escape? In what ways has he failed? "She can continue her torment. I will not break."

I huff in frustration. "Why can't y-y-you see that I'm trying to help y-you?"

I do not realize I've stepped closer until a quiet *pop* sounds in my ears, followed by an abrupt change in air pressure.

Low laughter coaxes the hair along my nape to stand on end. "Foolish mortal," he says. "You should watch where you step."

I look down. A faint line of soot sketches the stone underfoot. My gut cramps with understanding, and dread like I have never known. It is a symbol of protection, established to bind the god's power—most, but not all. He goaded me enough to step forward, causing my shoe to disrupt the line. Now that it is broken, so too are those bonds.

The deity unfurls to his feet with a clink of chains. I gasp and stumble backward, for there is no other word to describe his size except this: overwhelming.

Heavy, broad shoulders stretch the black fabric of his worn cloak, which snaps around his braced legs, clawed by a wind heavy with damp. He is at least a head taller than me, maybe two. The dark inside his hood fully conceals his face.

A massive hand reaches toward me, and I recoil, turning away in anticipation of the blow. It never comes.

My lungs expand and contract, each fitful gasp paired with a dull twinge. *Run, Min.* But there is nowhere to go. Forcing down a wad of bile, I look up at the deity. Through the shadowed interior of his cowl, I sense his gaze, a direct, piercing thing.

"What are you?" I choke out.

"I am Eurus, the East Wind," he responds, a hum of ancient winds and eroded stone. "The storms are my palette. The wind is my brush. I command them both. And now," he murmurs, "I command you."

A silvery band ensnares my waist, pinning me in place. I open my mouth to scream, but it's as if a thin sheet of air seals itself over teeth and tongue, cutting off any emerging sound. I struggle to no avail. Eventually, the pain of my reopened wounds becomes too great. I fall limp, trembling, as a breeze slips into my pocket.

"Take it, bird," coaxes the East Wind. "Set me free."

The sleeve of his cloak retracts. Lady Clarisse's key ring dangles from a thin rope. His hand is wide, pale, fingers distinctly masculine, with surprisingly clean nails. "How d-did y-you—?"

"That employer of yours is overconfident. The shackles suppressed the majority of my power, but not all of it." He sounds darkly pleased with himself. "But the enchantments on the shackles prevent me from unlocking them myself. Only a mortal can do so." He thrusts the key against my chest. "Before she returns."

Even if I were to escape, the nearest estate is half a mile south. And anyway, what would I say? That an imprisoned god attempts to break free from the tower where he is kept? They would think me mad.

"And if I r-r-refuse?" I whisper.

His exhalation drifts across my face. It smells of sweet rain. "I don't want to hurt you." The tendril squeezes my torso tighter. My ribs groan in protest, and I bite back a cry from the added pressure on my wounds. "But I will, if I have to."

Death by a thousand cuts, or death by a single blow? Lady Clarisse I can weather. The East Wind I know nothing of.

My hands tremble so severely it takes multiple attempts to insert the key into the lock at the prisoner's wrists. The chains tumble to the stone with a violent crash. The manacles encasing his ankles follow. A wave of power detonates, driving forth a screaming, rain-drenched wind that claws at my hair and skin and clothes. When it dies, I'm left hollow with guilt. Everything her ladyship has worked for, gone with but one betrayal.

"G-go then," I manage through chattering teeth. "I d-did wh-what you asked. Leave now."

"Oh no, bird." Eurus draws me closer, into the startling heat of his massive body. "You're coming with me."

His arms band around me. They are like pillars of stone, or wood, or something equally inflexible. My struggles revive themselves as he blasts open the door. Another gust shatters the window at the top of the landing. In my shock, the keys slip from my hands. Plastered to his chest, my ear shoved against the hard plate of his sternum, I go rigid in his arms.

For below, there awaits the sea. Look at how she churns. Her vicious temper, those dark, watery hands scratching at the rocky cliffs, waves frothed like saliva below. My tongue swells, blocking my airway, for the immortal has climbed through the shattered window onto the steeply slanted rooftop, its panes crusted in salt, slick from recent rain.

Now I begin to thrash. Now I writhe and hammer and beat at the deity who holds me captive. My stomach lurches as the prisoner strides to the very edge of the roof. The water. I can feel its sting in my throat, inside my nostrils. There is no ground, no solid earth, only the wide, swallowing sea below.

"Wait," I whisper. "Please—"

He leaps.

5

Down, down, down we plummet, the frigid air cutting at my face, and the sea swelling like a growth in my vision, until it is all I know. A wave arcs high, lashing toward me. Seconds before we make impact, I squeeze my eyes shut.

Abruptly, the downward motion jerks to a halt, and my stomach drives upward into my throat from the unexpected change. My eyes snap open. Somehow, we begin to climb. I cling to my captor with clawed fingers, only vaguely aware of how he stiffens beneath my touch. Overhead, there is the sky, its stars dusted like pollen in the wind. My mind whirs, unable to process why we failed to hit the water, until two dark shapes framing the East Wind's back draw my focus.

Wings.

Their breadth is vast, perhaps twice the length of his already impressive height. A thin gray membrane stretches over the long, curved bones. Inlaid across the top: ebon scales. Their texture appears similar to hammered copper or tin. They cast an iridescent shine in certain slants of light. Fearsome, to be certain.

I was not aware that gods possessed wings. The Mother of Earth certainly doesn't. She wears a simple cotton dress, her dark hair piled high upon her head, hands coated in dirt. The Master of Sea is equally humble in a long shirt and breeches, his only means of flight the sails of his ship, which he uses to shape the tides. This immortal, this *East Wind*, is so unlike them. Who is he? Where does he hail from?

A drop in altitude sends a weightless swoop through my belly. My fingers dig harder into his muscled shoulders, and I tuck my face against his neck to shield myself from the wine-dark sea below. We bank hard, catching an updraft of wind, which props us higher than I thought was possible. Over the East Wind's shoulder, the green rooftops of St. Laurent fade into black velvet, each loud *whump* of beating wings propelling me farther from home.

Soon, Lady Clarisse will return. She will make herself a cup of beauty tea, steeped for four minutes exactly. Then she will climb the stairs to the northern tower and find the cell door agape, the prisoner gone.

And then? When she discovers that I, too, have vanished, will she connect the pieces and assume I unlocked the prisoner's cell? The idea makes me ill. She would not believe me capable of such disobedience, would she?

Time spins out, but eventually, sunlight splashes the eastern horizon. Below, I spot a boulder shaped like a bird of prey—an eagle—erupting from the water. Then a rocky island comes into view, its edges worn smooth by seaside winds. But it is what surrounds the island that sends my stomach into a heaving, fear-stricken heap.

A gray, malevolent mass. A great storm circling the scrap of barren earth, its blackness broken every so often by lightning. The East Wind flies straight toward it, and I freeze, eyes squeezed shut as the first flecks of hail pelt my face.

Or rather, that is what I expect. When the precipitation fails to hit my skin, I crack my eyelids to find a protective sphere enfolding us as we fly safely through the churning air and dousing rain, into the eye of the storm.

Within the squall's heart, an immense, stately edifice sprawls along the exposed rocks like a skeleton washed ashore. It is hewn from dark gray stone, made darker by the sheen of water dampening its lower walls where the waves beat at its foundations. The structure could easily encompass the entirety of St. Laurent. There are hundreds of tall windows, dozens of balconies, a collection of towers and courtyards enclosed by high walls. But I spot not one tree or bush, no green to break the monotonous gray. I wonder whether I will leave this place alive.

My heart threatens to punch through my sternum as we begin our descent. I didn't realize how thoroughly chilled I was, all these hours flying in the thin, frigid air. Sea spray has fully drenched my dress, my socks and loafers, hair and skin.

For someone so large, the East Wind slips through the tall, fingerbone rocks encompassing the fortress with fluid ease, banking toward a high tower protruding out over the sea. He glides through the open window and sets me onto the ground.

The moment he releases me, I dart to the other side of the room, arms wrapped around my middle. Now that we are free of the lightless prison cell, I am able to see my captor clearly for the first time.

The East Wind is indeed immense. His worn cloak covers him head to toe, but if I focus carefully, I can almost distinguish the shape of his face within that hood. He stands with legs braced, arms hanging loose at his sides. Heavy boots encase his feet. He overwhelms. He steals the air.

And yet, my attention shifts to his wings. Partially extended, the upper bones arch high over his head. They are considerably scarred.

"Why d-d-did y-you bring me h-here?" I ask through chattering teeth. "Wh-why didn't y-you just escape by yourself? Why go through all th-this effort to t-t-t-take"—my voice cracks, gut twisting with shame, that I cannot even utter the simplest words without fumbling—"me from m-my home?" I shiver, wishing for a coat to warm me.

His coarse voice bleeds from the cowl of his hood. "Fire."

I blink in confusion. "Wh-what?"

A red glow blossoms to my left. I startle, shrinking against the wall. But it is only the fireplace. "H-h-how—"

"I require your skillset."

I open my mouth, snap it shut. "M-m-my skillset?"

"Your knowledge of poisons, specifically."

Already, the flame begins to heat the room. My shivering abates. I tell myself not to be grateful for the warmth. I would not be in this position if he had not dragged me from my home. "But ... I'm j-just an apprentice."

"Do you honestly believe that?" he asks calmly.

If Lady Clarisse says I am only fit for an apprentice's work, then that is all I will ever be. The only way I can become a qualified bane weaver is if she chooses to promote me. I am still hopeful that will one day occur.

"Your employer is a stupid, self-centered fool," Eurus says. "She wouldn't recognize talent if it was located under her very nose. I've been observing you for months now. You are far more adept than that woman realizes. Your skills mark you as a bane weaver, even if your title does not."

The full weight of the immortal's gaze blankets me. If only his hood were not blocking my view of his countenance. It is a strange, uncomfortable feeling, knowing this prisoner was able to learn the extent of my skills by listening through a steel door. I'm not sure what to make of it.

"I d-do know about p-p-poisons," I admit, "but I d-d-don't know anything about using immortal p-parts to create them, as my lady does. All that I know, I l-learned from my grandmother." I lick my lips. Lady Clarisse loathes questions, but ... "Wh-what do you need the poison f-f-for?"

The East Wind cants his head, the motion eerily similar to that of the falcons nesting in the high cliffs. "I, too, have been wronged by the people in my life. It is time they paid for it." He turns, his cloak whipping about his legs. "Warm yourself by the fire. I'll return shortly."

He departs without a backward glance, launching himself out across the black waters that churn.

I crouch in a shadowed corner, knees against my chest, arms wrapped tightly around my legs. Since the divine's departure, the moon has bedded down, the earth having released its tenuous hold on the sun. The air warms, and the sea's crashing rings through the open window. I close my eyes on a sudden wave of dizziness and press my spine harder against the wall. The water is far. I am safe.

From that specific threat, at least. The East Wind claimed he required my skillset. I will be used. In what ways? When he is dissatisfied with my work, will he unfurl the lash? Will he lock me outside amidst a lightning storm, exposed to the elements? Lady Clarisse particularly enjoyed that one.

Round and round and round my thoughts spin. My teeth resume their chattering, and I gather my legs tighter to my chest. The motion splits open the scabs on my back. I bite the inside of my cheek, swallow down the yelp of pain. It seems the healing tea has finally worn off. With my body having drained itself of adrenaline, every ache, old and new, makes itself known.

Back at the estate, I would be spending the early hours of morn preparing client orders, brewing simpler remedies, those that did not require immortal ingredients. Her ladyship did not trust that I would not hoard those sea-nymph hairs and banshee scales and fair folk names for myself. Perhaps she was right to withhold trust. Were it not for me, the prisoner would not have escaped. And I would not find myself stranded and alone.

If I'm correct, Lady Clarisse is supposed to meet Prince Balior again tomorrow. She told me nothing of their initial conversation, though of course I was not expecting her to. What will happen now, when the prince learns the East Wind has escaped?

Eventually, exhaustion must drag me under, for I startle awake, my neck twinging from having fallen asleep upright. The tower is bright, its walls coated in thick yellow sunlight. I glance around blearily, wiping the sleep from my eyes. Something has changed. There, on a small table near the door, a dish of food has appeared.

Frowning, I push to my feet. A hearty stew fills the shallow bowl. Beef chunks swim in a thick sauce paired with onions, mushrooms, and cloves of garlic: beef bourguignon.

My stomach clenches in hunger. Nearly a day has passed since I last ate, but I can't trust that it isn't poisoned. Regretfully, I turn away, taking in the room.

One door, shut, locked. One window, wide and arched and garbed in teal curtains, gusts of salted air swirling into the small space. There is a simple wooden desk and chair. Against the opposite wall, a narrow cot. My trepidation deepens. Does this god expect me to live here now? Will he confine me in this highest tower, a nightingale in a cage?

Something shifts to my right. Through the window, a vague form glides over the water. I scurry to the other side of the room as fast as my wounds will allow, turning in time to witness the East Wind snap his wings closed mid-flight and drop through the open window, landing on silent feet. When he straightens to his full height, the top of his hood nearly brushes the ceiling.

I sense, rather than observe, the weight of his gaze. Instinct dictates I look elsewhere, but I force myself to maintain eye contact. Steel in my shoulders, in my spine. He stole me from my home. I was only trying to help him.

Eventually, he swivels his head toward the table. "You didn't touch your food."

My molars grind together, a slow back and forth. If I were of a more courageous nature, I would strike low and quick. "For obvious r-r-reasons."

A beat of silence passes. "You think it's poisoned."

"I'm n-not sure, but I'm certainly n-not going to find out."

Eurus considers me for a time. It is impossible to know what he thinks of me. "Why would I go through the trouble of bringing you all the way here, only to kill you? I told you I have need of you."

His question pokes holes in my nerve. I falter. "I-I-I don't know. I-I-I imagine y-you have your reasons."

He shakes his head, takes a step forward. When folded neatly along his spine, only the crowns of his wings are visible, slender bones and thin gray skin. "The food has not been tampered with."

"Your w-word means nothing to me," I snap. Where this sudden mettle has sprouted from, I'm not sure, but I embrace it eagerly. "You s-stole me from my home, locked me in this tower—"

"I did no such thing."

My lungs hollow out, squeezed with an emotion so utterly unfamiliar it takes a moment for it to process: anger. "So n-now I'm a liar?"

"I presume you did not attempt to open the door."

I open my mouth. It hangs there, soundless, then clamps shut. He is right. I assumed it was locked.

"Go on," he says. "Try the handle, if you don't believe me."

My eyes flick between door and god. But—fine. I walk the short distance to the door and turn the handle. Unlocked, as he claimed.

I shake my head, unable to hide the pink warming my face. "This m-means nothing. I'm s-still your captive, aren't I?"

His silence is not reassuring.

Moments later, my stomach gurgles. The East Wind huffs with impatience. Picking up the spoon, he slips it into the sauce, drawing the utensil into his hood. When he pulls the spoon away, it comes out clean. "Does that prove the food is safe to eat?"

The spoon vanishes. A fresh, clean utensil materializes beside the bowl. I frown. First the fire, and now this. Do this deity's powers extend beyond those storms and winds he mentioned?

When I refuse to move, Eurus lifts the bowl and glides toward me. His boots thud against the floorboards, and firelight glances off the scales of his wings, like oil on dark water. I try to back away, but my injured shoulder hits the wall, making me wince. He halts beside me and sets the meal on the desk. "You are hurt."

It shouldn't matter that he noticed. Lady Clarisse certainly never cared to. "The wounds w-will heal." It is nothing I haven't suffered before.

"And that is acceptable to you?" he demands.

This has nothing to do with whether or not it is acceptable. *It is simply reality.*

"I didn't h-hear you deliver the food earlier," I say, eager to shift the conversation in another direction.

He peers at me, perhaps noting my intention, but doesn't mention it aloud. "I didn't deliver the food." He moves to shut the window. "The manor is enchanted to meet your every need."

With the roar of waves muted behind glass, I am able to relax slightly. "Pardon?"

"The manor." He gestures around the room. "Whatever you need, just ask, and it will procure it for you."

Then it was the manor that lit the fire. It must have also left the meal. Such a marvel could only belong to the divine. "You have no servants, n-no attendants?" I question, at last reaching for the beef bourguignon. I shove a spoonful of meat into my mouth and very nearly moan in pleasure. Oh, that is delicious. Far better than Lady Clarisse's crumbs. Somehow, despite having sat out for many hours, the food is still hot.

"None," Eurus says.

So, he lives alone on this barren rock.

"While I was gone," he says calmly, "I returned to your village. My intention was to kill your employer."

The rich broth coagulates into a paste plastered across my tongue. I swallow and return the spoon to the desk, my hunger evaporating. "And did y-you?" I whisper.

"Unfortunately, she evaded me." He crosses his arms over his chest. "She seemed to have anticipated the attack. I assume this isn't the first instance of an immortal escaping her? Or enacted revenge?"

It was long ago. One of the fair folk managed to slip away after stealing Lady Clarisse's name, using it as leverage until she opened their cell door. Later, they returned, slinking into her bedroom while she slept. They would have pierced her heart, but she was ready. She pierced theirs first.

"If y-you had told her wh-wh-what she wanted to know," I argue, "she might have let you w-walk free." It sounds pitiful, even to my ears.

The East Wind's laughter is one of roughened scorn. I flinch, for the sound is chilling, edged by sharp points.

"I'm constantly amazed by how blind you mortals are. You would rather stick your head in the sand than face the truth. That woman is evil."

My face stings with rising heat. "That's n-n-not true," I say, though they are feeble, these words. If I am to have a home, if I am to remain close to Nan's memory, then I must abide by her ladyship's instructions. As she often touts, there is no room for compassion in the herbal arts.

"Shall I describe the hot coals shoved into my mouth, the branding on my bare back? Shall I describe," he goes on, voice hardening, "the mutilation I endured, the severed fingers, their slow regeneration? Or how about the acid thrown in my eyes, the daily whippings, the blood pouring from my body in sheets? Shall I—"

"Stop!" I'm panting, a cold sweat beading along my hairline. I dab it with a shaking hand. "No m-more. Please." What I feel is beyond illness. It is a rot that has taken root.

We stare at one other in silence. I cannot see his eyes, but I feel the rage vibrating off of him. He doesn't understand. I am only doing what I can to survive.

"How l-l-long do you intend to keep me h-here?" I whisper hoarsely. Months? Years? Am I to live out the remainder of my days isolated in this highest tower above the sea?

My mind goes to all the things I will miss. My weekly stroll into town. Master Alain's kindness, gossip snatched from front stoops and open windows. The churn of soil beneath my hands. Nan's spirit, touching every overgrown grapevine in the garden. Her ginger scent, which I swear I smell on particularly frigid mornings. Freshly baked baguettes, which we would tear in two and slather with homemade blackberry jam. All those memories, clouding the air of the estate, the place I love most. A home that will be sold, soon enough.

"You will never return to your old life," the East Wind states. "I suggest you forget about St. Laurent. From this moment on, you are under my employment. In return for your services, I will feed you, clothe you, provide a roof over your head. You may not find a home here, but you will not be mistreated."

My breath comes short. Feast or famine, slap or caress. It is no choice at all. "We m-must have d-d-different definitions of m-mistreatment," I dare say. "Everything you've done so f-f-far has been mistreatment."

He considers me, this immortal. "Allow me to amend. I will never raise a hand to you. But should you decide to deceive me, you will quickly realize how dire the consequences can be."

I cannot, will not, accept that. Somehow, I must return to St. Laurent. There might still be an opportunity to repair my blunder. Perhaps I might become the woman Nan always saw within me, hidden deep.

"Come," says the East Wind, turning toward the doorway. "The day is long, and there is much to learn."

6

"How adept are you at making poisons?" Eurus asks, directing me down a corridor on the second level of the manor.

The summer I came to live with Nan at her estate, she placed a mortar and pestle into my hand. I haven't looked back since. "I can manage," I say.

"That tells me very little."

I glare at the East Wind's back, where his scaled wings sit flat along his spine. With his long-legged stride, I'm forced into a trot. "If you want a more detailed r-r-response," I say, "you need to ask a more s-specific question." The slap of my shoddy loafers is abruptly muffled by the long, worn rug stretching the length of the hall. Tall, elegant windows panel one side, offering a view of the island, where sandy footpaths wind down the protruding rock to the strip of beach below.

He grunts, quickening his pace. The East Wind is . . . *irked* by my challenge? "Allow me to rephrase," he says. "How much of your employer's work was hers, and how much was your effort?"

All teas made in-house are touched by my hand, every one of them. "M-most teas, brews, and poisons w-were created by me."

"But she takes the credit."

Admitting this feels like a betrayal to my employer. There would be no apothecary without her. She informs me of this often enough. "I'm j-just her apprentice."

"Mm."

The corridor empties into a vaulted chamber. My breath hitches, and I peer upward at the spherical glass ceiling overhead. The East Wind crosses into an opposite hallway, but I linger, taking in the luxurious, cushioned furniture, the walls featuring a surprisingly eclectic collection of framed art. A sitting room, perhaps? The manor is surprisingly clean. I spot neither dust mote nor cobweb, smudged glass nor grime. Nan's estate is cluttered on the best of days.

I hurry after my captor. At least my clothes have dried, though the pain of my wounds is still a distant nuisance. As for the manor, there is an unnerving vacancy to the space. No flame brightens the ample fireplaces, no bodies occupy the halls. I question how long it has sat empty.

I finally catch up to Eurus as he rounds a corner. "Can you s-slow down?" I huff.

He halts, waiting until I draw alongside him. "Are there certain poisons that require immortal parts for their creation?"

"No." My thoughts drift to *The Practice of Herbal Remedies*. Sometimes, brews would take months to produce, the proportions modified until Nan deemed them satisfactory. Lady Clarisse hasn't the patience for that. According to her, two canines extracted from a certain hound hailing from the realm of Under possess the same numbing properties as combining three parts red sand, one part willow branch, and three parts glacier ice. When creating Ivory—one of her ladyship's most popular beauty teas—with the latter group of components, the draught must steep for seven weeks. But with the teeth? Only three days.

"I w-wasn't allowed to access those ingredients anyway," I add, glancing sidelong at Eurus. As if sensing my attention, he shifts his hood in my direction. My heart stutters, and I snap my gaze straight ahead.

As we pass the third or fourth dining room, I glance through the open doors. Walls paneled in blue silk cool the space. Giant tapestries hang alongside oil paintings bordered in ornate gilded frames.

"So you know enough to create poisons with natural materials alone?" the East Wind remarks after countless minutes walking in silence.

"I do." It is how one manipulates the roots, stems, and buds that changes a brew's character. Whether one slices stems vertically or horizontally, whether the flowers are crushed or crumpled or rolled or diced, at dawn or at dusk, in sun or in rain. The cycling of sun and moon, the acidity of the soil, the frequency of watering—so much affects a plant's nature. I decide whether those elements lead to everlasting love or a slow, agonizing death.

I suppose I never realized the power that holds.

We turn a corner. Down to the first level—lower. As we descend into a dank, dim stairwell, the slap of water draws my focus to the bottom steps. The lowest level of the manor has been entirely flooded by sea water. A small boat, tied to a wooden post, rocks to and fro.

My tongue feels as though it has swollen to thrice its normal size as the East Wind climbs into the vessel and settles onto the bench. "Get in," he says.

I am frozen, a broken stone having risen from the earth. "I can't," I whisper.

He stares at me. The darkness of his hood blends easily with the low light. "What do you mean you can't?"

"I'm afraid of w-water, remember?"

Liquid licks the walls of the submerged chamber. It reeks of salt. My pulse climbs.

"That is not my problem," Eurus responds in his toneless rasp. "Close your eyes, if you must." He gathers the oars, slotting them into place. "I want no further delay."

"Why can't you f-f-fly there?"

"My wingspan is too broad for some of the smaller passages. Now get in."

I have been here before. Hesitate, and suffer the consequences. The bruising on my chest and back throbs, a reminder of what occurs should I step even a toe out of line.

I climb into the vessel on shaky legs. My shoe catches on the lip of the hull, and I go sprawling, a brushfire igniting across my back where the fabric drags. The boat rocks. A splash sends me cowering. Only a thin layer of wood separates me from the ice-slickened water.

The East Wind loosens the rope with a tendril of wind. Once released, the boat bobs, the current pulling us down the leaden passage.

"Wait." My hand lashes out, clamping the closest thing in reach: the East Wind's wrist.

He stiffens, tears his arm away with a jagged exhalation. I swallow and shrink lower. It appears the East Wind does not like to be touched, or at least not without his consent. "S-sorry."

"Keep your distance," he growls. "Now close your eyes." The oars cut the water. "Breathe."

Behind my eyelids, there is darkness. Within that darkness, there is the memory of hands dragging at my flesh, the burn of salt in my throat. Floundering, thrashing, clawing. Then, a drifting, velvet peace.

"I can't breathe," I whisper hoarsely. "The w-w-water . . ."

"Listen to my voice, bird." Something heavy cups the back of my skull. His hand? "I won't let you drown." There is a pause. My nape prickles beneath a scrutiny I cannot see. "Remember that I have need of you."

I shiver, my mind small and distant as the East Wind circles the oars, propelling us backward through the passage. If I do not think too deeply on who this voice belongs to, I'm able to focus on its timbre, which is coarse, yet strangely soothing to my fractured mind.

Every so often, there is a light splash. It is the Master of Sea, mocking me. He tasted six-year-old Min's fear and now seeks to claim what was promised: a young child forced beneath the waves, a sacrifice in exchange for the return of a beloved husband.

At the next bend, my body leans into the East Wind. I should withdraw, but there is something stabilizing to his presence as we cross this uncertain water. Heat blankets my spine, and over time, my shivering tapers off. He sits stiffly against me, but doesn't pull away.

Hours or days or months later, the boat knocks against solid land. The vessel dips as the East Wind disembarks, but I remain in place, eyes squeezed shut.

Suddenly, he grasps my upper arms and hauls me from the boat. Once Eurus sets me on stable ground, I peer up at him, some of my earlier wariness having dissipated. I cannot remember the last time I was consoled. I do think he comforted me, in his own way.

"This way," he mutters gruffly.

I'm led up another staircase, down a stone corridor, all murk and depths, but thankfully dry enough. My loafers clip out a frenetic pace.

From shadow, there is light. We arrive at an open chamber, the air perfumed by moss that clumps the smooth paving stones underfoot. Meanwhile, an entire stretch of wall has succumbed to its springy tufts. Overhead, the stone ceiling is partially caved in, almost as if something blasted it apart. The jagged opening has since been covered by a layer of stained glass, which filters the light into beams of fuchsia, olive, and mustard.

The chamber houses a large garden with raised beds. I recognize the more common herbs of rosemary, lemon verbena, basil. Yet there are some plants I don't recognize. Curiously, I touch one such leaf: heart-shaped, with a deep orange blossom. I frown, mentally flipping through the pages of *The Practice of Herbal Remedies*. Could this be meolan? I've never seen it in person. Once dried, its petals can heal all manner of ailments of the lungs.

A sparrow flits toward its nest in the cracked wall. To my right, a trough has been hewn into the floor, allowing a stream of water to carve through the space. It seems the garden has been contained to the manor to protect it from the salt-drenched air beyond. I glance at Eurus, who studies me as I dip my hand into the stream. When I lift my fingers to my mouth, I am startled by the lack of salt there. "It's fresh," I say in surprise.

"For as long as you are in my employment," the East Wind says, ignoring my comment, "this will be your workshop. Here, you will find all manner of plants and herbs, in addition to tools, oils, stone and glassware, a hearth. If you require additional supplies, the manor will procure them for you. Now. What are the three most potent poisons you know how to create?"

I scan the overgrown garden. It is certainly extensive, but it will take time to identify what, exactly, grows here. "Fable, Goldenrod, and Eastern Blood."

"And out of those three, which is the deadliest?"

I hesitate, feeling suddenly uneasy by the direction of this conversation. "That depends." I link my hands together at my front, feeling much more grounded now that I am surrounded by plants. "Some bane w-weavers claim Fable to be the deadliest. It works quickly to paralyze your n-nervous system." Lady Clarisse favors Fable for its particularly agonizing deterioration. Cruel, but effective. "Others s-swear by Eastern Blood."

"What are their properties?"

I pause. What are the consequences of divulging this information? Eurus claims my knowledge of the herbal arts is significant, but only because he lacks it himself.

As though sensing my reluctance, the East Wind extends his wings, their massive shadow eclipsing me entirely. Scarred skin, stretched taut across hollow bones. He has received his fair share of hurts.

"Let me be clear," Eurus articulates, in a voice that allows no argument. "If you withhold information from me, you are making your life decidedly more difficult. Grant me your cooperation, and you will not suffer here."

I shuffle back a step to place distance between us, my gaze watchful. Indeed, I have suffered enough these long years. I am grateful Nan never had to witness it. "Fable w-works quickly, and though it is not deadly, it c-causes the drinker such incredible p-p-pain that many seek to end their suffering through other m-means. Eastern Blood has n-no specific taste or scent. Once it is consumed, y-you may begin to feel dizzy, but a decent night's r-rest will cure that. The following week, your muscles m-might feel w-weak, you might have difficulty w-walking, but again, a hot meal will do wonders."

I lick my lips as the East Wind's large hand drifts toward his thigh. Those long, pale fingers curve slightly, as though seeking something tangible to grasp.

"By the third week," I continue, "you will lose y-your sense of smell, then your sense of taste. Your throat will feel s-sore, as though you've caught a cold. Days later, you will pass in your sleep, with no outward indication of the cause of d-death."

"I see." He rubs at his face. A lock of dark hair falls forward, which he tucks away. "What, in your opinion, is the most powerful of those three that you listed?"

His question takes me aback. "My lady believes—"

"I didn't ask for her opinion," he cuts in harshly. "I asked for yours."

I blink at him, wide-eyed. This is a jest, no? Yet the moments pass, and he continues his uncomfortable scrutiny. He wants my opinion, for however little it is worth.

Nan would say Goldenrod. She always knew best. But having observed Lady Clarisse for a decade now, I have learned that pain has its place, it has its power, and that power should not be ignored.

"Eastern Blood," I tell him. "It is slowest to t-take effect, but there is no antidote, and it is the only one that invariably leads to death."

He gives me a slow once-over. At least, I think he does. I wonder what he sees. I wonder if he finds me lacking. "How long will it take you to produce each of those poisons?"

I make a mental calculation. "Goldenrod w-will be completed by tomorrow evening, so long as my w-work is uninterrupted." This last bit, I speak with a pointed look. "Fable will require at least two weeks to complete, though sometimes it takes up to f-four, depending on how much sap can be b-boiled out of the black pine root. Eastern Blood requires five to six w-weeks. This is, of course, dependent on whether I have all the necessary ingredients on h-hand."

I sense his discontent and ponder how it might soften or harden his expression. "It is cutting things close, but ... very well. You will produce each of those poisons," he tells me. "But I want a triple dose of Eastern Blood."

Dutifully, I nod, even as the knowledge that I will be contained here for weeks stirs my panic. There must be a way to get in touch with my employer. Perhaps I can use this time to find out where the East Wind has hidden his god-touched weapon. "What is expected of m-me? Am I to remain in that tower until you call for m-me, or . . . ?"

"I'm not here to monitor you," he says. "You are free to explore the manor at your leisure. My only requirement is that you report to me with your progress at the end of each day."

Admittedly, it is more freedom than I had in St. Laurent. Her ladyship only permitted me to venture into town once a week. "Where will you be wh-while I'm working?"

"I have some loose ends to tie up," he says vaguely. "I will be gone most days. If you need something, the manor will see to it. But I want to reiterate that there can be no delay, understood? I will need these poisons as soon as possible, ahead of my return to the City of Gods."

My fingers tighten, bunching the fabric of my dress. City of Gods? But I do not ask. It is unlikely he would respond anyway. "Understood," I whisper, head bowed.

He pivots, striding back down the corridor from which he emerged. I watch him go, until there is no distinction between darkness and god.

Five oleander cuttings, pale pink blooms crowning long green stalks, line the weather-beaten worktable. It has been shoved against a wall carpeted so thickly in moss, I cannot see the stone beneath. Overhead, the stained glass has dulled. Its fiery reds grow clouded, its mustard hues reduced. The air smells of a storm.

Carefully, I snip away the leaves to collect the chalky sap oozing from the stems, taking care to avoid agitating my wounds. My stomach growls. I ignore it. After the East Wind's departure, I took it upon myself to explore the garden—mostly searching for a way out. It was more expansive than I first assumed, containing all manner of vegetables and herbs, common and rare, cultivated in realms distant and near. A smaller, secondary antechamber housed a variety of grain, including wheat, rye, and corn. There was even a greenhouse fashioned from panes of glass. Inside, three rare orchids tilted their painted faces against the steaming air. Two I recognized. The third I did not.

I snip another leaf, catching the dripping sap in a round jar. Unfortunately, my only exit seems to be the boat. The other two existing passages have been bricked up for reasons unknown.

In the hours that follow, I collect enough sap to fill the entire jar, perhaps three cups' worth. I slice and crush and blend until my hands cramp, my half-frozen fingers tipped blue. The changing seasons are born from the Mother of Earth, who demands the land fall dormant in order to bring about rebirth. Many claim the goddess is fickle, delaying or expediting growth depending on her moods, but I have never believed that. So long as I extend gratitude for each plant harvested, I trust that she will provide.

In truth, I enjoy the solitude. It is my only opportunity to fully relax. Though I have been stolen from my home, I cannot deny the slow rhythm of my heart in her ladyship's absence. There is no threat amongst the moss and weeds. They demand nothing of me.

A sharp clatter startles me. I jerk around, scanning the area. On a nearby work bench, a bowl of stew has appeared, along with a hearty slice of bread. The manor. It must have sensed my hunger.

I pick my way toward the hot meal curiously. No sign of the East Wind. He made his point earlier—why would he seek to harm me when he requires my services? And I *am* hungry.

The stew is filling, seasoned with rosemary and thyme. Chunks of meat melt in my mouth, and I eagerly munch through a few softened potatoes before dragging the bread through the rich broth. It warms me from fingertips to toes, and I consume the entire bowl before setting it down with a gratified "Thank you."

The bowl vanishes. A glass of water appears in its place. I take a tentative sip before draining it. Moments later it, too, fades. I feel a swell of gratitude toward this strange, enchanted place. It cares for me, which is something I have rarely encountered over the last decade.

"Do you happen to know a way out of here?" I ask the manor.

The small stream splashes once, twice, thrice. A shallow wave curls toward the garden's entrance, as if gesturing me to follow. I'm led to the flooded corridor, where the boat dips with the current.

"I can't," I whisper. "Is there another way that doesn't involve water?"

A few leaves stir around my ankles. They sweep behind me, coaxing my attention back to one of the walls in the main chamber. The leaves scatter upward.

"I can't go through," I explain. "The passage is blocked off."

The leaves stir again.

I shake my head in confusion. "I don't know what you're trying to tell me." My attention flicks upward, and I pause. The manor isn't directing me to the wall. It's directing me to the small opening in the upper corner, wide enough that I may be able to squeeze through.

I stare at the hole in frustration. Too far to reach. Even if I were able to slip through the opening, where would I go? I remain trapped on this island with no means of escape.

A soft scuff of sound sends me darting back to the worktable. I stand with my back to the wall, scissors clenched in hand: a pitiful weapon.

Eurus emerges from the open corridor, wings tucked against his back, long, faded cloak snapping around his legs. Worn, calf-high boots of black leather thud against the uneven stone, and I bite the inside of my cheek. The sting grounds me.

The East Wind stops a stone's throw away. "Well?"

I blink in stupefaction. "Well wh-what?"

"Are you done?"

I decide that I do not like this immortal. Not only did he abduct me and force me into his employment, he seems like someone who finds little pleasure in the world.

"I told y-you," I reply, "some of the poisons will require many weeks. It has only been a f-few hours."

A crude wind tugs at my braid. He is displeased by my response. I need not witness his expression to know that. But what, specifically, displeases him? That I have the gall to challenge him? I retreat a step, gaze wary.

But he only grunts and says, "Tell me of your progress."

With effort, I force my fingers to loosen around the scissors. Stupid. As if I have the courage to use a weapon against him. "Right n-n-now, I'm gathering the ingredients for Goldenrod. I'm nearly done extracting the s-sap from oleander. Once that is complete, I'll grind peppercorn and two roots from the b-bashling sedge."

He approaches the worktable. The air wavers around him, but it is softer, this emotion, his winds humming not with impatience, but intrigue. I suppose I never realized how unusual my skillset is. Lady Clarisse frequently reminded me that everyone and everything is expendable, including me.

"This bashling sedge." He points. "What is its purpose?"

Not a test. Not a means to put me in my place—I think. "It paralyzes one's n-nervous system."

"Paralysis?" He considers me. "That could come in handy. You are quite certain you cannot complete the poisons sooner?" he asks, angling toward me.

"Quite," I clip out. He stands so close I'm forced to tilt back my head to meet his enshrouded gaze. When I shift slightly to the right, I catch the pale crescent of a cheekbone emerging from the shadows of his hood.

"Why do you n-need these poisons anyway?" I ask him. And why so urgently? "You're a god. Why not kill whoever has w-wronged you with your god-touched blade?" Though it goes against my every instinct, I turn my back on the East Wind and return to extracting the oleander sap. The curve of my nape tingles from the weight of his stare. "Or have you misplaced it? Is that why you're r-r-resorting to poisons?" I prod with a nonchalance I do not feel.

I am not expecting him to respond. Less than a day I have spent in this deity's company, yet I have already pinned him as closed and cold. But the East Wind surprises me by saying, "Do not worry yourself about my ax. It is well hidden under layers of enchantments."

So the weapon is somewhere in the manor. Where might the divine hide their beloved weapons? Surely not under their mattresses?

"As for the poisons," he continues, "it is not just one god I wish to kill. It is twelve of them."

My hands still. No, I did not misunderstand. The clarity of his words was a sharp-edged blade.

Setting down the paring knife, I turn to face him. "You seek to kill y-y-your own kind?"

Except . . . I frown at him. What am I missing? Gods are eternal. It is they who dictate life's currents, whether rainfall or drought, a bountiful catch, an abundant hunt. They cannot be killed by something as insignificant as a collection of chopped buds and crushed roots.

"I do," he says with no hint of remorse. "And you will help me do so." Without a farewell, he heads for the flooded corridor.

I blink at his retreating back in indecision. Beyond the garden walls, there is the overwhelming roar of rupturing waves. "Wait!"

He halts, an ear cocked over his shoulder.

"How am I s-supposed to get back to my room?"

"Use the boat," he rasps tonelessly.

"But—"

He's gone.

A brown flutter cuts across the space. I track the sparrow, watching in longing as it plucks a blade of grass from the tangled growth and returns to its nest. My grip on the knife coils. Tight, tighter, white-knuckled, fingers crushing the wooden hilt. Every second that passes is a second closer to Lady Clarisse selling the estate. This god thinks he can demand things of me? It is time to work. Time to return to St. Laurent.

Slamming the knife against the table, I stride for the hole in the wall. Utilizing the cracks between the stones, I heft myself higher— shredded back be damned—grappling for any nook or ledge. My fingers slip across small pebbles, then grab hold.

When at last I reach the top, I peer down into a walled courtyard below. Three large birds with ink-tipped wings sit on tall, wooden perches. It is then I notice the colored rings circling their slender legs: courier birds.

Lady Clarisse will be hearing from me, and soon.

7

Sunlight slaps me awake. I lurch upright, wincing as my torso flares in agony. I press a hand to my chest, atop my bruised sternum, and gradually, the world takes shape. A mattress, soft beneath me. My clothes from yesterday, still worn.

The previous afternoon returns to me in fragments. It took all my courage to board that boat in the garden so I could return to the lone tower with its singular window. There, I collapsed, exhausted beyond measure. I wished to forget the day and its preceding night.

But the morning is bright, and this is no fantasy. Beyond the open window, the rupture of water on rock explodes skyward, the churning storm just beyond. No creak of old wood, no hiss of steam over the hearth, no aroma of diced herbs.

Hunger coils in my stomach as I climb from bed. Judging by the sun's position, it is quite late. Her ladyship required that I begin work at dawn—sometimes earlier, and my duties always kept me busy well into the evening. Teas to brew, plants to harvest. I am half expecting her to barge into the room, lash in hand, for my tardiness.

It is then I notice a small jar of salve resting on the bedside table. No note. The manor must have left it for me.

After carefully dabbing the salve onto my back and chest, I push to my feet. It is strange, falling asleep in a proper-sized bed, in a proper-sized room. It reminds me that I was once worthy of this, in my youth. These days, I am only good enough for a broom cupboard.

When I peek behind a wooden partition in the corner of the room, I discover a large tub, complete with soap and towel. After peeling the filthy clothes from my skin, I step into the scalding water, sink into its heat with a gratified sigh. The pile of garments vanishes moments later.

Washing doesn't take long. I braid my hair and don the blue dress, black stockings, and undergarments that have appeared, neatly folded on a nearby chair. The dress is a tad long, but that can't be helped. At least it is clean, without holes.

A strip of parchment flutters in my periphery, drawing my attention toward the desk. I peer down at the scrawled message, frowning.

You have the day to complete your work. I expect an update when I return.

A thread of vexation pulls taut in my gut, and I flip the message over. Neither *please* nor *thank you*. As it is, nothing could force me back into that boat. And anyway, the poisons must steep. Excuses? Perhaps. But no one is here to scold me. With the East Wind's absence, this might be my only opportunity to explore the manor thoroughly. Wherever his ax is hidden, I will find it.

Snatching a quill and pot of ink, I pen a message.

The East Wind took me. I know where his weapon is hidden. The estate has not been sold, has it? Send word by courier bird.

My hand trembles. Ink slips from the quill's sharpened tip and blots out *hidden*. Should I rewrite it? No, it is legible, if a blatant lie. Lady Clarisse never has to know. By the time I receive a response, I will have hopefully found the East Wind's weapon. It is my only leverage if I am to purchase the estate.

"Could you please show me how to get to the aviary from here?" I ask the manor.

Something plucks the note from my fingers, waving it before my nose. I snatch it back and tuck it safely into my dress pocket. "It's a message," I whisper, "for my family. I ... don't want them to worry." Surely an enchanted manor cannot discern the falsehood in my voice?

The door eases open, as though the manor is satisfied by my answer. I follow the flickering wall sconces down the spiraling stairwell. One of the oil paintings to my left wiggles on its hook. My mouth curves, and I follow the manor's clever communications, around a corner into a hallway paneled in dark, polished wood.

Here, the art is varied and intentionally curated: canvases depicting pastoral scenes in oil, busts shaped from glazed marble balanced on pedestals. The more I study the manor, the more I get a sense of her character, those varying shades. Gray, certainly, for there is much stone, but some walls are covered in wallpaper, some wood, and the rugs are plentiful. She—the manor—is cultured, refined, if a bit eclectic, shabby around the edges.

The manor directs me through an open doorway. I'm too busy absorbing the sights to pay much attention until the door clicks shut behind me.

"This isn't the aviary," I mutter in confusion.

The window curtains flutter, but the door does not reopen. Clearly, she wants me to explore the room.

The rug underfoot muffles my footsteps as I approach the massive oak desk. To my surprise, I find only a blank sheet of parchment and a clean quill resting along its edge. Seems rather sparsely furnished for a study. For that is what this is, I realize. The East Wind's study.

With a slow spin, I survey the space with fresh eyes. The floor-to-ceiling bookshelves are organized by size, with the largest tomes on the lower shelves, the smaller volumes on the upper. The room smells of yellowing parchment and something darker that I recognize as the god's own scent.

Something flaps near the window: an oil painting, though the canvas has been slashed beyond recognition. I peer closer. Four men are seated around a large fountain in a city square. Curiously, only one of the men has wings.

Despite searching high and low, I find no sign of any weapon, ax or otherwise. I sincerely doubt he would leave it out in the open, though I question why a god would not carry his prized weapon on his person.

"You wouldn't happen to know where the East Wind has hidden his ax," I ask the manor, "would you?"

I receive no response. It is as I thought.

I slip back into the dimly lit corridor, its walls papered in faded yellow silk. I explore each room on the second level, every dining room, sitting room, powder room, washroom, laundry room, bedroom—all eight of them—and library. Many of the rooms house impressive collections of oil paintings, enough that I wonder if the East Wind doesn't have a partiality for the medium. Only one door is locked. His bedroom? I will need to find another way in.

The manor then directs me outside. Wide, stone steps descend down a sloping lawn, its grass withered, likely due to its proximity to the sea. I hurry across an overgrown pathway leading to an old wooden door set into a high stone wall. Inside, I find the aviary.

One of the birds glides down to me as though having been summoned. I tie the message onto its leg, saying, "Deliver this to Lady Clarisse in St. Laurent." Then, because I am not quite sure if it understands me: "Thank you."

The bird spreads its wings. Air stirs at its departure, and I watch until it is swallowed by the distant horizon.

At midday, hunger forces me into the kitchen.

It is spacious and well-stocked, the clay tiles underfoot providing a much-needed warmth. A table draped in a thread-worn tablecloth is joined by four mismatched chairs. The window above the sink frames the island's crags and cliffs. When I run a hand along the wooden countertop, it comes away clean.

"Do you by chance have fresh bread?" I ask the manor. St. Laurent is known for its breads, pastries, and cakes. It is something I sorely miss.

A subtle wind rattles a narrow door behind the kitchen table: the pantry. Grains and preserved fruits and hunks of aged cheese. There—a baguette wrapped in parchment paper. I pull it down with a soft crinkle. It's still warm.

A pang hits, as does a memory. I sit at the kitchen table of the estate, my legs too short to reach the floor. Nan, dressed in a lavender blouse, tears pieces from the baguette we bought in town. There is butter, preserves, honey, all stored in porcelain bowls. My grandmother always gave me the crusty heel, along with a forehead kiss and a hearty, *Eat up.*

"Is there jam?" I murmur to the manor.

A small glass jar slides to the front of the shelf. After locating a knife, I cut into the warm bread and spread strawberry jam into its soft crannies, consuming the chunk in three bites.

A white linen napkin materializes on the countertop. I wipe my fingers, eyeing the bowl of fruit near the sink. After some consideration, I select a peach for myself.

"What are you doing?"

I startle and whirl around, the peach slipping from my grasp. It hits the tile with a soft *thump* and rolls, striking the toe of a large, scuffed boot.

The East Wind dominates the doorway, the tattered ends of his black cloak fluttering around his calves. The air shifts, shedding softened ease for something decidedly more deadly. I can all but feel it bend and waver around him in palpable fury.

"I w-w-was getting s-s-something to eat," I manage, retreating behind the table.

He picks the peach off the floor, strides toward the counter. The slow fall of his footsteps rattles the kitchen window. "If you're hungry," he snaps out, "ask the manor to make you something. Don't touch things that do not belong to you." He then begins rearranging the bowl of fruit. He removes the apricots, apples, and tangerines, carefully tucking each one back into its proper place, with the peach balanced on top.

That done, his gaze sweeps the countertops. There, the torn baguette. And beside it, strawberry preserves coating the knife in a glisten of red sweetness. A low growl sounds, and he's across the room, wiping down the counters and replacing everything as it was.

"I d-d-did ask," I say to him, voice quavering. "I th-think the manor w-w-wanted me to find the kitchen myself."

"That's ridiculous." He rinses his hands in the sink, wipes them dry with a rag. "Did you receive my note this morning?"

"Y-y-you mean the one t-telling me to get to work?" How could I forget?

"Well? Do you have an update?" He turns, pinning me with eyes I cannot see.

I bite the inside of my cheek. "N-not yet. The poisons are s-steeping now."

He tosses up an arm in frustration, and although he stands on the opposite side of the table, I recoil.

Slowly, Eurus lowers his arm. He stares at me. It is too quiet.

"I said I would never raise a hand against you," he utters. "I meant it."

It is not the words that matter. It is the raising of an arm, the curl of fingers into what could be a fist. "S-sorry." The East Wind is no stranger to my employer's treatment, but shame threatens regardless, that he sees how weak I truly am.

As though recognizing the aggression of his stance, Eurus relaxes somewhat. He says, in a noticeably gentler tone, "There must be something else you can do in the meantime. Can you harvest your next ingredients? As I mentioned before, there can be no delay. We must reach the City of Gods before the month's end, otherwise ..." He clenches his jaw and falls silent.

I swallow around the chattering of my teeth, wondering where this City of Gods is and why he is so desperate to travel there. *We*, he said. I do not like the sound of that. "I n-n-need to eat something first. Then I w-will w-work." How many times have I gone to bed hungry, my stomach in knots over having failed to complete the day's agenda in a timely manner? Too many to count.

"Very well. But after that, I expect to be updated on your progress."

I nod stiffly, watching him from across the table. "I w-wasn't aware you felt so s-s-strongly about fruit," I mention, only partially in jest.

"I like everything in its place," he explains with a stilted tone. "I decide. No one else."

I watch him scrub the counters, the sink, even the cabinets. He likes his kitchen tidy as he likes his study tidy, and perhaps all rooms in the manor. "I understand."

His head snaps toward me. There is an uncertainty to his posture as he refolds the cloth and places it by the woodfire stove.

"Back home, I have a chest full of m-my grandmother's things," I tell him. "I wouldn't w-w-want anyone to t-t-touch them either. I suppose that's wh-why I wandered into the kitchen," I continue, hoping my willingness to share will similarly encourage him. "I used to c-cook with my g-g-grandmother when I was younger. But I h-h-haven't cooked in a long time."

"Because you lost interest?" he asks.

"I don't h-have the t-t-t-time." At his pause, I go on, my stutter strengthening the more I try to repress it. "I w-w-work w-well into the n-n-night sometimes—" My throat closes, and I look down at my feet. "S-s-s-sorry."

"What are you apologizing for?"

"My st-stutter."

A warm breeze skims the back of my neck. A subtle pacifying. "It does not bother me. I think your voice is nice." There is a pause, during which I am not sure how to respond. The last thing I expected from the East Wind was a compliment. "Are you ashamed of it?"

My face heats. "My l-l-lady says—"

"Why do you listen to anything coming from that witch's mouth? She is horrible to you, and to others."

"She has her r-r-reasons."

"Which are?"

None are particularly convincing, now that I think about it. And the one truth I might reveal carries too much shame. "Everything sh-she does is to make me into a b-b-better apprentice. She s-s-said if I work hard, she will make m-me a full-fledged bane weaver."

I sense his unexpressed scoff. "You actually think she would do that for you?"

I want to say yes, but truthfully, I am uncertain. "After Nan d-died," I whisper, "I had no one else. My lady is the only f-f-family I have."

"And you feel that is reason enough to overlook the anguish she causes others? She tortures innocents. She shot me down as I was flying over St. Laurent, did you know that?" He jerks his head. The sharp line of his jaw appears, then is swallowed by shadow. "Hired a huntsman to do her dirty work. Whatever coated the arrowheads, it nullified my powers. She tied me up, tossed me into the back of a cart like chattel. When I awoke, it was in the darkness of the tower, my ankles and wrists shackled." The East Wind stares me down. "She doesn't care about you. And you are a fool to think she ever would."

I shake my head even as guilt renders me breathless. Her ladyship's methods of capture are brutal, inhumane. Which is exactly why I do not wish to know about them. "I'm s-sorry you endured that."

"I'm sure."

Before he can slip away, I ask him, "You keep m-mentioning the City of Gods. Wh-where is it?" By the Mother, I cannot think of traveling even farther from home.

"That is not your concern at the moment. The sooner you finish the poisons, the sooner your obligation will be complete. Eat up. You've work to do." He departs without a farewell.

A low, ragged breath escapes me. The East Wind is wrong, so very wrong. "He d-doesn't understand," I whisper to the manor. And he never will.

Where does that leave me? I am bound here against my will, yet I cannot stay. This is no life. This is a cage.

In minutes, I'm back in the tower, standing before the open window. There is the sea, cutting her vicious teeth on the rocks below. St. Laurent awaits. There must be a boat moored somewhere nearby. The thought of rowing through the storm surrounding the island makes my stomach roil, but if this is my only means of returning home, I will have to risk it.

Swinging one leg over the sill, I grip the salt-bitten frame in both hands, trembling. My breath sputters out of me. When I attempt to slide my other leg through the window, my balance wavers.

Blackness blots out my vision, and my grasp on reality slips as the sea spews foam. I clutch the window frame with all my strength. Quicker my heart thrums, a skittering rhythm caught behind my ribs. This was a terrible idea. And now I find myself frozen, unable to climb back inside.

Minutes or hours or days later, the door opens. The East Wind crosses the threshold and promptly goes still.

What must he see when he looks at me? A thin, bird-boned woman, caught between freedom and captivity. Tears trickle down my reddened face. My trembling intensifies as he advances toward me, long legs eating the ground in less than two heartbeats. A whiff of salt and something darker surrounds him.

Gently, he touches my chin, angling my face toward his hood. "Did you think to free yourself from me, bird?" He speaks quietly, yet always with that threatening edge. The tips of his fingers graze the curve of my jaw. I shiver beneath the fragile touch. "I already told you there is nowhere for you to go."

That had been my intention, and yet— "I'm stuck," I croak.

He reaches for me. Swift—too swift, his movements, the immortal speed. I flinch, accidentally leaning farther out the window. I claw at the frame and manage to right myself before toppling backward, gulping air. I will fall. My body will break across the waves. I will know only darkness.

The East Wind does not reach for me again. "I'm not going to hurt you." His demeanor has gentled, if I'm not mistaken. "I'm going to pull you back inside. Take my hand."

My muscles pulse erratically. I can't pry my fingers free. "The w-water—"

"Don't look at the water," he orders. "Look at me."

What am I to look at, exactly? There is no face, no expression, no sense of identity. His hood hides all, a void sucking any and all light.

But—better than the sea. Better than drowning. Since I can't make out Eurus' expression, I'm forced to read him in other ways. The tilt of his head. Points of tension in his body. How his legs are braced—ready to pull me in.

I reach for him. He retreats, then halts, as though battling his own instinct to shrink from my outstretched hand. In this moment, another of his shadowed layers peels away. Someone hurt him. How? In what capacity?

Before I realize he has moved, I'm pulled from the window and set on my feet. Immediately, he releases me.

My legs tremble so severely I'm forced to lower myself onto the ground. "I c-c-can't go back to the g-garden," I garble, the words choked by my useless tongue. "The water . . . I c-can't do it. I'm s-s-sorry."

Tentatively, I peer at him through my eyelashes. He lifts a hand to his face with a sigh. The motion pushes back his hood enough that a lock of black hair pokes out. "I will see about finding another way for you to access the garden."

I should not feel gratitude toward this immortal. But it is so small a thing, to be known, to have my fears heard, arrangements made with my comfort prioritized. "Thank you," I whisper.

"What of your progress?"

"Th-there is one ingredient I still r-require for Eastern Blood. It is called nightshade and it is g-grown in the realm of Under. Lady Clarisse has s-s-some, back at the estate," I offer too quickly.

His head snaps toward me, and I promptly shut my mouth. "And if I allowed you to go there to gather the nightshade, you would not attempt to slip from my grasp?"

"N-no." I force down a swallow. "It w-would be the fastest w-way to acquire what we need."

"As I said before," Eurus replies darkly, "you should forget your home. You will never return."

As if I need a reminder. I can only hope my message arrives to Lady Clarisse safely. If she learns that I live, might she try to save me?

The East Wind dips his chin, pinches the bridge of his nose with a sigh. "We will travel to Kilkare. It is a town located in the realm of Carterhaugh. There, you will find your nightshade plant."

I knead my arms in uncertainty. I've never traveled so far west. It would be a reprieve to leave these high stone walls, but— "Will w-w-we be traveling by boat?"

"We'll fly."

8

The air is breathlessly cold. Curled against the East Wind's chest, I listen to the steady *whump whump* of his wings, the ebon glitter of his scales reflecting the light. He holds me as though I am weightless, one arm slotted beneath my bent knees, the other bracing my lower back. The strength of him cannot be denied. His body has been honed, cut, carved out. Despite this, I'm held gently. Somehow, these two realities do not blend together, one sharp, the other dull.

We abandoned his island of isolation hours before, crossing the sea westward. Below, she waits. She thrashes and she howls. This god is no safe harbor, but I cling to him.

"Have y-you visited Kilkare before?" I ask, pitching my voice over the wind.

We dip lower. My stomach surges into my mouth, and I dig my fingers deeper into his shoulders until the sensation ebbs. He tries yet fails to shrug away my touch. "No."

The terseness of his reply exposes a discomfort I do not understand. Not that I expected in-depth conversation, though it would certainly make the journey more pleasant.

On and on and on we fly. My hamstrings twinge from the discomfort of holding myself in place, but I dare not stretch my legs for fear of slipping. I'm beginning to wonder if we will stop for a break when Eurus says, "We're past the sea."

He's right. The cliffs sketching Marles' eastern border are at last behind us. I'm relieved to leave the water behind.

Peering through my lashes, I search for shape and definition within his cowl. The glimpses I've been granted thus far are crumbs. I've an odd hunger for more. "Why do you live the w-way you do? I can understand the need for solitude, but y-you live on an island that is nearly impossible to reach. It makes me think you are avoiding s-s-something."

"I avoid nothing," he all but snarls, but his arms remain secure around me. "I like my space and my freedom. I do not care to give that up."

I frown, for I said nothing about sacrificing one for the other. "Is that wh-why you keep your face hidden?" I ask. "Because you do not w-want anyone to know you?"

His wings thrust us forward, fast, faster. Yellow-green streaks below—the forest and fields. My eyes sting from the rapidity of our pace.

After a time, Eurus slows. "The hood is a necessary precaution," he explains. "Some things the world is not meant to see. Some truths too brutal. Some wounds too deep."

We stop for the night in Aburgan, a region in western Marles known for its production of fine oil. The inn roosts atop a hill, cast in amber light from the setting sun. Its surrounding fields are plentiful, the air tinged with the musk of pressed olives.

The East Wind checks us in, to the wariness of the innkeeper. Separate accommodations, thankfully. After wolfing down a delicious roast in the commons, I return to my room to wash away the day's salt and sweat. I try the door: locked. The window: locked. It seems Eurus has covered all locking mechanisms with a layer of impenetrable air, preventing my escape. He is wise to have done so.

I succumb to exhaustion, falling into a dreamless sleep, and wake well rested. After breakfast, Eurus offers a brisk "Let's go" before ushering me out the door. Scooping me into his arms, he launches skyward, and we're off.

Before long, Marles' rolling pastures begin to diminish, the land patched with dried grasses, bare rock. The sun boils down. My eyes find the horizon, that seam of earth and sky. In the distance, the air wavers over red stone, a glaze of heat. Cracked earth transforms into expansive hills of sand. It is unlike anything I have ever witnessed. A land completely devoid of water and life.

As though sensing my wonder, the East Wind murmurs, "Ammara."

"Excuse me?"

"We have passed beyond the boundaries of Marles and now travel over the realm of Ammara." A slight tilt of his wings steers us northwest. Our combined shadows ripple below.

"It's . . ." But the words disintegrate. They are too trivial to properly venerate this unending plain. I am eclipsed in its greatness. "Have y-you visited?"

"On occasion."

Gradually, Eurus descends closer to the sand. I marvel at its palette of hues: red and ochre, yellow and tawny and gold. Now that we've left the higher altitude of Marles, sweat springs beneath my arms and at the backs of my knees.

"I was traveling back from Ammara when I was captured," he replies, in subtle surrender to my thirst for knowledge.

And just like that, all the desert's brightness dulls, as if coated in a fine layer of dust. "Oh." I remember the day of his capture. Lady Clarisse had returned to the estate with a manic grin crimping her mouth as two men carried the hooded stranger through the back door. I didn't know then that she had captured a god. I thought he was just another immortal, same as all the rest.

Eager to redirect the conversation—for this is, indeed, a conversation—I say, "What business did y-you have in Ammara?"

The East Wind angles upward, and a powerful flap of his scaled wings sends us soaring ever higher. "If I answer," he growls lowly, "will you stop asking questions?"

I nod.

"I was visiting my brother, Notus."

I stare at him. "You have a brother?"

"I have three."

Of course. That oil painting I stumbled across in his study portrayed four men, yet only one with wings. Could they be the Anemoi that her ladyship mentioned? Might his siblings also possess power over the wind? And if what he says is true, then Eurus is not the only deity occupying the mortal realms. "What is Ammara l-like?"

"Dry."

The urge to roll my eyes is strong. Somehow, I temper it. "Well, it *is* a desert."

"What I mean," he says, "is that Ammara has been fighting a drought for more than two decades. The annual floodwaters have ceased. Crops are in decline. The people suffer."

Unsurprisingly, there is little compassion from him. He is simply stating the facts. "For someone who hates to venture f-from his island, you seem to know a lot about Ammara's state of affairs."

"I should, considering I was the one who took Ammara's rains."

I startle in his arms. "You s-stole the rains from Ammara?"

"I stole nothing," he clips out, arms tightening at my back. "It was a fair trade. Their king was desperate, and I needed those rains to strengthen the protections around my island. He could give me that, and in exchange, I granted him his heart's desire."

The storm, I realize. Eurus stole Ammara's rains to feed the massive storm enveloping his manor.

"You're saying you d-d-doomed an entire realm to suffering because you needed more *water*?" It is absurd. It is sickening. "Those are life-giving rains. Y-you stole them." And likely took advantage of a poor mortal king. The man's desperation must have been immense, to willingly condemn his kingdom. I wonder what Eurus provided him in return.

He scoffs. "Not water. *Power.* And you would not understand."

Oh, I understand. It is clear the East Wind lacks any consideration for others, any compassion at all. He values influence above all else.

The reminder that I am but one more pawn on his board fatigues me. I rest for a time, though I am never able to relax fully in this god's embrace. When I open my eyes, the desert has been replaced with a vast tract of forest. We bank hard, veering toward a clearing on the outskirts of a small town. Eurus cups the back of my head as his wings flare out, slowing our descent. He touches down with all the care of a seamstress threading the eye of a needle.

The relief of returning to solid ground cannot be understated. I love the solidity of the earth. I love the bedrock and soil, the plains and mountains, valleys and hills. Change is slow with feet on the ground.

Eurus jerks his chin, and I follow at his heels, eyes wide as we venture down a busy market street.

It is not the shops I notice first, but the people. They are dressed in browns and whites and greens—shades of the earth. They clad their bodies in sturdy cotton and lightweight linen. There is no delicate silk or lacy frills, nothing extravagant about their manner of dress. The bright click of heels has been replaced with heavy boot tread.

As for Kilkare itself, we have exchanged the corroded metal rooftops of Marles for thatched coverings, chimneys sprouting coils of smoke. The doors to the chapel lie open. A tuneful hymn drifts from the candlelit interior.

The East Wind ducks down a small side street, glancing left, right, left again. More than one civilian stares as he passes. Then again, a massive, winged figure *would* attract attention.

Halfway down the road, he again peers over his shoulder.

"Is someone following us?" I ask.

"No."

By the Mother, he is not very convincing. "Then wh-what is it?"

His strides lengthen, forcing me into a trot. Ahead, a family halts at a market stall to purchase fruit. The East Wind advances without slowing, forcing the family to scatter or be trampled. My mouth pinches at his disregard for others. "There is someone here I would like to avoid at all costs."

Interesting. Eurus does not seem like the sort of person to run from anything. "Who?"

"My brother." A grimace coats his words in oily discontent. "But we'll be gone before he learns of my visit."

"Is this the same brother you v-visited in Ammara?"

"No." He glances down an alleyway before pushing forward. "Unfortunately, the most obnoxious of my brothers lives here."

Shortly after, we reach a shop with a powder blue door. A polished wooden sign hangs in the front window: *Chamomile & Sage*.

A warm, lemony fragrance hangs like a cloud over the threshold. There is every manner of herb, flower, and root, all stored in jars, baskets, and tins. The chaotic nature reminds me of my workshop back in St. Laurent. It comforts me, even as homesickness roots deep in my belly.

A woman wearing wire-rimmed spectacles and a patched dress regards Eurus warily from behind the counter. "May I help you?"

He steps forward, the top of his hood nearly brushing the ceiling. One of the shelving units shudders from the might of his footfalls. "We're in need of nightshade."

The woman pushes her glasses up her nose. "Nightshade is under restricted use. Due to its hazardous properties, prospective buyers require the permission of the Bringer of Spring. This is to ensure the plant will not be used for any ill—"

"What did you say?" Eurus demands. Slowly, his wings open, ink-blot scales glittering like a thousand minute eyes.

The shopkeeper pales before him. "I s-said—" She swallows. "You need to speak with the Bringer of Spring. He is the bridge between Under and Carterhaugh and lives on the other side of town—"

"Let's go," Eurus snarls at me, spinning toward the door. One of his wings hits a shelf. Glass shatters in the wake of his departure.

I scurry after him. He strides ahead, shoving people left and right as though they are of no more significance than dead leaves caught in an updraft of wind. But the throng is dense, my stature slight. Soon, I am swallowed, his dark hood lost amongst the crowd. By the time I turn the corner, I've lost sight of the East Wind.

Someone jostles me, and I hurriedly step aside, out of the immediate flow of traffic. Did he slip into a shop, maybe? Or would he return to the clearing?

Then I pause. Wait. He's *gone*. For the first time in days, I am free.

Turning, I race in the opposite direction, cutting down a trail that veers into the forest and runs parallel to a broad, sinuous river. After stopping to drink my fill, I hurry onward, picking my way over the root-strewn ground until I spot a building whose chimney belches smoke. I dart toward the open double doors and duck inside, panting, hand pressed to my heart.

"Can I help you?"

I gasp, spinning around to face a curvy woman studying me with unexpected kindness.

"Sorry," I whisper. Only now do I realize I've slipped into what appears to be a forge. A gray haze veils its large, stony mouth, white smoke drifting from its coals.

The woman lowers a mallet onto the anvil. Her hair is brightest flame. It tumbles over her broad shoulders in large ringlets, her pale, freckled face smudged with soot. A cowhide apron protects the cotton dress beneath.

"Are you in trouble?" She immediately shuts the wooden doors.

"Um." I wipe the perspiration dotting my brow. The ash-soaked air sticks inside my lungs. "There's a man looking for me. I do not wish to be found."

The woman's earthen eyes harden with distaste. "Then we will make sure he cannot find you. You'll be safe here," she says. "Let me find my husband, and then we'll see what we can do for you. What's your name?"

I lick my lips. "Min."

"Stay here, Min. I'll be back shortly."

As soon as the door creaks shut, my thoughts plummet into an endless spin. I'm safe, or so that woman claims, but for how long? Can I trust her, or anyone in this town? I spotted no ring on her left hand. Does she have a husband, or was that, too, a lie?

I hunch lower to the ground, arms curled around my middle despite the sweltering heat. Eurus has likely noticed my absence. Once he finds me, he will not let me go, not for anything. It will take weeks, possibly months, of travel to reach Marles. Though I still lack the East Wind's god-touched ax, I know the location of his manor. That should be enough to appease Lady Clarisse and convince her not to sell the estate, for now. Needless to say, I cannot stay here.

Easing open the door, I peek outside. Trees and swirling winds. The river that runs clear. Keeping to the cooling shadows, I skirt the forest path until I return to the edge of Kilkare. Its crowds have swelled beyond its muddy streets—men hauling sacks of grain on sweat-dampened backs, a harassed mother carting pails of fresh daisies. I spot a merchant tossing crates into the back of a wagon—an ideal hiding place.

"Pardon, sir?" The gentleman lifts his head, squinting against the brightness. "Are you leaving town? Do you have room on your cart for me to hitch a ride?"

Abruptly, the sun goes dark. My hand lifts, eclipsing the scorching orb overhead. A winged creature circles above, as a vulture does over a fly-swarmed carcass.

Shrinking into the shadow of a nearby building, I watch the East Wind spin oh-so-slowly, low, lower. He searches for one thing only: the bird that has fled its cage.

Eventually, Eurus veers off. Only when I lose sight of him do I sag against the wall, knees knocking.

"Miss?" The merchant peers at me in worry. "Were you still wanting a ride?"

I press a hand to my stomach. I feel sick. "No." Too risky, with the East Wind circling overhead. *What to do, what to do?* The ginger-haired woman and her forge at the edge of the forest—I should have stayed. It may be too late now, but . . . I have to try.

Keeping to the shadows proves difficult at high noon. The alleyways provide temporary shelter, but eventually I'm forced to cross the road, the forest just ahead.

It is the scent of brine that alerts me. My gaze snaps upward where the East Wind searches, and I freeze—my first mistake. His hood angles toward me, and he dives.

I dart for the nearest alley. *Hide. Run and do not stop.* For this is a hunt, and the East Wind seeks his prey.

I am crashing through gatherings, hurtling around beggars, leaping over carts. A cooling tendril snags my ankle, and I stumble, hitting the ground. But I'm up, pushing myself to the brink of what I can sustain. Around another corner, across a busy intersection. I duck into a shop smelling strongly of leather and crouch beneath a shelf. The woman—a book binder, judging from all the parchment and thread—gapes at me from her position behind the counter.

"Please," I pant. "Pretend I'm not here." I was not meant for running. I was meant for slicing, grinding, stirring, crushing, boiling. With a shaky hand, I wipe the sweat dampening my face and neck.

The door opens. I freeze.

"Where is she?"

The shopkeeper licks her lips nervously. "Good day to you, sir."

The East Wind crosses to the counter, searching with those unseen eyes. The door stands open. A crowd has begun to gather in the streets.

"We can make this easy, or difficult," Eurus says in his coarse rasp. "I'm looking for a young woman with black hair and brown eyes. Where are you hiding her?"

"I have seen no such woman. As you can see, my shop is empty."

"What of that curtained doorway? What are you hiding behind it?"

"Sir, please—"

As the East Wind slips behind the curtain, I dash outside, but as I hit the muddy road, the door explodes behind me.

I scream, darting between two buildings. Dust puffs beneath my flashing soles. The steady *whump whump* of his wings vibrates like thunder through me. I duck as the East Wind swoops low, his hand just skimming my shoulder.

He snarls a curse, the narrowness of the space between the buildings forcing him upward, lest he crush his wings. Spinning, I flee in the opposite direction and find myself at another intersection. Which way was the forest path? I choose a course at random. My lungs strain, each heaving gasp collapsing into the next as I turn down an alleyway, then stop.

Dead end.

A wave of air slams me against the ground. Dirt crunches underfoot. I flinch, eyes squeezed shut. My muscles lock, body curled inward for the cut of the lash, a swift kick to the leg. Whatever the punishment, I will endure it, as I have always done.

An unexpected warmth washes the entirety of my spine in heat. A helpless whimper slips out as the East Wind's broad hand comes to rest at the base of my nape, his fingers shaping the curve like a heavy collar.

"Why do you flee, bird?" The dark, velvet-wrapped croon sends a shiver skating across my skin.

My molars grind together so hard they squeak in protest. I am many things. Brave, I am not. "Why d-d-do you th-think?" I whisper, and wonder if I have secured my own doom.

Slipping his hands beneath my arms, he lifts me to a standing position. I struggle to catch my breath.

"Well, well, well, what do we have here?" someone drawls from behind us.

The East Wind stiffens. Rather than face the newcomer, he eases closer, the length of his torso plastered to my back. My heart skips a beat. When I try putting space between us, his hand keeps me in place.

"If even a word of our arrangement is spoken," he whispers to me, the heat of his breath tickling the shell of my ear, "I will return to your pitiful town and flatten it without a thought. Do we have an understanding?"

I am acutely aware of how small I am in comparison, how frail. I nod jerkily, and he releases his hold. A cooling wind sweeps between us, drying the perspiration beading my skin.

The East Wind turns to regard the newcomer, a slight man with springing, gold-streaked curls and skin kissed by a summer sun. He wears an olive, thigh-length tunic, brown breeches, and calf-high boots. His eyes are the pale shade of jade.

"Zephyrus," the East Wind clips out.

The man is all smiles, though his gaze flicks to me curiously. Beyond the mouth of the alley, people have begun to congregate. "Eurus! Is that any way to greet your own brother?"

Brother. I blink at the green-eyed man, or rather, god. Seeing as I have yet to view the East Wind's face, I cannot say whether they resemble one another. I know only a handful of details about my captor. Black hair and pale skin. A strong jaw. Does Eurus possess the same jeweled eyes as his sibling? Are his teeth as white and straight?

The man—Zephyrus—eases closer. There is a lightness to his limbs, a grace to his movements. "It's been a long time, no?"

"Not long enough."

A flash of teeth, there and gone. "Good to see not much has changed over the centuries. You're still as rude as ever."

"And you still stick your nose in places where it does not belong," Eurus grinds out.

His brother purses his mouth in thought, then shrugs. "Fair enough." He then shifts his attention onto me. It is open, this face. A warm, boyish countenance. "And who is this?"

I've barely parted my lips to respond when the East Wind grips my arm in warning. "None of your business," he snarls.

Zephyrus rolls his eyes. "If that's how you want this reunion to go, fine. But why are you here, Eurus? You're a long way from Marles."

"Calm yourself, brother. I'm not interested in meddling with your pitiful mortal existence."

Wait. *Mortal?* So Zephyrus *isn't* a god? How is that possible?

The East Wind wavers. I sense his hesitation. Stay, or go? In the end, he says, "We're here to acquire a plant called nightshade. Apparently, I must get permission from *you*."

Zephyrus' green eyes sharpen. "Nightshade?" His voice has thinned. "For what purpose?"

"That's none of your business either."

I shift beneath Eurus' touch. Though I am uncertain whether he is aware of the gesture, he tucks his thumb against my wrist, alongside the pulse fluttering there.

"You're fond of that phrase, aren't you?" Whatever humor had brightened Zephyrus' features has dimmed. "Will you punish me, punish us all, for the remainder of our lives?"

This is an old wound, built in layers of timeworn skin. Eurus has not forgotten. Neither has Zephyrus. I wonder when they last spoke.

"I told you before that we didn't know," his brother goes on. "We had no idea—"

"Enough!" Eurus barks, bristling. "This was a mistake. We'll find the plant elsewhere." Brushing his brother aside, he strides for the main thoroughfare, towing me along. The townsfolk that have gathered scatter in fright, clearing the way.

"Wait," Zephyrus calls.

Stiffness winds the muscles of my captor's arm into knots, his fingers twitching against my wrist. "What?"

"Have you heard from Notus?"

And the tension spirals higher, locking the joints of Eurus' shoulders, the lower span of his back. "No. And I don't care to."

Lies. Eurus mentioned meeting his brother in Ammara, prior to being captured. I glance between the two men in caution—well, one man, one god. If there is to be bloodshed, I intend to keep my distance.

But for whatever reason, the East Wind stalls our departure. "Why do you ask?"

"The beast has escaped the labyrinth," Zephyrus says. "Word is that it's looking for you."

There is a silence. I've a desperate need to yank back the East Wind's hood so that I might gaze upon his expression, whether impassive or puzzled, irritated or worried.

"I see." His grip on my arm loosens, but I'm not foolish enough to flee twice. "Notus told you this?"

"He sent me a message," Zephyrus confirms, arms crossed. "I assumed he sent a message to you as well, and to Boreas."

Four brothers. Eurus, Zephyrus, Notus, and Boreas. Do they, too, hold power over the winds, or storms?

"I never received a message," Eurus says.

"Really? It was sent to Marles—"

"I wasn't there," he snaps, then takes a breath. "I was returning from my visit to Notus when I was captured. I've been imprisoned for the last three months and only recently escaped. Not that you, or anyone, would have stepped in to help me. Isn't that right?"

Green eyes flick to the East Wind's massive wings, their thin gray skin and overlapping scales. "We would have helped you," Zephyrus murmurs, "if we had known. Eurus—"

"I don't need your pity," he growls.

His brother appears deeply troubled. To his credit, he does not retreat. "The beast travels with a man named Prince Balior," he continues, kicking the toe of his boot into the dirt. "Notus claims you know of him?"

I straighten in interest. Prince Balior: the gentleman who arrived at the estate late last week. Lady Clarisse also mentioned a companion he traveled with. Could that be the beast Zephyrus is referring to?

"I know who Prince Balior is," says the East Wind. "But why should I care about the life of a mortal?"

"According to Notus, he now wields the power of the gods," Zephyrus states, expression whittled into subtle aggravation. "He seeks to expand his realm. It is possible he will invade Carterhaugh, the Gray, maybe even Marles. He must be stopped."

"When we were banished from the City of Gods," says Eurus coolly, "we were granted the right to our own realms, our own lives, our own space. I have no obligation to Notus, to you, or to Boreas. These problems are not mine."

"But they will become yours, eventually," Zephyrus counters. A cloud passes over the sun, momentarily shading the deserted alley. "If what Notus says is true, few in the mortal realms will be able to stand against the prince. Boreas, Notus, and I no longer possess our powers."

"Because you were weak," Eurus snarls, and if I'm not mistaken, the dim obscuring his hood blackens further. "Because you allowed your foolish hearts to undermine your power. Do not place the responsibility onto me simply because you were too stupid to see otherwise. You chose this."

At this, the corner of Zephyrus' mouth slants into his cheek, a gesture of bitter emotion. "Yes, I fell in love with a mortal woman. I have no regrets. I doubt Boreas and Notus do either. All I wanted was to inform you of what was coming. Can you imagine what would happen if this prince managed to infiltrate the City of Gods? It would be catastrophic."

"Maybe that is what the council deserves," Eurus says, "after all the pain they caused in banishing us from our home."

With that, he scoops me into his arms and springs upward, as though he wishes to escape his brother as much as I wish to escape him. I clutch the back of his neck, my face tucked close to the opening of his hood. Even in brightest day, nothing penetrates the interior.

We fly east, back toward Marles. With the sun having pulled from the earth, the air has warmed, even at this altitude. The East Wind falls into a preoccupied silence. I can all but hear the twisting amalgamation of his thoughts.

After a time, I tentatively ask, "The City of Gods was your h-home?"

To my surprise, he responds with nary a growl or scoff. "It is where my brothers and I were born. The realm where all deities reside."

"What will happen if Prince Balior reaches your homeland?"

He cups the back of my head as we bank right. "I don't believe he will. It is all but impossible for a mortal to enter the realm."

I consider mentioning that Prince Balior visited Lady Clarisse, but I do not want to add kindling to the fire of Eurus' anger. "How can you be sure? Your b-brother said he wielded the power of the gods. Wouldn't that make it easier for h-him to access their realm?"

"My brother says a lot of things," he mutters. "Most of them rubbish."

It didn't sound like rubbish. There was true concern in the Bringer of Spring's voice.

"I noticed Zephyrus doesn't have w-wings," I say, deciding a change in subject is for the best. "Is that because he was made mortal?"

"I am the only one of my brothers with wings," he replies, so low that it is practically inaudible. "Mortality has nothing to do with it." Before I'm able to respond, he grits out, "Zephyrus should not expect me to solve the world's problems just because I alone retain my power and immortality. Where were my brothers when I needed them? When I became a subject of numerous sick experiments? They could not be bothered to see what was in front of their very eyes."

The vast tract of forest streaks below as horror rolls through me. *Experiments?*

With anger rises a torrent of words, more than the East Wind has ever offered me. All those edged emotions, forever locked away, now set free. "Zephyrus made his choice. He did not have to choose mortality. He could have kept his heart. It seems my brothers are equally weak when it comes to love."

The sentiment reeks of bitterness. "I do not view love as w-weakness," I say.

But Eurus isn't listening. He has turned inward, his thoughts his only companions as we drift through clouds. "I'd heard Boreas fell first," he mutters to himself. "A mortal woman from the Gray. Decent with a bow, or so I've heard. The North Wind, my eldest brother, made mortal!" He releases a sharp laugh.

"Next was Zephyrus. Imagine, the wicked Bringer of Spring falling for a woman of the faith? I could not believe it." His chin brushes the top of my head. It feels as though his body curves around mine fully, as though I am shielded within his strength. "But Notus was the greatest surprise, having rekindled an old love. He seems happy, if not completely vulnerable. Once, he had been the South Wind, god of the eternal summer breeze. Now, he is nothing."

So Eurus doesn't care to interact with his siblings, yet he keeps tabs on them. Something in him yearns for connection, whether he realizes it or not.

"I alone remain standing—the last of the Four Winds. It is why I've gone to great lengths to conceal my ax, for it is the source of my power. I've hidden it in the last place anyone would think to look."

Curled against his chest, my ear pressed to his heart, I consider these words.

. . . the source of my power.

. . . great lengths to conceal my ax . . .

. . . last place anyone would think to look.

Where would one store an ax? An armory. What is the opposite of an armory? A place untouched by violence. So . . . a garden? A library? Though one could argue the written word to be the sharpest tool of all.

"I may walk through life alone," the East Wind adds after a time, "but at least I will never again find myself vulnerable. At least I have a choice."

There is more, I think. Much, much more in these cracks that run deep. But I am not foolish enough to press him. "We w-will return to the manor, then?"

Firm wingbeats lift us higher until the trees lose their singularity and fall into a swirling mass of green. "Seeing as Kilkare failed to provide us with nightshade," Eurus says in frustration, "we will return briefly to St. Laurent to acquire it. This is the last component needed to complete Eastern Blood, yes?"

I nod, my heart swelling with tentative hope. Home—just over the horizon.

The pale spire of St. Laurent's cathedral breaches the surrounding wood, crowned in the reds and golds of early autumn. A few townsfolk peer upward, their attention drawn by the massive winged shadow overhead, a woman caught in its arms. By the time the estate comes into view, morning has given way to mid-afternoon. Its wild grounds sing to me, and I grip the East Wind's broad shoulders to stabilize myself as we touch down inside the iron fence encircling the property.

The structure appears even more dilapidated than I remember. Garden tools lay strewn across the ground, partially hidden in the overgrown grass. The sight irks me. Those were Nan's tools, and she took excellent care of them, as do I. Her ladyship's neglect has worsened over the years.

When Eurus strides down the dirt path toward the front door, I race after him with a piercing "Wait!"

He slows, turning to face me.

"Um." I clear my throat. "We n-need to go through the back."

There is a beat of silence. "You mean to tell me you're not allowed to use the front door?"

Slowly, I shake my head. "The front door is for g-guests and clients only."

"As it turns out, I *am* a guest." Turning the handle, he holds the door open for me. I can almost imagine his eyebrows raised in challenge.

It is a peculiar sensation walking through the front entrance. A sense of belonging, of welcome, of worthiness to be here, in the place I love most. We continue through the foyer into the kitchen. A fresh loaf of bread sits on the rickety table next to a basket filled with zucchini, carrots, and potatoes. Everything appears exactly as it was when I left.

In the workshop, the door leading to the basement is locked, which only occurs when her ladyship leaves the estate. Why isn't she here? Unless ... is she investigating available flats on Market Street? With only three days having passed since my abduction, she could not have bought another place of business so soon.

I could risk fleeing to town, but it is doubtful I would reach the road before Eurus caught me. He has already proven the lengths he will go to bind me to him in all ways. No, if Lady Clarisse is away, I will need to delay our departure until her return. She managed to capture this god once. She can do so again.

"You have five minutes," Eurus commands, pacing the workshop. "For every minute you go over, I will blast a hole through the roof. Understood?"

A bead of sweat slithers down my neck. My mind is already on the chest at the foot of my cot, where quill and parchment lie. "Yes. I'll b-be quick."

The East Wind stalks upstairs, likely hunting Lady Clarisse. As soon as he disappears, I scamper back into the kitchen, scanning the counter for the letter I sent via courier bird. I don't see it amongst the pile.

"While we're here," he calls to me from the level above, "grab whatever personal items you may need. We won't be returning."

If the message isn't here, either her ladyship never received it, or she burned it. This may be my only opportunity to contact her directly.

Nightshade is stored in a box under the kitchen table. I pull it out, clip a few dried flowers from the stem. They are deep crimson, with mouth-like protrusions erupting from the center of their petals. After tucking the plants inside a small envelope and slipping them into my pocket, I hurry upstairs to pull my rucksack from the chest, then a quill, parchment, and ink.

My lady—

"Bird?"

My hand cramps from how tightly I clutch the quill. Ink splatters across the parchment.

He took me. I have his ax. He—

A drawn-out groan of wood—the top stair.

I lunge toward my cot, accidentally knocking over the bottle of ink, and slip the note under my pillow. In seconds, I toss three sets of clothes into my rucksack, a few undergarments, extra stockings, and Nan's *The Practice of Herbal Remedies*. I spin around, ramming head-first into a hard, broad chest. "S-sorry," I manage.

His attention flits around the cramped space. "This is where you slept?" he asks in borderline disgust. "This hovel?"

I shrink against the wall in shame. "It w-w-was the only r-room available."

"There are half a dozen bedrooms in this estate and that witch put you in a *broom cupboard*? Where are the rest of your clothes?"

I draw his attention to my pack—away from the spilled ink slinking across the floor. "Th-this is all I h-have." Most of my dresses are hand-me-downs from Nan. Though the long-sleeved, cotton garments are reflective of Marles' current fashion, a select few are the more traditional gowns worn in Jinsan, with their short, wraparound jackets and long, voluminous skirts, which Nan brought with her to Marles, a young mother of seventeen.

Only then does Eurus glance away. I sense pity. "Fine. Let's go."

I follow closely at his heels. Step by step, my dread thickens. I can't be sure Lady Clarisse will spot the note. She rarely enters my bedroom except to slap me awake. I should have stuffed the note in my pocket and dropped it on the way out the door.

"Wait." I catch the East Wind's sleeve. He braces himself against my touch. "I f-f-forgot something."

"Too late." He tugs me onto the front porch. "We have delayed long enough."

No, no, no, no. If we leave now, her ladyship might never know I returned. Might never know I *want* to return, or that I'm sorry I disobeyed her. If she sells the estate, I will have nothing.

"Please," I whisper. "I don't w-w-want to l-leave my home. Take the n-n-nightshade. Here." I shove *The Practice of Herbal Remedies* into his hands, the manual that I have read front to back countless times, in guttering candlelight and by the brightness of the open window, when the moon is a coin of polished silver. "This book w-will tell you everything y-you need to know about the p-poisons. I'm sure if you r-r-read through it, you would be able to create th-them yourself." Granted, the manual is written in a completely different language, but—"You don't n-need me."

To my surprise, the East Wind tucks the book inside his cloak. "On the contrary, bird, I very much do."

Wrapping my upper arm in one large hand, he hauls me down the stairs of the front porch. I dig in my heels. "W-w-wait." Energy balloons inside me, and I break free of his grip, bolting down the footpath.

Three, four, five steps, and a coil of silvery air snags my ankle, halting me. My struggles grow increasingly desperate. I'm clawing at the noose when movement in my peripheral vision alerts me to another's approach.

Lady Clarisse races toward me down the road, dropping her bags of produce in the process. "Min!"

"My lady!"

I'm caught, lifted high off the ground, the world falling away. I scream, thrashing in my captor's grip as tears streak my face. Her ladyship's shrinking form grows ever smaller, for we are soaring eastward, toward the sea and its punishing winds.

But I don't stop fighting. He will not take me, not again. Lunging, I sink my teeth into the East Wind's shoulder, and he swears, trying to tear free of me. I bite harder, cutting through fabric, flesh, until blood coats my tongue.

I'm clawing at Eurus' hood, demanding to see the face of the god who cares nothing for my life, when he snarls, releasing me in his attempt to shield his face. I plummet with a scream.

9

THE WAVES REACH UP, SWALLOWING ME WHOLE.
I'm dragged down, through salt and lather, a thousand roiling bubbles. The water invades, its stinging chill setting fire to my throat and chest. A great swell slaps me sideways, and I'm spinning.

My body seizes, caught in the memory of a bygone time. My mother's nimble hands, forcing my head under, the blood drawn from her arms as my nails bite deep. I choke, flailing in an attempt to reach the surface, but the current forces me into further depths. Light wanes, squeezed into the smallest pinhole as shadows coax me into surrender. My limbs twitch. The world darkens.

Something snags my hair, yanking me in some unknown direction. I kick feebly, but my legs are so heavy, caught in my water-logged dress. Past, or present? Reality, or memory?

My head breaks the surface, my ears aflood with the shatter of waves and brute winds. The sea releases my stiff, frozen limbs, my dress sagging around my limp frame as Eurus hefts me into the air. His open palm slams my back. Water gushes from my throat, and I vomit as he grips me from behind, wings flapping to hold us aloft.

"Stupid mortal," the East Wind growls. "Do you have a death wish?" He shakes me like a doll. "You could have hit the rocks."

I hack so forcefully I'm certain I'll crack a rib. I gasp, shudder, gasp again. Alive, alive, *alive*.

"Will you cooperate," he spits, "or shall I leave you to the sea?"

My teeth chatter, a sharp *clack clack* that drives knives into my skull. If I fail to respond, will he abandon me to the water? The thought is terrifying enough that I grip him tighter, arms winding around his neck, face pressed to his damp shoulder. The rough weave of his cloak is oddly grounding.

"D-d-d-don't l-l-l-leave . . ." I shudder and bury into his wide chest. "D-d-d-don't—"

The East Wind sighs, yet says nothing more as we veer toward his island that stands alone.

The cold has consumed me: breath, blood, bones. No matter the blankets piled high, no matter the height of the flickering fire, my body will not warm. The chill has fully infiltrated my mind.

It is dark. Night, that pillow of star-studded velvet, cushions the sharp rocks of the island beyond the open window of the tower. Curled in bed beneath layers of wool, my muscles twitch incessantly. The manor adds another log onto the fire. When my teeth continue their chattering, the window snaps shut, glass rattling from the force.

"Thank you," I whisper earnestly.

Following our arrival at the manor, the East Wind had deposited me on the bed. "Fire," he'd barked, and the fireplace had exploded with heat and light. A small mountain of blankets materialized at the foot of the cot. He'd heaped them over my frigid form, ordered me to stay put—as if I actually had the energy to wander—then departed.

I'm not sure how many hours have passed. I drift in that peculiar realm between waking and dreaming. I am six years old and twenty-two. I am drowning, panicked, soaring, saved. Sometimes I startle awake, drenched in a cold sweat. In these moments, another blanket appears on my bed, a reminder that the manor is here, with me.

The creak of the door alerts me. I peer at the East Wind through heavy eyelids, shivering, always shivering. Candlelight and shadows pock the walls.

He strides to the window, having failed to notice my watchful regard. There he stands, a cloaked pillar in the gloom. For whatever reason, I find it difficult to look elsewhere. Firelight limns his wings, each black scale absorbing the glow until they smolder like hundreds of diminutive suns. Their coloring is not true black, I realize. In certain angles, there is orange, violet, sage. He still wears his cloak, though it appears to be dry now. Why not remove it, unless he has something to hide?

The more pertinent question is: Why do I care? He is my captor, with the power to crush all that I hold dear. And yet, the East Wind saved my life. I'm not sure what to make of it. Granted, this god has need of me. Or rather, the poisons. It is not a true kindness, my rescue, but I am grateful all the same.

"Are you well rested?" Eurus suddenly asks.

The grating of his voice spikes my pulse, and he turns in a fluid motion. He knew I was awake. Did he feel my eyes on his torso, the flared tips of his wings?

I swallow painfully. Sound is muffled, as though I am still underwater. "I th-th-thought you'd l-left."

Eurus approaches my bedside. I stare into the darkness beneath his hood, trying to trace the shape of his countenance. Moments before dropping into the sea, I'd exposed a portion of his face, the rise of a discolored cheek. "Your lips are blue." Then he reaches toward me, one large, pale hand exposed as the sleeve of his cloak pulls back. I recoil so quickly my shoulder slams into the bedpost. The East Wind falls motionless. Finally, he lowers his hand.

"I said I wouldn't hurt you," he says, tone softening. "You need to get warm."

"Then b-build the f-f-fire higher. Or ask the manor to g-g-give me m-more blankets."

Another wool blanket plops onto the pile. I blink. "Thank y-you," I whisper.

"Stubborn woman," Eurus growls. "Enough of this." Dragging me forward, he gathers me against his chest. The cold has so thoroughly stiffened my muscles that my attempts to shove him away prove futile.

The threads of his cloak scratch my cheek, yet, in surrender, I am thawed, slowly, fingertips to toes. The sea clings to him, but a darker scent emerges as well, a mellow musk that is not unpleasant. Over time, my heartbeat slows. My eyelids lower, and I am floating, wavering. Tossed and dragged under.

I gasp, my eyes snapping open. Where is the air?

Something brushes along the curl of my spine, languid, hot to the touch. "The sea is far," Eurus murmurs, with a gentleness I did not think he was capable of. "It cannot touch you."

Releasing a shuddering breath, I sag fully against him. "I feel it on m-my skin," I whisper hoarsely.

"And whose fault is that? Had you not fought me, you would not have slipped from my grasp."

If my throat were not so completely ravaged from swallowing salt water, I might laugh for how warped his perspective is. "In what world would a woman taken against her w-w-will *not* fight her captor?"

He is quiet, but it is the sort of quiet offered to contemplation, space granted to allow thoughts to settle into their decided forms.

Carefully, the East Wind asks, "You said your mother tried to drown you when you were a child. Why?"

What does it matter? I wonder. "My father w-was a fisherman," I whisper. "That's how he and my m-m-mother met. Each week, she purchased fish from him at the market. According to Nan, my mother never cared for children, but my father loved m-me, and I do believe a part of her loved me, too, when he was alive." I frown, unable to guard against the melancholy settling like a fog over my heart.

"A storm capsized his boat. My mother was d-devastated. I can only imagine the difficulties in raising a daughter alone. One day, she cracked. Dragged me down to the beach and sh-shoved me under." I shudder. "In return for sacrificing me, my mother hoped the Master of Sea m-might return the husband she'd lost."

Of course, death is not kind. One cannot call back someone who is already gone. It hurts, knowing I was not enough to love, but I was enough to sacrifice.

"She sounds nearly as bad as my father," Eurus comments.

And what had Eurus' father done to him? "Why didn't you kill my lady wh-when you had the chance?" I whisper drowsily. Sleep, that peaceful rest, beckons.

"Because she needs you. And I figured it would hurt her more, knowing I have taken you from her. Knowing you are mine."

My face warms. I turn it into his shoulder so he cannot see how that word—*mine*—flusters me.

"Rest, bird." The East Wind disentangles himself. "If you have need of something, the manor will see to it."

He slips out into the hall as silently as he arrived. I study the closed door long after he has gone.

The next morning, I'm woken by an intense bout of coughing. My still-bruised sternum twinges from the force of my hacking. Beneath the blankets, I shiver, my sweat-slickened skin feverish to the touch.

Sunlight pours through the window. It is well past dawn, I realize in shock. I never sleep so late. Then again, my slumber was fitful. Too hot, too cold. I doubt I got more than a few hours' rest.

As I sip from the glass of water on my nightstand, the East Wind stomps into the tower, a rough breeze trailing his entrance. "Why are you not up?" Legs braced, arms crossed over his chest. His displeasure is plain.

I stare at him from beneath the stack of blankets, feeling too poorly to react to his anger. "I'm not feeling well." The words are garbled, my throat painfully scratchy, as if stuffed with fistfuls of sand.

"That can't be. You received enough rest." He heads for the window. Admittedly, it is a lovely day, with blue skies and nary a cloud. Perfect weather for gardening. "Get up," he says. "We have work to do."

He means *I* have work to do. "I can't."

"What do you mean, you can't? I told you the poisons must be completed before we travel to the City of Gods."

"I'm s-sick!"

"And?"

Oh, dear. He hasn't the slightest clue what it means to feel unwell. I imagine immortality comes with certain benefits. "Have you ever suffered from illness before?"

"I am a god," he states, as though the answer were obvious.

That settles things. "When mortals become ill," I explain, my lips cracking painfully, "our bodies need food and rest to r-recover. If we push ourselves, we may make ourselves sicker."

His wings rustle in what I believe to be impatience. "So you need, what ... more rest? Something to eat? Did you ask the manor to make you lunch?"

"I was sleeping."

"Get her some soup!" he barks toward the ceiling.

A warm shimmer of air tightens around me, yet no soup appears.

"You could act a little m-more appreciative of the manor's efforts," I point out. "She's doing you a favor."

I can all but see his eyebrows lift toward his hairline. "*She?*"

"Yes, *she*," I say with a glower. Perhaps illness has granted me courage in addition to this terrible chill. The manor feels like a maternal figure. Thus: *she*. "You should be grateful she is h-h-helping you at all."

"I gave this place life," he growls, beginning to pace. Once he reaches the door, he pivots, striding back to the window. "If anyone should be grateful, it's this damned, useless building!"

Well, the manor certainly isn't going to do him any favors *now*.

"Hello?" Eurus waves a hand. The hem of his cloak rises high enough to reveal the fabric of his trousers. "Did you hear me? I require soup for the mortal."

"Perhaps if you ask nicely," I offer, enjoying his frustrations more than I care to admit.

"The manor is under my power. It bows to *me*."

I shrug. If he cannot see reason, I am certainly not going to waste my breath convincing him.

When the soup still does not appear, the East Wind rubs the back of his neck, then sighs. "Please, can you get the mortal soup?"

Nothing.

He utters a colorful string of curses before barging down the stairs. It is quiet but for the wet creak of my lungs. "Why didn't you deliver the soup when he asked?" I say to the manor.

That warm caress wanders into the strands of my hair, tugging the black threads playfully. I smile and settle deeper into the pillows. "You're right," I say. "He needs to learn some respect."

Sometime later, Eurus returns bearing a bowl of soup. He plops it onto my lap with a growled, "Eat."

All the aches and pains of yesterday's ordeal conspire with the still-tender wounds across my back as I slowly push into a seated position. As soon as my throat closes around the broth, my stomach heaves, threatening to reject the substance. I cough, spewing the vile liquid into the cloth napkin I hastily use to cover my mouth.

"Well?" he demands.

It is poison. Every last drop. The taste is horrendous, like ... like earwax mixed with spoiled meat.

"It's delicious," I croak.

Eurus gives a satisfied grunt. He rolls his shoulders, as if working out the kinks following hours spent toiling over a hot stove.

Carefully, I set the bowl onto the bedside table. "I'll finish it l-later."

Eurus stands there in uncertainty for a moment. He steps toward the door, almost in retreat. "Rest," he tells me. "The sooner you recover, the sooner you can return to work."

After he departs, I sag into my pillow and scrub the taste of the broth from my tongue. That was absolutely, without a doubt, the most disgusting meal I've had in my life. What did he put in it? Feet?

Something large and feathered whisks through the window into the tower. I nearly tumble from bed in surprise. A large bird perches on the back of a wooden chair.

The note. Lady Clarisse!

I toss off the blankets and remove the message from the bird's leg.

Min,

I'm pleased to know you have the god-touched weapon in your possession. Where are you keeping it? Where has he taken you?

—Clarisse

I can't help but feel disappointed in my employer's response. There is no mention of whether the estate has been sold. She hasn't asked about my wellbeing either. But ... she is pleased. I can still fix the mistake I made.

I scrawl a hasty reply.

The East Wind has taken me to an island somewhere northeast of St. Laurent. On it, there is a great, isolated manor, protected by many enchantments. The weapon is here with me, but it will take some time to get away without his knowledge. Will you hold off on selling the estate? Could you send someone for me?

Once I've sent the bird off with my message, the linens on my bed flap furiously in a bid for my attention. I peer upward. "What?"

The sheets snap out. It is a frustrated motion ... I think.

"I'm not doing anything wrong," I say to the manor. "What would you do, if someone abducted you from your home and forced you into service?"

The bedsheets settle and smooth themselves over the mattress. Even a sentient building, it seems, understands that perspective.

"All I'm doing is getting in touch with her ladyship. It's important. She's going to sell the estate where I grew up, where my grandmother grew up. It's all I have left of my family." Clutching my elbows, I peer out the window. The sea is calmer today, but no less vicious. And yet— "Nan would have loved this place," I whisper to the manor, dashing away a stray tear. "She loved the wildness of things, the raw power of the natural world. She used to sing me one of the lullabies from her homeland about the changing seasons." Tentatively, I pick out the first few verses, the language clumsy on my tongue. "You would have liked her."

One of the frilly curtains lifts to dab at my wet cheeks. I release a watery laugh. "Thank you."

My eyes then drift toward the abandoned bowl of soup. If Eurus returns to discover that I have not finished the meal, he will no doubt take offense—or accuse me of deliberately prolonging my illness. Best to hide the evidence. Only under pain of death would I risk another mouthful of the vile concoction.

My limbs tremble with weakness, but I've strength enough to shuffle downstairs to the kitchen, his bowl of soup in hand. My mouth parts in shock.

It appears as though the entire pantry has exploded. Vegetable scraps litter the counter, which is painted with spills of various textures and hues. Flecks of red sauce have splattered the wall behind the woodfire stove, with cookware strewn about. One such pot spews a gas that smells faintly of cabbage. I gag, slapping a hand over my mouth. And Eurus takes offense at *my* untidiness? What a hypocrite.

I shove aside his mess to make space for myself at the counter. Although the manor provides me delicious meals at my request, now that I'm in the kitchen, I cannot resist the urge to cook, to *create*. It has been too long since I've even touched a cooking utensil. Not since Nan was alive.

After locating a cast iron skillet in one of the cupboards, I toss a hunk of butter inside, then scour the pantry for supplies. Two squashes and an onion? That will do. I slice them thinly, toss them into the pan where the butter now sizzles, emitting a nutty aroma. Next, I grab a hunk of beef and cut it into small chunks.

"What are you doing?"

My hand jerks. Only quick thinking saves me from amputating a finger. Throwing the beef into the skillet, I slap the knife onto the counter and turn to face the East Wind, whose large shape blackens the kitchen doorway. "Can you please n-n-not startle me like th-that? I could have lost a finger."

"You have ears," he tosses back. "Use them."

Mortal ears. But this immortal is unlikely to see my perspective.

I have every intention of ignoring his presence, but his footsteps near. A great shadow blankets me as I carefully chop parsley. His wings shift with a soft whisper.

"If you're going to scold m-me about making a mess," I say, "I would suggest thinking twice."

He is quiet—too quiet.

I shake my head. "Let me guess. Usually, the manor cleans up after y-you, but she has refused that, too. Am I right?"

"Why are you cooking for yourself?" he rumbles. "I made you soup this morning."

My stomach growls louder as the scents of sauteed onions overpower Eurus' toxic sludge. "I m-mean this as respectfully as possible," I say, sprinkling a smidge of parsley into the pan, "but have you *tasted* your soup?"

"Of course I've tasted the soup!" He sounds affronted. "It's a perfectly acceptable soup. You're being ungrateful."

That stings. I've been extremely appreciative. I've said my thankyous, which he has ignored. "I appreciate the effort, but I n-need to eat something that doesn't make me want to vomit."

He hisses his displeasure.

"Take a bite then." I offer him a spoon, gaze direct, borderline challenging. I could never have spoken to her ladyship in this manner. She would reward my insolence with a slap across the face, followed by a beating.

"I don't need to prove anything to you."

"Then I win by default."

He snatches the spoon while the soup gives another wet gurgle. Scooping up the sludgy, yellow substance, he brings it to his mouth and promptly chokes, spitting it back into the pot. Laughter threatens. I clear my throat, expression wiped clean.

Eurus hurls the spoon into the sink without comment.

At least my meal is done. I transfer chunks of perfectly seared meat and sauteed vegetables onto a plate, topping the dish with extra parsley before taking a bite. The meat is tender, with a slight char. The onions' sweetness rounds out the taste. It seems I still remember what Nan taught me.

The East Wind angles his head toward the fruit basket, as if checking to see whether I've pilfered another peach. "I assume," he says, "if you are well enough to cook a meal for yourself, you are well enough to travel?"

A piece of squash sticks to the back of my teeth unpleasantly, and I lower the fork onto the counter. "Travel?"

"We're going home."

10

"Home?" I whisper. And oh, how my heart soars.

"Not *your* home," he clips out, wings stirring in irritation. "Mine. The City of Gods."

The sinking sensation in my chest hits hard. Lady Clarisse has always stated that if something is too good to be true, it usually is. Stupid, to have hoped. "I see." After all, he has mentioned it before. "And where is th-this City of Gods?"

"Far," Eurus replies. After dumping his scraps into a wastebin, he carries the dirty pots, bowls, and utensils to the sink. He glares at the mess, probably waiting for the manor to clean it up, but—as I suspected—she has decided not to enable him.

Grumbling, the East Wind wanders off. He returns carting a bucket of water, which he uses to wash his crockery. It is quite domestic of him.

"How far?" I press him while he dries a bowl and sets it aside.

"The City of Gods cannot be accessed by a simple trek across the mortal realms." He glances sidelong at me. I straighten, my face warming for reasons I cannot name. "But to answer your question: farther than you can comprehend."

This isn't how things were supposed to go. Traveling to a completely different realm, one inaccessible to mortals...my apprehension deepens. Will Lady Clarisse be able to receive my messages? And what of the East Wind's god-touched weapon? Does Eurus intend to bring it with him on the journey, or will it remain hidden in the manor?

"What about the p-poisons?" I ask. "Only Goldenrod is complete—"

"I don't want Goldenrod," he interrupts. "I want Eastern Blood."

Right. A triple dose to punish those who have wronged him. "Now that I have nightshade, I can complete the poison, but it still n-n-needs weeks to brew."

"We haven't the time," he says. "The Council of Gods is hosting a tournament, and I've just received word that all participants must complete their registration by tomorrow." After drying a pot, he returns it to the cupboard before turning to survey *my* mess.

I shrink, though I have done nothing wrong. "I w-was planning on c-c-cleaning up," I mutter.

When he vacates the area, I carry my dishes to the sink and begin to wash them. All my life I have bent to the wills of the strong, the wise, the elder. Today should be no different. And yet, it is not enough. Not for me. "I don't understand. What tournament? Why go to the city before the poison is ready?"

"The council hosts a tournament every few hundred years," Eurus says. "Seeing as it will last for several weeks, that is plenty of time for you to finish brewing Eastern Blood while I compete for the prize: a favor granted to the victor by the Council of Gods themselves."

"And you w-wish to be granted this favor," I say in understanding.

"Yes."

The opening of his hood tracks me as I dry the cast iron skillet with a cloth and place it back into the cupboard. My gaze flicks from Eurus, to the cupboard, back to Eurus. "I put it b-back in the right place, didn't I?"

"You did," he grumbles.

I allow myself a small, satisfied smile. Internally, of course. I do not want the East Wind to think I care for his approval.

Only a few utensils remain to wash and dry. As I soap up a wooden spoon, I say, "Didn't your brother say you all were banished? Wouldn't that bar y-y-you from returning to the City of Gods?" Beneath his scrutiny, I find myself hastening to complete my task. Lady Clarisse would often watch me work, pointing out my failings with scathing remarks. The sea may separate us, but I cannot deny the power she holds over me.

"It would, had the council specifically barred those exiled from the tournament. A gross oversight, but unsurprising."

There is a coarseness to his inflection that speaks of old wounds. I decide not to press it. "And you wish for me to poison, what, a *god*?" The thought makes me ill. What if it is the Mother of Earth? The Master of Sea? How will it impact Marles, should they disappear? This goes so far beyond what I was raised to believe: respect for all life, compassion, kindness toward others. Nan would be heartbroken to learn I went against those principles.

"My intentions for the poison are of no concern to you," Eurus says.

Of course.

With the dishes clean, I wipe down the sink and countertops. That done, I hang the cloth from its hook on the wall. "I w-w-won't do it."

"You will." The East Wind takes a step closer. Those wings unfold, adding to his height and breadth. My every instinct screams at me to quail in the presence of this predator. "You are under my employment. If I need you to brew a poison, you shall brew it. Or have you forgotten that your simple town will fall should you refuse to cooperate?"

"Employment implies r-r-recompence for services." Miraculously, I manage to speak without choking. "I'm j-just a captive h-h-here."

He moves—too swiftly. A blink, and he is pressed against me, one massive hand curled around my throat. He squeezes. Not enough to cut off my air supply, but enough that I feel the resistance when I swallow. *Stupid girl. What is wrong with you? Have you any sense? Were you given rocks for brains?* Her ladyship's scathing affronts are never far.

My frail wheeze stirs the fabric of the East Wind's hood. His fingers twitch, and he leans closer, until darkness brushes my face and I can all but taste the sea foam coating my teeth.

"You are mortal," he rumbles lowly. "Fragile. I can crush you with but a thought."

"You can," I agree. "But you w-w-won't." Eurus saved me, whether or not it was for his own gain. He cared for me, or tried to. "Without m-me, Eastern Blood will remain unfinished. Whatever revenge you seek, you w-will not get it."

His hand loosens, thumb tucked beneath the edge of my jaw. "Perhaps." His response quakes along my bones. "But you have given me the means to create it myself, haven't you?" With his other hand, he pulls a slender volume from the folds of his cloak.

I inhale sharply. *The Practice of Herbal Remedies.*

"This book was your grandmother's, was it not?" He skims the book cover to cover before tucking it back into his cloak. "It would be a shame to lose an heirloom so valuable."

"Give it b-back," I whisper.

"I will give it back when Eastern Blood is complete and I have claimed victory in the tournament."

Even if the East Wind were to follow the rules exactly as written in the book, the poison would, in all likelihood, fail. Some things can only be known through experience: the exact pressure of a knife blade, the proper method or direction to stir. My skills are valuable. He has need of me. And I, too, require something from the East Wind. Until I learn where his ax is hidden, I must accompany him.

"In all the days trapped in my cell, tortured out of my mind," he says, "I watched, and I listened, and I learned. That woman worked you like a damned dog, and not once did you try to fight back. You, who have teeth of your own."

For a moment, the shadows inside his cowl seem to fade, just briefly. There, coming into focus, is the glimmer of two dark eyes. "Why?" he demands. "Why do you let her treat you so horribly? Why do you seek to return to that life?"

The question settles all its uncomfortable edges alongside my ribs. When I attempt to shove the feeling aside, my nerves worsen. I can provide a partial truth. It will not change anything.

"My lady is s-selling the estate," I murmur. It hurts, speaking aloud what I fear most. "It is wh-where I grew up. Where my grandmother raised me. I can't purchase the estate unless I r-return."

"She promised to sell you the estate?" Eurus asks skeptically.

"Yes." In exchange for information. Not that he needs to know that.

A curl of darkness feathers against my cheek. "Don't you need funds to purchase property?"

"I have some coin s-saved." A pause. "I received an inheritance following my grandmother's passing. Her ladyship doesn't kn-know of it." Which is to my benefit, as far as I'm concerned. "Once I've purchased the estate, I could open my own practice, if I w-wanted."

"Is that what you want?"

I shiver, and my throat pulses against his palm as I swallow. If the East Wind—a powerful immortal—trusts me enough to create poisons correctly, maybe others would request my services as well. But I would not create those beauty teas her ladyship is so fond of. I would not be a slave to vanity, seeking to alter what the gods have bestowed. My remedies would be different. They would heal—physically, mentally, emotionally. "It would be nice," I whisper. "I think."

Leaning back, the East Wind removes his hand from my throat. "Then allow me to suggest a trade of sorts."

My hands seek movement, but I have already washed the dishes, cleaned my mess. I suppose it couldn't hurt to wipe down the counters again. "A trade indicates a f-fair and willing exchange." Somehow, I do not believe that is his intention.

"Finish making the poison," he says. "Help me win, help me get revenge on the ones who wronged me, and I promise to free you and return you home."

It is too easy. Too good to be true.

"You cannot kill a god by mortal m-means," I point out. Even I know that. The poisons Lady Clarisse concocts can weaken divine beings, maim them, but they live on unless a god-touched weapon is used against them. "Whoever you are targeting, they will not succumb."

"You do not need to worry about that," Eurus replies. "Focus on brewing Eastern Blood. I will take care of the rest." He regards me steadily before offering his hand. "What do you say, bird? Do we have a deal?"

I must be the realm's biggest fool, agreeing to poison one of the divine. But what choice do I have, really? Freedom exists at the end of this treacherous road, my promise fulfilled. And so I accept the East Wind's touch, my hand swallowed against his large palm, my fate sealed.

11

It turns out the City of Gods is not a place one can fly to—unless you're one of the divine. It exists seemingly on a different plane of existence, one separate from the mortal realms. Unfortunately, the journey is long, and according to Eurus, we haven't the time to fly. Our only option is the nearest doorway leading from the East Wind's island, which can only be accessed by boat. Thus, we have descended into the lowest level of the manor, where the sea has flooded its stony core, and the slop of the tide tunnels down into my teeth.

"It's all right, bird." Seated on the bench of the small vessel rocking to and fro, the East Wind offers his hand. "The journey will not take long."

Perhaps, but it takes only a few minutes to drown.

My fingers tighten around the strap of my rucksack, which contains my clothes and the supplies required to complete Eastern Blood. Reaching out, I allow Eurus to pull me onto the boat. The vessel dips, and he stiffens. Only then do I realize I've clamped onto his shoulder, the scalloped edges of his left wind brushing my forearm.

We push off. Huddled in the bottom of the hull, I inhale through my nose, exhale through my mouth. Twin oars cut the opaque water. My teeth begin to click incessantly as my grasp on reality weakens.

A sudden heat blankets my form: the East Wind's wing, splayed over me. The scales are slender, coated in a high shine, and hard as small, overlapping coins. My breathing eases; the chattering of my teeth tapers off. I want to cry for this kindness. It is wrong, I think, to feel gratitude toward my captor.

The tunnel splits. We ease right, eventually reaching another water-logged stairwell. I practically fling myself onto the steps, the slickened stone solid beneath me.

"This way," Eurus says.

I stumble after him. At the top of the stairs, we reach a locked door carved of wood. It pulses with a strange energy.

I lick my lips nervously. What awaits us in the City of Gods? Nothing good, I fear. "Will your brothers be participating in the t-tournament?"

"No." He brushes the handle, a curl of aged brass. "The tournament is open only to the divine. Had my brothers been of sounder mind, they could have used this opportunity to return home—permanently."

"What do you mean?" I ask.

"I told you that whoever wins the tournament is granted a favor from the Council of Gods." His voice grates subtly, bristling with sudden aggression. "I intend to win, and when I do, I will ask the council to end my banishment so that I may return to the City of Gods at will."

I see. "It seems we *both* w-want to return home." And if I speak a little more forcefully, well, surely he cannot blame me?

Silken laughter slips around my limbs and spikes the hair along my neck. He then gestures to the door. "My brother, Boreas, helped fashion this entry for me. Since he was responsible for our banishment, I demanded payment from him, a means to our homeland. I haven't used it since."

The door opens with an aged squeal. I blink against the sudden brightness. Across the threshold lies a vista worthy of a painting, for there are brushstrokes of deep green; blots of rose, apricot, and peach; a palette of wildflowers whispering in a sweet wind. No rock, no gray, no churning storms. No water as far as the eye can see.

In marvel, I trail Eurus across the threshold, vaguely aware of the door shutting at my back. We stand on the rise of a grassy knoll overlooking a shining city nestled in the surrounding foothills, the air possessing a subtle bite. A skinny footpath sketches a line through the high grasses. Autumn dusts the trees in red and gold, orange and brown. The brittle light exhibits the waning days, their descent into winter.

"If I'm to aid you in your m-mission," I say suddenly, "shouldn't I know more about what I'm getting myself into? What exactly does the tournament entail?"

He gestures me forward, and we stroll shoulder to shoulder down the path, amber reflecting off the city's peaked rooftops as if from a multi-faceted jewel.

"The tournament will be split into three trials. Only a certain number of contestants advance to each subsequent round," he says as we pass through the shade of the surrounding forest. "Many perish in the attempt."

"You can be killed in the tournament?" Shock and dismay.

"Yes."

"But doesn't that throw the w-world out of balance?" If a god is lost in the games, how will the crops grow? Who will regulate the weather, the currents? And what of fertility, or those dependent on the hunt?

Eurus leaps over a fallen tree. I'm forced to clamber up and over, dropping onto the other side.

"I suppose," he concedes. "Being one of the divine is a little like what you mortals call having a profession—new deities are born every day, and there is always someone willing to fill an empty role."

I see. "It makes sense then, to win." Or at least stay alive long enough not to lose.

The East Wind nods, cloak swirling around his legs. "A favor from the Council of Gods is a boon. There is very little they cannot—or will not—do."

Then it is a boon indeed. If *I* were granted a favor, I would wish to have Nan back. Life was easier with her alive, the air impossibly sweet with potential.

"Understand this," Eurus says. "You are a mortal in the realm of gods. They will see you as easy prey. They will try to bend you to their will. By the time you realize what is happening, it will be too late. Trust no one."

I press a palm to my cheek. My skin is warm—too warm. Why did I agree to this again? "I have no p-p-protections, is what you're saying?" Only a flimsy promise, the hope of a day without shackles.

"You will be safest in the palace, where the competitors are housed. You should not venture beyond the grounds unless I accompany you."

By the time we reach the city proper, perspiration dampens my neck and underarms. Residential properties lay claim to these farthest corners of the valley, all constructed of gleaming white stone, complete with hidden courtyards, tamed lawns, and wrought iron balconies. The air smells musky, like overripe fruit. Residents of every shape, culture, and complexion roam the wide, cobblestone lanes, each some nameless goddess or god.

We merge with the flow of traffic. I do my best to take everything in without stepping on anyone's foot. Before I met the East Wind, I'd never traveled beyond the boundaries of St. Laurent.

Across the street, three deities take refuge in the shade to share their most recent purchases. A few steps later, a drunkard wearing a loose white robe stumbles through the throng, slurring something about kings and gold. I do a double take. He has hooves in place of feet and long, furry legs. I scurry after Eurus, wondering if I am going mad.

And the structures fall away, and the cobblestones stretch forth. There, a burbling fountain. And there, a small park edged in mist. A crooked lane boasts the large glass windows of a bakery, a collection of tables and chairs occupying the front porch. There, the divine gather, fingers curled around steaming mugs, some swathed in elegant silks with unique prints, others clothed in blood-spattered armor or threadbare rags as they chatter amongst themselves. It seems even the gods love their gossip.

We pass through a crowded square where many have set up shop, including a long-haired sculptor who chisels a slab of marble into the curve of a woman's waist. The detailing is exquisite. Lifelike, almost. At a neighboring stall, an intricately carved box rests on a stone plinth. Without understanding why, I reach for it.

"Don't touch."

I flinch back. My hand drops, and I fold my fingers against my palm where they will not do harm.

The East Wind snaps the lid shut. "A music box. Harmless to the divine, potentially deadly to your mortal ears."

I nod, though my throat has cinched tight, allowing neither word nor breath to escape. *Don't touch.* Lady Clarisse was especially fond of that phrase.

The crowd thickens around the entrance of an impressive two-story temple, bougainvillea crawling up its cracked facade. Many place offerings on the steps, the stone smoothed by the press of a thousand feet. I wonder how that works, exactly. Surely the gods do not worship themselves? Or . . . maybe they do?

It is only after we've turned down a less crowded street that I realize none glance in our direction. "They don't see us," I remark, "do they?"

"No. My brothers and I were struck from the books following our banishment, which means we are undetectable to those around us. Once we reach the palace, however, my name will be reinstated for the duration of the tournament. As for you, Min—you are mortal. Too insignificant to attract notice."

I'm opening my mouth to respond when Eurus halts, and I blink in bewilderment. Two gargantuan gates stand open. They are forged from hammered bronze, sculpted into elegant curls. Beyond lie substantial, grass-cloaked grounds. Pebbled footpaths crisscross the rolling hills, and a manicured lane stretches from the entrance gates to the palace, circling the marble fountain planted at its front.

Then there is the palace itself: extensive, stately, refined. A collection of pearled walls, delicately crowned towers, and shaded verandas appear to have been woven from moonlight's glowing threads. It stretches eight—no, nine—stories. Each boasts wide balconies and capacious terraces, arched windows dressed in filmy curtains, and bridged walkways occupied by deities whiling the afternoon away. The East Wind's manor is downright diminutive in comparison.

As soon as Eurus and I pass through the gates, the divine swing their heads in our direction, halting mid-stride.

The East Wind goes rigid beside me. I shrink against him, seeking the enemy I know over the enemy I do not. All my life I have walked the earth unremarkable and plain. Here, I am a curiosity, dare I say, unique.

"Is that woman *mortal*?" someone whispers in horror.

A pouty-mouthed goddess covers her nose with a sneer. "She reeks."

"She doesn't smell *that* bad."

A rush of trampling feet, like bloodhounds on a hunt. The divine surround us, scandalized conversation muffled behind hands or murmured into neighboring ears.

"Let's go." Eurus grabs my arm, hauling me along.

"But—"

"Keep walking." He slips his palm against my back, propelling me forward. Our difference in size is comical, and it takes little effort for him to direct me down the road, where one goddess has called her two hounds to heel.

"Eurus? Is that you?"

A tall, buxom woman parts the crowd. The long dress cinched at her waist is dyed all the colors of the sea's hidden depths—a lovely complement to her olive skin. She wears slender heels studded in what I believe to be diamonds, all sparkle and shine. I stare as her eyes catch mine. They are yellow, like a cat's.

"Demi." The East Wind sounds aghast. It's perhaps the first time I've heard him caught off guard. "What are you doing here?"

She arches one beautifully groomed eyebrow. I can't stop staring—those heels, that gown, the cascade of dark ringlets over her shoulders, the lush, scarlet-painted mouth. She is effortlessly striking. "I'm here for the tournament, of course. I assume you are, too."

"I am."

"What an unexpected surprise." The goddess then scowls at our audience. "Away, all of you. Scat!" The crowd breaks apart to sounds of disappointment. "Vultures." But she smiles, shifting her weight onto her other leg. "To think how quickly a few centuries pass. I would say you haven't aged a day, but it's a little difficult to tell with that hood covering your face."

The East Wind's hand drops from my back. "You certainly haven't aged."

Smoky laughter slips from between her perfect white teeth. "It takes work to look this good, love." She peers at him, and something sharp and uncomfortable pokes at my innards. I glance away, feeling as if I am intruding on their exchange. "We'll have to catch up soon. You'll seek me out?"

There is a pause. Then: "I will."

Though the goddess peers at me peculiarly, she continues onward, the sway of her body reminiscent of rippling silk. I question the way Eurus studies her retreating form. He did not seem particularly enthused to see this goddess.

The moment we enter the palace, a scrappy fellow races toward us, head buried in a pile of documents. With his twig-like limbs, he looks akin to a prepubescent boy, though he is likely many millennia old. "Hello there, and welcome. I'm the tournament coordinator, so if you need anything, please let me know. Once I have you checked in, you'll ..." He lifts his head, nose wrinkling. "What is that *smell*?" Then he blanches, having recognized who stands before him. "Eurus?" A slow, bewildered blink of his long-lashed eyes. "You're here, you're—" He flips through his documents furiously.

"The announcement stated that the tournament was open to all deities," Eurus clarifies. "No exclusions."

"Ah ... hmm. Yes, that is true, but ..." The coordinator consults his notes, lower lip caught between his teeth. "It seems you *do* have a right to enter the tournament. That is ... well. Let me see what rooms are available."

We stand in a massive foyer, multiple curtain-draped corridors leading deeper into the palace. Three women climb the curved, central staircase, hands sliding along the gleaming banister. They wear long white shifts and swords strapped across their backs. Their hair is red as flame. Sisters? As one, they glance at Eurus, then at me. The tallest woman mutters something to her companions. They laugh and continue to the level above.

I suppose news of the East Wind's arrival has spread. Some of the other competitors cannot resist passing through the foyer for a closer study. I shy from the sapphire gaze of a massive centaur, its large hooves clopping against the tile as it disappears down one of the halls.

"We do have a single suite on the fourth floor that is available. It should fit your, er—" He glances at the East Wind's wings. "Needs."

My attention snaps back to the coordinator. "We need two suites!" I blurt.

Only then does the god look at me. His eyes widen. "A mortal?"

"She is my assistant," Eurus clips out.

Assistant. Right. I imagine *bane weaver* is a bit off-putting, especially to those Eurus intends to harm.

"But she is mortal," the coordinator repeats.

"And?" The East Wind glowers at the smaller god until he drops his eyes. "There are no rules barring mortal assistants. I have checked."

"That's true," he murmurs, flipping through his documents nervously. "Very well. Two suites—"

"One. My assistant and I will share."

The blood drains from my face so rapidly I sway, hand raised in an attempt to shield myself from the idea of the East Wind and me cloistered in a room together. "B-but—"

The coordinator motions for us to follow him up the stairs. I clutch the back of Eurus' cloak, vaguely aware of the passing doorways blurring in my periphery. Our suite is located at the end of the corridor. The East Wind pushes inside, shutting the door in the coordinator's face.

As soon as we are alone, I collapse onto a cushioned chair, eyes closed. Strangely, I yearn for the manor. How she always provided me food, or blankets, shifting pieces of furniture in her unique form of communication. This . . . this was a mistake.

"Bird." When I squeeze my eyes tighter, Eurus sighs. "Min."

It is a reluctant unfolding, but eventually, my heartbeat settles, and I open my eyes, straightening in the chair.

The suite is far more spacious than I anticipated. Windows span the far wall, green curtains tied back to welcome the sun. They grant a stunning view of the city in autumn. Red maples brighten the green spaces, and the mountains have begun to turn as well, all the colors of the earth.

The walls are painted a warm, dandelion yellow. A handful of smaller chambers branch off the main sitting room, which houses low sofas, a fireplace, cozy blankets draped over the backs of stately armchairs. A partially open door reveals a washroom, while a set of double doors lead to a large bedroom.

"Sharing a suite is a necessary inconvenience," the East Wind states, studying me from his position near the door. "I cannot trust the other contestants not to pit you against me."

There is a roiling beneath my skin. I cannot discern its flavor—anger, helplessness, frustration, all three? "I gave you my w-w-word that I'd help you w-win," I reply tersely.

"You also promised your former employer that you would follow her instructions, yet here we are."

He is not wrong. I chew the inside of my cheek and consider the words I must use to defend my character. In the end, I swallow them down. "Where am I supposed to s-sleep?" Certainly not in that bed with *him*.

"There is another bedroom behind you." He points. "That can be your workspace as well."

Seems reasonable. I think. "You're sure this w-won't be uncomfortable for you?" I glance at him, but only long enough to feel the brush of his gaze. "Sharing living quarters, I mean?"

His hesitation is so brief I wonder if I imagined it. "No." He stares at me. It has a strange effect on my body. "Why would it be uncomfortable?"

I don't want to say it. He will make me say it. "I'm a mortal w-woman of marriageable age, and you are—" A giant amongst men. "A god. Won't the other contestants talk?"

He peers down at me with an air of disdain. And yet—that hesitation. "Do not convince yourself this means anything at all, bird. You are my assistant. Nothing more."

I've had sexual relations with men before. Well, *man*—singular. Curtis used to deliver milk to the estate. I was seventeen, and I wanted to know what it felt like to be wanted, just once. Unfortunately, our relationship did not last. Lady Clarisse did not like to share me, so my experiences were rushed, secreted, and only occurred when she was out of town. "Fair enough." As long as I know my place, and he knows his.

The East Wind pushes open the door to my bedroom. The mattress is smaller, but I am not a large person. And I do not have wings.

"Will this space suffice?" he asks.

It is larger than my bedroom back home, that's for sure. It even has a proper bureau to store my clothes. No dust. Someone must have cleaned recently. A single window filters the light. "I can use the dresser as my w-worktable . . ." I trail off, thinking of what Eurus intends to do. "And you're serious about poisoning twelve gods?"

"Why wouldn't I be?"

He's right. When has the East Wind ever spoken in jest? I've never met someone more averse to joy. "Think of the r-repercussions. What happens when they are gone?"

"I am not concerned with how this will impact the mortal realms. The City of Gods will endure."

I fall quiet. How is it that twelve deities wronged him? But in the end, it is not my problem. If Eurus intends to kill these gods, that is his prerogative. I am here to complete a task, to birth poison. Only then will I walk free.

"Let us lay some ground rules for the duration of our stay." He lifts a finger. "First, you will remain in this suite at all times."

Here is what I know: I was lonely at the estate. Yes, I had her ladyship, and once a week, my journey into town, but my dearest friends were my herbs, crushed and rolled, pruned and boiled and dried. No matter how I wished plants could speak, mine was the only voice I heard.

"Y-you expect me to s-stay here until the tournament is complete?" My molars clamp down. *Use your words, stupid girl.* How is it her ladyship's cruel barbs manage to haunt me across realms? "Why can't I m-m-move around the palace? You s-said I would be safe here, as long as I don't g-go into the city."

He stares at me. I stare back—until I don't. I look out the window, but the heat of his gaze lingers on my cheek, eventually dipping to my neck where the pale skin flushes pink. It is not a captive's place to determine the boundaries of their cage.

"Very well."

My head whips toward the East Wind in surprise. He changed his mind?

"You may explore the palace at will," he says, "but keep to the grounds. If anyone approaches you, inform me immediately. The stakes of this tournament are high. We all want a favor from the council. As a general rule, no harm may be done to contestants outside of the trials, but that doesn't apply to assistants, and the divine possess little honor. Some competitors may take your wandering as an invitation to meddle."

I nod. It's strange to think that less than two weeks have passed since I released the shackles on the East Wind's power. Now I am to mingle with these highest celestial beings. "How m-many competitors are th-there?"

"We will see at tonight's banquet." He rolls his shoulders; the motion stirs the air, its rain-sweetened scent out of place so far from his island. "Keep your wits about you. Assistant or not, you are still mortal: easy pickings, easy prey." He stares at me for a long, unbroken moment, long enough for my face to heat. "Trust no one. Not even me."

12

"So. What interest does the East Wind have with a mere mortal?"

I angle toward the brown-skinned goddess who questioned me, face tightened by a smile that fails to reach my eyes. She sits across the long dining table that seats over a hundred competitors, in addition to the Council of Gods. Tonight's welcome banquet has been set in one of the palace gardens, beneath a pergola intertwined with small rosebuds. It is, to be fair, lovely, if a bit brisk.

I've managed to make it through three courses unscathed, but the goddess now pins me with a set of violet eyes. Their coloring is remarkable, like shadowed caverns with hidden depths.

"I'm not sure what you mean?" I whisper in confusion.

"Oh." She frowns dramatically. "Don't tell me you mortals are as stupid as you look."

A bark of laughter erupts from somewhere down the table, and I flinch. All evening, I have endured slurred gossip and scathing remarks, the smiles that assure friendship, the eyes that promise suffering. Maybe if I ignore her, she will leave me alone.

"He's gotten you pregnant, hasn't he?"

I startle so badly my fork clatters against my plate. "Wh-what?" I peer at Eurus, who sits directly to my left, but he doesn't give any indication that he overheard, focusing solely on shoveling kale into his mouth. He hates this dinner nearly as much as I do. "No. That's n-n-not, um..."

The goddess smiles, then shakes her head. "Don't sound so appalled. It is more common than you think." She shrugs. "But you're right. You're too meek to catch the East Wind's interest." She slips a cube of squash between her lips, severing the flesh with a snap of teeth.

I watch her chew in unease. My nerves began to fray hours ago, my system so flooded with vigilance I cannot even properly enjoy the meal. After sipping from my glass of water, I glance at the impressive, bare-chested deity sitting at the head of the table. Long, white-blond hair hangs over his muscled shoulders. His sun-kissed skin ripples as he gesticulates to his neighbors, and a set of what appear to be lightning bolts rests in a basket near his chair, within reach. Might he lead the Council of Gods? He is certainly formidable enough.

"So. What realm do you hail from, mortal?" the violet-eyed goddess asks me. She dabs at her mouth with her scarlet napkin.

"Um." I poke at the pile of vegetables with the tines of my fork. "Marles."

"Marles. Yes, I can hear it in your accent. You've a lovely voice, has anyone ever told you that?" Before I can respond, the goddess peers at the East Wind. "Do you not think she has a lovely voice, Eurus?"

His utensils smack the edge of his plate with a harsh clang, and he clears his throat. "I... suppose." Through the gloom coiling within his hood, the intensity of his gaze hits. "It is quite nice," he murmurs.

I'm so taken aback by the admission that I hurriedly shift my attention back to the goddess, asking, "Who are y-you, if you don't mind me asking?"

Her grin stretches wider than is natural. "Let's just say I'm someone who deals in a bit of witchcraft now and then."

"Don't talk to the witch," Eurus murmurs in my ear.

The heat of his breath feathers the curve of my nape, and my awareness of his proximity sharpens. Thankfully, the woman—witch—shifts her attention elsewhere. "What am I supposed to d-do?" I mutter. "I can't be rude. She's just making small talk."

"Small talk counts as talking."

Imagine that.

"If you want m-my cooperation," I say, surprised by the irritation lacing my tone, "I would appreciate it if y-you stopped trying to control everything and everyone around you."

I can all but feel the East Wind's scowl as I sip from my goblet of wine. Well, too bad. There is more at stake than this tournament. As I have come to learn, home is not guaranteed.

The fourth course is served: pork tenderloin roasted in an apple glaze. I dig in, if only to avoid the many eyes cast my way. The duller my actions, the swifter they will grow bored.

"You didn't answer my question," the witch says. Lifting her silver goblet, she drains its contents, licking a droplet from the corner of her wine-slickened mouth. "What interest does the East Wind have with a mortal?"

"If you m-must know," I reply, ignoring Eurus' warning growl, "I'm his assistant."

"His assistant? How darling." Her lips peel back, revealing two extremely sharp canines, thin as sewing needles. "Why, exactly, would a god need assistance from a mortal?"

I regard the woman over the rim of my goblet. Could this be one of Eurus' targets? What could she have done to him that would drive him to murder?

In the end, I play the game the divine dearly love to play: I gift her an answer without information. "I suppose you will have to w-wait and find out."

I return to my meal, but not before catching her smile that is not a smile. Hopefully my insolence will not elicit her wrath.

Every so often, my attention drifts to the goddess from earlier—Demi, now clothed in an exquisite crimson gown softened by orange and ochre pleats. She sips daintily from her glass, observing the attendees with a keenness that reminds me of Lady Clarisse.

As though sensing my gaze, she glances sidelong at me. I drop my eyes, wipe my fingers on the cloth napkin. By the time my attention returns, she is looking elsewhere—at the East Wind, though he does not appear to notice, his hood turned toward the lightning god. My eyes fall to Eurus' hand. It is curled white-knuckled around his fork.

The lightning god pushes back his chair and stands. He is, quite simply, gargantuan.

"Friends, council members, competitors—welcome." Deep and resonant, his voice carries out over the garden hedges. "You all know why you're here. Soon, the tournament will commence. One hundred and ten of you will have the opportunity to gain what few are granted: a favor from the Council of Gods."

Demi raises an eyebrow, mouth pursed as she regards those seated. The air is a muddle of hope and desperation, trepidation and wonder. The trio of ginger-haired goddesses I spotted earlier exchange whispered discourse. The largest bears a shaved head and small, beady eyes. Her sharp-toothed grin is positively terrifying.

"As you well know, there will be three trials," the lightning god continues. "The first is trial by combat. In order to move on to the second round, you must survive long enough to pass through the door located in the arena."

His gaze sweeps the table, his eyes ancient, like eroded stone. When it comes to rest on me, I swallow hard, but it moves onward, lingering on Eurus. "The only rule is this: once you enter the arena, you cannot leave until the round is complete. Whatever happens on the field is permanent—even death."

A sudden rise of murmurings unfolds.

The lightning god gifts his audience a close-mouthed smile. "The first trial will take place in four days' time," he goes on. "Best of luck to you all."

The fifth course is served: roast duck dusted with gold flakes. A small mountain of potatoes accompanies the protein, as well as sugar-glazed carrots, their scraggly green tops crisped from roasting.

The divine dive into their meals, some forgoing utensils entirely.

One broad, muscled god wearing dented armor snaps a thigh bone in half and sucks the marrow from within. Internally, I wince. No one appears disturbed by the behavior. Indeed, even a few silk-draped goddesses follow suit. Meanwhile, the East Wind continues to observe the lightning god long after he has taken his seat.

The din of conversation resumes. I tune in for a time, both fascinated and appalled by the in-depth discussion surrounding the quickest way to fell a god depending on one's weapon. Then another dialogue catches my attention.

"He couldn't possibly reach our realm," one god explains to his neighbor a few seats down. I strain my ears. His voice is but one thread of a hundred. I pluck it from the masses. "Only the divine have the ability to enter the City of Gods."

"Then what of the mortal woman breaking bread with us right now?" one of his companions—a withered-looking deity with gray hair—snaps.

I hurriedly wipe my mouth with my napkin.

"Good point," the god concedes. He frowns, nudging the scraps across his plate. "Apparently, this mortal prince travels with a beast that was once one of our own. Do you remember when it was exiled, confined in the mortal realms? Well, it has since escaped the labyrinth where it was detained and seeks revenge on whoever imprisoned it."

Wait. Didn't Zephyrus mention this beast to Eurus? He claimed it was looking for him. Is that because *Eurus* imprisoned it in this labyrinth?

The withered gentleman—gentlegod?—sips his wine thoughtfully. "Not that I'm dismissing your story," he goes on, "but I don't ever recall one of our own who was physically abnormal or *beastly*, as you say. Unless you count Eurus!" The ancient deity wheezes at his own joke.

My eyes cut to the East Wind. He gives no outward indication of having overheard the comment, but I understand this immortal as one who shows nothing of himself, not even his countenance. What do they mean by *abnormal*? His wings?

"But there was!" a goddess cuts in. "Remember the sacred bull?" She drops her voice, juts her chin toward a figure dressed in dark green robes overlaid by fishing nets, who is seated in a chair carved from coral. "*He* gifted it to that mortal king."

A one-eyed crone clothed in a threadbare shawl points a long, jagged fingernail at her dinner companion. "The bull copulated with the king's wife, and a monstrous child was born. Do not forget who advocated for this child to be exiled from the city."

Three, four, five pairs of eyes flick toward the East Wind. And thus, my suspicions are confirmed. But why would Eurus send one of his own to be imprisoned? What sordid past does he hide?

I'm so engrossed in the conversation that I fail to notice dessert has been served until a faint whiff of rot stings my nostrils. As Eurus sinks his fork into the slice of lemon cake, I slap aside his utensil. He recoils into the back of his chair, one arm lifted against the unexpected strike.

The garden falls eerily quiet.

I fear moving too suddenly, breathing too forcefully. Adder's Bite: a commonplace poison used to numb a person's senses, weaken their tether to reality. Generally, it is scentless, but citrus oils effectively draw out the odor of rancid meat. With the amount of wine consumed this evening, most would fail to notice.

Eventually, the East Wind lowers his arm, grips his knife with curled fingers. I imagine his expression, a blending of fear and humiliation. "You'll have to excuse my assistant," he clips out, the smoke of his voice boiling with suppressed rage.

Cackling laughter tunnels down into my eardrums. My face warms, and I hunch closer to the table. "I d-d-didn't mean . . . I s-smelled . . ."

"I think," the East Wind says, "it would be best if you excused yourself." This, followed by a softly snarled, "*Now.*"

Lurching from my chair, I stumble along the table, clinging to whatever shred of dignity remains.

"Can't you control that mortal of yours, Eurus?" someone drawls as I brush past.

There is a pause. "Mortals are slow to learn, as you know."

I press a hand to my mouth to stifle the hitch in my breath. Slow, like some brainless animal in need of training. Her ladyship called me slow. Slow and burdensome and dull.

Once inside the palace, I veer toward the central staircase, desperate for the seclusion of my bedroom.

"The divine are notorious assholes."

I spin around. A trim, dark-skinned god leans against the wall, arms folded, one ankle tossed over the other. His tight brown curls have been shorn close to the scalp.

"And you, my dear? Why, you are paired with the most notorious one of all." His gray-eyed gaze drags upward, from the tips of my toes to my distraught expression. "A mortal assistant. How curious. How very curious." Pushing off the wall, he takes an intricately carved staff into his hand. "You are too soft a thing to be dallying with beasts." He offers me a long-stemmed rose with flourish. "For you."

Seeing as I do not want to offend, I accept the flower with a nervous smile.

"I confess I was observing you during dinner," the god says, "though I do not believe you noticed me."

I shake my head. "There w-w-were many people p-p-present." The soft pink petals brush my cheek. It helps calm me. "Are you participating in th-the tournament, too?"

"That is the intention." With a twirl of his staff, he bows gallantly. "My name is Arinogimus, but my friends call me Arin."

I dip my chin in acknowledgment. "Nice to m-meet you, Arinogimus."

"Arin, please."

I glance around nervously, but we alone occupy the hall. "Arin, then."

"Will you tell me your name, or am I to wait with bated breath?"

"Min," I whisper, for I am used to giving what others ask of me.

"Well, Min, I imagine you are eager to return to your quarters, so I won't keep you. If you ever need help, don't hesitate to seek me out." He winks at me. "Luck to you, Min."

Though my legs itch to flee, I force them into an unhurried amble as I continue up the stairs and down the corridor. I do not want to act more like prey than I already am.

After nearly an hour searching the halls, I finally locate our suite, stumbling inside to find Eurus planted in the middle of the main chamber. He whirls to face me. "Where have you been?"

I close the door warily. My bedroom is located a handful of strides to my right, but to reach it, I must pass the East Wind. "I got l-l-lost."

"Lost." I hear the curl of his mouth, a borderline sneer. My muscles pull taut. "How difficult can it be to find the suite?"

"There are over three hundred r-rooms in the palace," I say. "I've only w-walked the halls once. You can't presume m-me to know my way so s-soon after arrival."

"You expect me to believe that? Where were you really?"

"I just told y-y-you," I growl between clenched teeth.

"Where did you get that flower?"

I glance down at the rose in surprise. I'd forgotten I was holding it.

Frowning, I toss it onto the dining table. "One of the competitors g-g-gave it to m-me."

Time drips out, and still the East Wind stares. "Ask yourself, bird. Why would one of the divine gift you a flower?"

"I don't kn-kn-know," I choke out. "You ask me these questions as if I have the answers, but h-h-how am I to know anything when you tell me n-nothing?"

"Whoever gave it to you probably suspected you would bring it back to our suite. What if it has been tampered with?" he presses, taking a step forward. The shadow of his wings cloaks me, soles to scalp. "What if there is some toxic coating along the stem, which would weaken me if I touched it?"

The gift was odd, but I hadn't considered the implication. My mind, grappling with the humiliation of that dinner, sought only the shelter of tranquility. My shields were lowered. I let someone in, perhaps to the East Wind's detriment. And yet, I have done nothing wrong.

"Th-th-think what you w-will," I say, "but he w-was only trying to c-c-comfort me after how you treated me at dinner."

"How *I* treated you?" Eurus thunders. "You ruined a perfectly good meal. I wasn't even able to eat my dessert!"

"Did y-y-you even ask yourself *why* I s-s-slapped the fork out of your hand?" I manage. "Do you think I like s-s-slapping utensils from people's hands for *fun*?" I was only trying to help him, and he tossed me to those slavering wolves. I am silly enough to feel hurt over it. Perhaps Lady Clarisse is right. I am a brainless fool. "I apologize if I s-s-startled you, but s-s-someone laced the cake with a poison called Adder's Bite," I go on, fury churning with hot shame. "Clearly, someone wants y-y-you out of the way. Why are y-you punishing me for trying to h-h-h-help you?"

Those last words I spit vehemently, like small, sharp stones. My skin buzzes with a strange combination of apprehension and satisfaction. By the Mother, that felt good.

"I didn't know," he says. "I was trying to protect you—"

"No," I growl back. "You h-h-humiliated me."

"*I* humiliated you? You humiliated me!"

"N-not purposefully." My voice cracks. "You either trust m-m-me, or you don't," I say, pulling away to place much-needed space between us. "But I w-w-won't be treated like your enemy. I told y-you I would help. I *want* to return home. Why would I risk th-that?"

He can't answer, or won't. In the end, it makes no difference. The sound of silence is all the same.

"I'm going for a w-walk," I say.

"Bird—"

Brushing past him, I slam the door shut behind me.

13

I RETURN TO THE GARDEN, BECAUSE THE NIGHT-BLOOMING JASMINE and the star-cloaked night are content to let me be. As I enter one of the hedge mazes, I imagine it is the estate grounds I wander, tall bushes of lavender skimming my knees.

A deep ache throbs beneath my sternum. Longing? Sorrow? The palace is not the estate. It means nothing to me. And yet, I may wander without threat of the lash, or whatever harsh punishment Lady Clarisse managed to concoct. It is nice to know peace, if only for a little while.

Despite all signs of the banquet having been removed, my attempts to shunt aside thoughts of the East Wind don't work. They never do. I fear I have confined myself in an even smaller cage. I must remain here until the tournament is complete, the East Wind's victory claimed. And if he does not win? What then? If by some miracle I'm able to return to St. Laurent, I pray her ladyship is merciful.

"Lost, are we?"

I startle and whirl around. A curvy woman with a generous bust slinks around one of the hedges, eyeing me with a hunger that sets my teeth on edge. The goddess we met earlier today. Demi.

"I ... guess I am," I reply, taking one step backward. Leaves poke my back, the hedge blocking further retreat.

The goddess ambles nearer, still wearing that dazzling, sunrise gown. She is tall, far taller than I am, and easily overwhelms the space.

"I didn't catch your name earlier." Her yellow eyes flash in the dark. "Eurus didn't offer it."

He wouldn't have. I'm not sure why that disappoints me. "It's Min," I say.

"Min. How quaint." The goddess holds out a slender hand ornamented by delicate gold rings. "Demi."

I shake her hand. Callused, like mine. It is something I did not expect.

Abruptly, she tugs me forward, nose pressed to the crown of my skull with a deep inhalation. The hem of her sleeve brushes my arm, and I shiver. "You smell of chervil." She releases me, head canted in interest. "What realm do you hail from, Min?"

I glance toward the maze entrance, where gloom beads along its branches, amongst the leaves. Eurus assured me I would be safe, so long as I remained on the palace grounds. Then again, someone tried to poison him tonight. "Marles," I reply.

Lush mouth pursed, Demi picks at one long, painted nail, saying, "Lavender fields and vineyards, fresh bread and soft cheese." The powder dabbed around her lashes has darkened them to a sultry coal. "You worship the Master of Sea and Mother of Earth, is that correct?"

I blink. "Yes. Well, mostly the Mother of Earth, as do most farmers. Sailors worship the Master of Sea."

"You're a farmer?" She arches a brow. "You certainly don't look like one. Though I suppose that would explain why I smell chervil on you."

"No, I'm not a farmer. I—" But I can reveal nothing more. I have likely said too much as it is. As Lady Clarisse never failed to remind me, silence is best.

The goddess' mouth stretches corner to corner, seemingly amused by my reluctance. "Secreting information already? You are wise, Min from Marles. I think it's just *precious* that Eurus has taken a mortal lover."

My eyes pop wide. "Lover?"

"Of course. That is why you're here, isn't it?" She peers at me beneath lowered lashes. "Don't be bashful, love. If anything, you should be *celebrating*. The number of women who have hoped to find themselves in Eurus' bed is many. You have accomplished what few have been able to."

"Eurus and I are n-not, um, lovers. I'm just his assistant."

Pleasure brightens that lambent gaze, and she tosses back her head, teeth parting around a cascade of warm, rolling laughter. "That's what they all say."

This conversation grows increasingly uncomfortable. Exactly what sort of numerical value does *many* represent? Not that I care to part the curtains of the East Wind's sex life. He is ageless, after all. Likely a great number of conquests. I imagine the sum to be substantial.

"So tell me, Min from Marles." The goddess, Demi, reaches overhead to pluck a flower from the wall of interlocking leaves at my back. The bloom, doused in a beam of moonlight, seems to enlarge in her palm, the petals elongating. I stare in shock. "How is it that you have found yourself entangled with the East Wind, and during the tournament no less?"

A subtle curl of her fingers, and the flower's snowy edges blacken. "Begging your pardon, madam, but I'd rather not say."

"Not into gossip, are you? That's probably for the best. To be fair, I did not think Eurus would grace our homeland again, but here he is. I'm particularly happy to see him."

Her fondness for the East Wind is undeniable. I feel small in the presence of this deity. Small and overlooked. "You knew each other, long ago?"

"That's one way to put it." At my blank stare, she elaborates, with a relish that borders on violence, "We were lovers."

"I see."

"Does this upset you, knowing Eurus and I once shared a bed?" A scarlet fingernail *tap-tap-taps* against her defined bicep. The toes peeking from her sandals are painted a dusky pink.

"No." But a pang sharpens beneath the hard plate of my sternum. It is not jealousy, exactly. More like . . . envy? Yes, that must be it. I envy this goddess her freedom and poise. "Why w-would it?"

"Why indeed." Her eyes narrow, and sweat blooms beneath my breastband. Eurus was right. I should never have left the room. Four walls to keep me in—and others out.

The goddess sighs then, dropping the flower onto the grass and crushing it underfoot. "I wondered if you would do me a favor, Min."

"A favor?"

"I'm supposed to meet some friends in the city for lunch this week, but one of them canceled last minute. Would you care to join me?"

My mouth parts, hangs open a moment. "Oh, um . . ." In St. Laurent, wandering Market Street brought with it mixed emotions. The joy of freedom, however brief, yet paired with this, always, was longing, melancholy, for I was separate from those gathering in the cafes, always on the outside looking in.

"Don't worry about the cost. Everything is already paid for," she says, noting my hesitancy. "And just between you and me, the palace can get a bit stuffy. The city is much more fun." Unexpectedly, her eyes soften; their yellow glow dims. "How does that sound?"

The East Wind ordered me to keep to the grounds, yet I do long to see more of this alluring realm. "Can I ask you something first?"

"Of course." Demi leans forward, an eager participant in our conversation.

"Why do you want to have lunch with me?" After all, she was at the welcome banquet, scheming, observing, strategizing. "I won't reveal anything to you about Eurus, so if that's the r-reason you're asking, you will have to find your information elsewhere."

"You claim you are not lovers," Demi says with savored intrigue, "yet you defend him as fiercely as though you are." Then she does what none have done in my life, save Nan: she frames my face in her warm, roughened palms, studying me as though I am a young pup in need of a firm hand.

"There is mettle in you, Min from Marles." The goddess nods in satisfaction. "You will need it amongst these immortals. And no, I'm not asking you to lunch to press you for information. I'm asking because you smell of chervil, and it is my favorite scent in all the realms."

With the first trial less than a week away, there is nothing to do but wait.

Following the humiliation of the banquet, I elect to receive my meals in the suite, sitting cross-legged in bed as I arrange the ingredients for Eastern Blood across my bedspread. The brew itself warms over a burner, with my notes and tools arranged neatly on the dresser. With nightshade finally integrated, the poison must simmer for another ten days before the next ingredient can be added. During this time, Eastern Blood gives off a rather putrid reek. The East Wind has made his distaste for the scent known.

"Well, if I had *The Practice of Herbal Remedies*," I'd told him yesterday, "I could find a solution to mask the odor."

He refused to hand it over. Unsurprising. If I must suffer the stench, so must he.

Turning from my work, I stare out the window, searching for a messenger bird, but I fear they are unable to reach the City of Gods. If I cannot communicate with her ladyship, how am I to purchase the estate and preserve Nan's legacy?

As for the East Wind, he comes and goes at odd hours. Occasionally, I see him lounging on the sofa in the common room, poring over accounts of past tournaments. Or perhaps *lounge* is the wrong word. The East Wind perches. Settles. Not lounges. Never lounges. For the most part, we coexist, each keeping to our respective bedrooms. Rarely does he greet me when entering the suite. Rarely does he bid me farewell.

While smoothing the petals of a chamomile flower, a clean, herbaceous scent drifts across my nose. My bedroom door lies ajar, offering a partial view of the shared washroom: door shut, steam seeping through the crack beneath.

I hear the slosh of water, the East Wind's gratified sigh. I swallow, my skin tightening at the sound. Who is the East Wind without his cloak? Sometimes I question whether he truly *is* a god, for I have never seen his face in full. All that I am given—the rasp of his voice, the motion of his hands and fluidity of his movements—paints only the haziest image.

Another splash jolts my system, and I slide to the edge of the mattress, hurriedly plant my feet, a grounding in the earth. Why am I listening to the East Wind bathe? No, I've plenty to occupy myself with.

Pushing to my feet, I move to my workstation. Head bent, I grind down the root with painstaking slowness. *It must be the finest of powders,* Nan would say. *Too many clumps, and the root will fail to fully dissolve.*

The washroom door creaks open. I swallow, refocus my attention on crushing the last of the fibrous rhizome as Eurus steps into my bedroom without bothering to knock. I bite the inside of my cheek against a sudden swell of irritation. For all he knew, I could have been half-dressed!

"One of the competitors is having a small gathering at their residence this evening," he says. "It's a good opportunity to study the competition. I probably won't return until tomorrow."

I continue with my grinding. Even at this distance, I smell the soap on his skin: rosemary, black pepper, goat's milk. "Very well." His absence certainly makes no difference to my day.

When the silence stretches to the point of frayed threads, I turn to glance at his hooded form. Water beads along the bones rising from the center of his upper back. My eyes drop. His feet are bare. The sight unnerves me, and I promptly resume my work.

"Is there something else you n-need?" I say, only a little breathlessly. "Is my chopping disturbing you?" Lady Clarisse always complained about how loudly I worked, as if one can shop herbs *noiselessly.*

Eurus steps closer so the warmth of his body buffets my flank. I continue twisting the pestle in half circles. With little enough space in the bedroom to begin with, the East Wind's considerable physique all but commands the small chamber.

"Why do you continue grinding the powder?" he asks, a warm exhalation stirring the hair atop my head. "It's already as fine as it can be."

So he thinks. "If the poison is to be successful, it m-must dissolve into the bloodstream instantaneously. Only the finest powder will suffice."

"It looks fine enough."

Inwardly, I scoff. The things Nan could teach him! "A proper poison is both science and art. You cannot r-rush it."

"If it's already ground up," he goes on, "it would be more efficient to move on to the next step."

"Why don't you let me focus on wh-what I do best," I snap, "instead of offering your opinion on something you know nothing about?" The swiftness of my rebuttal, the severity of my tone—today, I will not be pressed into the earth like an errant pebble.

Eurus leans down, the hood of his cloak angled toward me. "Take care to remember who it is you speak to," he murmurs.

As that darkness shifts, the skin along my arms prickles with some unnamable emotion. The East Wind need not worry.

I will never forget.

The city center is marked by a large square to which all roads lead. Strolling alongside Demi—dressed stunningly in slender white trousers, pink heels, and a sage green blouse—we explore the various shops, browsing all manner of flowers and soaps, teas and jewels, fabrics and books, perfumes and shoes. Bells ring unceasingly as doors open and shut, open and shut.

The goddess tugs me into yet another clothing boutique, where a gaggle of women complete their purchases at the front counter. I finger my threadbare dress self-consciously, all too aware of the runs in my stockings. Someone sniggers. I wince and duck my head.

Demi slides an arm around my shoulder, glaring at our audience. "Something to say?"

The women exchange a wordless look, then exit the store with their bags in tow.

"Try not to let them bother you," Demi offers. "The one with the black hair?" She lowers her voice. "Her mother chained her to a rock, poor thing."

Too overwhelmed with gratitude to speak, I allow the goddess to lead me toward the back of the boutique. While I take a seat on a padded bench, Demi stands before a long mirror, a gown in each hand: one green, one blue. The latter appears to be fashioned from rippling water. The former sparkles with an intensity that rivals the sun.

"For the victor's banquet," she explains. "It's putting the cart before the horse, I know, but I need an excuse to buy something beautiful." Lifting the green dress in front of her body, she adds, "I'm leaning toward emerald, but I do love the cut of the navy gown. What do you think?"

"I think you'd look good in anything you chose to wear," I say, and I mean that sincerely. She is every shade of striking, and I can't fathom why she would choose to spend her afternoon with me—unless she seeks information about the East Wind.

The goddess quirks her mouth, but its curve fails to touch her eyes. "You're sweet. Too sweet for Eurus, as far as I'm concerned. You truly don't have a preference?"

"It's not the gown that makes one beautiful."

She turns. There is something different about her face. Before I'm able to grasp whatever emotion has exposed itself, she sniffs, dabs beneath her eyes with a square of cloth. "Are you trying to make me cry?" Then she shakes her head. "Maybe you are his assistant after all."

Another moment hemming and hawing, and she selects the green gown. It costs two thousand gold coins. For that price, one would think it were sewn entirely from emeralds.

As it turns out, it is.

We return to the chaos of the streets, and I allow myself to relax for the first time since my arrival. Though the sun beats back the chill, my skin stipples in the shade, and I rub my bare arms, wishing I'd remembered my coat. Sometime later, we pass a cart selling hot cider and jars of honey, enveloped in a cloud of cinnamon-scented air. I gaze longingly at the drink, but of course I've no coin to purchase one.

Before I understand what is happening, Demi buys two ciders and offers one to me.

"Oh, I couldn't," I protest.

"You can, and you will. I insist." She doesn't relent until I accept the drink for what it is: a gift. "You know what complements cinnamon surprisingly well?" Demi asks over the rim of her cup. I shake my head. "Blueberries."

"Blueberries?" I take a sip. The intense apple flavor warms my throat and belly.

"Yes. It helps highlight the taste of the fruit." She winks at me. "Give it a try sometime."

We continue onward, wandering the market for a time. It seems that there's been a recent harvest, for there are tables laden with squashes and gourds, turnips and carrots. Demi is kind enough to purchase a jar of honey for me, despite my protests. At one point, someone stops to ask her how often they should water the new ornamental plant they've purchased. I observe the interaction carefully. Though she seems genuinely interested in spending time with me, I hardly know her. How can I trust that her intentions are pure?

"Can I ask you something?"

The goddess casts me a sidelong glance. Kohl intensifies the yellow of her irises. "Of course."

"You said you haven't seen the East Wind in centuries. What was he like back then?" I should not be so fascinated by my captor, but I find my questions multiplying the longer I spend in his company.

She shrugs. "Not much has changed. He was less closed, maybe. Then again, pain affects everyone differently."

"What pain?"

At this, the goddess smiles, albeit sadly. "I love gossip as much as the next deity, Min from Marles, but that story is not mine to tell."

I tuck my tongue into my cheek thoughtfully, ignoring the growling of my stomach. "Then I assume his banishment is off limits as well?"

"Oh." She flaps a hand dismissively. "That is no great secret. Eurus, along with his brothers—the Anemoi, they are called—helped overthrow our previous governing body and bring the current Council of Gods to power. But not long after, the council turned on them. The Anemoi were deemed traitors and thus banished."

I may not particularly like the East Wind, but the punishment seems unjust to me. It must hurt to be barred from entering one's home. "I don't understand. Why would the council banish the Anemoi if they helped them gain control? It doesn't seem fair."

"The divine are rarely fair." She speaks fondly, as though referring to a small child's antics. "The council was paranoid the Anemoi would one day turn against them, so they were banished. It was a shock to the community. Oh—avert your gaze, love, lest you be turned to stone." Demi cups a hand over my eyes as we pass a gray-skinned woman standing on one of the benches, spouting insults at any man who dares venture too close. Two serpents coil her shoulders and upper arms.

Once we are beyond the gray-skinned woman and her verbal abuse, Demi lowers her hand. "But you're right," she adds thoughtfully. "It wasn't fair what the council did. I imagine it to be a difficult life, living out eternity alone."

"I don't believe his brothers are alone," I say, recalling Eurus' conversation with Zephyrus. "They are mortal now, and all are in committed relationships. Eurus is the only one who is not."

The goddess halts, eyebrows winged all the way up to her hairline. "Mortal? But that would mean Eurus' brothers relinquished their power, or it was taken from them." At my confusion, she elaborates, "See, often—but not always—a god's power is tied to a specific object. Eurus and his brothers each possess a weapon that acts as a conduit to their power. If the weapon was destroyed, then theoretically, their power and tie to immortality would be, too."

Interesting. How very, very interesting. "And this is common knowledge?"

"On the contrary, it is relatively unknown. Best to keep that information hush-hush, if you know what I mean."

So if her ladyship destroyed the East Wind's ax, he would be made mortal. Although, *would* she destroy his ax? Once he is mortal, I can't imagine his blood would be of any use to her. Perhaps, if he is killed by his god-touched weapon, his blood will retain its divine properties long enough for her to create that potion of immortality. The power of a god, extinguished. It is difficult to imagine.

Sometime later, we arrive at an outdoor cafe tucked inside a shade-dappled courtyard. As Demi veers toward a table in the back, I halt in surprise. "Arin."

The gray-eyed immortal unfurls to his feet. I frown in confusion, for Demi has taken a seat at his table. *He* is the friend we are to meet for lunch?

Arin casts the goddess a look I cannot hope to dissect as he resettles in his chair. "You didn't tell me Min would be joining us."

Demi unfolds her napkin across her lap. The vibrant hues of her outfit grant her the appearance of a flower herself, one of many dotting the courtyard. "I wasn't sure if she would agree to it."

As a well-groomed server arrives to pour wine, Demi covers my glass with one bejeweled hand. "Do you have anything less potent?" At the server's bewilderment, she elaborates, "We're dining in the presence of a mortal." She smiles, and the immortal—a young fellow with antlers sprouting from his skull—stares at me for so long I grow uncomfortable.

Eventually, he dips his chin in assent. "Let me see what else we have." He disappears and returns, pouring a clear, sparkling liquid from a copper pitcher. It is the sweetest, most refreshing water I've ever had the pleasure of tasting.

"May I get you something to eat?" the server asks.

"What do you think, Arin?" Demi angles toward her friend, cheek resting in her open palm. "Spotted elimna? Or how about a bowl of fruit. Min can sample all sorts of flavors! At the very least, she should try the pasta. Or . . . you know what?" She turns to the antlered attendant. "We'll have one of everything on the menu."

The server departs. I, however, gape at Demi. "Are you sure that's not too costly?"

She flaps a hand, leans back in her chair, one leg tossed over the other. Her pink heel hangs, slapping the sole of her foot as her leg bounces. "Cost is irrelevant. You should experience everything our realm has to offer. I can't imagine Eurus is playing tour guide with you."

"Speaking of which, I haven't seen you around the palace much," Arin states with honed focus.

Yes, because Eastern Blood requires frequent stirrings at this stage. But I shrug, saying, "It's n-not exactly safe for me to wander alone."

Arin nods in understanding. "With news of this Prince Balior, I dare say I would not want to wander alone either."

"Quite right," Demi quips, turning to me. "Though if you ever want company, love, you can always visit me. Room twenty-two, second floor."

It is a welcome offer, though I am not without my suspicions. But I settle in, basking in the warm sun, songbirds flitting amongst the bougainvillea. Is this what it feels like to know peace?

The server returns with our order, and soon, the entire table is covered in a variety of foods. Arin and Demi transfer small servings onto their own plates. I hesitate, unsure if I'm allowed to do the same. After a few moments, the goddess sets down her fork.

"If you are hungry," she says, "you should eat."

It is spoken meaningfully, which makes me question whether it is food she refers to, or something more, something cowering beneath the surface of my skin that I cannot yet expose.

So I eat. Mostly with utensils, sometimes with my hands, when required. I eat until my stomach strains, I eat until my taste buds grow numb, I eat for the simple joy of exploration. It has been a long time since I've shared a meal with others. It heals something in me to realize Demi and Arin enjoy my company. Imagine if Nan could see me now.

As I shove another spoonful of dessert into my mouth, Arin stays my hand. "I'd slow down on the iceberry cream," he says with a teasing smile. "It's known to cause gastrointestinal issues when eaten in large quantities."

"I hope I'm not interrupting."

My throat closes, and I sputter, spraying food across my plate. Arin's eyes gutter like extinguished coals.

I swivel in my seat. The East Wind looms over our table, having drawn the attention of those enjoying lunch in the courtyard. His anger is palpable, expelled outward from his hulking frame in waves of ravenous heat.

"Eurus." The goddess rises, arms spread, her smile cutting enough to rival a freshly sharpened blade. "If I had known you would be joining us, I'd have made the reservation for four."

"I'm not here to join you," he clips out.

"Yes. I forgot about your abhorrence of happiness," she responds sweetly.

The East Wind's cloak snaps in a rain-scented breeze. "I'm here for my assistant."

"Maybe so, but you can wait until we're finished eating."

"That's all right," I blurt out. "I'm d-d-done eating."

The goddess studies me closely. "You're sure?"

"Yes." I look to Demi, then to Eurus, back to Demi. One cloaked in darkness, the other swathed in color and light. "I sh-should go with him."

"That's what you want?" Demi presses, with a pale touch against my arm.

I nod vigorously. Her skepticism is plain, but she doesn't seek to change my mind. Instead, she reaches into her purse. Six, seven, eight gold coins clatter onto the table. "This should cover lunch." She glances at Arin, who has yet to remove his gaze from the East Wind. "Shall we?"

As soon as they vanish around the corner, Eurus growls, "Stay away from Demi."

He provides nothing more. No explanation, no reasonable evidence to support his stance. He commands and assumes I will fall in line. A part of me—a very large part—wants to. If I make no waves, there is no risk of capsizing. But I enjoyed my time in Demi and Arin's company. Am I to trust Eurus' perspective simply because he hammered it into my will?

"Are y-y-you going to tell m-me why?" I prompt.

"She is divine," he snaps, guiding me down an unfamiliar street. "No other explanation is needed."

I lengthen my stride to keep pace. "What is the r-r-real reason?" Why single out Demi? What, exactly, is their history? If they were once lovers, something must have come between them. "Did she b-break your heart?"

Eurus nearly trips over his own feet. He grunts, forces a path through the throng with his winds. A handful of the divine slam against the shop windows with cries of outrage. He ignores them. "She did not break my heart. She broke my trust. I believed she wanted what was best for me. But she showed her true colors. Never again."

If anything, his response manages to paint a more obscure image of his past. But I drop it, for now. "Wh-what about Arin?"

"What about him?"

"He is also divine—and a c-c-competitor."

We veer toward an area of the city with garlands of dried flowers strung between the rooftops. The East Wind walks so fast I struggle to keep up. He does not trust, this god. How I wish I knew what expression creased his features. So much is spoken with the eyes.

"I'm not concerned with Arin. But Demi—" His shoulders creep upward toward his ears. "I warned you to stay inside the palace grounds," he growls. "Do you have a death wish?"

The East Wind does not care for me, I remind myself. He only cares for what I can provide him. "It w-w-was just lunch," I puff.

"You know nothing of Demi, or Arin. They are gods, bird. Everything they do is for their own gain. Who is to say you would not have been in some unfortunate accident that left you dead, the poison unfinished?"

Now *my* irritation begins to churn. "So you want m-m-me to avoid Demi. Fine. But have y-you considered the benefits of me s-spending time with her?"

Gods and goddesses leap from our path, granting the East Wind a wide berth. He seems to bite his tongue, but eventually, he relents. "I . . . did not consider that."

Shocking.

"What do you suggest?" he asks.

The stitch in my side tunnels deeper. If I push my legs any faster, I'm convinced they will collapse. "Allow m-me the freedom to spend time with Demi, and I can see if she has heard of anything regarding the w-weaknesses of the other competitors. Maybe about the t-t-trials themselves. You would n-not need to remain in the d-dark." After all, what is one more thread in this web of lies?

Placing his hand at my lower back, the East Wind steers me through the worst of the crowding. The flutter in my stomach is as unexpected as it is unwelcome.

"So long as you continue your work on the poison," Eurus says gruffly, "I suppose it wouldn't be the worst thing for you to spend time with Demi, if you think you can get her to open up. It could prove useful to know her whereabouts, what she's up to, her interests." He nods to himself. "Just be careful, bird. You are mortal, easily broken. I would not wish you to come to harm."

14

FAR WEST OF THE PALACE, IN A STRETCH OF OPEN GROUND, STANDS the arena.

The immense stone structure is a feat of engineering. Its outer walls curve up and in, the center hollowed out, exposed to the elements. Below, a great field marks the heart of the stadium, tier after tier of stands rising gradually higher to surround its grassy center.

My pulse kicks hard, provoked by the bellow of a hundred thousand spectators. The roar is both declaration and promise. Today, blood will be spilled. It will soak the grassy field. It will splatter the walls and streak flesh.

Gripping the railing in front of me, I lean forward on the bench, scanning the hundred-plus competitors spaced equidistantly around the field's perimeter. There is every color and shape of immortal: elegant denizens, hybrids of beast and man, some that look no older than children, though I assume they are as ancient as the rest. On the far side of the arena, the red-headed trio stands as a single unit, armed to the teeth. Another goddess with pin-straight, midnight hair and light brown skin shields herself behind a veil of deepest night, while a many-headed creature of serpentine appearance stretches their legs. I don't see Eurus anywhere. We parted ways at the arena entrance without so much as a *Good luck*.

Four levels above me, shaded beneath a white tent, sits the Council of Gods. I recognize the lightning god, never far from his basket of lightning bolts. Two fair-haired deities, one male, one female, chatter idly with one another, the latter restringing a beautifully ornate bow.

Another god slouches in his cushioned chair, goblet in hand, peering down at the field through weighted eyelids. My brows creep upward in surprise. Of those present at the welcome banquet, he was the most disruptive, having consumed multiple flagons of wine before the second course had been served. I would never have guessed he was a member of the council.

Lastly, seated at the far end, almost like an afterthought, is a scrawny, disfigured man, his face etched in soot. Two of the dozen chairs are empty.

As someone settles onto the bench beside me, I glance over, then stare. "Demi?" I blink. "What are you doing here? Aren't you competing?"

The goddess eases back with a snort, legs crossed, curves adorned in an elaborate violet gown more appropriate for a musical recital than bloodshed. "Gods, no. I know my strengths, though there's nothing quite like watching the other deities have their entrails ripped out."

This last comment she voices with great relish. I shift uncomfortably on the bench. "Surely you don't mean that?"

Demi continues to monitor the field. "Why wouldn't I? A little bloodshed never hurt anyone."

What did I expect? We come from two separate realms, Demi and I. We may as well be fish and bird, stone and tree, sky and earth.

"I've already placed my bets," she goes on, unaware of my internal turmoil. "My money's on the Fates."

"The who?"

She points to the red-headed trio. "Extremely vicious. They would be more than happy to hack up the competition. I do worry about some of the weaker participants though. Unfortunately, some will pay a steep price."

Her ominous tone draws the hair along my arms to fine points. "What do you mean?"

"Only fifty contestants will make it to the next round. And I suspect a great many of those who don't will die in the attempt."

I knew the tournament could be deadly, but it sounds far more horrifying uttered aloud. "And you enjoy this?"

A half-hearted shrug, and she turns, leveling me with those pale, yellow eyes. "Something you should know, Min from Marles. The divine grow bored quite easily. What better way to entertain ourselves—and increase the stakes for those participating—than to demand immortals fight for their lives, as mortals do?"

I shy away, if only to mask the repulsion twisting my features. The East Wind warned me of the gods. I elected not to listen. Moving forward, I must take care with who I interact with and in what capacity. Eurus was right. None can be trusted.

"I just . . ." My voice softens. "I didn't think . . ."

"Well, what can you expect of those who live forever? We have seen all there is to see, accomplished all there is to accomplish. We are worshiped and adored, but even that loses its luster, in time." Demi gestures toward the Council of Gods seated in the stands. "Some enjoy the tournament more than others. Take Apollo, for example." She points to the blond man seated beside the equally blonde woman. "He does not savor the violence, but his twin sister loves it. Then again, she *is* a huntress."

"Two of the chairs are vacant," I observe.

She offers a vague hum of assent. "One of the council members is currently investigating the mortal everyone's been talking about: Prince Balior."

I straighten to attention. "What about him?"

"Well," she says, foot bouncing as it hangs, "it seems that his power is somehow linked to the beast he travels with. Some worry he might be able to cross into the City of Gods. We haven't much information, aside from that."

"And—" I lick my lips. "Is this of concern to you?" Has Lady Clarisse involved herself in something far more insidious than I first believed?

"At the moment, no. But change is constant. First, we must see what this Prince Balior wants. There's no point in dwelling on it until we receive more information. The investigation is ongoing. Thankfully," she adds, gesturing to the field, "we have the tournament to keep ourselves occupied."

Right. The tournament. As I scan the field for Eurus, Demi expounds on what the first trial will entail. Open battle. Its purpose? To establish hierarchy. Here, participants will divide the weak from the strong. In the end, only fifty will move on to the second trial. The rest will be disgraced, or dead.

"I don't see Eurus," I say.

"Far right, love."

There—a set of scaled wings. They expand and contract a few times, as if he is stretching the muscles in his back.

"How will he fare against the others?" I ask Demi, thinking this is a good opportunity to gather information.

One corner of her mouth slants into her cheek. "Don't tell me you're worried about him."

I am less worried for his wellbeing and more concerned about going home. "I'm curious. Most of the participants carry weapons, but he carries none."

"Eurus has his rage. That will fuel him. A banished god has much to prove."

True—but she didn't exactly answer my question. "Who do you think will be most difficult for Eurus to beat?"

The goddess purses her lips, considering each of the contenders. "The Fates—and Arin."

Of all the immortals, Arin is one of the slightest, and one I have admittedly overlooked. "Why Arin?" Even as I speak, I spot him below, positioned between two hulking brutes, each armed with no less than ten blades, their monstrous hands tipped with frightening claws. Arin appears downright diminutive in comparison.

"He may be a lesser god, but do not underestimate him." Her eyes flick to mine. "Arin will do anything to win."

I understand that desperation, though I wonder what, exactly, is at stake for him. "What powers does he hold?"

"He has an affinity for the healing arts. That staff of his? It can heal all manner of illnesses. But it also has the power to draw the strength from one's body, or even to insert an ailment into the bloodstream, though I have not witnessed it myself."

"That's . . ."

"Thrilling?" Demi's eyes brighten with excitement. "I do love an underdog."

As the lightning god pushes to his feet, a hush sweeps the stadium. Demi, seemingly unconcerned, waves over a food vendor from one row behind and purchases two bags of roasted chestnuts—one for me, one for her. I accept mine without complaint, too nauseated over the impending battle to rebuff her offer.

"One hundred and ten of you have gathered to make your stand," the lightning god bellows, his voice booming throughout the arena. "Unfortunately, only fifty will move on to the next trial."

At this, the audience stirs, an unease slinking through the creaking of benches and crunching of food concessions.

"Your objective," he continues, lifting one of his crackling lightning bolts, "is to outlast the other competitors, who will fall by blade or power, weakness or blood loss, surrender or grievous wound. When we are satisfied that enough blood has been shed, we will open the door at the center of the arena and allow fifty of those still standing to pass through."

As the announcement takes hold, I observe the participants checking and rechecking weapons, scanning those foes nearest to them. Eurus assesses the Fates across the field. The shortest of the trio wields a scythe. The tallest brandishes a gleaming black whip. The last bears no weapon, but brown leather wraps her knuckles, and her fiery hair has been braided in a crown across her skull. With a sinking sensation in my gut, I realize that they, too, possess wings.

"You fight to claim something for yourself," the lightning god roars, feeding the crowd's growing frenzy. "You fight," he says, "to win."

A thunderous assent shakes the arena.

"Competitors, take your marks."

As the Fates glide to the far side of the field, a short, stumpy god with a dented breastplate hobbles after them. An old injury in the leg? Already, he is at a disadvantage.

"Who are you betting on?" Demi asks eagerly.

I continue to watch Eurus, the bag of chestnuts crumpled inside my sweaty palms. They are all predators in the ring, but the East Wind's lack of motion is particularly eerie, a stillness amongst the impatient and the keen. He needs me—but I need him, too. He is both protector and captor, my only means of returning home. "Eurus, I guess."

"A reliable choice."

I glance over to see her exchanging coin with the group sitting behind us. It is all so very casual, betting on the lives of her friends.

The lightning god lifts a hand. "Begin."

An ear-splitting crack rends the air. There is a great rush toward the field's center, all one hundred and ten competitors bearing swords and maces, axes and rusted shields. Many are accompanied by animal companions, whether hawk or owl or dove, fox or snake or dog. Then, a spray of blood, a wretched scream: the first kill.

I'm not sure where to look first. Arin locks staffs with a much larger opponent. The Fates work as a team, driving their weapons into hearts, stomachs, throats. Two gods collide at the far wall. One punches a mass of fire toward his foe. It hits a transparent barrier, and the fire-god's opponent flees, ducking blows in his attempt to reach safety on the opposite side of the arena.

"What was that?" Demi screams at the fleeing god as she shoves to her feet. Her dark hair springs from its confinement, and red paints her face. "Are you a coward, or are you a conqueror?"

Our neighbors holler their agreement, shaking fists and flinging food into the stands below. I shrink further into my seat, horrified beyond measure, yet unable to look away.

The stadium rumbles, and I clutch the railing in confusion as a cyclone plummets downward, whipping up a thick haze of debris. Gray clouds boil overhead, spitting hail and a stinging rain. A bolt of lightning strikes three competitors at once. They collapse, dazed, as I squint against the driving rain. In the center of the cyclone stands Eurus, the storm his to command. He lifts his hands, and the tempest sweeps the field. It drags three, five, seven competitors inside its spiral before spitting them out in pieces.

Dead litter the ground. The air is a great red cloud, a coppery miasma. I cover my eyes against the suffering, but it makes no difference. I am back at the estate, Lady Clarisse venturing belowground. Sometimes, the screams would stretch for hours until the voices failed, disintegrating under constant strain.

My fingers spread, and I peer through the spaces between. One deity dressed in an ornate robe locks blades with a blue-haired goddess. Her skin glows in shades of brightening sunrise, the intensity enough to burn her opponent's eyes to dust. He claws at his face until someone rams a spear through his chest.

Across the arena, a wild-eyed goddess nocks an arrow to her bow. The East Wind, whose back is to her, does not recognize the danger as his wings unfurl and he takes to the sky.

"Watch out!" I scream.

The arrow cuts the air, swift and clean, embedding itself in his shoulder. Cloak flapping around him, Eurus locks onto the goddess who shot the arrow. A two-headed ax appears in his hand, and he dives toward his adversary, dodging a second arrow, a third. I gasp, leaning forward. His ax. It's *here*.

The goddess bares her teeth, stabbing at him with one of her arrows. He dodges easily, slips behind her, and decapitates her with one brutal slash.

The head bounces, rolls. I gag as her body crumples. The stadium quakes with another wave of deafening noise. Meanwhile, Demi has made herself comfortable, legs resting on the back of the bench in front of us. She laughs and tosses another chestnut into her mouth.

Eurus blasts hail at a gray-skinned woman with snakes slithering along her limbs—the goddess Demi and I spotted the other day in town. He calls down a thundercloud that seethes with white lightning. Using the rain as a shroud, Eurus evades the snake goddess' great yellow eyes, speeding low toward the ground until she loses interest and seeks another poor soul to turn to stone.

And still the battle rages. Two gods fall, their wings ripped off. Another collapses onto the ground, not one, but *three* daggers protruding from his chest. Several deaths are added to the growing tally: a beast with its belly split open, a god impaled by a spear. The more violent the tournament becomes, the louder and more piercing the screams.

"Oh, come on!" Demi cries, lurching forward. "Use your shield to protect that skull of yours! Or do you lack the brain to recognize that?"

I stare at her, eyes wide.

"Pardon," the goddess says, lips curved coyly as she settles back and resumes her languishing. "I sometimes get, ah, *heated* about sports."

She and I have a different definition of sport.

A great many deities now lie strewn across the blood-soaked grass, either gravely wounded, or dead. One goddess with the lower body of a canid lunges at Eurus, who uses his winds to divert her into the wall. He pins her, ax in hand, and cuts her throat.

I look away, breathing in and out, slowly. "How much longer?" I whisper to Demi.

She touches my back in comfort. "Nearly done. I can't imagine the council would let it continue for much longer."

Death, or surrender.

"Oh," the goddess whispers in horror. "Oh, no."

There, in the middle of the arena, the East Wind battles against some beastly creature. I thought Eurus was a giant amongst gods, but this behemoth is the largest I have seen, towering nearly as high as the arena wall. His skin is a lumpy gray, and his single reddened eye churns in the center of his forehead like a vast, boiling sun.

I gasp as he pins Eurus to the trampled grass. The East Wind kicks out unsuccessfully, trying to twist free with a wildness that speaks of a deep-seated fear. Using his ax, he slashes at the god's beefy forearm. At one point, his hood falls back, revealing a shock of black hair, but I'm too far away to discern any individual facial features.

A violent wind hammers into his foe's wide chest. There is a splintering crack, and the god releases him.

The East Wind launches himself skyward, narrowly dodging a flaming arrow, before plummeting back toward the ground. He flips mid-air and lands with a sickening crunch on the back of the god's neck.

I recoil from what Eurus does next. Even Demi curses beneath her breath, her bag of chestnuts forgotten, scattered at her feet. "Oly should have known better than to touch him," she murmurs.

I look to her. It is safe, this face, lovely and pristine. "Why should he have known better?"

She doesn't answer me, her attention fixated below. The East Wind has abandoned his winds for his ax. Bone crunches; blood sprays. I cover my mouth with my hands as he hacks the immortal to tiny pieces.

The Fates, having vanquished their most recent opponent, regroup and spear toward Eurus.

"Behind you!" I scream. "*Eurus!*"

He's tackled by three at once. They roll, their kindling hair flickering against the dark of his cloak. He catches two around the neck, slams them into the ground. The third, he punches in the stomach.

A horn sounds, and the Fates scatter. Moments later, Eurus' legs give out.

I gasp as the air shimmers across the field. A door has materialized at the center of the arena. Those nearest to it have already begun stumbling through, but those still locked in battle have failed to notice. My fingers dig into my thighs as the screams peak.

The East Wind pushes up onto his knees. He bows forward, struggling to stand. I chew my lower lip as competitor after competitor sprints or hobbles past him.

"He's not moving," I say. "Why isn't he moving?" Leaning forward, I belt, "Hurry up, Eurus! I never figured you'd be the slowest one on the field!" Harsh? Perhaps. But, injured or not, he needs to make it through that door.

He's up, his wings spread. A few great beats send him soaring over the field, straight through the open doorway. Satisfied, I resettle myself, catching Demi's quirked eyebrow in the process. "What? He was moving too slowly."

She shakes her head, actively fighting a smile.

"The first trial has reached its end," booms the lightning god. "Those that have passed through the door are granted entry into the next round, which will take place seven days hence." With that, he returns to his chair. Meanwhile, the competitors that survived stumble toward the door leading from the field.

"Well," Demi quips beside me. "That finished sooner than I'd hoped."

Lunging from my seat, I hurl myself down the stairs, shoving aside those making toward the exit, the elation high and the air bristling with static. When I reach the lowest level of the stands, I search for an access point onto the field, yet find none.

I am likely breaking all sorts of rules, but I vault the arena wall. My feet hit the blood-soaked mud with a squelch. Hand pressed over my mouth, I race toward the open doorway, dodging severed limbs and crimson puddles. My loafers slide across the drenched grass, but I manage to cross the threshold, entering what appears to be an infirmary.

I find the East Wind lying on one of the many cots, his cloak in tatters. In seconds, I've reached his bedside. "Eurus."

"Hello, bird," he grinds out. "Come to . . ." He hacks a wet cough. "Finish me off?"

I gaze down at him. My fear has morphed beyond its hovel, wrenched into a thousand minute points. His cloak may very well be shielding a fatal wound. "You're hurt. We need to remove your clothes."

"No." He catches my wrist. His fingers quaver, then fall away. "No," he whispers again.

Stupid immortal. "Fine," I grit out. "It's y-your death."

"The divine possess extraordinary healing capabilities," he counters in a strained voice.

"Not against a god-touched weapon." And speaking of god-touched weapons . . . his ax lies a few feet away, resting on a small side table. I swallow. When he isn't carrying it with him, it must be secreted somewhere in our shared chambers. If I can find where it is hidden, perhaps I can smuggle it back to St. Laurent once our bargain is fulfilled.

Eurus shoves himself upright using one hand. "I'll be fine."

I doubt that, but I hold my tongue. "Then let me at least help y-you up." When I reach for him, however, he slaps my hand aside with a low growl.

I stiffen, but there is no fear now, only a great fury that claws at my throat, rises to mask my vision. He has been through much, but I, too, have suffered. While I may not be of divine origin, I am still a person worthy of respect.

"You s-s-stubborn, arrogant, divine idiot," I growl. "Why can't you see that I'm trying to help y-you? To save your sorry life?"

The East Wind regards me from his collapsed position, breathing erratically.

"What I don't understand," I whisper, "is how you still treat m-me with such callous disregard, after I've done my hardest to help you, to work with you in whatever capacity you demand. I am trying my b-best. But you make it so hard to like you, so hard to be generous with you, so hard to be understanding. No m-matter my efforts, you will not even give me an inch." My voice quavers. I can be strong, I think. Even I have my limits. "You don't want m-my help? Fine. But good luck dragging yourself back to the r-room."

Turning on my heel, I march from the infirmary. Not once do I look back.

15

From the northern tower, there comes a scream.

I startle awake, heart stampeding in my chest. The gloom of the broom cupboard blots my vision. It is dark, always dark. I fist my blanket nervously, but the texture is all wrong. The fabric feels silken, almost slippery. I drop it as my surroundings come into focus.

A tall window framed by luxurious curtains, and walls decorated in patterned paper. There is no squeak of wood, no seaside gales hammering fists against the aged bones of the structure. The palace, I realize, rubbing at my eyes. The City of Gods.

The scream comes again, fracturing into a thousand shards before dissolving into a pained groan. Alarm grips me, yet I slip from bed, move barefoot across the room to carefully ease open my bedroom door. Beyond: darkness. The low sofa, smudged, and the dining table a gray silhouette seated near the cloaked windows. When a low whimper sounds, I startle. It came from the East Wind's bedroom.

It has been an unspoken understanding that we do not intrude on each other's space. And yet, day after day and year after year, I beheld Lady Clarisse's gruesome methods of torture. What did I do? Nothing. For months, I'd closed my ears to the East Wind's suffering, and I regret it to this day.

I'm across the main chamber, palm pressed flat against his door. A gentle shove nudges it open.

The East Wind's bedroom is perhaps three times as large as mine, with a massive bed, a chest of drawers, four windows, and a small sitting area. But it is the immortal occupying the bed that captures my attention.

He lies curled in a ball, legs twisted in the blankets. His back swells and deflates in a rhythm as unceasing as the tides. His unfurled wings drape his cloaked body, scaled tips bowed over the side of the mattress to skim the floor. Even in sleep, Eurus refuses to remove his cloak, though it appears to have been washed since the first trial.

Hello, bird. Come to finish me off?

The East Wind's comment from days earlier hangs like a thundercloud over my head. I pry it loose, roll it pensively between my palms until a corner or rough edge draws my attention to its momentary imperfection. What, exactly, did he mean by suggesting I was there to kill him? Why do his words linger? Why do I shelter them against my chest, as though having sensed their injury?

Eurus rolls onto his back with a soft groan. His hood has fallen back, exposing the edge of his jaw, the curve of his chin, and his mouth, softly parted. I stare. His lips are full, yet there is some discoloration around the left corner. As I watch him sleep, his hands clench and unclench against his stomach. "Father." He gasps for breath. "I didn't mean..." He jerks hard, then falls still, panting.

"Eurus." Crossing to his side, I reach for his arm, yet pull back before my fingertips brush skin. What was it Demi had said during the tournament?

Oly should have known better than to touch him.

I lower my hand, let it hang slack at my side as these seemingly small fragments of his past slide into place. He was abused. Of that, I am certain. Is that why he wears his cloak at all hours? To hide whatever welts or scars mar his skin?

Eurus emits another murmured plea. He twitches, kicks out his legs. His distress does strange things to my heart. I realize I do not want to see him suffer. At least, not tonight.

After grabbing the smelling salts from my room, I return to the East Wind's bedside, waving them under his nose until he stiffens and his arm shoots out, hand fisted. I duck, barely avoiding having my nose crushed as he blasts a forceful gust around the room.

"It's me," I gasp, gripping the bedpost. "Min."

Eurus falls motionless, his breathing coarse. Eventually, he sags into the pillows, a hand pressed to his brow. It is an age before he speaks. "What happened?"

I rise, tugging at my nightgown self-consciously. Thankfully, he is too distracted to notice my bare legs. "You were having a n-nightmare."

He is quiet as he processes my words. Already, the darkness recedes as my vision adjusts. "Did I . . . say anything?"

This conversation is most delicate, a sharpened edge dragged along a thread of silk. "You mentioned your father," I whisper.

He tugs his hood forward, further veiling his face. I've the maddened notion to push it back fully, reveal what he so desperately shields, but I do not particularly care to lose a hand. "I see." He clears his throat. "Did I say anything else? Anything about the council?"

"No." My curiosity demands more from him. "Why would you mention the council?"

"Because their lives are the ones I plan to end."

"What?" I gape at him. "You're going to poison the Council of Gods? You're going to kill th-them?" But of course, he has already provided his answer. There is only one question left to ask then. "Why? I thought you wanted a favor from the council."

The East Wind slides to the edge of the mattress. "Yes," he says. "I *am* here for that. When I win the tournament—and I plan to win—I will ask that they reinstate my title during the victor's banquet. Seeing as I am disgraced in the eyes of the council, winning is the only way to guarantee my invitation. And it is at the banquet where the council will gather in one place, allowing me the opportunity to kill the ones who banished me in one fell swoop."

"But if you're no longer banished, why—"

"Because they did not protect me!" he roars, shoving to his feet.

I stand stock still, gaze wary as he clutches the bed frame with both hands. *Run*, I think. Yet I see how he trembles. He is an animal, cowering in the corner of its cage. "In what w-way?"

Eurus sags forward in defeat, wingtips dragging along the ground. I might brush their delicate arches if I were not afraid of spooking him.

"The previous council—the one my brothers and I fought to overthrow, well, they knew my . . ." He shakes his head. "They knew of my suffering. And they chose to do *nothing*." This last word, spat with venom. "I had hoped that by defeating the council and installing a new one in its place, things would be better. But they turned against me and my brothers, banishing us. And this new council has proven itself just as corrupt as its predecessor. It is time for the institution to end."

A softness moves through me. Pain I understand. I understand, too, how one's lungs can shrink, and there is not air enough in the world to remove the weight crushing your chest. "So the Council of Gods n-not only failed to help you as a child, but they b-banished you and your brothers as well?"

"Exactly. Which proves the council as an institution has too much power as it is. Clearly, they do not use it for the benefit of our people, if I have been doubly failed."

Maybe, maybe not. But I know better than to argue. "So what's your plan?" I whisper.

"Once the poison is complete, it will be added to their meals at the victor's banquet. Three weeks later, they will fall ill, as you claimed. While they are indisposed, I will visit each of their residences and carve out their hearts. And it will be finished." He releases a huff of air. Laughter, I believe, though it has twisted onto itself, this ugly mutation of joy. "Think of me what you will," he says. "Let it be one more reason for you to despise me."

"I think you are in m-much pain," I say, "and looking for ways to heal it."

His head snaps around. My breath hitches, but I do not retreat.

Eventually, Eurus sighs. His wings droop. The sight saddens me for reasons I cannot name.

"All I know," he says, "is that I am tired. I am ready for this to end."

I prod the silence carefully, testing its shape. Tough, like the belly of a goat, yet there is a bit of give. He is not completely closed off, this god.

Without a word, I scurry to my bedroom, digging through my supplies for a small vial, which I offer him upon my return. "Here," I whisper.

The East Wind stares at the object with reproach. At least, I believe that is what he does. "What is it?"

"It is a draught to bring easy sleep."

"I don't need help sleeping," he growls, then strides toward one of the windows and tosses the curtains aside. Moonlight whitens my vision, and I duck my head, eyes watering from the unexpected intensity.

"There is no shame in it," I reassure him. "Sometimes we n-need these things—"

"I said I'm fine!" he snaps.

I glare, but he does not notice, for his back is to me, the scales of his wings reflecting the pooling light like hundreds of minute stars. "You're not f-f-fine," I mutter. "Not even close."

Eurus scoffs. "You have no idea what you're talking about."

"I do kn-know, Eurus. But continue w-weaving that story for yourself, if it makes you feel better." So many days of his poor treatment, and I have reached the threshold of what I am willing to accept. It is freeing to speak my truth.

Slowly, he turns to face me. My heart hammers; my face warms. I am not small. I am empowered.

"You may have stolen me from my h-home," I whisper, and somehow the darkness is tempered, fashioned into a fabric rich with depth. "You may have threatened me, coerced me, taken advantage of m-my goodwill. But I have slept better in the last few weeks than, well ... truthfully, I cannot even remember. And maybe I am y-your captive," I say, voice strengthening as I stare into the empty space of his cowl. "Maybe I am nothing more than a weak mortal. But at least I have purpose n-n-now. And that is something I have rarely felt in my life—ever."

And so I hold out the sleeping draught. Sometimes, we must fight. Others, surrender. "As I said, there is no shame in it. Whatever wounds y-you carry... grant yourself peace from them, if only for a night."

The darkness between us coils, drawing the East Wind across the room until he stands before me. My mouth goes dry. My spine begins to tingle, and I fight to calm my sporadic heartbeat. His large hand curls around mine, so that we hold this draught that is both blessing and curse.

Low and throaty, he says, "Very well, bird."

The East Wind has never let me in. But this time, he takes what I offer, climbing into bed and draining every last drop. By the time I pluck the empty vial from his slackened hand, he is already asleep.

The next morning, the East Wind elects to take breakfast with me in our suite rather than the dining room with the remaining contestants. Thus, Eurus sits across the table from me, pouring himself a cup of tea.

As I fill my plate, I cast him a wary glance. The blackberry jam is fresh, slightly acidic. I slather it across a warm croissant. The East Wind's energy, that dark, simmering thing beneath his skin, has dulled. There is no breeze to hint of his emotions. Indeed, it seems as though he feels nothing at all.

History has taught me to keep my mouth shut. I will eat my breakfast, and he will drink his tea, and we will share the space and the silence until he departs. But I have been thinking about last night's incident since the sun irradiated the whole of the sky. A singular moment of vulnerability, the East Wind's defenses stripped, brought low by whatever nightmare stalked his mind. It cannot be ignored, or forgotten.

"How are you feeling?" I ask quietly.

Eurus adds a spoonful of sugar to his drink. The silver utensil clinks against the rim of the cup. "Better." He hesitates. "Your voice... helped calm me down. It was... pleasing."

Heat pinkens my cheeks. Eurus gives compliments sparingly, and to praise something I have despised my entire life, this shameful stutter? It smooths some jagged-edged fragment in me. "Th-thank you."

He sets down his spoon. His cloak has been repaired, stitched and patched together. I see it for what it is: security. "I'm reconsidering my participation in the tournament."

I pause with my jam-slathered croissant halfway to my mouth. "What do you mean?" And what would that mean for me if he decides to remove himself from the running?

Eurus stares down at his tea. Then, moving slowly as though it pains him, he takes a sip. "As you know, I haven't returned home in a long time. It is bringing back unpleasant memories. I . . . don't like being touched. Especially when I am held down."

What child would, if it was followed by pain? Eurus may be a man grown, but he was not always. We carry those wounds with us. "I w-won't tell anyone about last night, if that's what you're worried about."

"You would have every right to. After all, I stole you from your home, manipulated you into helping me claim my revenge."

He did. But I must focus on what *is*, rather than what *was*. Eurus must win. Only then will I return home. "We all have our pain," I say. "It is nothing to be ashamed of."

"How freeing it must be to live as a mortal, all your faults on display for the world to see." If I'm not mistaken, there is a melancholy to his tone. "Do what you will with the information," he says, draining his tea. "I will be gone most of the day. The Council of Gods has invited the remaining contestants to lunch; I plan to gather what information I can on their strengths and shortcomings. With the second trial to take place at the end of the week, I haven't much time."

Which reminds me. "Are you aware of the properties of Arin's staff?" I take another bite of my croissant.

"I've heard that it is related to healing in some way." Then his voice sharpens. "Why? Did you learn something?"

"Apparently, his staff has the ability to sap an opponent of their strength. It can also inflict ailments on a person."

"Ailments?" His voice darkens. "I will keep that in mind."

With that, he pushes to his feet. Generally, the East Wind departs without farewell, but he halts at the threshold of the suite, glancing back in hesitation. "The sleeping draught was helpful," he says. "Thank you."

Then I am alone, as I am most days. Only now, I am almost disappointed to see him go.

I take my time clearing the dining table, placing the dishes and leftover food in the hall to await collection. Meanwhile, Eastern Blood continues to simmer on my dresser. Not long now until it is complete. Only when I am certain Eurus has truly gone for the day do I make my move.

A gentle pressure against his bedroom door. I expect the lock to catch, but to my surprise, the hinges swing open.

His bed is neatly made. I peer beneath the wooden frame—also spotless, though I know he has declined the palace's cleaning service on account of the poisons. As for his dresser, I pull open the top drawer, blink down in surprise. Tunics, tidily folded, in a variety of colors. Dark green, gray, black, white. Another drawer holds breeches. I suppose the East Wind *would* wear clothes beneath his cloak. Another drawer contains socks, also folded into pairs. But no ax.

It is as expected. Despite my empty hands, I must touch base with her ladyship. I worry she will interpret my lack of response as a reason to move forward with selling the estate, if she hasn't already. I've spotted no evidence of messenger birds, but perhaps I have been searching in the wrong place.

After leaving Eurus' bedroom as I found it, I decide to wander the palace, eventually finding myself in the kitchen. It is all warm wood, its walls painted the deep shade of a lightless forest. A small fire crackles in the hearth.

Movement draws my eye toward a table stretched along the wall, and Demi hard at work kneading dough. At the scuff of my loafer, her head snaps up.

I freeze. She, too, is unnaturally still. We stare at each other in uncertainty. If I'm not mistaken, wariness touches her eyes, a shield I cannot begin to penetrate. "Good morning, Min from Marles."

"Apologies," I whisper. "I didn't mean to disturb you."

Her shoulders relax, just a touch. "Typically, when one says good morning," the goddess remarks, continuing to dig the heels of her palms into the sticky ball, "the proper response is to say good morning back."

She lifts her head then, her expression strangely tentative. Curls of dark hair spill over one bare shoulder, a healthy flush warming her olive skin and powdered face. Instead of the extravagant outfits I have come to expect, she wears a plain gray dress and leather sandals.

"Sorry—"

"Ah!" She lifts a hand. "No apologies."

I dip my chin self-consciously. Lady Clarisse would have scolded me for the interruption. "What are you making?" I ease closer. Onions—julienned—piled in a bowl. There is also grated parmesan.

"Cheese tarts," Demi replies. "They're Eurus' favorite. Also, brioche. I could use some help."

And why should it matter that Demi knows Eurus' preference for baked goods? It shouldn't, but the sudden twist in my gut proves otherwise. "I'll probably mess something up," I murmur.

She raises an eyebrow. A bit of flour dusts her nose—her entire front, actually. "You have never baked before?"

"I used to, when I was younger. My grandmother taught me."

"Then what makes you think you would mess up?"

Shall I reveal to her the burn marks and the scars? Shall I offer up my left hand, its thumb slightly bowed from where her ladyship broke it as punishment for failing to add an ingredient to one of her beauty teas? Maybe I do not need to share the particulars of my life. Maybe Demi sees for herself what I have endured.

But she does not press. Rather, she refocuses on her kneading, saying, "Do you know that I have a daughter?" At my surprise, she tosses me a quirked grin. "Yes, I realize I may not *look* it, but I have been a mother for many centuries. She's a darling young woman, though too naive, I'm afraid."

"Why is she naive?"

"She trusts too easily. I have tried explaining to her that to trust is to make yourself vulnerable, but she doesn't listen to me." Demi shakes her head. "She's at that age. Everything I do embarrasses her. I fear there will come a day when I am not able to protect her, but what can I do?" A long, tragic sigh follows. "I suppose what I'm saying is . . . you are young. You will make mistakes, but you will learn."

I glance at the goddess' elegant hands: relaxed, lacking tension. Safe. "I don't want to take up your time," I venture.

"You haven't, and you won't. Come." She waves me over, offering a white apron to match the one she has tied across her shin-length dress.

"If you're hungry," I point out, "couldn't you ask the cook to make you something? It would avoid staining your clothes."

"What if I prefer getting my hands dirty?" It is spoken in a way that suggests I am not the first to advise she let others work in her stead. "There's something gratifying in doing things for oneself, don't you think?"

I nod. She handles the dough competently, after all. "I didn't mean to imply you weren't capable. I guess I assumed you would prefer someone else to handle those things for you."

A sad bitterness clouds her expression. "And why wouldn't you?" she murmurs, more to herself than me. "I have given you no reason to believe otherwise."

Sensing a shift in mood, I focus on tying my apron while Demi separates the dough into two halves and sets one before me on the wooden table. Although Eurus would prefer I use the opportunity to gather information on his competitors, I would rather spend time with Demi without the pressure to use her in some way.

"What did you bake with your grandmother?" she asks.

"Oh, all sorts of things. Breads, muffins, pastries. We would bake croissants on Sundays. I preferred mine with chocolate, but Nan loved raspberry jam." I smile, recalling how we would each sample the other's creations, our fingers sticky with sweetness, and begin to knead, a forceful motion of the arm. "Sometimes, Nan would sell her pickled vegetables in the market, along with her teas."

"Teas?"

"Yes. My grandmother was a superb herbalist. She taught me everything I know about potions."

The goddess slows her kneading, expression curious, more like her old self. "She taught you to make potions?"

Only then do I realize what I have uttered aloud. My stomach curdles, the apprehension sour in my throat.

Demi lifts the ball of dough, slams it down onto the table. I jump. She does it again, having fallen into quiet contemplation.

Stupid. No one must know that I am a herbalist, much less a bane weaver. Surely she would not think deeper on the matter. Herbology is not an uncommon trade. As far as she is concerned, I am just a mortal with a passion for plants.

"Can I ask you something?"

Demi smiles as she continues working the dough. Every so often, I catch a whiff of verbena and wonder if I am imagining it. "That depends, love. Is it a favor you're asking for?"

"No. Well, not exactly." I hammer my fist against the dough, as Nan taught me. "If I wanted to send a message to someone in the mortal realms, how would I go about doing that?"

"A lover?" The goddess winks at me. "There's no shame in that."

My face warms. "No lover," I whisper. "Just someone back home who is worried for me."

"Your grandmother?"

"No. Nan passed years ago. It's . . . for an old acquaintance."

With the dough properly kneaded, she sets it aside to rise in a cloth-covered bowl. "Seek out the Courier. He is the only one able to dispatch messages across realms."

The Courier. "Where can I find him?"

"He's usually found in one of the nearby taverns. I can take you to him."

Too effortlessly, agreement rises to coat my tongue. *Yes,* I might say. *That sounds perfect.* Except Demi is close to Eurus, and I don't want her knowing of my contacting Lady Clarisse. "Meaning n-no offense," I say, "but I would really prefer to deliver it to the Courier myself."

The goddess appears more curious than upset. "You are an enigma, Min from Marles. But . . . very well. Seek out a tavern called The Blind Oracle, west of the palace. And keep your wits about you. Eurus would have my head if you came to harm."

I return to the suite, but only long enough to pen a message.

My lady,

If you have written to me since my visit to the estate, I have not received your message. Eurus has taken me to the City of Gods. He has his god-touched ax in possession, but I am not sure how to take it.

I pause, quill hovering over the last line. No, that will not do. I cannot give her ladyship a single reason to doubt me. I scratch out that last bit and replace it with: *Please know I am doing all I can to return to St. Laurent with the weapon, as promised.*

Unease slides through me. This was my purpose: to grow close to the East Wind. To build trust enough to gain access to his god-touched ax. But that was before a sleeping draught passed into his hand, that moment of hope and tentative surrender. Before I learned how deeply Eurus ached.

My hand trembles and the quill slips from my grip. Why this guilt of betrayal? Eurus has done so much worse, having stolen Ammara's rains, subjecting its people to drought, his plans to poison the council. I would be *saving* lives by handing him over to Lady Clarisse. If I am to one day open my own apothecary, then assisting her ladyship is my only means of seeing that dream realized. The estate must remain in the family. It must become mine.

Quickly, I finish scrawling the message.

Any news about the estate? You have not sold it, have you?

Your humble employee,
Min

With the letter in hand, I go in search of the Courier. Down the stairs, across the foyer, over the lush green lawn with its impressive topiaries. The palace has three gates: south, east, west. Eurus and I entered via the southern gate, closer to a more residential area of the city. I utilize the western gate and soon find myself wandering an area that has fallen into neglect.

Or perhaps neglect is not the right word. Here, the two-story buildings are fashioned from the same white stone as the rest of the city, but murals have been painted across their textured surfaces. One wall depicts a desolate wasteland of cold, a black citadel piercing its white canvas. Farther down, the illustration portrays a muscled god facing a three-headed beast.

In what seems like an attempt to bring color to the area, many of the doors have been painted as well. Although the fountains have run dry, they have been repurposed as planters that now boast collections of anemone, narcissus, and climbing wisteria.

The road grows cracked. Stone disintegrates to dirt, dust, mud. Here, there are shadows and places to hide, hooded forms gathering in those lightless areas. Beyond the next intersection, I spot a wooden sign swinging from a porch overhang. The Blind Oracle. Relief propels me up the steps.

A group of deities stumbles out the door. Two dark-skinned men drag a half-conscious immortal across the porch and down the stairs. A rush of stale, smoky air follows. My nose wrinkles, but I push inside the dimly lit tavern.

It is all gloom but for a few strategically placed candles. The tavern itself is half occupied, veiled behind the smoke unspooling from slender pipes. It smells a bit sour, like spoiled milk. Discreetly, I scan those gathered at the tables. A few patrons take notice of my presence. Most continue their gambling. This would be far easier if I knew what the Courier looked like.

"Taken a wrong turn, mortal?"

I turn toward the man behind the bar. God, rather. He is spindly, with arms like a spider's legs. He dries the inside of a copper mug with a rag, seemingly unperturbed by my presence. When his eyes lock onto mine, I stumble back in horror. His pupils are slitted, like a snake's.

"Um." I lick my lips and take a step forward. The soles of my loafers peel away from the layer of dried liquid coating the buckling floorboards. "I'm looking for the Courier. I was informed he might be here?"

The creature—beast, immortal, whatever he is—peers into a far corner. "He's here." He jerks his head at a man with short white hair, seated with his back to me. "He expecting you?"

"Not exactly."

The serpent-eyed barkeep studies me for a time. Is that a tattoo peeking from his shirt collar? "Takes bravery to venture into these parts," he says. "You sure you know what you're doing?"

"Y-yes." Absolutely not.

He grunts, sets aside the clean glass. One of the patrons seated at the bar signals him, and the barkeep pours whiskey into a smudged tumbler, sliding it down the counter into the man's awaiting hand.

As I begin weaving toward the Courier, the barkeep calls, "Wait. Take this with you." I turn. He offers me a glass filled with ale. "A bribe," he explains.

"I don't have coin."

"It's on the house."

"But—"

"I'm not in the mood to scrub blood off the floors tonight," he clarifies. "Give it to the Courier. You'll be glad you did." Then he returns to his drying.

"Thank you," I whisper.

Head held high, I cross the room, skirting lopsided tables and deities playing darts, more than one patron passed out across a bench or chair. The snow-haired god plays cards with three others covered in tattoos. I curl my arms against my chest, feeling distinctly out of place in my dress and loafers. "Excuse m-me."

It is chilling how immediately conversation dies. Not just this table, but the whole of the room falls beneath the hush.

The snow-haired deity turns in his seat, and my throat clamps down on a budding scream. I've never seen such eyes: pools of liquid silver lapping at half-sunken eyelids.

He wears a scarf that is every color and no color at all—green, yet when I peer closer, it seems to shift hue: blue, indigo, deep orange. An intricately carved pipe rests in a shallow dish to his left, smoky remnants uncurling from the burned leaves within. His companions watch me unnervingly.

"Are you the Courier?" I ask.

Those silver eyes slide down to the glass of ale I hold. Recalling the barkeep's warning, I offer him the drink.

He lifts an equally white eyebrow, but accepts the offering and takes a sip. "Eurus' mortal." His blurred voice pours past a thin, unsmiling mouth. "I have heard of you."

I swallow as the back of my neck tingles beneath the scrutiny of those in the tavern. "Good things, I hope."

"That depends on your definition of good."

That is fair, I suppose. Though I elect not to ponder the matter too deeply. "I apologize for disturbing you, but I was advised you were the person I must speak to if I wanted to send a message to the mortal realms."

"Indeed." This intrigues him. *I* intrigue him. "And you wish to send a message?"

In answer, I pass over the letter, secured by a wax seal.

The Courier lifts the parchment to his nose and inhales, his eyes flickering like moonlit pools. "Salt, yeast, aged cheese, wine. Marles, but . . . east Marles." He takes another sniff. "Brine. Hmm. St. Laurent?"

Slowly, I nod, my apprehension too great to be impressed.

He taps the folded parchment thoughtfully against his palm. "I can deliver this for you. But it comes at a price."

"I haven't any coin," I whisper. If he refuses to deliver, how am I supposed to get in contact with Lady Clarisse?

"Oh, it's not coin I want." He picks at his nails. Both his wrists are tattooed with snakes. "Perhaps we can come to some arrangement. I will need to think on it. Mortals have their uses, after all."

I do not like the sound of that. But what choice do I have, really? It is the estate, or nothing. "The message is urgent," I press. "It can't wait." Perhaps I should have accepted Demi's request to accompany me. I doubt the Courier would demand payment from *her*.

He tucks the letter into his cloak pocket. "Tomorrow, I will deliver it. I expect payment upon my return."

16

*S*TUPID.

I'm too nauseated to pay much attention to the passing gods and goddesses as I make my way back to the palace. Can the Courier be trusted? Who is to say he will not break the seal and read of Eurus' downfall before it occurs? If he were to inform the East Wind of my plans, Eurus would never let me walk free.

The door to my suite is a welcome sight. I slip inside, shutting out the dread that hounds me. Back pressed against the door, I release a heavy sigh. What's done is done. In the meantime, I will wait for Lady Clarisse's response and focus on completing Eastern Blood.

Shrugging off my coat, I pad across the main chamber toward my bedroom, the amber of late afternoon streaming onto the thick patterned rugs. Framed by the window curtains are the city's countless squares, vines clambering up walls of white stone, the antique faces of apartment buildings. Something like longing tugs at me. All my life, I have been content with what St. Laurent has to offer. Now I begin to wonder if something is missing.

As soon as I enter my bedroom, I stop.

The East Wind stands with his back to me, the hem of his cloak stirring around his long legs like a hundred licking tongues, wings tucked tightly against his spine. He stands before the cauldron of

Eastern Blood, consulting a book he holds in his hands: *The Practice of Herbal Remedies*.

"Your notes are quite detailed," Eurus observes without turning around. "Meticulously organized." The parchment emits a soft hiss as he turns a page with a blunt fingertip. It depicts a table showcasing how long one must boil the root called heaven's tears before it breaks down into a paste.

"You can read Jinsean?" I ask in surprise. The manual is written in my grandmother's native tongue.

"I am a god," the East Wind replies. "I understand all languages."

At last, he turns. It is strange to see him standing beside my unmade bed. The twist of the sheets, proof of how poorly I slept after waking to Eurus' nightmare. "You made me believe you knew only the basics. That you were still learning as an apprentice. But your notes suggest the expertise of a master bane weaver."

"Those aren't my notes," I say. "They were m-my grandmother's."

He peers down at the manual, brushing the edge of a page in thought. "Your grandmother knew what she was doing."

"She did," I manage through a thickening throat.

"You miss her."

I nod, sensing his attention on my face. "Every day."

"She treated you well?"

I choke out a laugh. "Of course," I whisper. "She loved me."

Eurus shifts his attention back to the manual, though I suspect it is because the sentiment makes him uncomfortable. Does he know what it feels like to be touched with a gentle hand? To know all of your days are washed in security and warmth?

"Tell me of Cornflower Hills," he demands brusquely, pointing to the bottom of a page covered in my own miniscule handwriting.

Wariness brushes my body's every edge. Surely it is not a lesson he is after? "It is a b-brew used to expel dark spirits from one's body," I explain, drawing nearer so we stand shoulder to shoulder, peering down at the book.

"I've never heard of it."

"You wouldn't have," I say, flipping the page. It falls open to a comprehensive sketch of a hyacinth flower. "I created it myself."

Though the East Wind angles toward me, I keep my focus on the drawing. This brittle parchment, this shaded charcoal, this endless, obsessive scrawl notating measurements, symptoms, cures. Nan's entire life's work. And someday mine, if I am worthy of it.

Eventually, he shifts his focus back onto the book. I tell myself I am relieved.

Though our hands do not touch, their difference in size is comical. And yet, I am curious ... What would happen if I shifted my hand slightly to the left?

When the curve of my smallest finger grazes Eurus' wrist, he goes still.

I dare not breathe. My lungs feel as if they are crumpling from within as the East Wind rotates his hand, his pinky curling subtly around my own.

"For what purpose did you create this poison?" he asks, with a breathlessness I fail to miss.

"It was my lady's idea, actually." Well, sort of. In truth, the idea was mine, but she insisted on taking credit for it. "She'd c-captured an immortal that ..." The fingers of my other hand twitch, curl into a ball. I recall this prisoner. She kept him chained in his cell for nearly six months. "On second thought, it's probably better that you don't know."

"I see." His distaste cannot be misconstrued, and he withdraws his touch. I already mourn the loss. "How many poisons in this manual have you created yourself?"

"A few dozen," I mumble.

"And did your former employer know of this?"

"Some, n-not all." Higher and higher I would have soared. But her ladyship kept me caged, my wings forever clipped.

The East Wind ponders for a time. "Here is what I don't understand." He traces the sketch, each curved petal. I watch the trail of his finger, mesmerized by the motion. "You are kind, intelligent, yet you became a bane weaver, of all things. Do you enjoy harming others?"

I stare at him, cheeks hot to the touch. "It wasn't like that w-with Nan. Her work revolved around healing. It was good, it was ... people traveled from all over Marles for her teas," I say, voice softening in memory. Some days, upward of thirty customers would walk through the front door. Lady Clarisse is lucky to receive twenty a week, and most only come for her beauty teas. "There was n-never an ailment Nan couldn't treat."

"So why hurt when you can heal?"

I do not *hurt* as he suggests. Not deliberately. "Her ladyship dictates what brews we m-must make. As her apprentice, I am expected to follow her lead."

"But it brings you no joy making poisons," he says.

Why must I continue to overturn these harder emotions? Disappointment plaited with self-doubt, all their shine coated and cracked with overuse. "If not for my lady, I would not have a h-home. And I definitely wouldn't have the knowledge I do now." And she's right, isn't she? I am slow. I do not learn quickly. Chopping, slicing, pressing, drying—with these tasks, I am only adequate.

"But you've said most of your knowledge came from your grandmother," Eurus points out. "So which is it?"

Something tugs behind my sternum, the shallowest ache. The deeper I fall into poisons, the farther I feel from Nan. Perhaps it is better that she is no longer alive to witness what I have become. "Her ladyship says I should kn-know my place."

"Why do you listen to the venom that witch spews into your ears?" he asks, but without the caustic tone I've come to expect.

"Because it's true."

"Do you honestly believe that?"

Yes. It is a noose, this word. It is her ladyship's hand curled around my throat, demanding surrender. But I cannot force something I do not feel in my heart is true, can I?

Since leaving St. Laurent, I have more than proven my abilities. How can I reconcile that with Lady Clarisse's unfair assumptions? "I-I-I ... I'm n-not ..."

The East Wind's silence speaks volumes. It tells me who I was to this god days before is not who I am to him now.

"Here." Snapping *The Practice of Herbal Remedies* closed, he hands it to me. "It's yours."

Our fingers brush as I accept his offering, thoroughly confused. "But I thought you w-wanted it as leverage."

"You promised to help me," he reminds me. "Can I trust you to keep your word?"

Concealed within his hood, his eyes capture mine. I can feel it, the heat that is intensity, and the focus that is perhaps the finest of his weapons. My heartbeat stumbles in an attempt to right its rhythm. I'm certain he can hear it. "You can."

"Then there is no problem I can see."

The East Wind is not all thorns. There are moments of gentleness to him. It does not seem right that he should be killed for the cost of immortality. After all, it is not everlasting life Lady Clarisse seeks. It is power and protection, a desperate grasp for control. Somehow, I do not believe the death of a god to be the answer.

"Where did you go today?" he asks.

I'm surprised he does not know, considering I am a popular topic of conversation amongst the divine. "I spent some time with Demi in the kitchen making bread. And cheese tarts." I bite the inside of my cheek. "She said they were y-your favorite." And why does my throat suddenly constrict around this admission?

The potency of his gaze is enough that I can all but see his eyes through the masking shadows inside his hood. They would be dark. Glassy, like obsidian. "I enjoy them." A pause. "Does that bother you?"

"N-no," I say. What are the odds Demi would mention to Eurus my interest in sending a message to the mortal realms?

"Hm." He sounds as if he does not believe me. "So how is Demi?" He speaks casually, though I sense an earnestness beneath. "Did she seem relaxed, or ... ?"

I frown at Eurus, feeling suddenly uncomfortable. What does relaxation have to do with gathering information? "I guess. She seemed her usual pleasant self."

"Did you learn anything of significance during your time with her?"

"No." Though I did not bother asking. I should feel guilty, but I cannot regret the lovely afternoon. "What about lunch?" I say, eager to turn the conversation away from the goddess. "Did *you* learn anything significant?"

The East Wind shrugs. It is an unnervingly human gesture. "I learned what Arin intends to ask for as his favor if he wins the tournament."

I set the manual aside to check on Eastern Blood. "Oh?"

"His sister suffers from debilitating seizures." Eurus watches as I test the poison's color against a chart in the book. Currently, it is an olive shade, but as it continues to boil, it will transform to a deep gray-green, eventually settling into the color of red wine. "There is no cure. He intends to ask the Council of Gods for help if he wins."

While my knowledge of the divine has been limited thus far, my observation exposes a common vein: selfishness. That Arin wants to win for the benefit of his sister's health is touching. With his affinity for healing, it must be frustrating that he cannot help her himself. "I think that's very n-noble of him."

Eurus snorts. "You believe him?"

I stiffen and lower the strip of dyed paper onto the dresser. "You don't?"

"Of course not. It's clear he's lying so that others lower their guard."

Not that I know anything about Arin, but I choose to see the light instead of the dark, if I can. "He d-does have a sister, right?"

The East Wind's wings stir, then settle. A whiff of salt pervades the space, which generally occurs when he is flustered or frustrated or battling some other tumultuous emotion. "Yes, though I have not seen her since my banishment."

"Shouldn't you give him the benefit of th-the doubt?"

"Why? He is a competitor."

Or an ally, should Eurus choose to reach out rather than retreat into isolation. "Arin isn't a bad person. He's doing what is r-right by his family."

"So you're siding with him? Do you believe his *nobility* takes precedent over my vengeance?" His next words emerge as a snarl. "I suppose I should count myself lucky you are here at all."

A familiar numbness takes hold of my limbs. I must shrink, but to shrink is to move, to draw the enemy's eye, the flat of their palm, a raised fist. But I forget that I am not powerless. Eurus cannot get his revenge without the poison. Only I am skilled enough to complete it.

"I w-w-won't have you speak to me that w-way," I whisper as my pulse flutters like a bird freeing its cage. "As for counting yourself lucky, y-y-you forget I am not here of m-my own volition. Or did you fail to r-remember th-th-that you forced me into y-your *employment*, as you continue to call it." I'm trembling. If only my tongue remained unaffected, my words untouched by stutter. In this moment, it is enough to know I have the strength to challenge Eurus at all. "I don't know why I'm s-s-surprised. Of course you would regard Arin as the enemy. You, who d-doomed thousands in Ammara to suffer, because you believed y-y-your need for isolation was more important than their l-l-lives. To you, everyone is y-your enemy!"

The East Wind has gone still. "The matter of Ammara's drought does not concern you, bird."

"Maybe n-not, but I still don't understand how you can live with so little r-remorse. Doesn't it bother you that people are suffering, dying? Perhaps even your own b-brother?" My every impulse screams *retreat*, but I edge closer, reaching for his arm. My hand halts a hairsbreadth away. There, my fingers hover, just on the threshold of touch. "Will you not r-return what you have taken," I whisper, "and give life back to the earth?"

"It is not so simple." The rasped response draws bumps along my arms. "If I go back on my word, then what does that say about me?" He does not give me the opportunity to respond. "It says I am weak," he growls. "The power must always rest with me."

How wrong he is, how confused. "When you refuse to see the error of your w-ways, you are no better than the ones that hurt y-you." Gently, I press the pads of my fingertips to the underside of his wrist, where the sleeve of his cloak ends. "You are one of the divine. The people of Ammara are mortal. You could ch-change their lives for the better. Real, lasting change."

He pulls away. "The deal was made years ago. It is already done."

"Can't you change your mind?"

For one indeterminable moment, he neither moves nor speaks. "I thought you were on my side, bird."

As if a captor and his captive could ever work together. "Just because I h-have agreed to complete this poison for you doesn't mean I have no conscience. I am my own p-person, I . . ." My teeth begin to chatter. I clamp them down. I am not defeated. I am standing, and will continue to stand. "I'm going out."

"Bird."

But I'm already across the suite, the scent of burning chasing me out the door.

Lifting my fist, I knock.

Or rather, that is the intention. Before my knuckles make contact with the wood, however, I balk. Room twenty-two, second floor, as Demi said. Now that I'm standing on the other side of her door, I question my sanity. What of the first trial, the roar of deities having gone feral over battle? She, too, had lusted for blood. Imagine what she would do to an injured bird or lame fox, as I often perceive myself in this City of Gods.

But my interactions with Demi have thus far been harmless. She has been kind to me, open. My heart speaks *trust*; my mind warns *peril*. Always, I have heeded the latter. Now, in the dark hours before dawn, I choose the former.

My knock echoes, folding onto itself as the deserted corridor swallows evidence of my presence. Then a lock tumbles, and the ornately carved door is pulled open.

Demi, dressed in a gauzy sleep robe, blinks her long-lashed eyes, as though convinced I might be an apparition. "Min?"

She is bare-faced. Without the powder and paint coating her cheeks, I notice her skin is a bit rough, as if she spends ample time outdoors—which does not necessarily fit the image of a well-dressed goddess in heels. Then again, I am not certain what power Demi presides over. She's never told me. And I've never asked.

"Sorry to wake you," I murmur, hands clenched at my front.

"It's no trouble, I was just resting," she says, appearing both intrigued and concerned. Her lazy posture unkinks itself into something straight-backed and keen. "Did something happen?"

I bite my lip. Still, the tears rise, a stinging pressure behind my eyes. "Can I stay with y-you tonight?"

As the last vestiges of slumber dissolve from her features, the sharpness of her gaze grows sharper still. "Come inside," she says, holding the door open. I shuffle across the threshold, shoulders hunched.

Her suite is far more personalized than the one I share with Eurus. The fireplace mantel boasts small trinkets: stones and feathers and dried flowers, all gifts the earth provides. Articles of clothing have been tossed over many a chairback. An assortment of plants reach leafed tendrils toward the windows and across curtain rods.

I'm impressed. Demi has managed to make this temporary space a home in less than two weeks. She may not be participating in the tournament, but many attendees prefer to reside in the palace until a victor is announced, due to the arena's proximity.

"Tea?" she asks, leading me to a quaint seating area.

"Please."

I settle into a comfortable armchair while she puts a kettle on the stove. Through the window, the moon hangs swollen and full. When the kettle screams, she adds tea leaves, allowing them to steep before pouring me a cup. The tea's warmth gradually thaws the ice in my chest.

"What is that taste?" I ask. "That hint of licorice. Not anise..." Once more, I take a healthy swallow, letting the flavor suffuse my tongue.

"Heathersworth," Demi replies.

My eyebrows climb so high I would not be surprised to find them lost behind my hair. "You know of heathersworth?" It is an extremely rare herb, found only in Under.

After lighting a candle—a guard against the waning day—she takes a seat across from me, curvy legs tucked beneath her sleep robe. She pours herself a drink, takes a sip. "Let me guess. I don't seem like the type of goddess who knows her way around a garden, right?" She regards me with a haughty jut of her chin. There are many kinds of shields, after all. I recognize this as hers. "Did you know heathersworth is used by some cultures as a sedative?" she asks.

"I didn't." Though I do know it helps slow one's heart rate, so this does not surprise me.

"We women are more than just looks, Min." She sets down her cup. Then, as if having changed her mind, picks it back up and drains its contents. "We have skills, knowledge. We are worthy of praise. I imagine your Mother of Earth welcomes appreciation every now and then."

She is trying to tell me something. I cannot put my finger on it, only its hazed edge. "I thank the Mother of Earth for every successful harvest," I say. "Without her favor, I doubt Marles' soil would be as rich as it is, our vineyards as abundant."

The strain around Demi's mouth eases. "I enjoy speaking with you, Min from Marles. Not all my friends care to talk of plants and harvests. They much prefer eating, shopping, gossiping, and the like. They invited me out for drinks tonight but—" She shrugs. "I suppose I wasn't in the mood. And I appreciate my alone time, perhaps more than I let on."

Indeed, she appears comfortable dressed down, at ease after a long day.

"But we're not here to talk about me. We're here to talk about you." Her expression reflects a fierce intrigue. "What happened?"

"I don't know," I whisper, setting down my drink. Now that I've given myself distance, I find it difficult to recall the details of our argument. "It was just Eurus being Eurus." By which I mean rude, inconsiderate, pacing like an animal in a cage. "I can't tolerate it anymore." And I shouldn't have to.

"I see." The goddess pours herself another cup of tea and sits back, hands framing the porcelain. Without her usual face paint, she appears younger, more approachable. "Did he do something in particular that bothered you?"

Yes—and no. There is much I might say, were my circumstances different. But I am forbidden to expose the true nature of our relationship. I cannot speak of Eastern Blood. And where has my bargain with Eurus left me? Trapped in this realm of gods, no allies, no friends. It hurts to find my situation no different than it was back home. Am I not worthy of something better?

"If you must know," I say, fiddling with the fabric of my dress, "I d-didn't choose to come here."

She cants her head, and I've the distinct impression of being cornered, as a hare is forced into its burrow. "What do you mean?"

I could stop there. I could excuse myself and return to my suite with Demi none the wiser. But perhaps it's time I place my trust in another. "I'm not here as Eurus' assistant. I'm here as his c-captive. I was taken from my home in St. Laurent. Eurus and I . . . made a deal."

"A deal?" Her gaze sharpens.

I nod. "If I agreed to assist him during the tournament, he would set me free and return me h-home."

Nervously, I watch the goddess' features. I search for a pleat of skin around her eyes, a bend of her mouth, anything that might indicate how she receives this revelation.

"I'm sorry you've found yourself in this situation, Min from Marles," she at last replies. "Believe it or not, I do understand what it means to be a captive, though only from what a beloved member of the family has told me."

My confusion must be plain, for she goes on, "I mentioned my daughter before, but I did not tell you that she was stolen from me. Yes.

Stolen by a god of darkness. Trapped in his realm for months, allowed to return to me for only part of the year, to bring an end to winter's chill. There is nothing I can do."

"That's horrible," I say, appalled. "The Council of Gods will not help?"

"The council does not meddle with individual affairs," she says with a strange lilt I recognize as irony. "And that is why it is pointless to bring your plight to them, if that is what you were hoping to do."

That is, in fact, the last thing I intend to do. "I know they would not help a mortal. But I thought, maybe there was something you could do to help m-me?" I lift my eyes in hope. I am not beneath pleading my case.

Demi sighs before setting down her cup of tea untouched. My stomach is too twisted into knots to consider drinking anything. I wonder if Eurus even cares that I have left. It is a subtle rash against my skin, the thought that he does not.

"Historically, the divine keep our orders separate from the mortal realms. It is for everyone's protection. That you have been brought to the City of Gods is unfortunate, but I fear my hands are tied."

I nod, feeling entirely too small for this conversation, though I know it is not Demi's intention. It is not my fault, after all. It was never my choice to make.

"Is there nothing you can do?" I ask.

She shakes her head, mouth pressed into severity. "No. By our laws, you belong to Eurus, and we gods do not take lightly to things being taken from us. We have gone to war over less."

"I'm not an object," I challenge. "I'm a person."

"The divine do not see it that way."

"Well, the way they see it is despicable," I hiss out. Then I blink. Too harsh, these words. Too many points. "I'm s-sorry. I don't know what came over m-m-me."

"I do." She chuckles. "You do not feel heard. Don't ever be sorry for speaking your mind, love. There is no other way to live." She then picks up her cup, brow knit in contemplation. "Perhaps it's time you learned the truth."

I sink lower in the chair, feeling worse than I did upon entering the room. "Not to offend, but I didn't come here for advice about how to speak up for myself. I came here because I thought you m-might understand where I'm coming from."

"I hear you, Min." Demi levels me a gaze filled with so much compassion it eases the tension strangling my muscles. "But I wasn't referring to you. I meant the truth about Eurus' past."

"Oh," I manage weakly.

Demi sighs. It is a sound of prolonged suffering, yet acceptance, too. "It was around Eurus' sixteenth year when he and I first became lovers. That was also the year Eurus' father took a particular interest in him. He was . . . not kind." She frowns in a preoccupied manner. "Very few of the divine possess what you would call *nurturing* tendencies. But Astraeus was something else entirely."

Steam wafts upward from the pale-yellow tea, which tastes of grass and sunlight, brightest spring rolling across my tongue. It is an uneasy contrast to the darkness of the goddess' words. "In what way?"

"He was brutal, ruthless, uncompromising. And he saved the worst of his wrath for Eurus. There were many days I saw him slathering salve over fresh bruises or nursing a recent break. As you can imagine, such treatment took its toll over the years."

I do not need to imagine. I have lived it most of my life.

I hastily set down the cup, fighting for breath. It is too warm, the air stagnant. A bead of cold sweat wends its way down my spine.

I'd suspected that Eurus' past involved abuse or neglect. But to have it confirmed, to hear of the horrendous treatment he endured at the hands of a person who should make him feel worthy, secure, loved . . . The East Wind and I are more alike than I realized.

"But that was not the worst of what Eurus faced," Demi says softly.

My fingers grip the tops of my thighs. "What, exactly, did he face?"

The goddess' features lie in shadow as she stares into her tea with faraway eyes, her skin having paled.

"A few months into our relationship, Eurus began to change. He grew detached and suffered from seemingly random outbursts of rage. I heard from Notus—one of his elder brothers—that Astraeus had taken Eurus away, far from the city. When Eurus returned, he was gravely wounded."

I press a hand to my clammy forehead. It feels as if every past wound and break and scar has ignited across my body, rendering me breathless with pain. "In what way?" Only in pushing through the ugliness of the East Wind's abuse will I truly understand him.

"There were strange scars on his back. When I asked him where they'd come from, he refused to tell me. In the weeks that followed, intimacy between us declined. He would not let me touch him. And then he began to cover up, eventually donning the cloak he now wears. He grew mute, often not speaking for weeks." Her eyes glisten in remembrance. "One particularly stormy autumn, Astraeus again took his son away. When they returned months later, Eurus had wings."

My mind struggles to make sense of it. "How—?"

"Experiments," she clips out. "Conducted by his own father to twist Eurus into some beastly creature. Eurus tried cutting them off—multiple times. But the wings always grew back."

I can only sit there, tongue slack, mind encased in a white fog. "Why would his father do such a thing?"

"I'm not sure. Eurus never spoke of it." The goddess taps the toes of one bare foot against the table. "But it changed him."

What does it mean that my heart aches for him? "Is it true that the Council of Gods refused to intervene?" That is, after all, what the East Wind claimed. One of the reasons he plans to enact his revenge.

Something flits across Demi's lambent gaze. It is gone before I have the opportunity to decipher it. "As I said, the Council of Gods does not intervene in private affairs on principle. Their duty is to uphold the realm. And in the City of Gods, there is no law against a father punishing his child."

Punishing? "We are talking about abuse," I whisper, horrified.

"I never said this world was kind," Demi replies, her gaze hardening. "Remember that you are mortal, Min from Marles. But the divine?" She shrugs. "That is just how we live."

I'm woken by the *thunk* of a lock, the creak of hinges. Low voices, muffled beyond the walls of the guest bedroom in which I now sleep.

"No, you can't see her," Demi hisses. "Come back tomorrow."

"It *is* tomorrow," Eurus snarls with an aggression that could only belong to an incensed predator. "Midnight has come and gone! The second trial begins at noon."

"And?"

"And I require her presence, seeing as she is my assistant."

I roll my eyes only an instant before I hear the goddess snort. Too stubborn, this god. "I believe you are confusing *captive* with *assistant*. Min did not choose to work for you. She told me everything."

Drip, drip, drip goes the quiet, like a wound bleeding out.

Pushing upright in bed, I peer toward the soft glow coming from beneath the bedroom door. This flimsy slab of wood, all that stands between the East Wind and myself. "What did she tell you?" Eurus demands.

"*She* has a name, and it is Min."

An unexpected rush of gratitude warms me. It is not Demi's duty to shield me, but she has stepped in when I sorely need it.

The East Wind sighs, a sound of surrender. "What did Min tell you?"

"That is for me to know and for you to never find out. Let me be clear: the council has no interest in the affairs of a mortal, but I certainly do. If any harm comes to her, there will be hell to pay."

"So, you finally grew a backbone." Despite the words, there is little heat behind them, almost as if the fight has gone out of him. "Tell me, Demi. Where was the council when *I* needed them? How am I to know you will not harm her to get to me?"

Fisting the blanket, I draw it up to my shivering chest as the goddess scoffs. "I would never lay a hand on her. She is good—too good for you, as far as I'm concerned."

When the East Wind speaks, it is slow, stilted with shame. "You are probably right about that." Then he swears. "I know it may not seem like it, but I am doing my best to protect her."

My palm lifts to cover my heart, which skips a beat. It is the strangest thing, but I believe him.

"Maybe you are," Demi concedes, "but what happens if you perish in the tournament? What will happen to Min then? You know the council will not allow her to stay."

"You don't need to worry about that. I intend to win." His wings stir with a delicate clatter of scales beyond the bedroom door. "Tell Min to meet me at the arena following breakfast." A beat of silence passes. "Please."

"I will. And Eurus?" There is a pause. "I'm sorry. For everything."

He responds, almost too quietly for me to hear, "I know."

The door shuts, and I roll onto my back, staring up at the darkened ceiling. I feel my pulse behind my eyelids, in the roots of my teeth. The East Wind belongs to this darkness, and I've the maddening notion to burst through the door and call him back. There is comfort in his presence. But there is a danger, too. Because sometimes, I yearn for things I dare not name.

Soon, waves of tawny light paint the bedroom walls. Forcing myself from bed, I shuffle into the main chamber to find Demi seated at her breakfast table, an impressive spread laid before her. Today, she is dressed in velvet, gold trimming the sleeves and neckline. "Good morning." She gestures to the empty chair across from her. "Care to join me?"

I sit. The windows lie open. The curtains stir and birdsong twitters in the distance, the city sparkling like a jewel as the world wakens.

"How did you sleep?" she asks while slathering jam onto her bread.

"Well, actually." The bed was both soft and spacious, a cloud to lay my head upon. "Thank you again for letting me stay here." I pour milk into my tea and stir it with a small metal spoon. It clinks gently, a fragile chime.

"You're welcome, but please don't think it was only a one-time offer. You may stay here for as long as you need."

My throat tightens. "Thank you, Demi. But I don't want to intrude—"

"Min. Look at me." I dutifully lift my eyes. Hers glitter like cut citrine. "I mean it. Stay here for as long as you need. I enjoy the company. How many can say they've shared both breakfast *and* lunch with a mortal?" She grins.

"If you're sure..."

"I'm a goddess, am I not?" She gives a haughty sniff. "I'm always sure."

My mouth quirks. I'm coming to learn Demi. For whatever reason, she is curious of mortals.

"How are you feeling about yesterday?" she asks.

I shrug, take a bite of the creamy eggs I've spooned onto my plate. "I know what I must do." Once the East Wind claims victory, I'll be free. The more I think about it, maybe he *does* deserve having his heart cut out by her ladyship for what he has put me through. Except, the thought squeezes my lungs to the point of pain. Which doesn't make any sense.

What is worse? My image of home has grown clouded. Even if I am able to purchase the estate from her ladyship, would I have the means to build my own business, or would she run me into the ground before it had the chance to blossom? Distance from Lady Clarisse has made me realize I am more relaxed than I was. I do not flinch at every passing sound. But I have nowhere to go, no one else to lean on.

"These eggs are very good," I tell Demi, smiling. Though I would expect nothing less from a goddess who knows her way around a kitchen. "What's that spice I'm tasting?"

"Nutmeg," she says, rather pleased. "It's my secret ingredient. Things taste better with a little sweetness, don't you think?"

For whatever reason, my thoughts wander briefly to Eurus. I immediately stamp them out.

Following breakfast, Demi and I head across the city toward the arena. We merge with the outpouring of deities, spirits high and a hunger for blood sweeping like brushfire through the throng. More than one god or goddess reaches out to pet my hair. Demi slaps their hands aside with a growled, "Mind yourselves!"

By the time we reach the entrance, the announcements are already well under way. I struggle to hear over the jostling.

"... fifty are still in the running, but only twelve will face the third and final trial."

The lightning god's voice booms and crackles, erupting across the expanse. I strain my ears to catch the rest, only half aware of Demi elbowing people aside, one of her hands gripping my arm to prevent me from getting trampled by those in the corridor leading to the stands beyond.

"In this trial, your powers will be nullified. That includes your godly strength and speed, your protective scales and feathered wings, your special talents, any and all enchantments. This is to even the playing field. Your determination alone will decide who is strong enough to push through the pain and fatigue.

"In addition, the protections offered to you through your divine blood will be masked. By which I mean, death may find you at any point, and through various means, as it does for mortals. For many, it will not take long before your will crumbles. The question is, are you tenacious enough to reach the exit before it does?"

A roar quakes the bones of the arena. The ground trembles underfoot.

"In order to move on to the final round, *both* you and your teammate must pass through the door—"

"Min."

I whirl, a hand pressed to my heart. The East Wind is a boulder amidst the current, braced and unwilling to yield. His newly patched cloak is borderline ragged in the harsh noon glare. "You st-startled me."

When he doesn't respond, I drop my hand. No matter the guilt that nags, I've nothing to apologize for. I did nothing wrong. *He* should be apologizing for treating me so disrespectfully.

But Eurus clears his throat and glances elsewhere. The crowd gives him a wide berth. "Nice weather," he mutters.

My expression twists. "Absolutely," I say. "A great day to die."

Eurus snorts. My mouth twitches, but the smile falters. Why am I surprised by his unwillingness to discuss last night's spat? I should not be so eager to expect change.

"Good luck out there," I tell him, and I mean it, I do. He needs his revenge. I need the estate.

"Can I have a minute of your time?" he requests.

I look to Demi as someone elbows me in the back. The goddess shakes her head in irritation. "Will you be all right?" she asks me.

I nod. "I'll come find you."

With a final scowl of warning to the East Wind, Demi ventures down the corridor toward the stands. Once out of sight, his hood snaps toward me. "You need to come with me."

"What?"

The horde thickens, forcing me into his chest. His arms wrap around my back; my palms land on his chest. When I attempt to retreat, I find my way blocked by the rambunctious crowd.

The East Wind loosens his arms, but doesn't drop them completely. I am still sheltered for a while longer. "They informed us last night," he explains. "We each require a teammate in the second trial. Otherwise, we forfeit."

"What are you saying?"

"I'm saying you're competing with me."

My mind has frozen. His words skate over its surface. "That's not funny," I croak.

"It wasn't meant to be."

"I can't go in th-there." I spin around, but Demi has since vanished. "If you chose someone else—"

"I can't trust anyone else!"

As he peers down at me, I've the absurd notion to cover my heart. I am too exposed beneath this immortal's scrutiny. "It must be you, bird."

A sudden wave of dizziness drags at me. I sway. "But—"

"We don't have time," he presses. "We need to get to the field before the trial begins."

"Have you forgotten that I'm m-m-mortal?" I manage, each word a rumpled wheeze. "I'll die!"

"You won't." In this, he is absolute. "I will not allow it."

My throat stings with the rise of bile. I'm going to vomit. "How are y-you supposed to protect yourself and m-me at the same t-t-time?"

"Listen to me, bird." Catching my jaw, he gently tilts it upward. The roiling of my stomach settles as the press of his fingertips warms my chilled skin. "Only twelve contestants move on to the third trial. We need to be in the top three. The higher we place, the more of an advantage we have in the final trial. Understood?"

I jerk free of his hold. His hand hangs there momentarily before dropping to his side, fingers still curled, as though preserving the shape of my face. "I'm not like y-you," I say. "I'm not all powerful."

"You have power, too, in your own way."

And what power is that, exactly? The power to cower and hide? To sidestep, never facing anything head on? To continually lie to myself about who I am and what I want? The East Wind expects nothing short of a miracle. Whether by arrow or ax, sword or knife, I will surely fall.

"Don't think about what people expect of you," Eurus says. "Think of what you want—then claim it for yourself."

"*Competitors, please take your marks!*"

I glance down. My poor, battered loafers. If I knew I'd be competing in the tournament, I'd have worn sturdier footwear.

"Please, bird . . . Min." The East Wind's voice deepens, becomes that sound I first heard through the steel door of his cell, an abrasive rasp that at times felt like a physical touch. My belly quivers; my breasts peak. I hurriedly cross my arms over my chest, eyes wide at my reaction to his proximity. "I need you. Not Demi, not anyone else. Just you." He hesitates, then drags a fingertip down my right cheek. "I have not forgotten my promise to return you home."

Think of what you want—then claim it for yourself.

In this moment, I am not thinking of St. Laurent, or Lady Clarisse, or the estate, or Nan. I am looking at the East Wind, and I am thinking that he smells so acutely of the sea . . . and I am not afraid.

"I will help you," I say.

No time to waste. Catching my hand, he drags me through a side door and down three flights of stairs. Two brawny immortals guard what I assume is one of the entrances onto the field. They look to Eurus, then to me. "This your teammate?" one asks.

"Yes."

The guard snorts, but opens the door. Eurus drags me through, and we take our places along the perimeter of the field. From this position, I realize how massive the arena truly is, a hundred thousand spectators screaming above, the air violently alive. As for the field itself, in front of each competitor and their teammate, a shut door has appeared. I assume we are to step through once given the signal.

From his seat amongst the Council of Gods, the lightning god lifts a hand. "Begin!"

The doors open. Fifty competitors lunge through the doorways, along with their partners. I glance down at where Eurus grips my hand—my only lifeline.

"Trust me," he says.

I do not, yet what choice do I have?

Together, we step through.

17

We are suspended on the jagged edge of the world.
Straight ahead: the sea. Its black span spits white foam as it branches and curls, drawing those ruffled collars beneath its surface. A coarse wind drags at my hair and stings my eyes. I squeeze them shut, nausea coating the back of my throat. This is a dream. It's not real. I am safe. I am *safe*.

But the rush and roar of water collapses my strongest shield. No matter how far I travel, the sea always finds me.

I force my eyes open. The field has been transformed, the stands of the arena screened behind a thick wall of haze, the roar of attendees muffled behind whatever enchantment has taken hold. Overhead, the sky is a vicious gray-green, and waves thrash against the cliffs on which we stand. Many of the forty-nine competitors and their teammates have already begun to climb down the bluffs, including the three redheaded Fates.

"We'll need to act quickly!" Eurus shouts into my ear. "See those boats?"

Eyes slitted against the wind, I spot a collection of wooden vessels moored to a small dock, which juts from an island located perhaps a half mile from shore. And far, far out to sea, beyond the island—a rise of rock. It is there the door awaits, its gilded frame beckoning.

"Can't we f-fly?" I shout back. Already, dampness has flecked the fabric of my dress, and I shiver, teeth gritted against the frigid autumn air.

"No powers," Eurus reminds me. "No wings." His hand comes to rest against my lower back, and my eyes widen. I'm not even sure he realizes he's touching me. "We'll have to reach the boats another way."

Descending the cliffs, he means. I inspect the terrain, but no alternate routes lead to the beach. A few competitors stalk the precipice, hesitant, as I am, to begin that perilous climb.

Heart thundering, I step forward, peering down at the toothed rocks below. To fall is to die. "Are y-you sure—"

"How should w-we do this?" I ask. "Should I—"

An arrow hisses overhead. Eurus catches me around the waist. We hit the ground.

"Did you see where the shot came from?" he barks.

One of his hard thighs slots between my legs, pressing upward against their juncture. It is a hard, heavy heat, and my mind whites out from the contact. An unexpected pulse of warmth floods my pelvis.

"Bird?"

My cheeks sting; my throat goes dry. "N-no . . ."

Thankfully, I spot the arrow in my periphery. I reach for it, yank the stone tip from the damp earth, and sniff the yellow substance coating the head. Nutmeg and . . . broth of violet.

My fingers spasm, and I release the arrow with a muffled curse. "The arrows are coated in poison."

"Can you identify it?" he replies, and the warmth of his breath dives beneath the neckline of my dress, soothing my pebbled skin. As he shifts against me, I stiffen, heat and cold twining through muscle, ligament, bone. Eurus goes still as well.

"Um." My palm rests against his chest, but he doesn't immediately pull away as I expect. "Do you think y-you could . . . ?"

I'm not able to take a full breath until Eurus pulls himself off me. There I lie, staring at the sky, gasping for air. My thoughts feel akin to shredded cotton, possessing neither substance nor shape. What is wrong with me? What ailment do I suffer from?

As I force myself to stand on wobbly legs, another cold gust cuts through my dress. "They've used Ashes to Ashes. It kills instantly." Immortal or not, whoever is hit by the poison-coated arrows will die.

He swears, spins around to study the landscape, as do I. Arrows spear through the air, unaffected by the wind. One deity is hit near the spine. He hangs by mere fingertips for one breath, two, before he slips. The drop is long. His body splinters into a thousand fragments of bone.

"Climb onto my back," Eurus orders. One, two, three arrows spear toward him. He ducks to avoid being impaled.

I can't do this. "I'll fall," I whisper.

"You won't fall. I won't allow it."

"You can't know for certain."

The East Wind angles toward me. "Look at me," he demands.

If I die, then Nan's dream dies with me. As for Lady Clarisse, she will never know of my demise. Would she care? Dull, stupid Min, out of the picture at last.

"Bird."

His suppliant tone coaxes my gaze upward. The edges of his cloak ripple, and shadow spills from inside his cowl. A glint of light, like the sheen of a single eye, lures my focus. For one breathless moment, I am staring into Eurus' shining pupil.

"I won't let you fall," he murmurs. "I promise." He catches my wrist, shackling it with his fingers. "Climb onto my back."

"And expose m-m-myself to the arrows?"

This silence bears the peculiar shape of a pursed mouth. "Very well. Hold on to my front. You will be well shielded."

He is the East Wind, he is undying, he is my captor, but here, now, he is my protector, my teammate, reluctant or not. If we are to successfully survive this trial, then I must trust him, for however little his trust is worth.

Trust is thus the press of two bodies: mortal and divine. It is my arms draping his neck, my legs wrapped around his solid waist, the lack of tension in his frame as he accepts my touch. It is the stuttering rise of his chest, those massive hands curving around the backs of my thighs. It is my face tucked against the curve of his neck, the only warmth to be found on these exposed bluffs.

Carefully, Eurus kneels, crawling backward until he reaches the ledge. I squeeze my eyes shut, emit a small, breathless squeak as he lurches, lowering himself until we are fully vertical, clinging to the overhang.

Thunder erupts. The rock shudders. I clutch Eurus harder, torn by two warring desires: to burrow deeper into ignorance, to open my eyes and see. A muffled scream pierces the thickening gloom—yet one more competitor tumbling to their death.

It begins to rain.

In seconds, I am drenched. The heavy cotton hangs off me like bags of old skin. Arrows cut the air with increasing frequency, but Eurus angles nearer to the cliff face, protecting me from any projectiles. He fumbles for a handhold, swearing softly beneath his breath, and I realize how difficult it must be to bear both our weights. There must be something I can do, some way to help him.

The moment I force my eyes open, my vision wavers. The sky seethes darkness, and wooziness loosens my hold around the East Wind's neck.

As though sensing my slackened grip, he snaps out, "Min!"

I sag backward against the rock. The water is all around, its hiss deafening. My tongue stings; my throat is on fire. I choke for breath, drowning on dry land.

"Min, listen to me."

"I feel faint," I whisper.

"I know," he says. "But the water can't touch you. You're safe. Do you hear me? Listen to my voice." And the East Wind cups the back of my head, cradling me against his broad, muscled chest. Vaguely, I realize that cannot be possible unless he clings to the cliff with only one hand.

"You're safe," he reassures me. "I won't let anything happen to you."

And he proceeds to tell me a story as he maneuvers downward, though I do not immediately recognize it as such. He tells me of his time in Marles, his visits to the vineyards and old, cobbled villages. His velvet voice slips through my bloodstream, its low thrum like a pulse.

But the story is cut short as he jolts wildly. My skull strikes the rock, and I recoil with a soft cry of pain. Beneath my palms, the muscles of his upper back spasm.

Tentatively, I open my eyes. An arrow protrudes from his shoulder. "Eurus."

"Pull it out," he snarls through gritted teeth. His entire body trembles. "Hurry."

"But—"

"Do it!"

My sweaty fingers surround the slim piece of wood. As the East Wind exhales, the muscles of his back slacken, and I yank the arrow free.

"*Fuck!*"

It takes some awkward maneuvering to draw the arrowhead close enough to inspect through the rain. Surprisingly, a green, rather than yellow, substance coats the tip. It smells of cherries.

"Larkshin," I whisper.

"Another—" He bites back a hiss of pain. "Poison?"

I release the arrow, watch it tumble onto the rocks far below. "Yes." Better than Ashes to Ashes, at least. "It is a poison of paralysis. It will begin with y-your legs and quickly work its way through your system until it reaches your heart. You have maybe an hour before collapse, if that."

The East Wind grunts, having braced himself against a short overhang. His fingers dig into the wet stone, and small pebbles shake loose around his boots. I wipe strands of hair from my dripping face, squinting into the distance. "Two people have reached the beach."

He mutters a few choice words before descending another step. I tighten my legs around his waist and try not to think of how intimate our position is.

As he searches for a foothold, a splash of pink catches my eye through the gray deluge.

"Wait." I grip Eurus' shoulder. He flinches, and I yank my hand back, having forgotten about his wound. "Sorry. There's a sandflower to your right that can help slow the p-poison. If you can get me close enough, I might be able to reach it."

Eurus shuffles horizontally across the rock, nearer to the weeds. He stops, and a full-body shudder grips him. "I can't go any farther. My legs are beginning to turn numb."

"I'll be quick." Leveraging myself upright, I anchor one hand to his unwounded shoulder, the other reaching as far as I'm able, until my shoulder joint burns from the strain.

"Bird."

Another inch of reach, and my fingertips brush the petals. Eurus attempts to lean closer, but the trembling in his arms worsens. "Almost . . . there," I whisper.

"I can't hold on for much longer."

I'm pulling the stem from the crevice when fire tears through my upper arm. I scream, wrenching backward and slamming into Eurus' chest.

He grunts and lists sideways. One of his feet slips. We drop. I yelp, but he catches himself, gripping the rock for all he's worth. "You're hit."

An arrow bulges from my bicep. I stare blankly. The sweet perfume of cherries tickles the back of my throat. "It's only Larkshin. I'll be fine." For now. "Let's just focus on r-reaching the beach."

Miraculously, the East Wind maintains his strength for the remainder of the descent. As soon as we touch down, my knees give out.

I turn to find Eurus having collapsed, his cloak completely soaked through. "Chew," I demand, ripping the roots from the weed and thrusting them into his hand. While he swallows, I consume the roots as well before snapping off the arrow shaft jutting from my upper arm. If we make it through this trial alive—and I sincerely hope that we do—then I will need a healer to remove the head.

Another crack of thunder rolls across the landscape. At least on solid ground, we are shielded by the cliffs, arrows falling like a silver rain from above.

Only a handful of contestants still cling to the rockface. Some attempt to crawl toward the shoreline, their legs already paralyzed.

A few battle the ferocious sea current, cutting through the waves to reach the small island where the boats are docked. One of those competitors is Arin, I realize. Upon reaching the dock, his teammate jumps into the boat, and they're off, rowing for all they're worth toward the door.

Five vessels remain.

"We'll have to swim," Eurus says, pushing upright. His legs wobble, but he remains on his feet.

My tongue sticks to the roof of my mouth. I peel it free, swallow the wad of saliva that follows. "I'll w-wait on the beach while you get the boat."

"You can hold on to my wings," Eurus cuts in. Without giving me a chance to respond, he jogs toward the shoreline.

I dart after him, shouting, "I'm not getting in the w-water! You'll have to come back for me. I'll wait here."

The East Wind whirls to face me. The storm is relentless, hammering our backs with sharp rain and hail. A flash of white tears through the bloated clouds, followed by a ferocious *crack*. My ears ring dully.

"Why do you continue to let fear dictate your life?" he demands. "You have the opportunity to free yourself, yet you sit in your cage while the door stands open. This is your chance to get what you want. Will you let it pass you by?"

"This isn't what I w-w-want," I cry. "This has never been about wh-what I want! This is about what *you* want, and what I n-need to do to make that happen."

He stares at me. The tide sweeps the sandy incline, swallowing our shoes, ankles, calves. Meanwhile, a handful of competitors dive into the water farther down the beach.

"Maybe I was wrong about you," Eurus says. "Maybe you are nothing more than a coward."

I press my fingertip against the insult, testing its ache. *Coward.* The old bruise runs deep.

"I never asked to be h-here," I shout, fighting tears, "but you forced m-m-my hand. You said you needed m-me. You said I w-was the only one you could trust!" The hurt is doubly edged, for I *wanted* to believe him, deep down. Wanted to believe that some deteriorating part of me might be revived if the sentiment were true. "What did you expect from m-me? Did you think I would m-m-miraculously overcome my fears simply because you *demanded* it of me?" I'm a fool. A fool to think he might win, a fool to think he might change, a fool to think there is something softer beneath that cloak, shoved far, far back from any illumination. Mostly, I am a fool for letting myself believe the East Wind might have grown to care for me, in his own way.

"Think of me wh-what you will," I state with a strength I did not believe myself capable of, "but I'm staying here. It's your decision wh-whether you come back for me."

The East Wind remains unmoving, but the blackness inside his hood deepens, if I'm not mistaken. "It seems I don't have a choice," he growls, "do I."

"You always h-have a choice," I counter. "But my life is not y-y-yours. It's time you realized that."

To our left, another contestant completes his descent from the cliffs and flings himself—and his teammate—into the sea. This immortal doesn't appear to have been hit by a poisoned arrow. His arms and legs propel him forward with a complete lack of effort.

Eurus emits a low oath. Without waiting for my response, he dives into the sea.

I watch him cut through tumultuous waters, every rising peak and plunging valley attempting to shift his course. Far beyond, the Fates and their companions have reached that elusive door, slipping from sight.

I glance toward the island in worry. Only four boats remain. The first is claimed by a god with eel-slick skin. The second, a goddess with azure locks. She cuts the rope, grabs the oars, and leaps into the vessel. It spins, the stern crashing into its neighbor. As the goddess and her teammate row away from the dock, the damaged vessel slowly takes on water, eventually sinking beneath the waves.

And then there was one.

Back and forth and back and forth, I pace the shore. If I do not acknowledge the growing numbness climbing my legs, then it cannot be real. My throat swells, drenched in brine. One deep breath, followed by another. Gradually, the blackness surrounding my vision retreats.

At last, Eurus reaches the island. But he is not the first to do so. Another deity has reached the final vessel and struggles to loosen the rope mooring it to the dock. Step by step, the East Wind stumbles across the rocks. At one point, he trips, catches himself on the shriveled branches of a warped tree.

The competitor successfully unties the rope. Eurus, recognizing his narrowing window of opportunity, puts on a burst of speed, but fails to notice the deity's companion leaping from behind a tree, sword lifted.

"Behind you!" I scream.

The East Wind spins, the curved head of his ax cutting across his foe's throat. The man falls. His divine companion scrambles into the boat, but does not get far before he meets the same fate.

I press my fists to my mouth, having returned to pacing. Waves rush the shore, soaking my loafers further. At this point, the remaining competitors are either in the water, rowing toward the door, or dead. I alone stand on the strip of beach.

Grasping the oars, the East Wind shoves them into the waves that toss him high, threatening to capsize the tiny vessel he now commands. Unfortunately, Larkshin has begun to weaken his limbs. The rowing motion of his arms stops and starts as he attempts to navigate around those fighting the waves. He's halfway back to shore when two flaxen-haired immortals latch onto the side of his vessel.

Their weight drags one side of the boat toward the water. Eurus snarls, kicks one of the immortals into the sea. The woman flounders, and I watch, sickened, as she claws at her companion in an attempt to keep her head above water. They sink beneath and do not resurface.

As soon as his vessel hits the sand, I leap inside. Eurus casts out, rowing as hard as he can through the floundering competitors. One immortal manages to grab hold of the hull. I pry his fingers loose, and the waves do the rest.

Thrice more, desperate contestants attempt to board our vessel. I kick them away, watch them drown. Only when we are safely out of range does Eurus slow, panting.

"You need to row us to the door . . ." A low groan squeezes past his throat, and he hunches forward. "Take the oars, bird."

The boat tips, and I scream, clutching at his shoulder. Eurus must be truly under the poison's spell if he fails to react to my touch. When a second, larger wave barrels toward us, my stomach bottoms out. It grows and it grows, like a grasping hand reaching over us. I close my eyes. If I am to die, I would prefer not to witness it.

Chilled fingers seize my face. Their icy touch burrows beneath skin, and my eyes fly open.

"Take the oars," Eurus urges again.

Shaking my head, I flinch away. "I can't do this m-m-myself."

"You can, and you will," he pants, voice gradually petering out. "If you wish to return home."

He dangles St. Laurent like a carrot before a horse. Does his cruelty know no bounds? And yet . . . he is right. I *do* wish to return home.

Wordlessly, I pry the oars from his stiffened fingers. Another wave breaks over our vessel. Arctic water showers us, and I bite the inside of my cheek hard enough to draw blood. *I can do this. Just keep rowing.*

It is not the East Wind who rows our fragile vessel to the door suspended in the middle of the sea. It is a mortal woman from Marles, cutting through tumultuous waters, hands white-knuckled around the oars until her arms give out.

18

A BARRAGE OF WIND BLASTS OPEN THE DOORS TO OUR SUITE. The East Wind stalks inside, the frayed hem of his cloak snapping around the scuffed leather of his menacing black boots. I pause warily at the threshold, watching him pace. His spine is a rod of iron attaching hips to skull. His shoulders—bunched, coiled with repressed rage—creep continually toward his ears. Soon enough, he will wear a channel into the floor.

I trace the scar on my bicep where the wound from the arrow has smoothed over. Following the second trial, the final twelve were taken to the infirmary, where they were treated and released. Having completed the second trial in last place, Eurus and I were the last ones to be seen by the healers.

"Last place isn't how I imagined I'd be entering the final trial," the East Wind growls.

After a moment, I step inside and shut the door. Pacing and pacing and more pacing: door, desk, sofa, table. As he passes before the window, the shadow of his body momentarily eclipses me. "I don't understand. You're a contender for the prize. Isn't this what you wanted?"

Eurus halts, pivots to face me, that hood seething with darkness, always. "I should have been first," he says. "I told you how important it was that I make the top three for the final trial. The advantage is enough to all but guarantee victory." His wings stir, the long, curved bones partially unfolding in a motion I have come to recognize as a desire to flee. "Instead," he clips out, "I find myself in last place, the odds of winning too slim for comfort."

Shaking his head, he turns to stare out the window. What does he see? Likely nothing. Not the gilded skin of this marvelous city, nor how the mountains cast violet across the valleys where the forest thickens and a ribbon of silver carves a slender path.

"I should have asked someone else for help," he mutters, his back to me.

Lamplight spills across the overlapping black scales encasing his wings. I stare at the hundreds of small, self-contained suns shining across his back, and wonder why I feel no joy at witnessing how beautifully the light is refracted. "You said you n-needed me," I murmur with a sinking heart. "That I was the only person you could trust."

"That may be true, but trust isn't how you win a tournament. Victory is not claimed by the weak."

"Are you insinuating *I'm* the r-r-reason you came in last?"

Eurus whirls around. "Had you not hesitated in climbing down the cliffs, we would have likely reached the beach first, unscathed."

Though my back seeks to bend, my mind will not allow it. It is of iron, tempered steel. It reminds me of how far I have come. "I did my best to help y-you. Had I not b-been present, you would have succumbed to the poison before ever reaching the d-d-door."

"If not for your delay," he tosses back, "I might not have been hit at all. Had you swum to the boat, I could have reached the door without having to return to shore for you."

I have often imagined an existence where fear of water did not plague me. Perhaps, in another life, I could have swum to the dock. But that life is not mine to claim. It never was.

"I don't know wh-why you're so upset," I say, and I'm ashamed to find my voice quavering, my fumbling tongue not far behind. "We f-f-finished. You got to the th-third trial. You still h-have a chance to w-win—"

"There is no chance," he says.

He will not give. It is everything or nothing.

"I h-hear you, Eurus. I'm trying to r-reassure you—"

"I don't need your reassurance!" he shouts, tossing up a hand. "What I need is competence. Certainty. Courage." He shakes his head at me, scoffs, then turns his back.

His blatant disregard for my feelings *hurts*. I am not perfect, but I am good. To think we'd made progress in building trust, however tedious the development.

"I d-don't appreciate your t-t-treatment of m-me," I grind out. "You could be k-k-kinder to—"

"I will do what I want."

Blood crawls through my chest, up my face, its heat splitting open my veins. His response has all the finality of a guillotine. History dictates I bury my words. I pack them into a tight, dense ball of everything I wish to say but dare not. By the Mother, when do I decide what is best for me? When do I begin?

Think of what you want—then claim it for yourself.

"Shut up," I whisper.

The air stirs. It tugs at the tips of my hair as, slowly, the East Wind turns to face me. "Excuse me?"

There is a fire in me. I see it now: spark to coal to licking flame. "You heard m-me."

"No, I don't think I did—"

"You are obsessed with revenge!" I scream, and by the Mother, does it feel good to rid my body of this poison, this festering resentment. "You will go to any l-l-lengths to get it—and then what? Have you asked yourself what will come after, wh-when the council is dead and you are free to return h-home? Have you considered the damage you will have wrought in your quest for vengeance? What of the lives y-you have destroyed, the families you have broken, the dreams you have ruined?"

My breaths come short. My skin, singed by the fury eating at my veins, feels feverish to the touch. Rage? No. That is too simple an emotion. "Have you asked yourself that?" I press. "Have you asked yourself at wh-what cost your revenge will come? You think things will change for y-you, Eurus, but the truth is, even if you kill the council and return home, you will still be the s-s-same person. You will continue to hold on to mistrust and judgment. You will live out your eternal life m-miserable and alone because you cannot find it in y-your heart to forgive yourself for what occurred."

"Forgive *myself*?" It emerges too quiet. A low, chilling hiss.

"Yes." I cannot—will not—waver. "Whatever torture you endured when you were younger . . . it's not y-your fault. Your father's abuse is not your fault. The council turning a blind eye—"

"You know nothing of my situation!" he roars, wings snapping open. A brute wind rocks the room. Books are flung from their shelves, and chairs topple onto their sides.

The door to my bedroom lies open, offering sanctuary. Although some small part of me longs to quail, retreat, hide, I do not. Eurus needs to hear this. He needs to know what I have only recently discovered for myself—that change is not dependent on external forces. It comes from within.

"Think of wh-what this is doing to you," I murmur. "Winning won't heal you. It won't change the injustices that have been d-done—"

"As if you have the right to speak of things like change."

A blink, and he is before me, looming, enormous, all-powerful. My back hits the wall. I've nowhere else to go.

"Before I took you away, you were a lowly apprentice, treated no better than vermin," he murmurs, head dipping low. "Two hands to stir brews, two legs to run errands. That's all you were to your old employer: disposable."

I flinch, a hand lifted to ward off the blow. It's not true. Her ladyship needs me. I have been diligent all these years. One day, she will see me as I am. She will understand what I have sacrificed.

But the East Wind goes on, each snarling insult cutting into me. "You allow that witch to abuse you mercilessly, yet daily you crawled to her, begging for whatever scraps she tossed your way. Did you expect her to *love* you?"

"I-I ..." My airway cinches shut. *Disposable.* "I-I-I—"

"Have you no pride, bird?" He shakes his head pityingly. "Have you no self-respect?"

His derision carves deep, through skin and muscle, down to where my heart's rhythm flags. I feel old in this moment. Old and fatigued. For what I have fought is a long, arduous battle, and I now stand on the killing fields, bleeding out, alone.

"M-maybe I have l-l-lacked self-respect in the past," I whisper, each word a distinct ache, "but I gain more and m-m-more each day. And I n-n-never pretended to be st-st-strong. I'm mortal. We are m-messy and naive and f-f-foolish. We l-live and d-die, create and d-destroy."

My voice fades. I might stop there. I might leave my thought unfinished. I might hand to him victory in silence. Might ... but won't.

"At least at the end of the d-d-day," I go on, face lifted toward his hood, "I can s-say that I'm t-t-trying. I'm able to s-s-see those bright places in the dark. I still search for them. I always w-w-will." Tears—they wend down my cheeks, drip from my chin. I let them come. It is a relief to oust the pain and know that I have not allowed suffering to harden me. "That you p-pity me matters n-n-not. Because I pity *you*, Eurus. I pity y-y-your callous nature, your single ambition to end the ones who have h-h-hurt you. But m-most of all, I pity y-your heart, for it is empty, and selfish, and cold. And it is the only company y-y-you will keep in your long, lonely life."

With those parting words, I brush past him, shutting the bedroom door soundly at my back.

Flinging myself onto the bed, I release a soul-wrenching sob, an outpouring of shame and fury-stricken grief. Eurus is right and he is wrong. I have distanced myself from Lady Clarisse, yet a part of me still craves her approval. I fear Eurus sees what I have spent the better part of my life trying to bury. That I am weak and unwanted. That I am as useless as her ladyship so gleefully claims. No matter my efforts, I will never be enough.

Later, my limbs strewn across the mattress like a collection of limp cuttings, my every emotion wrung dry, the soft creak of hinges reaches me. I tense, for the East Wind's tread is as familiar as it is unwelcome.

"Bird."

"Go away," I whisper brokenly.

His footsteps cease. Still, I sense his presence. "There are things I wish to say to you."

"I don't w-w-want to talk to y-you, or look at y-you, or be anywhere n-n-near y-you," I cry hoarsely. "So please, for once, w-will you do as I ask and let m-me be?"

Shoving my face deeper into the pillow, I purge this heat and bitterness, the weight encasing my heart and lungs, until my sobs disintegrate into pitiful mewls of pain. Clutching at the blankets with clawed fingers, I wish for healing, I wish for peace.

Predictably, the East Wind does not depart at my request. He nears, for the brine feathering his skin is so much more potent now. "I will go," he says, and this might be the first that I have heard sadness bleeding through his tone. "But before I do, I want to apologize."

My cries lessen as his statement trickles through the fog shrouding my good sense. Lady Clarisse never cared to apologize. "Is this a j-jest? If so, I d-d-don't appreciate it."

"It is no jest. I'm truly sorry for what I said." It is heavy, his regret. "It was cruel. And you did not deserve it."

"Th-then why did y-y-you say it?"

His wings rustle. It makes him uncomfortable that I have asked this. "I was . . . overwhelmed."

That is no excuse.

"I was afraid of failing the second trial, afraid that coming in last would prevent my victory. So I lashed out. I sought someone else to blame. But I was wrong. If not for your expertise in poisons, I would not have reached the boats at all."

He tells me what I already know. It does little to heal what is broken inside me.

After a moment, I roll onto my side, the cool air drying my sticky face. Always, the East Wind wears his cloak, never allowing me the opportunity to glimpse his countenance. "You were r-right," I choke out. But . . . it is done, my heart exposed, too aggrieved to shield itself properly.

"About what?" he asks gently.

"I'm useless. I'm—" My chin quavers. I bow my head, tears slipping down my nose. "I'm n-n-not worth the effort."

He steps toward the bed, one seamless, liquid motion. "That's not true, bird."

"Isn't it?" If I were worth the effort, wouldn't my mother have attempted to foster a relationship with me? Wouldn't she have showered me in all the colors of the world so that, even on the bleakest days, I would never fall completely into shadow?

Instead, I was gifted to the sea, I was abhorred, I was abandoned. I've spent years of my life breaking myself down to prove to Lady Clarisse that I am good, I am enough, I am worth others' time. If I could develop useful skills, if I could be dutiful and diligent, if I could be a ladder for her to climb, then she might finally see me as worthy. And maybe I would see myself as worthy, too.

The mattress dips beneath Eurus' weight. "The fault is mine," he murmurs. "I hurt you deeply, and I failed to make you feel safe. I'm truly sorry for that, bird. I really am. You are absolutely worth every effort."

"Says the m-man who cannot stand to be in the same r-room as me," I whisper bitterly. My eyes sting. I wipe the wetness away with the back of my hand, slumping deeper into the pillows. I'm tired, but I do not wish to be alone. I have been so lonely these past years. I dare say my heart no longer recognizes another's.

"I know this may come as a surprise to you," he continues in a soft tone, "but I am not usually one for company."

"You don't s-say."

He huffs. "I know I do not have a right to ask for your forgiveness. I have treated you in ways no person should be treated. Maybe I reacted so poorly because I recognize the truth in your words. My childhood was not a happy one. I have long blamed myself for what occurred." He plants one hand in the blankets near my thigh. Its heat radiates through the fabric, and my skin stipples, as though already anticipating its touch. "How much did Demi tell you—about my childhood?"

It is pointless to pretend. "Your father . . ." I cannot say it.

For an extended moment, the East Wind stares down at the pile of blankets. His hood then angles toward my feet, which peek from beneath the fabric. I tuck them away, suddenly self-conscious.

"My father was a hard man," he says, "but what can you expect from Astraeus, ruler of the sky at dusk? It was a great responsibility, and he was often irritable, tense. Most days, he left the house before sunset and did not return until well after daybreak.

"Over the years, his relationship with our mother grew strained, and that added to his unhappiness. I still remember the first time he hit me. I walked into the kitchen, and suddenly my ears were ringing, and I was on the ground. He said I walked too loudly, that I was disturbing him as he cooked."

His story is my story, I realize. Lady Clarisse was an unsettling balance of charm and aggression. She, too, would lash out unexpectedly.

"I was an adolescent when my father first took me away from home," Eurus continues lowly, and the pain in his voice cannot be masked. "He claimed we were to visit a distant relative of his. I was stupid enough to believe him." He shakes his head, scrubs a hand over his face. "Where did we end up? A distant temple where few traveled. It was there that he began his experiments."

My gut clenches at that word: *experiments*. "Demi said your father hurt you, but not your brothers," I say. "Why is that?"

He rubs the blanket between thumb and forefinger. A soft, gray light delineates the curtains screening the window, softening his darkened form. "Who can say why I was singled out? Perhaps my father thought he was teaching me a lesson."

I frown, considering not the words themselves, but their rise and fall, the briefest hesitation before his response. It feels like a partial truth, but I do not press him. Whatever shadows he harbors, they are his to bear.

"Did your siblings know what y-your father was doing to you? What of your m-mother?" One might hide bruises and breaks beneath clothing, but ultimately, scars reveal themselves in other ways.

"Over time, my father grew abusive toward my mother. Fearing for her life, she abandoned us. As for my brothers, they did not know what was happening to me until much later. I tried to hide it. I was ... ashamed." I hear his throat click as he swallows. "There must be something wrong with me, if I alone was selected for his torture. I must have deserved it, right? I must have deserved the pain and isolation."

Hearing Eurus speak aloud these fears, I realize it is not his fault, and neither was it mine. Why should the East Wind deserve punishment simply for existing? And why should *I* deserve such treatment from her ladyship?

"Your father is r-r-responsible for your wings, is that correct?"

"Yes. His experiments grew more twisted as the years passed. After that, I was unable to hide what I had become: some sick, twisted creature," he chokes out in disgust. "An abomination that did not belong in this shining city."

It is the pain contorting his voice that finally emboldens me to reach for the East Wind. In this moment, I am not thinking of the consequences my touch might bring. I am thinking that he has grown up believing he is unwanted, unloved, unworthy. I am thinking that he was a child, and I was a child, and love from our caretakers was conditional.

Catching his hand, I press it against my chest, atop my heart. Its pace stumbles, for the opening of his hood shifts toward me in surprise. If Eurus does not want my touch, he is free to retreat.

His fingers twitch beneath mine, then settle.

"You are neither twisted, n-nor an abomination," I assure him. On the contrary, his wings are lovely, unlike anything I've encountered before. They offer him a means of freedom, escape.

But he shakes his head. "My father may have made me what I am, but the Council of Gods allowed him to do it. And when the current council banished me and my brothers, after we helped them to overthrow the old gods ... As an institution, I cannot allow it to continue."

While I may not agree with the East Wind's decision, I understand. Maybe I am wrong. Maybe ending their lives *will* heal him, though I am inclined to believe it will not.

"I'm sorry you suffered," I whisper, teary-eyed.

His hand tightens around mine. "Do not cry for me, bird. Do not waste your tears on something that cannot be changed." He sighs then, draping the blankets over my shoulders. "Can I tell you something?"

I nod.

"I often listened for your voice, back in St. Laurent."

"Wh-wh-what do you mean?"

"For three months, that witch tortured me out of my mind. Most days it was too difficult to focus on anything besides the pain. But as the weeks passed, I found solace in the rhythm of your voice. It offered a kindness I had rarely encountered in my immortal life."

I find it difficult to swallow as my awareness of his body heightens, and I am once again reminded of how large he is, how absolute. I hadn't the slightest idea Eurus felt this way.

"Time passed, and my fascination with you grew." His thumb rubs along my raised knuckles. "This mortal woman, weak and cowardly, or so I believed. I wondered what you might look like, what your mannerisms would be, the subtleties of your expressions. I listened for the press of your footsteps. In the evenings, when you would wake to stir whatever brews needed tending to, I began to wish you would approach my cell. And then you did, and I frightened you, and I thought it was what I deserved: to scare off the thing I wanted most."

My belly quivers in response to his admission. So, my curiosity about Lady Clarisse's prisoner was not one-sided after all.

"You're not w-wrong about me," I whisper. "I am weak, cowardly." Then I wince, for who cares to admit such feeble traits? "After Nan passed, my . . . her ladyship bought the estate, relegating me to her assistant. She claimed I needed direction, claimed she would teach me all that she knew, so that one day I m-might take over the apothecary when I was ready." My mouth bends, sullen and resentful. "It was a foolish hope, to think I might prove myself to her l-ladyship. To think I might be proven w-w-worthy of the honor of bane weaver."

My eyes sting. Tears, again? I have tried every day of my life to be what Lady Clarisse wants, but in the end, I am only stupid Min, foolish Min, incompetent Min who is more a burden than a blessing.

"When will it stop hurting?" My words are garbled, choked by emotion.

The East Wind smooths a hand across the back of my skull. "When will what stop hurting?"

"Living."

Wordlessly, he gathers me into his arms, one palm cradling the back of my head. My breathing grows more erratic, stretched to a high keen that cracks against my teeth. The dim is all around us. The tears will not cease. They well and gather, sliding across the dips and hills of my face as, curled into his chest, I release back-breaking sobs.

A stream of warm air stirs my hair as the East Wind says, with a gentleness I yearn for, "I understand, bird. Living does hurt. But don't be like me. Don't pretend your pain does not exist, because it will eat at you. Eventually, you will no longer recognize the lonely creature you have become. I would not wish that for you. I would not see your kind heart grow cold."

"Is that what h-happened to you?" I ask, leaning back, though not far enough to completely remove myself from his embrace. With a tentative touch, I trace the frayed edge of his hood. "Is that why you refuse to show your face? Because y-you fear your own reflection?"

The East Wind holds himself in high tension. I can almost feel it, like a mist against his skin, spreading taut to encase his bones. "My scars remind me of a time when I was helpless and alone. I do not like to be reminded of that. It is not pleasant, my face."

"I'm sure it is not as bad as you th-think," I reassure him.

His laughter contains an unexpected trace of humor. "I am aware of what I look like, bird. Trust me, it's not a welcome sight."

I pluck a loose thread from the blanket, considering how best to ask for what I want. I would like to think our walls are lowered and mutual understanding reached. "Would you allow me to r-remove your hood?" If I am to look upon the East Wind, if I am to understand him fully, his armor must fall.

"I do not think that is the best idea. I would shield you from what lies beneath, if possible."

"What if I t-told you I don't care what you look l-like?" I counter. Before he can respond, I push forward. "I have seen ugliness in all forms, Eurus. Your features cannot scare me." I waver, for to live is to be brave, and I have never considered that a strong quality in myself. But I reach toward his hood regardless. Darkness consumes the tips of my fingers, which brush something smooth, yet softly prickled in texture: the East Wind's stubbled jaw.

He goes still, yet: "Go on," he murmurs.

Catching the edge of his hood, I draw it back. It falls away to reveal a head of thick black hair, tousled; a raw-boned face; dark eyes and wide cheekbones, like those ancient gods from Nan's homeland, forever enshrined in her holy books.

But that is where our similarities end, for the East Wind's visage is twisted and malformed. The entire left side is puckered by a stretch of old scarring. A portion of his hairline has receded where the damage is particularly severe. His left eye has been spared, though its corner droops slightly, smeared into the damage blotting his cheek.

Burn marks. I would recognize them anywhere. But they do not detract from the rest of his features. The right side of his face, largely untouched by scarring, reveals considerable beauty. His jaw is sharp and wide. The pupils of his eyes are clear. His mouth: long and of pleasing shape, one side soft, the other kinked with scarring. What of the rest of his body? Is it, too, marked by scars?

The East Wind begins to draw his hood back up.

"No, please." I catch his hand. For just a moment, our fingers lie curled beside each other's, like kits in a burrow. "Don't cover up."

He stares at me. It does funny things to my insides. "My features are too ugly."

"You're not ugly," I say. Then, quieter: "Not to me."

Reluctantly, he lowers his arms, granting me permission to continue my perusal. My body buzzes with sudden anticipation as I reach for his face and allow the tips of my fingers to coast along the raised, toughened skin, a gossamer touch.

His expression changes then, thawing into tentative pleasure as my fingertips travel along his jaw, up and across his unblemished right cheek. His eyebrows are straight, yet sparse. His nose slightly rounded at the tip. And I was mistaken. His eyes are so much richer than I first perceived, gleaming black stones shaded by short eyelashes.

And somehow . . . somehow, we have drawn closer. I'm not sure who moves first, but as the East Wind cradles the back of my head, he brushes a soft kiss across my cheek. The scarred edge of his mouth grazes my skin, and my head sinks beneath high waves, the sea drawn into my lungs. Two heartbeats later, Eurus pulls back. I blink at him, dazed.

"Rest, bird." After easing me back onto the mattress, he tucks the blanket around my form. "You deserve it."

As he shifts away, I catch his hand, peer up into a face that is both familiar and wholly new. "Thank you," I whisper.

His mouth curls, the disfigured corner pulled taut. "Don't thank me," he says. "I've done nothing to earn your gratitude and everything to earn your spite. But tomorrow is a new day. I'm going to make this right."

Then he is gone, and I am left with the warmth of his gift, this darkness that is his and mine to share.

Part 2

What the Water Gives

19

*IN,*

Keep an eye on the East Wind's ax. In the meantime, you must find out more about him—his weaknesses, what he cares for. No detail is too small as it may grant us leverage when it comes time to ambush him.

I have reached out to my contacts. Prince Balior has mentioned this island you speak of. Or rather, his beastly companion has. Do you know when you're expected to return to the island? What of any protections placed around it? I assume the East Wind employs a number of defenses.

I've a buyer for the estate. The deal will be done by the month's end. You have until then to get me the ax.

—Clarisse

Fingers trembling, I tuck the slip of parchment into the pocket of my dress. End of the month. That's less than two weeks away. Either I deliver Lady Clarisse the ax, as promised, or the estate goes. The thought of returning to Marles with no home, no place to rest my head, no earth to dig my hands into, slicks my skin in a cold sweat.

"Good news, I hope?"

I lift my eyes to the Courier, who has claimed a table in the back of The Blind Oracle. Smoke uncurls between us, hazing the bright silver of his eyes.

"Yes." I plaster on a smile. "I appreciate you sending for me."

Yesterday, a palace messenger passed me a note, a single scrawled line from the Courier requesting my attendance. I waited until Eurus left this morning before venturing into the city.

"It was no trouble," he replies, taking a long, sucking drag from his pipe. "Though I do expect payment."

I blink, startled. "Oh. Right." I'd nearly forgotten. "What would you like in exchange?"

The Courier exhales a white cloud sweetened by clove. "What can you offer me?"

"I'm not sure—"

"Come now. Surely there's *something* you're adept at?"

Lady Clarisse would claim I haven't the experience, nor the title, to tout my expertise, but I don't necessarily share that viewpoint anymore. "As it turns out, I am a bit of a talent when it comes to herbology."

"Herbology." He looks me up and down. "Like plants and such?"

"Yes. For healing." In the fringe of my vision, a patron jostles our table, clearly inebriated. I wait until he stumbles off before continuing. "Is there something you would like mended or restored?"

The deity taps a finger against his glass of ale. The tavern could use a fresh coat of paint, but at least the glasses are clean—mostly. "My wife is with child. I'm worried it will be a difficult birth. What are my options?"

"That depends. Are you looking for a calming agent when she goes into labor, or a tea that offers strength when it flags? I've also a remedy that will provide additional nutrients for the unborn child." Nan notated an entire section related to childbirth in *The Practice of Herbal Remedies*, her calligraphy precise and clean.

The Courier contemplates his decision while dragging on his pipe. That he is willing to try my remedies, having never heard of me before, gives me hope there is room enough for my healing teas in St. Laurent. "What would you recommend?"

"The strength tea sounds like it would help. It will take a few days to create, but I will return once it is complete."

The Courier opens his arms, a king amongst his subjects. "Then I await your return, mortal."

I exchange the smoky tavern for the dry autumn air of the city proper. That is now two deities aware of my abilities. I only pray the information does not make it back to Eurus. But it felt meaningful, I realize, helping someone else. Using my skillset for *good*.

I take a longer route to the palace, cutting through one of the public gardens. Interlocking leaves enfold me in utter quiet, drawing forth those particularly intrusive thoughts. The East Wind, whom I have successfully avoided thinking about these past three nights—or so I tell myself.

I'm not certain whether I'm avoiding him or he's avoiding me. Eurus is gone before the sun rises and does not return until the stars appear, if he returns at all. When eve cloaks the world, I lie awake in bed, door cracked open, listening for the rustle of his wings, the cadence of his gait. I wish for space. I wish for company. Neither brings me peace.

And if he were to enter my bedroom, what then? He kissed me, yes, but I am not so foolish to believe there was any deeper sentiment to the gesture. It was but a moment of comfort exchanged between mortal and god. And yet, I think of it: the scrape of his stubbled cheek, the spice of his breath as it stirred the hair floating near my ear.

I quicken my pace, traversing a small footbridge that arches over a burbling brook. Regardless of who, exactly, is avoiding who, Eurus and I need to discuss the next steps. The final trial is in five days. Then? The victor's banquet, a poisoned Council of Gods. The timing could not be better. Eastern Blood is nearly complete.

And after? Home. But what that will look like is something I have avoided analyzing for any length of time. Her ladyship expects a speedy reply, and I do not want to disappoint her. But the thought of giving her more information that will be used against the East Wind hooks into my insides.

By the time I reach the palace, perspiration dots my skin, and I dab my forehead as I veer toward the kitchen. Though Eurus is probably out, I do not wish to tempt fate at this hour by returning to the suite. My emotions concerning the East Wind are painfully turbulent.

Outfitted in a flowing cotton dress and having gathered her hair in a messy knot atop her head, Demi busies herself chopping vegetables. A pot boils on the stove. It smells of garlic and sage.

"Good afternoon, Demi."

Her head snaps up. Heat reddens her cheeks, and perhaps the knowledge of being caught in the kitchen once more. "Min, hello to you." After wiping her hands on her apron, she adds the vegetables to the pot. It bubbles over, hissing as liquid hits flame, and the goddess swears, moving the pot toward a cooler area of the stove. "How do you feel about soup for lunch?"

In answer, I grab an apron, joining Demi at the counter. Even without her heels, the goddess is still ridiculously tall. At this point, my presence in the kitchen feels like second nature. I can almost imagine Nan standing over my shoulder, gently guiding me in preparing my first dish of fermented cabbage.

Spices have been laid out, all the colors of a painter's palette. We work in tandem, silent but for the simmering liquid and delicate birdsong tumbling through the open window. Once the vegetables have finished cooking, Demi sets the pot aside to cool.

"Something is different about you." She scrutinizes me, her eyes threatening to pry back whatever shield surrounds me. "You seem . . ." Yet she trails off, properly stumped.

I shrug with all the nonchalance I can muster, then proceed to sort through the spices. "There is much to celebrate. Eurus made it to the third trial, which means he is one step closer to winning, and I am one step closer to returning home."

Though I pray Demi will drop the subject, I should know better than to dangle a sweet before a child and not expect them to snatch for it.

"No." She shakes her head, tugging at her lower lip in thought. "That's not it. There's something about your face. You're blushing." And suddenly, all is made known. Demi's eyes pop. "You and Eurus didn't . . ." She gestures vaguely. "You know."

My face grows so hot I would not be surprised were it to crumble to ash. "N-no, of course not. H-he's my . . . well . . . it would be extremely inappropriate, not to mention odd, considering he's holding me captive until this bargain is fulfilled and—"

"You are not a very good liar, Min from Marles." That smile pulls wide, wide, wide. "I believe you when you say you haven't lain with Eurus, but there are other ways to share intimacy besides with one's body."

I'm well aware. My experience with men might be limited to only a single sweetheart, but I have learned enough. "We kissed," I whisper.

"Kissed! On the mouth or . . ." She winks. "Elsewhere?"

I tap my cheek, throat too stricken to work properly.

The skin around Demi's sparkling eyes pinches, she is grinning so hard. "And were you satisfied with this kiss, or did you perhaps want more?"

"Um." Is it appropriate to discuss this with Eurus' former lover? "Well—"

"Of course, you don't have to tell me if it makes you uncomfortable," she goes on, gathering bowls from the cupboard. "Obviously, I know how Eurus is. He is distant, yes, but there is a surprising warmth beneath the surface."

The idea of Eurus sharing a bed with Demi is not a thought I care to ponder. "Right," I say, my smile wilting.

Slowly, I stir the soup. Their relationship was in the past. The *distant* past. Eurus harbors no great affection for her. Indeed, his behavior toward the goddess more closely resembles resentment, if I'm not mistaken.

"Min," she says quietly.

"Yes?" *You're fine. It doesn't matter what occurred between them. Just focus on the task at hand.* "If there's anything else you n-need added—"

"Are you jealous, love?"

The ache grinds, and I wince, releasing the spoon as I turn to face Demi, who is beautiful and confident and has such presence, and I cannot convince myself that Eurus would ever feel anything for me, someone weak and mortal and terribly small.

"I don't know." Truth. "The kiss didn't mean anything." Lie. "Eurus doesn't have feelings for me." Truth. "Our relationship is a means to an end." Also truth.

Catching my chin between thumb and forefinger, she lifts my face upward, perusing my features with an intensity that would concern me if I did not trust that she would not harm me. This close, I smell the perfume of her skin: dandelion greens.

"A means to an end?" The goddess appears concerned by my explanation. She reaches around me to stir the soup, then grabs a ladle. "I want you to be careful, Min. I'm telling you this as a friend. The gods care only for themselves. I do not wish to see your heart broken when you are so eager to share it with him."

"That's not ..." Fact or falsehood? I can no longer distinguish between the two. "I'm n-not sharing my heart with Eurus," I state firmly.

"If you're sure." One ladleful into each bowl, steam rising from the hearty broth. "If it's any consolation, you have nothing to worry about when it comes to Eurus and me. That was over a long time ago, and there was never any stability to it, truth be told." After carrying the bowls to the table, she gestures me over, and we sit. Sun pours through the window, and I can almost convince myself I am back at the estate, or perhaps the manor, whose kitchen overlooks the sea.

Slipping a spoonful of soup into her mouth, Demi cants her head, rolling the flavor along her tongue. "Not bad. A bit more pepper, perhaps." She swallows down a second bite.

"Can I ask why things never worked out between you two?" As soon as the words leave my mouth, I gird myself against what will unfold.

"Eurus does not trust easily." She looks at me, and in her eyes, I see their shared history, what was whole and then broken. "If you are lucky enough to receive his trust, know that it is a gift. I did not realize its value at the time, and I broke it."

"How?"

She shakes her head. "I learned—too late, but I learned. It is a fragile thing, trust."

I lower my spoon into the bowl, my appetite having fled. *Trust?* I am luring the East Wind to his demise. What was shared in the dim of my bedroom days ago . . . it meant something to us both, I think. I do not wish him to come to harm, but I lived a life before we met. I have dreams. Don't I deserve to see them realized?

"Oh, drat!" Demi suddenly cries, shoving upright. "I forgot I'm supposed to meet Arin and his sister today. I need to leave a bit early, due to the blockades in the north."

"Blockades?" I stare at her in confusion.

"For the protests. They've closed off the roads. You haven't heard?"

I shake my head and begin helping Demi clean up. She washes the pans. I toss the vegetable scraps. She wipes the counters. I scrub the bowls and utensils. It's nice sharing the company of another. Dare I say a friend.

"Apparently," she says, "this Prince Balior is becoming more powerful than the divine are comfortable with. Some claim he wants to take over the mortal realms, but evidence suggests he's searching for a way into the City of Gods. The beast he is said to be traveling with cannot be located. The protestors are demanding action from the council."

That doesn't sound reassuring.

"Some think that whatever dark bond connects them has allowed the prince to drain the beast of its power," Demi adds as she dries her hands with a thin towel.

"Will the Council of Gods get involved?"

"There will need to be a vote, but it probably won't occur until after the tournament is complete. The divine do not appreciate when their entertainment is interrupted."

Once more, I am reminded that Demi and I come from completely separate worlds. If Prince Balior seeks to infiltrate the City of Gods, then Marles may be spared from whatever horrors he is planning. It is entirely possible that Lady Clarisse is aligned with the prince. Somehow, with gods protesting in the streets, I don't think it would be wise to mention that to Demi.

I am drying the last of the dishes when the back of my neck warms, touched by a gaze I cannot see. Calmly, I return the bowls to the cupboard, then turn. The East Wind stands in the doorway, cloaked head to toe in black, watching me.

"Eurus." Demi offers him a smile. The sight twists my stomach. "Had I known you were hungry, I would have saved you some soup. Unfortunately, Min and I ate it all."

"I'm not interested in soup, Demi." He then shifts his attention onto me. "Can we talk?"

Considering he's spent the last few days avoiding me, this is a surprise. But I nod, following him out of the kitchen and down the corridor until we reach an empty study. He gestures me inside, then shuts the door.

I glance around the room, if only to grant myself time to consider what I might say. Windows paneled in dark velvet. High-backed armchairs and a gleaming oak desk. When we last shared space, I learned what his breath might taste like, were I to allow it to flood my throat.

"Where have you been?" Eurus demands.

Beyond the expansive panes of glass, the city gleams beneath an autumn sun. It is the most beautiful place I have ever laid eyes on, but it is soured by the East Wind's absolute incompetence at communicating.

"Let's start with a proper g-greeting," I bite out, turning to look at him. "I suggest *good afternoon*, although *good day* would suffice."

"Maybe mortals enjoy wasting breath on menial greetings," he says, "but time is not on our side, bird."

I shake my head. He listens, but he does not truly understand. "It would take such little effort on your part," I say, "to treat me m-more kindly. What was it you said again, about making things right between us?"

The time for cowering is past. Today, and every day hence forth, I vow to honor myself, expel those rotting doubts from my core, the ones that tell me in no uncertain terms that I am not worthy of decency and respect.

"I'm doing my best," the East Wind says.

"No," I say. "You are barely making an effort. If this is what you consider your best, then I'm leaving."

I brush past him, and his seaside scent drags me down into memory. A dark and drowning tide I did not fight, but welcomed. I falter, yet force myself toward the door.

"Wait."

For half a heartbeat, I consider pushing out the door, but I don't. Maybe I am too softhearted.

"You're right. I'm sorry. That was rude of me. I . . ." His voice hitches as he fights to collect his words. "I am not very good at this."

"*This*, meaning acting like a d-d-decent person?" I say, turning around to study him.

The East Wind lowers his head in what may be shame. "Yes. I'm sorry for that. You were gone this morning. I went looking for you. When I couldn't find you, I feared something may have happened."

He was worried, I realize. Worried—and tormented by the emotion. "I didn't think you would notice that I was gone."

He steps toward me, long legs swallowing the distance, until the heat of his body buffets mine. "Why wouldn't I notice?"

He is so tall I'm forced to tilt back my head. "Because you've failed to make an effort to speak to m-me the last few days," I stutter.

There was a time when I would have left this thought unfinished. I would not press for more. I would not seek answers, assuming I was not worthy of knowing them. But it is a new day. "Why have you been avoiding me?"

Eurus steps back in surprise. "I haven't been avoiding you."

"Really?" I laugh. I can't help it. If I am a terrible liar, he is worse. "Where have you been sleeping then?"

"I haven't been. Sleeping, I mean."

Interesting. So, what, he has been wandering the palace grounds, flying off to who knows where, all to prevent himself from sharing a suite with me?

"I wasn't sure if you needed space after what happened," he murmurs. "I thought it better to give it to you."

"You mean since the kiss."

"Yes."

I've the notion to push back his hood so that I might see whatever reaction has captured his features. That he considered my comfort is unexpectedly sweet. "I appreciate that," I say, "but the suite is your space, too. It's not like we're sh-sharing a—" I fumble the word. "Bed."

His wings unfold, though only partially, a brilliant canvas of shining black. "Of course we would not share a bed," he says, but the words are strained, their edges crude. "You are, after all, mortal."

Should I take offense to that? "Why should that matter—being mortal, I mean?" I move toward the desk, rifle through the stack of documents to busy my hands, which long to peel the East Wind's cloak from his body so that I might see what lies beneath. There is something wrong with me. How can I look upon my captor and crave deeper intimacy?

"It doesn't," he hastily replies, then clears his throat. "Regardless, I'm glad to see you're all right. You're still gathering information from Demi, I assume?"

Why does he care so much about the goddess anyway? She is not even competing in the tournament. "I don't w-want to deceive her anymore. She's my friend."

I am fully expecting a scoff or some other adverse reaction to my statement, but no one is more surprised than I am when Eurus captures my hand, offers it a gentle squeeze. I stare at the curl of our fingers, dazed.

"Do not forget that Demi is one of the divine, bird," he says. "Just ... be careful. Do not let yourself be lured into a false sense of security simply because she does not resort to abuse."

His words give me pause. Is that what I have allowed myself to do? No lasting bruises, so she must be safe, right? But words, too, are weapons. They do not need to be sharpened to cause damage.

"All I know," I say, "is that Demi has been a friend to me when I have n-never had a single friend in my life. I appreciate that you are trying to protect me, but I trust her."

"Trust will get you killed," he mutters.

"Not everyone is an enemy, Eurus, and there is more to life than revenge. You could be happy, too, if you chose. Only you can decide how you wish to expend your energy, whether to avoid the pain, or work through it and let go."

"And have you?" he presses me. "Let go?"

I cling. I reach. I attach. Lady Clarisse was that person for me. But is she that person still? I'm not sure. Ten years caught beneath her thumb, and only in the last few weeks have I come to realize how little she gave me.

"I don't know," I whisper as the battle between mind and heart renews itself. "But I dearly hope to find out soon."

20

THREE WEEKS AGO, ONE HUNDRED AND TEN CONTENDERS SAT AT the welcome banquet. Now, a scant twelve competitors remain.

Despite the reduced attendance, the dining table, set beneath one of the garden pergolas twined with night-blooming jasmine, is adorned in brass and shining gold, every utensil having been polished to reflect the haze of candlelight. A rich, olive tablecloth offers a backdrop to the variety of fare served. Some are familiar, like chicken confit and ratatouille. Others are foreign: strange fruits I have never seen, fowl that is neither goose nor duck, quail nor hen. One dish crisps over an open flame.

Eurus and I sit side by side at the table, with Arin to my left. The three Fates are seated across from us, in addition to two other competitors, both burly warriors with scarred faces and shaved heads. Of course, the Council of Gods is present, as are additional guests, including Demi, who sits farther down the line.

Eurus and I spend the majority of the first course making small talk. At least, that is how it begins. Somehow, we navigate deeper, exploring his fondness for oil paintings—the reason so many grace the walls of his manor—and debating what makes the best cup of tea.

As the servants collect our empty plates, Eurus is pulled into conversation with his neighbor, and I turn my attention to Arin, who has kept to himself this evening. That concerns me, for the immortal is usually quite gregarious. "How are you, Arin?" I ask.

He attempts a smile. "I've been better, truth be told."

"Demi mentioned having visited your sister." I hesitate as the second course is served. It is none of my business, but— "How is she?"

He stirs the charred squash on his plate. The skin around his eyes appears bruised, suggesting lack of sleep. "Her seizures are occurring more frequently. At this point, there is nothing to be done."

"But she is immortal," I argue. "Shouldn't the seizures heal on their own?"

"It is true that our healing capabilities protect us from most wounds, and we are impervious to disease. But she was cursed long ago, and our healing abilities do not protect from dark enchantments. So long as my sister lives, she will suffer." He drops the fork onto his plate. Its sharp clatter draws the focus of those around him. "I try not to dwell on it."

It is not right that only one may claim victory. It leaves those like Arin, who wish only to help a loved one, dead, while others like the East Wind claim revenge. My heart aches to think of what Arin and his sister must bear if he is unable to win the council's favor.

A disturbance at the end of the table begins to draw others' attention. The Vintner—a malicious deity with yellow hair and a taste for wine—lifts his fourth (fifth?) glass in a toast, while tilting his chair onto its back legs. Unfortunately, the chair overbalances, and he crashes to the ground, his glass shattering. Servants rush forward with a flurry of napkins, which they use to mop his face and clothes.

Eurus snorts beneath his breath. "Damn fool."

After a few harried moments, attendants arrive to carry the Vintner from the garden. The moment he is gone, everyone breathes a sigh of relief, and the lightning god pushes to a standing position.

"First," he says in a voice that is as deep and clear as a forest pool, "I must congratulate you all for making it this far. You have persisted. That is no insignificant undertaking." He inspects the faces of those seated at the table, including mine. I blush and duck my head as he goes on. "Unfortunately, only one of you will have the opportunity to claim the prize: a favor of your choosing from the Council of Gods."

The remaining competitors straighten to attention, including the Fates who, thus far, have failed to show any interest outside of their own whispered discussion. In the corner of my eye, Eurus discreetly scans the table. Has he already finalized his plan for the council's demise? Of the twelve, who will be the first to fall beneath his blade?

"The final trial will commence in two days' time. There is no need to gather at the arena, nothing you need to do to prepare." A slow smile stretches his mouth. "The tournament will come to you."

A rush of puzzled whispers. Even Eurus appears befuddled. Leaning closer to Arin, I murmur, "I assume this is unprecedented?"

The dark-skinned deity nods. "I'm not sure what he means by this, but I suppose there is little point in ruminating. We will find out soon enough."

"For the final trial, you may use whatever powers, weapons, and surroundings are at your disposal to outlast your opponents and survive the obstacles the arena presents you. Only when one contender remains standing will the door reveal itself. But what comes between you and that door," says the lightning god shrewdly, "will determine whether you end the tournament in victory, or defeat."

The thought is sobering, and I no longer feel hungry. The East Wind must survive. He must end eleven immortal lives. He must end *Arin's* life.

It is kill or be killed.

Back in our suite, Eurus stands before the open window, his wings lax. After the smallest hesitation, I join him, staring out at the city lights.

It is a subtle thing, but his thumb skims the cotton of my dress where it meets my stocking. Heat blooms beneath my sternum, crawls up my neck. It would be easy to lean against him. Eurus would catch me, shelter me.

"Are you ready?" I whisper into the darkness.

The edge of his hood stirs, and I nearly reach up to tug it back, let the bright, bright moon cast the planes of his face in white. "No," he says. "But it must be done."

"You mentioned w-wanting the Council of Gods to reverse your banishment," I hedge softly. "Do you still want that?"

"Yes." He, too, speaks no louder than the lowest whisper. "Why?"

Was there a pause preceding his response, or did I imagine it? "Well ... it seems like you don't very m-much enjoy life in the city."

He shrugs, and something brushes the backs of my thighs. I startle, muscles tightening as warmth moves through my system. The edge of his scaled wing, I realize. He does not move it aside. Nor do I shift away. "It is the place where I was born. Why should I want something else?"

"But are you happy here?" When he does not respond, I press, "What if you used your favor differently?"

Now the East Wind faces me fully. I sense his suspicion, even if I cannot discern his expression. "Like what?"

"I was talking with Arin at dinner tonight." I clasp my fingers at my front so as to avoid tracing the bones of his wings. "He mentioned his s-sister. She is ill."

He regards me for an indeterminable amount of time. "Are you implying that I should use my favor to heal his sister?"

"Would it be so terrible?"

"The only way Arin's sister will be healed," Eurus growls, "is if Arin wins the tournament."

The notion is a swift kick to the gut. With Eurus dead, I would no longer be under his protection. They would come for me, these vultures, these wolves.

Wordlessly, I reach into my pocket, grasp the small vial of poison nestled inside. The opening of his hood angles downward, toward my outstretched palm. His massive hand curls around mine, Eastern Blood sheltered between.

"It is done," I say.

I expect him to release my hand. Instead, Eurus tucks his thumb against the inside of my wrist, where the pulse beats rabbit quick.

Lean forward. Close the distance. The desire to taste the East Wind's mouth is so compelling my teeth *ache*.

My tongue darts out to wet my lips. The weight of his gaze tracking the motion cannot be missed. "What is the plan?" I whisper.

Still, he stares at my mouth. Only when he glances elsewhere do I find myself able to breathe properly. "On the eve of the victor's banquet," he rumbles, "I will add Eastern Blood to the council members' drinks. Before the night ends, they will grant me my favor, my banishment reversed before they ever realize that poison weakens them. In the coming weeks, the Council of Gods will begin to fall. One by one, I will strike until they are gone. I will make sure that none suffer from their negligence again."

It is a wound, unhealed after all this time. It is not for me to decide how Eurus should repair it. However, I do not believe this is the answer. "What will happen when th-they are dead? Who will g-govern the city?" I ask.

"No one. It will fall to anarchy, most likely."

"And you are not troubled by this?"

"Not in the slightest."

My concern over the matter deepens, as does my guilt in playing a part in the collapse of the divine as we know them. "Eurus—"

"Please, bird." He lifts a hand. "Just for tonight, can we pretend we do not stand on opposite sides of war? I know you do not like it, but do not forget our bargain. I have something you want. You have something I want. For now, let that be enough."

He is right. I made my decision long ago. My mind will not change. Why should I hope the East Wind's would? "Understood."

I am acutely aware of Eurus' proximity, the heat of his long, muscular torso buffeting mine. I cannot be the only one struggling to breathe with any semblance of normalcy.

"The remaining competitors are going out tomorrow night," he abruptly states, voice strained. "Seeing as it is the final night before the trial, it is their last opportunity to let loose."

The change in topic takes me aback. "Let loose?" I did not think the East Wind was capable of such ease.

He crosses his arms, drops them to his sides, crosses them again. "Well, yes," he says gruffly. "I've noticed mortals are quite fond of the phrase."

I suppose he has a point. Our remaining days at the palace dwindle. The final trial, the victor's banquet, then: my return to Marles. Three days. That is all I have left in the realm of gods.

And then? A violent clash of mortal and divine. Following the East Wind's capture, Lady Clarisse will carve out his heart, all for the purpose of creating a potion that would extend her life indefinitely. The thought makes me horribly, unspeakably ill.

What if I ignored her message? I could pretend I never received it. Eurus would return me to St. Laurent, and with his banishment reversed, he could settle in the City of Gods. Without that god-touched weapon, her ladyship would in all likelihood refuse to sell me the estate. Could I live with that, my future undefined?

Whatever the answer, it is too complex a problem to solve tonight. "If you want to *let loose*, as you say, Eurus, I am not going to stop you." Though perhaps I'd hoped he would spend the evening with me. Foolish, to be certain.

"Bird." He stares at me long enough that I shift in place. "I'm asking if you would join me. Not as my assistant, but as my companion."

"Oh." I blink wide eyes. "L-like a—" I can't say it. I must say it. "Date?" I squeak out.

To my considerable shock, the East Wind shuffles his feet nervously. "I suppose that is something you mortals care for?"

I nod in response.

"Then would you do me the honor of accompanying me tomorrow evening?"

My every pore screams to reach out and touch him, grasp the fabric of his cloak, draw him close, toe to toe and groin to groin. By the Mother, there must be something wrong with me. "Y-yes! I mean—" I clear my throat. Too much enthusiasm? "I don't have anything to wear."

The East Wind gazes at me for two, three, four heartbeats. I can almost imagine his expression: a bit perplexed, a subtle softening. "Luckily, I know someone who does."

"I can't accept this."

The East Wind peers over my shoulder, comically large in the mirror's reflection. The drab black of his cloak looks out of place amongst the racks of jewel-toned gowns and diamond-encrusted accessories. Through the storefront windows, a small crowd has gathered, faces pressed against the glass. I ignore them.

"You can," Eurus says.

Demi pulled some strings. I'm not sure what she promised the shopkeeper, exactly, but the woman closed her store to accommodate a private dress fitting. *My* dress fitting. Granted, I only have the hour, but I never imagined I would be allowed such a privilege.

"I really can't." The silk of the blue gown pours like water over my body. "How much does this cost?" I imagine it to be exorbitant.

"Don't worry about the cost," he assures me. "If you like it, get it. It looks good on you."

The sapphire coloring *does* complement my pale skin and black hair. And yet, he likely doesn't understand what it means to be given something without expectation of recompense.

I bite my lower lip until the sting behind my eyes passes. Crying over silk. What is the world coming to? "I'll pay you b-back." Somehow. "Or I can wear a dress I already own." Plain cotton, but at least it is clean. My coat will conceal the small holes near the hem.

The East Wind eases closer, his chest brushing my spine. Heat floods my abdomen, and I straighten in the mirror, my expression flickering with an emotion better kept masked. If he removed his hood, might I see the ways Eurus was affected by our proximity as well?

"Is that what you want?" he asks.

I can imagine what Lady Clarisse would say. Keep your filthy hands off that fine silk, Min. You are good enough for digging in the dirt, but little else. "I don't know." Or perhaps I do know, but I'm afraid of accepting the idea that I deserve something this fine.

Eurus turns toward the shopkeeper. "We'll take it."

"What!" I spin around on the platform. "No, I can't. Really. I'll wear my own clothes."

But the goddess is already unbuttoning the gown. She proceeds to wrap it in delicate tissue paper before placing it in a box adorned with green satin ribbon. Eurus pays. It is a hefty sum, judging by the number of coins piled onto the counter. He offers me the box, and I hold it to my chest on our walk back to the palace, too overwhelmed by gratitude to speak.

Upon entering our suite, we hover in the middle of the chamber, staring at one another in uncertainty. We've less than two hours before we're to meet the other competitors in town. Time enough to bathe and dress, but little else.

My eyes dart to the washroom. "Should I . . . ?"

"I'll go first." He pivots jerkily, strides to the washroom, and shuts the door.

There is a splash, followed by a long, satisfying groan. Warmth skitters up my arms, for the sound is base, twined with all manner of pleasurable things. *He is bathing, and bathing is not sexual.* Except now I'm imagining the East Wind drawing the wet cloth across his pectorals, down his hard abdomen. Though I have never seen his torso, nor any glimpse of his body, I have been held against his chest, felt the strength in his arms. The East Wind's physique is unabashedly male, taut with untapped power.

Somehow, my thoughts wander to his wings. I never considered how Eurus fits into the tub. Does he drape them over the edge? Keep them submerged against his body?

Blowing out a breath, I force my legs into motion and cross to my bedroom window, shoving back the curtains. The City of Gods, striking as a whetted blade. I wonder how the manor fairs in the East Wind's absence. Is she able to occupy herself, or does she require his presence to function? It would not be so bad to return, if only for a short visit.

Unfortunately, my thoughts again veer toward the image of Eurus bathing. Rather than shut my mind to the temptation, I willingly follow it down and down and down into the dark, where experience lies in sensation, taste and sound and touch.

"Bird."

"Y-yes?" I cross my arms, drop my arms, wipe my face, straighten my clothes. Finally, I turn, but the doorway is empty. "Eurus?"

"In here."

Ah. I stride for the washroom. "Do you need something?" I press my ear to the cool wooden door.

He clears his throat. "In my haste to bathe, I realize I forgot to bring a change of clothes with me."

"Oh." Breathy and low. "Where—"

"In the dresser, back of the bottom drawer, there should be trousers and a long-sleeved gray shirt."

I nod exuberantly, which is silly, considering he cannot see me. "I'll get them."

I all but flee to the East Wind's bedroom, pulling open the lower drawer of his dresser. Recalling his desire for everything in its place, I remove the clothes he asked for without disturbing anything else, but a small notebook tumbles onto my lap, falling open to a random page.

Black ink, heavy scrawl. A single phrase, written over and over, top to bottom, page after page after page.

You are nothing.
You are nothing.
You are nothing.
You are nothing.
You are nothing.

Immediately, I close the book. My body feels shaky, scooped hollow of substance. Those words were not for my eyes. They were for no one. If this is what he thinks of himself ... I hurriedly stuff the notebook back into his dresser, wanting to be rid of those poisoned words.

"Bird?"

My understanding of the East Wind deepens to a frightening degree. I understand what it is to wake up each morning and know you are low, worse than low, not even worthy of acknowledgment. I understand, too, the difficulty in living your life around this truth. How parts must be stretched or lessened or locked away to accommodate this ravenous belief, which leaves air for nothing else.

Pushing to my feet, I return to the washroom. "Your clothes," I say through the door.

It cracks open, allowing Eurus' hand to slide through. Moments later, he emerges, lemon-scented steam clouding his back, beads of water clinging to the rising peaks of his beautiful wings.

But—his cloak. My heart sinks in sight of it, woven fabric draping him head to toe, for I had hoped he would go without, at least in the privacy of our suite.

As if sensing my shift in mood, Eurus comes forward. "What is it, bird?"

"Will you not remove your hood?" I ask quietly.

He glances toward the entrance of the suite. The set of his shoulders reminds me of a soldier readying himself for war.

"The door is locked," I reassure him. "No one will see you but m-me."

The East Wind is not easily swayed. Yet I ask him for this one thing, and he complies, pushing back his hood to reveal a countenance thrown into harsh relief in the late afternoon sun. The raised scarring crawls across his left cheek, the roundness of his chin, even to the edge of his sparse eyebrow. I recall meeting his brother, Zephyrus, and wondering how Eurus' appearance compared to that of the green-eyed, curly-haired mortal. The differences between them make me ponder what his other brothers look like.

Lifting a hand, I cup his face. My thumb sweeps the rise of his sharp cheekbone. A quiet agony clouds his features, skin drawn taut and mouth condensed into a seam.

"Is this the only place you have scarring?" I question.

"No." He stifles a shudder as I trail gentle fingertips along his jaw, down to the dip of his collarbone. "My chest and back, too."

And if I were to tug aside his cloak, might I witness these scars, and map their swells and divots? But of course, I do not. I have *some* propriety. "They appear to be burn marks."

Eurus leans closer so the flat of my hand curves around the side of his neck. This close, I can count the hairs bristling his jaw.

"They are," he whispers, eyes half-lidded, hazed black, black, black. "After my successful mutilation, my father wanted to create something even greater, some creature impervious to harm—fire and flood, sword and spear." The muscles of his throat contract beneath my palm. "As you can see, it didn't work."

"I'm sorry," I whisper.

The East Wind searches my face. "Why? You had nothing to do with it."

A small, sad smile bows my mouth, and I drop my hand, already mourning the warmth of his skin. "It's called empathy, Eurus. You should try it sometime."

He snorts and begins tugging his hood forward, but I stay his hand. "Wait." What, exactly, is there to fear in asking? Eurus is not Lady Clarisse. He will not lay a hand on me for speaking out of turn. "Have you considered attending tonight's event just as you are—without the cloak?"

He regards me in thinly veiled surprise. I swallow, wondering if I have overstepped, if I even have the right to ask this of him.

He says, in a rare display of vulnerability, "You have seen the divine, bird: flawless miens, unblemished skin. I don't wish to draw attention to myself. I know how unsightly my features are."

"They're not unsightly," I argue.

"They will stare."

"Only for a time. Eventually, they will get used to it, grow bored, and shift their focus elsewhere."

Eurus tugs at his hood self-consciously. "I would rather not."

Today, I am bold.

I step further into the East Wind's space until we are chest to chest and I am peering up at him. *You are nothing*, he wrote to himself. I have never read something so untrue.

"Our suffering does not make us ugly," I whisper. "The people that hurt us—*they* are the ones with ugly hearts. You were hurt, yes, but you endured and will continue to endure. That is a beautiful thing."

"And you," he says lowly, his eyes singeing me from soles to scalp. "You, too, have endured."

I have. I'm still here, still breathing. I may only be a mortal woman from Marles, but I try my best to do what's right. I was not broken then, and I'm not broken now.

"I like that your features are n-not perfect," I murmur. "I like that your face shows me of your life and helps me understand what kind of person you are and why." The longer I am caught within the intensity of his gaze, the more I am convinced I will burn and burn and burn. "The ridge on your cheek reminds me of the earth, which is beautiful despite its cracks. The color of y-your eyes reminds me of black opals." Rare in Marles, incredibly rare. "And I like your smile," I add teasingly.

Eurus stares at my mouth. "I never smile."

"I know." Naught but a whisper. My stomach is doing strange acrobatics without my consent.

"But your smile ... yours is one I would definitely remember," he murmurs.

I lose my train of thought at the curving of his mouth. "I should ... Um. I should w-wash ..." Snagging the gift box, I slip into the washroom and shut the door.

The bathing chamber is quite roomy, with a carved bench to place one's clothing, a sink and toilet, shelves of soaps and plush towels, a wall mirror, and an enormous marble tub sunken into the jade-tiled floor. After running myself a bath, I shed my clothes and submerge myself into the scalding water with a gratified sigh, enjoying how the heat scratches at my skin.

Arms, legs, chest, face—all scrubbed until they glow pink. When I am done, I climb from the tub, pull a comb through the long strands of my hair, dab powder and lip rouge onto my face, then slip on my new gown. It slithers over my skin like falling rain, bathing me in the most beautiful blue hue.

The back gapes open, in need of buttoning, but I struggle to secure the fabric. A sigh of frustration leaves me. If only my arms were longer.

"Everything all right, bird?" Eurus sounds as if he stands just outside the door.

Again, I reach for the fastening to no avail. "I can't get my dress buttoned."

"Can I come in?"

I suppose there is nothing indecent about it. I am dressed, as is he. And Eurus has very long ... arms. "Yes."

He opens the door.

I startle. "Your cloak." He has done away with it. In its place is a body that is even more impressive in fitted clothing. His long-sleeved gray shirt is tucked into the waistband of his trousers, a brown leather belt emphasizing the cut of his hips, and those boots he is never without. "You look n-nice."

Eurus rubs the back of his neck self-consciously. "Thank you." Our eyes catch and hold.

Head ducked, I turn, presenting him my back.

His touch, when it alights, sends a shivering cascade of sensation along my bones. The roughened tips of his fingers brush the vertebrae of my spine, each risen hill, and I tense, breath held as the warmth of his exhalation stirs the crown of my head. I expect Eurus to button the fabric. Instead, he grazes the lines of welts marking my back, all kissed by the cold leather of Lady Clarisse's lash. I shudder, fighting the urge to lean back into his solidity.

"Your wounds have healed well," he comments.

I nod. Too enthusiastically, perhaps. "The manor left me a strong healing salve. It helped with the pain."

Down, down his hand drags, halting at the base of my spine, the rise of my backside. I can't breathe, I can't *breathe*.

His hand falls away, and Eurus begins securing the buttons from my lower back to the stem of my neck. My heart beats with new awareness. The salve, and my wounds, and his observation of them. His knowledge of her ladyship hurting me. "The manor left me the salve," I whisper, "right?"

Still, the East Wind elects for a non-response.

"Eurus—"

"You were in pain," he explains. "It was the only thing I could offer you at the time."

I turn to face him. How can I not? Gazing into his eyes, I wonder how it is possible to judge someone so wrongly. The East Wind noticed my suffering when I'd believed him to be immune. "Thank you," I whisper.

He searches my face as I search his, likely for the simple pleasure of exploring its terrain. Then his attention slides lower, across the gown draping my body. The design does the impossible and grants me hips, even a small bust.

The East Wind's mouth curves in what is *almost* a smile. I dearly hope it is not the last. "You look lovely, bird."

The affection in his tone sets fire to my cheeks. "As do you."

He offers me his arm. "Shall we?"

Together, we depart the palace and wander the streets as eve bruises the eastern horizon. A winter-kissed breeze coaxes out heavy coats, including my own, but I revel in the sting on my skin, the tip of my nose, all reminders that I am alive.

The divine purchase hot chocolate, mulled wine, roasted nuts. A few strangers glance curiously at Eurus in passing, unable to recognize him without his hood, his cloak open at the front. Most, I'm pleased to note, do not spare his scars significant attention.

Eventually, we reach a tavern called A Thousand Ships, its porch illuminated by the glow of oil lamps. From inside, a percussive drumbeat accompanies a string ensemble, and the lively jig calls for a toe-tapping good time.

The door swings open. Out stumbles a three-eyed god, who narrowly avoids crashing into Eurus. Catching the porch railing, the man straightens, squinting at this newcomer for a long, uncomfortable moment.

"Something you want to say?" the East Wind growls.

The man opens his mouth, then clamps it shut, perhaps having come to the conclusion that speaking would not bode well for him. He shakes his head and shoves past us, staggering down the street.

I look to Eurus. "Ready?"

But he is not looking at me. He is peering through the front windows of the tavern, its every chair and booth occupied, its tables packed, few places to hide.

"Do you want to turn back?" I venture.

He brushes a finger across the scarring puckering his left eye, his grimace all the more frightening in the dim. "I don't know, bird." Inside, a glass shatters. The barkeep releases a string of expletives while the ensemble churns out its melodious merriment. "They will see."

"We all have our scars," I say softly. "There is no shame in them. Some just happen to be more prominently displayed."

"It is not so easy, bird."

"Isn't it?"

I see you, I think. *I am not afraid.* "Will you hide away in the shadows?" I challenge him. "Or will you finally face the light?"

A low rumble of frustration emanates from his chest. But when I say, "You are not alone," some of the tension leaves him, and the skin around his eyes smooths. With a deep breath, Eurus reaches for the door handle and pushes inside.

21

It takes less than a heartbeat for conversation to cease. As one, heads turn. I sense the desire to flee coiling in Eurus' limbs. Centuries he has hidden his face, yet tonight, the veil is lifted, his every brutal scar on display. It means something that he is here, exposed to the world. It means a great deal.

With what seems to be the entire tavern watching, I tuck my hand alongside his wide, callused palm. I have nothing to be ashamed of. I am no immortal, but I am dressed appropriately for the evening, as are all who occupy the establishment, a place of gleaming wood and glossy brass and old leather booths.

"Whatever happens," I whisper to Eurus, "remember that it takes strength of heart to show yourself in this manner. They cannot take that away from you."

A subtle quiver shimmers down his arm, through his wrist and fingers. The East Wind is resilient, but he is not unfeeling. He has closed himself off for so long he has forgotten what it means to form deep connections with others.

"Well, well, well, look who it is!" someone crows.

I startle, reality rushing forth to fill the gaps in our surroundings, as a man dashes toward us, his features somehow magnified: bulging eyes and a wide, slitted mouth, and red corkscrew curls flopping across his brow.

"Could it be?" the immortal exclaims. "Eurus himself? Why, I haven't seen you in centuries!"

He lunges toward the East Wind, who blasts the stranger clear across the room. The man crashes into a table, and playing cards explode in countless directions. Those whose gambling has been disturbed turn to glare at Eurus. Thankfully, a kind-hearted goddess helps the fallen man to his feet—then picks his pockets.

Her victim fails to notice, too busy brushing himself off with a good-natured grin. "Not one for affection, I see. But you do remember me, right?" He taps his chest with both hands. "Jem? We lived across the street from one another as boys?"

Patrons return to their gambling, their drinking, their conversations, the sight of the East Wind's bared face already forgotten behind the haze of ale and wine.

Meanwhile, Eurus considers the newcomer, head cocked. "You wore blue sweaters. Every day, even in summer."

"You remember!" He plucks at his—yes, blue—sweater before shifting his attention onto me. "And this must be the mortal woman everyone is talking about."

As I remove my coat, Eurus slides a hand across my lower back. The shock of his touch whitens my thoughts momentarily. "This is—"

"Min, there you are." Demi materializes as if from thin air. She is striking in a crimson gown. The gossamer material clings to every generous curve, and slender black heels place her a head taller than most. "Oh, Jem, I believe someone is calling for you." She flits her fingers toward the bar, which is so swarmed with clients I cannot see the barkeep. The immortal skips off, much to our relief.

"That'll keep him occupied," Demi murmurs conspiratorially, taking a sip from her wineglass. "I'm so glad you could make it. Min, you look radiant. Doesn't she look radiant, Eurus?"

Deliberately, she dips her chin at him, eyes smoldering beneath the fan of her lowered lashes. My gut knots itself, and I hurriedly look away. Demi assured me I had nothing to worry about when it came to her friendship with the East Wind. So why does my throat sting with bitterness?

"She does."

My head swivels toward the East Wind. His gaze has gentled, and he traces the scooped neckline of my dress with a callused fingertip before catching a tendril of my hair and tucking it behind my ear. When his fingertips brush the lobe, a fresh wave of heat splits my skin.

His touch does much to temper my envy of the goddess, enough that I can calmly face her and say, "Thank you again for organizing my dress fitting. I really appreciate you for that, Demi."

"It's no trouble. I'm happy to help a friend." She flutters her fingertips at a passing server, coaxing the man closer to provide a refill. "Arin and I have a booth in the back. Won't you join us?" She points to where Arin nurses a tumbler of whiskey. When he catches my eye, he waves. I wave back. The East Wind waves to no one.

"Actually, Eurus and I were going to grab a table for ourselves, if that's all right w-with you." I claim the East Wind's hand, vaguely noting his surprise.

Her eyebrows pinch with tempered humor. "I understand. It's the evening before the final trial. Who knows if it will be your last together?" Before I can begin to dissect that statement, she adds, "We'll be around, should you decide to join us," then saunters off.

Her parting instills a subtle agitation in my bones, the desire to call her back and demand an explanation. "What do you think Demi meant by *Who knows if it will be your last together*?" I ask Eurus, pitching my voice over a colorful riff from the guitarist.

"Does it matter?" He is still peering at our clasped hands. "As far as I'm concerned, this tournament is already won."

Fair point.

Eurus glances around the space. Unexpectedly, a table becomes available by luck. Or rather, the East Wind glares so hard at a group of deities that they abandon their table as though it is land ceded in war. I fight a smile as I take a seat, draping my coat over the chair back. "Was that really necessary?"

"It was." Rather than sit on the opposite side of the table, he selects the chair closest to me, wings splayed out in a cascade of ebony scales. Our knees touch. I pretend not to notice.

A server drops two tankards of ale onto our table. Eurus takes a healthy swallow. In the gloom of our isolated corner, I watch the length of his throat work, the play of ocher light dancing along the bridge of his nose and the cut of his cheek. It is a marvel to see flesh, to know he is real.

As though sensing my gaze, his eyes catch mine. I yank my drink closer, take a hearty gulp—and nearly spit it out. "Ugh."

"Not very pleasant, is it?" he asks, expression wryly amused.

My tankard hits the table with a dull *thunk*. "Not really, no. I thought everything here tasted of ambrosia."

"A common misconception. The truth of the matter is, the gods enjoy a foul-tasting ale every now and then."

"I can't imagine why," I choke out.

His mouth stretches wide then, parting around a set of beautiful white teeth. I stare at him, stupefied. "Your smile!"

It is gone by my next heartbeat. "Apologies." He sounds furious and hurt. "My scarring sometimes pulls my features into unpleasant shapes."

"It's not that. I've just . . . I've never s-seen it before." My ears tingle with heat, and my face, and my chest. "It's really quite lovely. Your s-smile, I mean."

He appears to have been made deeply uncomfortable by my admission. Fearing I have overstepped, I quickly attempt to repair the damage. "I'm sorry. I simply wanted you to know I don't see any part of you as distasteful, but I know I'm not always the best with w-words. I think you are h-h-handsome."

"Handsome," murmurs the East Wind thoughtfully. His eyes meet mine over the rim of his glass. They darken subtly, and my belly heats. "Do you know what my father used to say when I was a boy, in the hours after he had spent torturing me?"

I shake my head.

"He told me I was worth nothing, and that this pain was a gift. For millennia, I believed him. But having met you, I now see that the shame he felt toward me, the hatred and anger, was just a byproduct of the mistake my mother had made."

"What do you mean?"

He stares at a point over my shoulder. There is a distance between us, though he sits within reach. "I was not my father's son."

"What?" I lean closer, for his voice is swiftly buried under the cacophony of the tavern.

"My mother had an affair, though to this day I do not know with whom. Following my birth, I assume my father suspected something was amiss. He did not have proof, but he had his doubts. Like my brothers, I inherited my ability to control the winds from my mother. But I also inherited a power none in my family had—power over storms, rains, lightning. I was on the cusp of manhood when my mother finally admitted to my father the truth of my birth," he says. "He killed her, and the abuse began not long after."

One of the servers collects the empty tankards from a nearby table and hangs them over her curved horns before moving off. When I glance toward the booth Demi and Arin share, I detect the goddess staring our way. Quickly, I turn my back, wondering what she finds so interesting about our conversation.

"I'm sorry you suffered that alone," I reply, catching his fingers in mine. "Did your brothers know that you did not share a father?"

Tentatively, he allows his hand to relax against my palm. His wings stir and resettle. "I never told them, but I would not be surprised if Notus knew. Of all my brothers, he alone would be keen enough to make the connection."

"Might it be worth broaching the s-subject with him?"

"No." He shakes his head. "I have done enough damage already." Noting my confusion, he elaborates, "That mortal everyone's been talking about—Prince Balior? It is in part my fault that he has gained this dark power."

"Wait. *Your* fault?"

He gathers himself before saying, "Long ago, I imprisoned the beast—the creature he travels with—in a labyrinth built in Ammara's capital city. At some point, Prince Balior must have entered the labyrinth, promising to free it in exchange for siphoning some of its power. I did not think the beast would escape, nor did I particularly care."

"Why did you imprison it?"

His lips twist in some cruel imitation of a smile. "The beast was an abomination, the bastard progeny of a woman and a bull. It did not belong in the City of Gods. Or maybe *I* thought I did not belong, with my hideous mutation. I looked at that beast, and I saw myself."

"Eurus," I whisper.

"Look, what's done is done. I should not have imprisoned the monster, but it escaped regardless, and together with Prince Balior, it destroyed Ammara's capital—Notus' home."

Which was already suffering from drought, if I recall correctly. "But if you were in Marles, who was watching over the beast?"

Before he can respond, the door to the tavern rams open, and in stumbles a large group of blue-skinned gods and goddesses, their brows wreathed in laurel leaves.

"The mortal king of Ammara was willing to do anything to save the life of his newborn daughter, who was born frail. In exchange for Ammara's rains and the king's promise that he would maintain the labyrinth, I used some of the beast's dark power to borrow twenty-five years of life for the infant girl—but it was a cursed existence."

It is a slow thing, this emergent horror. I can only listen as he goes on, the depths of his selfishness and malevolence brought into sharp relief beneath the low lighting of the tavern.

"I thought I had washed my hands of it." As Eurus speaks, he looks elsewhere: the front door, the crowded bar, the couples dancing before the ensemble. Anywhere but at my face. "But years later, I learned the king's daughter had grown, and Notus had fallen in love with her."

"The child you cursed grew up to be your brother's *lover?*" I whisper in dismay.

A muscle tics in his jaw, and he traces his scarred cheek, chin to temple and back. "She wasn't his lover at the time. Then, she was only an infant. I didn't care about the consequences when I made my bargain with the king. I took Ammara's rains," he says in a tone I now recognize as remorse, "because I needed more power to fuel the storm surrounding the manor."

"To keep others out," I clarify.

"Yes." It is quiet, this word. Quiet and defeated. "I believed I offered nothing good—to anyone. Not to family, and certainly not to the world. So when my brothers and I were banished, I did everyone a favor, and I flew to a place I knew none would go, and it was there I built my life on the rock in the middle of the sea."

The clink of glasses fills the silence that swells to swarm us both. What do you say when the person you have grown to care for reveals mistakes from their past? Choices that have led to grave peril? The destruction of others' lives?

"What you did," I whisper to the East Wind, "was wrong."

He flinches, the fingers of one hand curling into a fist. "I know."

"But I understand."

He loosens a breath, and his other hand envelops mine, squeezing so tightly my bones creak. In times of drowning, we seek the rock, the pillar, the ledge. Tonight, I will be that rock for him.

"I've been thinking about what you said before, about the drought," Eurus murmurs. "You're right. My actions have consequences."

It is what I'd hoped for him. "What will you do?"

The toe of his boot nudges my ankle. Even that brief contact coaxes my pulse higher. "I know what must be done, but . . . I don't know if I'm ready. The storm is my protection. Yes, people are suffering, but—" He releases a self-conscious laugh. "Is it stupid that it makes me feel safe?"

"No," I whisper. "It's not stupid at all."

"A part of me wonders if giving up the rains will leave me open to attack. I'm not saying no," he adds hurriedly, perhaps sensing my apprehension. "I'm saying I need more time to decide."

It is more than I ever expected from the god who once spoke of others' suffering as though it were of no more significance than an unexpected drizzle.

We relapse into companionable silence. I drink the horrid ale, if only to prevent myself from doing something rash, like reaching for the East Wind instead.

"I want to apologize, bird." He swallows. "Min."

"Again? For what?"

The moment his black eyes capture mine is the moment I recognize that I have changed, as has he. I have despised him, I have loathed him, I have judged him, I have scorned him. But we are threads of the same loose weave, hardship fraying our lives. I cannot despise the East Wind unless I despise myself.

"For how wrong I was to judge you," he says. "For doing everything in my power to hurt the one person who might be able to help me. For failing to see that who you are is separate from who you work for. For not lifting you up when you needed it. For withholding gratitude and appreciation. For making your time here horrible. For taking you from your home." He trails off, his expression troubled. "And that is only the surface."

We could be in a tavern, or a ballroom, or a library, or the middle of the street. It wouldn't matter. My awareness of our surroundings has long since faded, and there is only the East Wind to anchor me to reality.

"I'm sorry," he says again, voice hoarsening. "For everything."

That he cares enough to admit his transgression shows how far the East Wind has come since our tumultuous beginning all those weeks ago. "Thank you, Eurus. Really. Thank you." I do my best not to peer at him too closely for too long. His face fascinates me.

Apparently, his is not the only face others find fascinating. I have been so engrossed by our discourse that I have failed to realize that I, too, have become an object of interest to the divine seated at the surrounding tables.

"They stare," I whisper.

"Because you are radiant, as Demi said," he murmurs. "There can be no other reason."

I shift in my chair, strangely breathless. "Or because I d-don't belong."

"What if I say that you do?"

My body leans toward him and the warmth that is promised. What does he mean, exactly? Belong here, in the City of Gods? Belong with *him*?

But it is a dangerous edge to toe, and so I retreat a step into safer waters. "What comes after?"

"After?"

"When the tournament is done. After you have won." *And killed the Council of Gods.*

His knee brushes mine. My eyes drop to the point of contact, his heavy thigh cloaked in the stiff fabric of his trousers, mine concealed beneath layers of silk. The clamor of the tavern dulls, as though steeped in a heavy fog.

"I promised I would take you back to St. Laurent if you helped me, and I keep my promises. Unless," he says with new intensity, "you have changed your mind?"

Weeks ago, I would have reaffirmed my desire to return home. Now, I question the decision. Should I wish to open my own practice—and I believe that I do—Lady Clarisse will do everything in her power to sabotage me. And then what? Homeless and out of work. Nan's legacy forever buried. "I don't know."

"Why do you want to return to your old employer so badly?" he presses. "You know she will return to mistreating you. It may even be worse than it was previously."

He is right. The moment I return, I will be punished. The only question is how severely.

"It's not that I wish to return to *her*, necessarily, but if I want to be promoted to bane weaver, then I need to return to the estate. Do you expect me to just leave and start over with n-nothing, at a place I have no ties to, with people I cannot trust to have my best interests at heart?"

"That witch has never had your best interests at heart," he argues. "And I question what will change, if anything, should you return to her."

"What do you mean?"

"What of the immortals she's taken prisoner? Will you return to your former life and do nothing as you did prior to coming here? Will you listen to their cries of pain and turn a blind eye?"

The churning in my gut hitches, for I can recall with frightening clarity how those cries broke against the walls of the estate. "I d-don't agree with her ladyship's t-treatment of immortals," I squeeze out, feeling suddenly small and pitiful, little more than the gunk wiped off the bottom of someone's boot.

"So what will you do to stop her?" His tone has softened.

"I d-don't—" I shake my head, throat stricken. He's right. For all the years of my life, I did nothing. I was forever frozen by the fear of being cast out, drowned simply for the idea of existing. "I-I-I—"

"It's all right, bird." Eurus cups my cheek, and I calm. "We don't have to discuss this right now."

Thank the Mother of Earth for that. Reaching for the ale, I drink deeply, then drop the tankard onto the table with a retching sound. "Truly, this is awful."

He chuckles. "Then why drink?"

Because it is less awful than granting space to the idea that returning to St. Laurent does not hold the same allure as it once did. Because I am not prepared to dissect the ways I have changed.

Here is what I know: I have grown to care for the East Wind, a man of brutish character, rigid boundaries, severe perspective, and gross misunderstanding—or so I thought. He is officious, yet wounded. He clings to control to build security within himself. He is a product of his environment, as am I, as are we all. But even the hardest stone erodes should water impact its surface frequently, over lengths of time.

"I'm going to get another drink," Eurus says. "Do you want something?"

My head tilts back to keep him in my sight as he stands, tucking his wings safely against his spine. "Water, please." I watch him leave. I'm helpless to do otherwise.

Settling back in my seat, I use the opportunity to peruse the crowd. Arin speaks with a flaxen-haired young man in a distant corner. At least, he *appears* young. A brown-skinned goddess, a bow slung across her back, makes an impressive picture as she slips through the throng, two wolves at her heels. Additionally, the Fates sit at the bar, conversing with each other. When one catches my eye, her hand drifts threateningly to the weapon at her hip. My stomach drops, and I hurriedly glance elsewhere.

Eventually, a new thread weaves itself through the rise and fall of conversation. Laughter, but like nothing I have heard before: hoarse with disuse, the grind of stone on stone.

I turn, and there he is, propped against a wall across the room as he lifts a full tankard of ale to his mouth, the gray fabric of his shirt stretched alluringly across his broad chest. The East Wind, laughing. He is magnificent. *Free.*

But there is Demi, having sidled close. With one hand propped on a sultry hip, she snorts out an answering titter. They appear to be having a merry time.

I turn my back, gulp my drink. Eyes closed, deep breath. I've never heard Eurus laugh before. It must take a woman—no, a *goddess*—who knows him intimately to draw out the sound I have most yearned to hear. How could a mortal like me ever hope to bring joy to the divine?

Except ... Eurus arrived with *me*. He bought *me* this dress, called *me* radiant, his focus on *me* alone as we spoke. He made me feel important. He made me feel *alive.*

I do not need to mask myself in another's shadow. I can claim space for myself, not as the East Wind's employee, not as his captive or mortal *pet*, but as Min, a bane weaver from Marles. Someone honorable and trustworthy and true.

Setting down my ale, I slip through the throng toward Eurus and Demi. As the goddess' voice reaches me, however, I halt, partially shielded behind one of the structural beams.

"You care for her." She taps her glass with a fingernail, yellow eyes narrowed as she regards her former lover. "It's all right, Eurus. There's nothing to be ashamed of. Plenty of us have had relations with mortals."

"It's none of your business," he growls.

"I disagree. Min is my friend, and as her friend, it's my duty—"

He pushes off the wall, wings flaring in warning. "She means nothing to me, understand? Once she helps me win the tournament, I'll have nothing to do with her, or you, for that matter."

There is a great buzzing in my ears, like a hive. It momentarily mutes the clamor of the busy tavern.

Then all at once, sound comes rushing back: the clink of glass, the shudder of the floorboards, the sigh of crisp air as the front door squeals open.

I feel sick.

"Look." Demi sets her wineglass on a nearby ledge. "There is no need to pretend. I see what is happening here. We all do."

His eyes flash dangerously. "There is no pretense. If I'm not mistaken, Min has already informed you of our arrangement. Is that correct?" Her silence is all the affirmation he needs. "Then you understand this was always a business transaction. I feel nothing for Min, and this is the last I'll speak of it. Do we understand each other?"

Someone jostles me from behind, breaking my daze, but I manage to catch the shock written across the goddess' features, hurt on my behalf. My throat swells. I suppose I now know who is truly my friend.

"I thought better of you," Demi scolds Eurus. "I thought you had changed, that your heart had softened."

"Don't talk about my heart," he snarls. "You know nothing of me, of my life."

She studies him calmly. "Min cares for you. How can you not see that?"

No more. I can take no more of this.

Spinning around, I shove through the crowd, jabbing aside bodies with my elbows, forcing a clear path toward the exit. Everything Eurus and I shared . . . it meant nothing. Here I was, thinking we had begun to form a connection, something deeper than the skin. *Stupid.* I was always going to be used. I would only be accepted for what I could provide. And I fell for it. Have I not learned?

The crowd parts, and there is the door, its silver bell a subtle shimmer. I quickly snag my coat. My heart feels like it has been wrenched in two, yet from that pain, a bright fury is born. All I have given, all the time and effort, the understanding and patience and yielding and distress, and for what? To be dismissed as though I am *nothing*? I have spent the better part of my life trying to escape that bottomless hole of suffering.

Now that the East Wind has expressed his genuine feelings toward me, I have no further scruples in handing him over to Lady Clarisse. What matters? The estate, Nan, my future. Regardless of who wins the tournament, I will not remain trapped here. There are things I must do, plans to put into motion. Eurus thinks I will help him willingly?

We will see.

22

I STEP OUTSIDE THE TAVERN INTO POURING RAIN. IT SLICKS THE cobblestones, drips furiously from the porch eave. Thunder cracks. The sky whitens, cleaved apart by lightning.

Head ducked against the onslaught, I carefully pick my way over the slippery ground, water smearing the city lights' reflections. In seconds, my coat is drenched, as well as the gown beneath. It is a chilled rain, a frigid soaking. Unfortunately, that can't be helped.

Few lamps illuminate the flooded roads. My eyes sting in the next chilly gust, and I bring my hands to my mouth, huffing into the cupped space to thaw them. As I exchange one shadowy intersection for another, my shoulder knocks someone in passing. Before I can apologize, they stride off, vanishing into the downpour.

While A Thousand Ships was festooned with customers and merriment, The Blind Oracle is all but dead, smothered in deep shadow. Only a handful of immortals occupy the space, most having congregated by the fireplace. Here, the music is of a more rudimentary nature: the grate of glass sliding along a tabletop, the crack of a log eaten by flame. I shiver, water dripping from my coat onto the floor. At least it is warm here.

Near the back, I spot the Courier's head of snowy hair. None have noticed the arrival of a soaked-to-the-bone woman—except for the barkeep. He scans me head to toe with those slit-pupiled eyes, but I do not flinch. Betrayal has lit the fuse, and oh, how I burn, and burn, and burn.

"Hello again." Approaching the counter, I offer him my sweetest smile. "Do you by chance have a quill and parchment?"

"Is it a love letter you're looking to pen?" he asks as he polishes the countertop. Another customer enters and selects a stool at the end of the bar. Without looking at him, the barkeep pours him a tumbler of liquor, sending it straight into the god's beefy hand.

"Of a sort." Though his gaze unnerves me, I force myself to maintain eye contact. "Well?"

Wordlessly, he passes over the requested supplies, but not without a healthy dose of suspicion. I quickly scribble my message.

My lady,

I apologize for the delay. The East Wind and I will not be returning to his island, but rather to the estate in two days' time, along with his god-touched ax. I am very much looking forward to returning home.

Sincerely,
Min

Message: folded. Wax: melted. Seal: pressed. Eight, nine, ten steps across the room, and I slide into the chair opposite the Courier, who is tossing dice with two ancient crones.

"Eurus' mortal," he says without looking at me. "Was wondering when you'd be back." He drops the dice onto the table. Both land on the number five. With a frightening grin, he collects his winnings, his competitors groaning at their misfortune.

"I've a message to send. It's urgent."

"And on the eve of the final trial, too," he says drolly. After counting his earnings, he takes a drag from his pipe, then blows a smoke ring into my face.

My eyes water, and I cough, batting aside the repulsive fumes while the Courier again tosses the dice. Double sixes. Either he has excellent luck, or the game is rigged.

"And what of my payment?" he asks after a time. "What of the strength tea you promised for my wife?"

I hunch lower in the chair, hands clamped in my lap. "It is r-ready. But I forgot to bring it."

"A likely story."

When one of his companions wins the next round, gleefully piling gold into their lap, the Courier's mouth pulls in dissatisfaction. He swipes the game pieces. "If you can make a double batch of the tea and deliver it by the end of the week, I can send the message tomorrow. Will that suffice?"

On the morrow's sundown, either the East Wind will have claimed victory, or he will be dead. Do I wish him to win? Yes, but only because it will mean a swift journey home. As for what he will face when we return to Marles, that is no longer my concern.

"It will," I say in relief. "Thank you."

"Don't thank me," the Courier murmurs. "I'm just the messenger."

I return to A Thousand Ships, drenched head to toe in rainwater, yet with heightened spirits, fresh conviction. I'm not sure why I convinced myself Eurus felt anything for me. That kiss we shared, though only a brush of lips against cheek—might it have been part of his plan to soften me, persuade me to see this bargain through? I suppose it doesn't matter. Soon, I will have returned home, the City of Gods a distant dream.

Thunder rocks the tavern as I shake cold droplets from my coat. The ensemble continues to perform onstage, a few couples swaying to the easy rhythm. I tell myself I will not search for Eurus, but unfortunately, I spot him and Demi slotted together against the wall, their heads ducked conspiratorially. He laughs. She laughs. How euphoric they appear, together again at last.

I turn from them, feeling shaky and nauseated. I need a drink. Something strong enough to take me from this place and this dark cloud of unhappiness.

Thankfully, someone vacates their seat at the bar. As soon as I claim the stool, those nearest me move off, muttering something about the stink of mortal. At least the barkeep offers me a glass of ale. I take a large swallow and nearly spit it out. Bitter—extremely. But an accurate reflection of my mood.

"May I sit here?"

I tap a finger against the glass with a shrug, not bothering to look at whoever is speaking to me. "I hold no title over an empty chair." As long as it's not Demi. Or Eurus. I don't think I can handle sitting next to either right now.

"How am I to know that?" the man replies, an indistinct shape in my periphery. "You mortals and your strange customs."

My ears strain in an attempt to pick up Eurus' laughter, but the racket is too overwhelming. "Our customs are no stranger than yours," I mutter.

He sighs. "I must be a bore if I cannot even get an attractive woman to look at me when we're talking."

His words pierce the fog of my foul mood, and I shift to face the stranger, whose crooked smile suggests amusement at the situation. I straighten in interest. He is quite comely, with dark skin and black hair curling around the collar of his white tunic. His eyes are an arresting shade of hazel green.

"Apologies." I wince. "My mind was elsewhere."

"I can see that." He gestures to the stool. "May I?"

"Please." I scoot over to make room, and he settles in, angling toward me so our knees touch. "My name is—"

"Min," he cuts in, warm hand overtaking my own. "You're a popular topic of conversation." We shake. His hand is broad, though still smaller than the East Wind's. And I am immediately irritated by the direction of my thoughts.

"Dare I ask what the gods are saying about me?" I have overheard my fair share of opinions. *Incompetent mortal, too stupid to live.* Some are convinced aligning myself with the East Wind will lead to my own demise. Others believe I will offend the wrong deity and be struck down.

He signals the barkeep. A glass of ale appears so quickly it may as well have materialized from thin air.

I quirk an eyebrow. The motion feels as though it belongs to someone else, someone far more daring than I. "Do you actually enjoy the taste of that?"

"This?" He holds up the glass, face scrunched. "Oh, no. This is horrid, truly. But that's the fun part." He grins cheekily at me, and my face heats, much to my embarrassment. "But to answer your question, the gods are saying all manner of things, really. Here I was thinking you were some old woman, too infirm to be of any use. But you are neither old nor infirm. You are," he says, "lovely."

I tighten my grip around the glass as a group of stools are overtaken by a gaggle of goddesses swathed in white. "What do you want?"

"Pardon?"

"There must be some reason you approached me in a crowded tavern. Do you and your friends have a bet to woo the mortal? If so, I do not appreciate the deception, Master . . ."

"Call me Kip," he says.

"Master Kip—"

"No Master," he says with a laugh. "Just Kip."

"Well, *just Kip*," I say, surprised by my own brashness, "if you're here to humiliate me, you're far too late for that." I gesture to the multitude of deities gawking my way. They underestimate me, all of them. They judge and they belittle. They know nothing of what I'm capable of. "And I would prefer to finish my drink in peace, if it's all the same to you."

His eyebrows climb all the way to his messy hairline. "Are you sure you're the same mortal everyone's talking about? Because you are not timid at all, as far as I can see."

It is definitely the ale. "Perhaps I was too harsh." This Kip fellow regards me without a hint of malice or cruelty, only a willingness to listen.

Which is more than I can say about my *employer*. "I've been warned time and again about trusting immortals. I was quick to make assumptions."

"You do not have to explain anything to me, Min." He flags down the barkeep. Seconds later, two full glasses of wine appear before us. "You're right about the gods. We're a horrible lot. I don't blame you for your suspicion." He gestures at the wine. "You might find this more to your liking."

"You're not one of the tournament finalists, are you?" I ask Kip, lifting the glass and taking a satisfying swallow.

"No, thankfully." This, paired with an impish smile. "I'm happy enough as a spectator. Though a betting one, if I'm being truthful."

He is not the only one, that's for sure.

A sudden uproar draws my attention to the opposite end of the tavern. An immortal with the face of a lion has begun to waltz atop one of the tables. The crowd cheers him on.

Inadvertently, my focus flicks to the corner where I last spotted Demi and the East Wind. No sign of them. Where might they have gone? Back to the palace? Some gloom-shrouded corner? It matters not. Eurus is free to go where he wants and spend his time with whomever he chooses.

"Would it be in poor taste for me to ask who you've bet on?" I ask Kip.

"No." He keeps smiling, this god, which makes my mouth bend in response. "It would be in poor taste not to."

I'm about to respond when a tendril of air teases the curve of my nape, and I freeze, heart aflutter. Moments later, I sense a wall of heat at my back, a presence that is both comfort and agony.

"Bird."

The rough grate of my name in the East Wind's mouth pebbles my skin. Outwardly, I am calm. Internally, lungs and heart are at war, each fighting to claim space inside my chest. By the Mother, am I so quick to forget what I overheard less than an hour earlier?

"Eurus," I clip out, sipping my drink with an air of indifference. "Where's your *dear friend* Demi?" The snide tone is so foreign it must belong to another. Why am I treating the goddess like an enemy? Demi is good. She is my friend.

Shoving those tumultuous thoughts aside, I gesture to my companion. "This is Kip. Have you met?"

The smaller, more affable god tilts his chin at Eurus. "Once, long ago. You likely wouldn't remember."

"On the contrary," the East Wind replies coolly, "there is very little I forget."

The musicians announce a brief interlude, and conversation rises to fill the gaps previously crammed with chords. As I take another sip of wine, Eurus steals my glass and downs the rest. He returns it to my hand as if it is perfectly normal for his lips to warm the same rim mine did seconds before.

I glare at him. "I was drinking that."

"And now you're not."

I draw myself higher in my seat. Clearly, I've done something wrong, though I haven't the slightest idea what. "You owe me another drink."

"It's time to g—"

"Now."

He frowns, taken aback by my demand. I suppress a victorious smile as he signals the barkeep, who is so overwhelmed by customers he does not immediately notice. Eurus scowls. Kip glances at me, an eyebrow raised.

"Another wine, please," the East Wind calls out. Two, five, seven tumblers are sent into awaiting hands. Only then does the barkeep pass Eurus a glass of wine.

He sets the drink in front of me. I blink down at it. "I was drinking white."

A vein throbs in his temple. It looks like a great, fat worm. The image tickles me, and I tamp down a snort of laughter as he demands another glass—white, *and make it snappy*.

Less than a heartbeat later, my drink appears. With a sweet smile at my surly companion, I lift the glass to my mouth and sip. To his credit, he waits for me to finish my drink before saying, "Let's go, bird. We're late."

"For what?" I wasn't aware we had other plans.

He leans forward then. The scarred edge of his mouth grazes the shell of my ear, and I inhale sharply through my nose, the desire to tilt my head back and allow him easier access warring with the impulse to shove him away, the image of him and Demi a brand behind my eyes. "I'll tell you when we get back to the palace," he rumbles.

Stay, or go? I look to Kip in indecision. "You're sure I need to be there? Kip could walk me back to the palace."

The dark-skinned immortal smiles brightly. "Absolutely—"

"No," Eurus snarls. "We go together."

Fine. I don't have the patience to deal with this, and I do not want to attract any more attention to myself than I already have. With a venomous glare in Eurus' direction, I slip off the stool and gather my coat.

Kip's smile tilts in sadness. "I hope to see you around, Min."

"Me, too," I whisper, but Eurus is already dragging me toward the door using his winds to nudge aside any who block our way forward. We push out onto the street, into the driving rain.

"Will you manhandle m-me all the way to the palace?" I snip. "Or will you allow me to walk on m-my own?"

He releases me. "Apologies." He does not sound apologetic in the least.

Do I move simply because another wills it? No. I am finished living for others. It stops here. "Why should I return with y-you? I was enjoying my evening. Just because you wish to return to the palace doesn't mean I'm obligated to."

"You are my assistant," he says.

"*Captive*," I correct him with a hiss, "and I have done my part. Eastern Blood is r-ready. All you need to do is win the damn tournament and dole it out like you intend."

The rain, which falls in heavy sheets, blurs the East Wind behind an amorphous gray stretch. "Speak a little louder, will you?" he growls.

I do not care. What was it he said all those weeks ago, when I was trapped by the desperate need to alter my fate? *Trust no one. Not even me.*

Lady Clarisse was right. I am the queen of fools.

Turning on my heel, I stride as quickly as possible through the rain-drenched streets. *Run*, I think. *He cannot catch you.* But it is one stupid thought after another. The East Wind would launch skyward, swoop low to snag me on scaled wings. I will not relive that indignity.

To his credit, he does not attempt to resume the conversation until we are back in the suite, door shut and locked. Gloom enshrouds the space as I toe off my damp shoes near the door. The evening held such promise. Now it's just a pile of shreds.

"Why are you acting like this?" Eurus eventually says, peering at me warily from where he stands by the dining table.

"Why am *I* acting like this?" I scoff. "How about taking accountability for your own actions f-first."

To this, he says, "All I want is to talk."

I begin searching for a means to light a lamp. "I believe our definitions of *talk* are vastly different. I say *talk* and m-mean discussion. You say *talk* and mean t-t-telling me what to do! And just so you know," I add, flinging a withering glare over my shoulder, "I didn't appreciate your treatment of me back there."

He runs both hands through his wet hair. "I'm sorry, I . . ." He sighs. "It was time to go."

"Says who?" I search the side tables, feel along the fireplace mantel. Where is the flint? "I was having a nice evening. What gives you the right to decide how I spend m-my time?" In my stuttering and sopping state, I do not pose much of a threat, but that cannot be helped. At least I am speaking my mind. It is, I think, everything.

"You are in my employment," he states. "If I say it's time to go, then it's time to go. That was the deal."

And he cuts continually deeper. "Right," I whisper. "Because it always comes back to what y-y-you want from me, is that it?" I brush past him. Eurus is who he is. I cannot change him, and I wonder why I even believed it was possible.

"Where are you going?" he demands.

"To bed." I shove my bedroom door open—hard. A picture frame rattles loose and hits the ground.

I'll clean it up in the morning. I need sleep, which is deaf and blind and will take me from this place. To think that in this moment I would trade the opulence of the palace for the estate's cramped broom cupboard. At least there I knew what to expect.

Eurus dogs my heels, sweeping into the room with a cloud of crackling air. "You don't want to talk?"

"Not really, no." I remove my rain-damp coat and squeeze water from my hair. Eurus monitors me without blinking, and for half a heartbeat, I wish for his hood to cover his face so that I will be spared the confusion and hurt I find there.

"Clearly I've done something to offend you," he grinds out.

"Yes, Eurus," I cry, whirling around. "Your entire *existence* offends me!"

He stiffens, and his eyes grow dark and wounded. His wings, those gleaming, arched peaks, slump lower toward the ground.

My stomach cramps. That was too far, even for me. I did not mean to suggest it would be better if he did not exist at all, but I fear I have done exactly that. "I'm s-sorry," I mutter. "That was unkind." And not true.

I rub at my eyes, suddenly exhausted beyond measure. "Look, it's been a long day. Let's get some sleep. We'll talk tomorrow." Though I dread what I might say. I could never have imagined desiring the East Wind in a romantic way. That I believed—hoped—he felt similarly proves how wrong I have been—about everything. "I think it's best if w-we take space from one another tonight."

"Space." He spits the word as I proceed to turn down my bed, fluffing the pillows to my desired softness. "Why, so you can find comfort in the arms of *Kip*?"

My hands pause on the fabric. Slowly, I turn to face him, strangely breathless. When I speak, there is no stumbling over my own tongue.

No, for once, my words are perfectly, succinctly clear. "Are you jealous?"

His black eyes flatten with a primordial chill. "You liked him."

He *is* jealous. Except that makes absolutely no sense. Why should he care who I like, when he made it explicitly clear he feels nothing for me?

"How could I like him?" I respond, far more wearily than I intend. "I do not even know him."

"But you wanted to."

"Maybe I did. He was nice, a good conversationalist, and seemed genuinely interested in getting to know me. The only reason I talked to him was because you abandoned me for Demi." And if I hurl it as an accusation, well, it is what I feel, and I will no longer mask that for his benefit. "Why should it matter that I was talking to him?"

"It matters," the East Wind snarls, crowding my space, "because you offered him your smiles when you've offered me none." His mouth dips near mine, and I inhale sharply, unable to resist the spice of his breath as it grazes my face. "Tell me why, bird."

He is very close now. Darkness feathers our skin, and it takes everything in me not to lean into his body, no matter how alluring the pull. What might happen were I to press my lips to his and slot my tongue between?

"Funny," I murmur. "I was thinking the same thing about you and Demi." Whom he clearly has relations with.

The sting of that realization hurts all over again, and I turn away from him. How did it all go so wrong, so quickly? I think that is what wounds deepest. For once, I was *happy*, and free. "Please," I say. "Just go."

The East Wind brushes past me without a farewell, without ... anything.

23

I WAKE IN DARKNESS.

Its thick, impermeable murk soaks into my eyes. Hard stone lines my back. Except, that cannot be. What of the plush mattress, the luxurious blankets and plethora of pillows? I inhale a mouthful of air tasting faintly of mineral. It chokes me, and I cough hard until my lungs clear, the first fragments of alarm stirring.

This is not my bedroom. This is not even the palace. The air stirs in a way that suggests I am outdoors. It lacks the autumnal, nutmeg-infused fragrance that clouds the City of Gods, and holds a chill reminiscent of exposed mountain peaks.

Moving slowly, I push upright into a seated position. I blink, blink again. The blackness does not lift. "Eurus?"

My voice carries, hits nearby walls, perhaps a ceiling. It folds onto itself and is gone.

Drip, drip—water in the distance. Where am I? What has occurred? Why do I not remember? I rub at my arms, for I have no coat, only a thin nightgown, no shoes, my hair falling loose down my back. Following my argument with Eurus, I slept, though poorly. Might this be a dream then?

Ears pricked for sound, I climb to my feet. My palm finds a damp wall. I pinch my arm, and the pain reveals my reality, all of it. Is this a cell? A burrow beneath the earth?

Slowly, I pick my way forward, one hand braced against the stone, the other outstretched as a precaution. My toes catch in a crack, and I stumble. Gradually, the gloom begins to lift. There, in the distance—a spot of gray.

The brightness coaxes me onward, and I lift a hand to shield my eyes as, at last, I emerge from a large cave into a cold and cutting wind.

It is day. High noon, according to the sun's position. I stand on a hill overlooking a dell, movement luring my eye below.

In an open forest clearing, two immortals cross swords. A small, lithe woman with violet hair combats a strapping man with two-pronged antlers erupting from his skull. They move with a swiftness I cannot track. Their blades bleed silver.

Competitors. I recognize them both. The deer-like immortal hacks at his foe, again, again. His next cut threatens to remove the woman's leg, but she dances out of range, receiving a slash to the thigh rather than a severed appendage. She parries his next attack, then sweeps under his guard. Her blade sinks hilt-deep into his chest.

The man drops to one knee, expression agonized. Yanking her blade free, the violet-haired woman decapitates her foe swiftly, one finite blow.

As I look away, a bell tolls. Its mournful clang draws the hair along my body straight up, and I wipe sweat from my forehead despite the frigidity. I'm not sure what the bell signals, but I do understand one thing. This is the final trial.

Once more, the arena has been transformed, in this instance a large tract of forest, unending hills, a dense swathe of trees enclosed in that same hazy enchantment that temporarily blocks the grandstands from sight. Beneath the wind, a muffled roar reaches my ears: the cries of a hundred thousand spectators.

Mother of Earth. How am I here? I assumed I would witness the event, but as a bystander. Surely I'm not a contestant? *I'm* certainly in no position to win. My presence must therefore serve a purpose, and there is only one I can think of for a mortal participating in these immortal games: *prey*.

Ducking behind a nearby bush, I take stock of my surroundings. Strange hoofprints mark the soil, overlapped by the occasional outline of a bare foot. At some point, some of the participants wandered this way, but there is no sign of them now, and—what is this?

A long strand of red hair is caught in my nightgown. No, *two* strands. The sight chills me. I know of only one—or rather, three—competitors with hair this shade of scarlet.

My presence in the arena is no accident. Here is what I know: only when the last competitor remains will the door appear. Regardless of the fury I feel toward the East Wind, allying with him is my greatest chance of survival. I must not delay.

As I slip toward the trees, however, I notice a large, dark shape sprawled across the forest floor.

A cloud of flies has already descended to feed on the goddess' eyes. I gag, a hand slapped over my mouth. Her gown has been slashed, heels broken, legs pieced at unnatural angles. Had the contestants been taken unaware, as I was?

Something snaps behind me. I whirl around, scanning the area. Whatever it is that lurks beyond sight, I do not wait around to find out.

I run.

Except I do not run far. Puffing hard, I lurch to a stop, brace a hand against an aged tree. The wood is dark here, the understory veiled in obscurity. It boasts peculiar plants and pale-winged birds. Every so often, the bell peals and dies.

It is foolish, this plan. Find the East Wind, yes, but how? He is one god amongst trees that number in the thousands. By calling out for him, I risk alerting the other contenders to my presence. Then again, even if he *did* know of my presence, why should he search for me? Why should he care?

Say nothing, Min.

Useless girl.

A waste of space.

My fingernails dig into the lined bark. My head threatens to burst its seams. All the years of my life, I internalized these words. I regarded them as truth. I was neither strong nor clever, prolific nor useful. I was stupid Min, useless Min, impudent Min, burdensome Min. And it was simply not true.

How many mortals would have survived this realm of gods, a flimsy bargain their only armor? I am not useless. I have my strengths. They may be different than those of Lady Clarisse, but that does not make them trivial, less than. She was wrong. I am capable *and* innovative *and* intelligent. I have the grit required to see difficult tasks through. If Eurus is out there, I *will* find him. This I vow.

A piercing cackle snaps my attention upward. A cutout in the leaves reveals the blue sky, its edges brushed the pink of coming sundown. Something flits past—something with wings.

I climb a nearby tree, hefting myself into the highest branches until my head breaks the canopy. As I catch sight of a figure in the distance, my heart surges, then plummets in equal measure. Not Eurus. Rather, it is one of the Fates, bow and arrow clasped in hand.

She circles the wood slowly, dropping gradually lower. No sign of the other two sisters. After a time, a strong beat of wings carries her west, and she dives. Three, four, five heartbeats pass. Then, a familiar scream of pain.

My blood runs cold.

I descend the tree as swiftly as possible. Quickly, quickly now. The light wanes, and the sky loses color. Fear that I will not find Eurus before night cloaks the wood drives me faster, farther over the spongy earth. I leap over a fallen tree, crash through thorn-tangled brush. A collection of sharp stings graze my back, arms, and chest.

But I do not falter. Darting through a grove of ferns, I spot dozens of arrows buried in the trunks of adjacent trees, in addition to one lying in the dirt. No blood coats the carved head, which means it missed its mark. I gingerly untangle it from the undergrowth, grasp it tightly in hand. This singular weapon, my only defense.

I follow the river for a time, then climb a hill rising from its bank. As I round a great, gnarled tree, I halt in surprise. A pair of trouser-clad legs stick out from the brush, and draped over the thighs: the threadbare fabric of a patched cloak.

The blood drains from my face so quickly I sway. "Eurus?"

Leaves crunch as I shove through the bush to where the East Wind lies, a scarlet pool seeping into the dirt beneath him. Blood oozes from the arrow lodged in his left shoulder. He was lucky it did not pierce his heart.

But why has he fallen unconscious? The loss of blood is too minimal to warrant this state.

Pushing back his hood, I examine the face that has begun to haunt me in my waking and sleeping hours. The slightly rounded nose and square chin, between which rests his mouth, parted wide enough to reveal a glint of white, even teeth. His eyes, closed, short lashes fanned across high cheekbones. The scars marking his visage, revealing a story of horror and neglect.

Gently, I trace one such eruption, the place where healthy and healed skin meet. The East Wind is naturally pale, but there is a sickly tinge to his complexion that worries me. I press a fingertip against his lips. They are unexpectedly chilled.

"Eurus." I shake him, hard. His head lolls.

I sit back on my heels. If he cannot wake, then something must be preventing him from doing so.

Leaning close, I inhale as he exhales, dragging the scent of his breath into my lungs. It smells of anise. I frown. Eurus despises anise. He told me once, after I brewed one of my stronger morning teas.

Carefully, I tug back one of his eyelids. In the white of his eye, the blood vessels appear engorged, like bloated worms. I study the sight with growing dismay. Many poisons utilize the plant, but only one causes this specific symptom.

Again, my attention returns to the arrow lodged in his shoulder. A murky substance coats the splintered wood. I brush my finger through it, lift it to my nose. Now I am certain.

Gray Snare: a freezing poison that lowers one's core body temperature. Should he face a contender in his weakened, hypothermic state, it is unlikely he would survive. Because the poison entered his bloodstream through a god-touched arrow, it could prove fatal.

Something rustles behind me then. I spin around, the second arrow clenched inside my trembling fist.

The wood has changed. Its shadows have lengthened, and a tree drops its leaves.

I squint into the distance. A fog-like substance slips through the understory. It swallows a second tree, and that, too, withers beneath its touch.

"Eurus!" I tap his cheek, but he does not wake.

Again, the bell tolls, scattering multicolored birds into flight. I yank his arm in an attempt to drag him down the hill, away from the creeping fog. I recall passing a cave a while back. It is the only viable shelter I can think of.

But—the East Wind. Enormous, overpowering, all brawn. And me: a woman, mortal. Moving him will be impossible with strength alone. But if I can drag him to the river, that wide bend of unhurried water, I could pull him along with the current until we reach shelter.

"Sorry, Eurus," I mutter, and shove him downhill with all my strength.

His body flops, back to chest to back, a laborious roll that soon gains momentum as the incline steepens. His wings snag against the vegetation, and he tumbles through a muddy pool, which coats him thoroughly.

When he rolls to a stop along the riverbank, I scramble downhill to check his body and wings for breaks. There are only surface wounds.

A distant shriek cuts the stillness as I scan the river with reluctance. The water is clear: I can see the pebbled bottom. It does not seem too deep, and the current is blessedly slow. It is not the sea, I remind myself. These waters are tame. There are no hands to hold me under, no salt to scour my throat and lungs.

After tucking the arrow into my waistband, I grab the East Wind's arms and heave. He doesn't budge. Well, what did I expect? The god is easily twice my weight.

I tunnel deep, down into the core of me. Not strength of body, but strength of spirit, strength of character, strength of mind.

A second yank slides him into the river on his back. The frigid water laps against my thighs like hungry tongues. The silty riverbed sucks at my ankles.

You are safe. Do not think of the water. Focus on saving Eurus' life.

Travel is slow, and the hours pass into darkness. Gripping the collar of the East Wind's cloak allows me to keep his head above water as I haul him downstream. Night sounds descend, each rustling branch dragging my awareness skyward, but no sign of that eating fog. Despite this, I cannot let my guard down. One of the competitors might be watching this very moment, awaiting the opportunity to strike.

At last, we reach the fallen tree where I recall spotting the cave. With the sun having set, the temperature has plummeted. My teeth chatter, loud in the dark.

Grabbing one of Eurus' arms, I drag him across the forest floor, aiming for the knoll marked by rising cliffs. Another heave brings us to the cave's entrance. I peer into its stony mouth. No sign of a competitor. I will take my chances.

Once I've dragged the East Wind inside, I kneel beside him. "This is likely going to hurt." When he fails to respond, I grip the arrow shaft, brace myself, and yank—hard.

Skin tears. The East Wind wakens with a harsh bellow, arms raised in defense.

"Eurus." I catch his arm. "It's me."

He curls the fingers of one large hand around my wrist—an anchor. "Min?" His eyelashes flutter, hazed in shock. "What are you doing here? What—"

"You have to stay awake."

"I'm trying," he rasps. "Why am I so tired? My shoulder . . ." He squints at the hole that weeps blood. "The trial . . . You can't be here. Why . . . ?" He trails off in confusion.

"You've been poisoned," I say, ripping a strip of fabric from the bottom of my nightgown to staunch the wound.

A slow, dazed blink. "I was hit by one of the Fates."

"Yes." And speaking of the Fates . . . "I think they're the reason I'm here. I found their hair on my clothes. They must have kidnapped me while I slept and—" What? Planted me in one of the arena caves? But how? Why?

I suppose it doesn't matter. All my efforts must now turn toward helping the East Wind, whose blood has already soaked the crumpled cotton.

Noting my grimace, he asks, "How bad is it?"

"If left untreated, you will enter a hypothermic state. The poison will rob you of warmth and ease of movement. Eventually, you will fall unconscious."

He is grim—too grim. "Is there an antidote?"

"Yes," I whisper, "but I haven't the components to create one." The rare root of vervesworth, found only in arid habitats, must be dried for two hours in direct sunlight, then another two over open flame.

If Eurus falls unconscious, it will likely be the end for me. I've certainly no hope of besting a god. When I am gone, no one will mourn me. Lady Clarisse may mourn immortality having slipped from her grasp, but she will not mourn *me*.

I press harder on the wound, watching his blood blot the fabric. My trembling persists. Even my bones feel frozen. "Your only chance of survival is to reach the door," I whisper. Then, with bitterness: "I'm sorry."

"What are you sorry for?" When I do not reply, he goes on, "Will you look at me, bird?"

I cannot. It is too treacherous, his gaze. I will fall into it like a darkened well.

"Don't worry," I say, still avoiding his eyes. "I p-promised to help you win, and I keep my word. We'll find the door. You will have your victory."

The air stirs sluggishly, as though the strength of his power has begun to weaken. "You are . . . angry with me?"

"This has nothing to do with anger, Eurus. I've only realized how much time I have wasted. The sooner we find the door, the sooner you can kill the council. You will have your revenge; I will have my life back." Though I cannot say what will happen when we leave the City of Gods, I do know this: I am ready to begin. "St. Laurent is where I belong."

The East Wind bites back a groan as he shifts position, curling partially onto his side. I continue to apply pressure, relieved when the blood starts to clot. "And what if I wish for you to belong with me?"

It pierces my most tender wounds, these words, these lies. And from that hurt, something sharp and uncompromising is born.

"I see wh-what this is," I say. "It is not enough that I have agreed to help you win, is it. You want something more? Well, I have nothing to give. You have already taken everything of value from me, and I refuse to belong to s-someone who is claimed by another."

"What?"

This feigned shock is just one more manipulation, I tell myself. I won't fall for it. "I will not repeat myself."

"Please, bird," he says, breath ragged. "What do you mean 'claimed by another'?"

As if he hasn't the slightest notion. But—fine. At the very least, it may offer me some relief.

"I never told you how w-wonderful of a time I was having at the tavern," I begin, my callous tone contradicting the gentleness with which I bandage his wound. "I enjoyed our time together. I felt like ... like myself. And I know that must sound silly to you, but I don't think I ever really knew what th-th-that felt like before that moment." Back in St. Laurent, there was no space for Min. I was forever obscured by Lady Clarisse's shadow.

"I was having a nice time as well," Eurus offers tentatively.

Right. I tie off the bandage, glaring at him. "I suppose that explains why you left me to speak with Demi." At his look of confusion, I add, "You were ..." *Happy. Present. Alive.* "Laughing," I manage to push out.

"And I realized you had n-never laughed with me, and maybe I wanted that. Maybe I thought you wanted that, too. You told me from the very beginning not to trust you. I didn't listen. I was your captive, and—"

As Eurus reaches for me, I shove to my feet, arms curled around my middle. Let the distance be my shield when I have none.

"What are you talking about?" he says in bewilderment. His expression tightens as he drags himself into a seated position, his breathing labored.

"I heard y-you. You told Demi I was nothing to you!" And oh, I cannot hold on to this pain any longer. It pours from my eyes and down my face. It splits my heart in two. "And I was stupid enough to believe otherwise. To think th-that you cared f-f-for me."

Eurus stares at me somberly, wings half stretched. "Bird."

"I didn't plan this," I croak. "I h-hated you. You, who stole me from my home. All you cared about was using me. Exploiting me like some draft horse, there to do your b-bidding. It s-s-sickened me. And yet, there must be something wrong with me. There has to be. It's the only explanation for why I f-found it in myself to treat you with compassion when you did n-not deserve it. Why I grew to care for you.

"And maybe that was m-my mistake," I go on. "Trusting that there was room for change in you. Thinking, wishing, hoping that I might be worthy of being cared for, or lo—" I swallow and change course. "Hoping that you had been changed by me as I have been changed by you."

Another mistake. Another stupid dream.

I shake my head, turn back to face the East Wind. He sits slumped against the wall, his brow crimped beneath a fall of limp black hair. His mask is the toughest I have encountered, but all at once, the veneer thaws and all is made harsh and bright. It hurts him, to hear these things.

"Please," he whispers. "Let me explain."

I tighten my arms around my shaking form. Too painful to stay, too risky to leave. In the end, my fatigued legs give out, and I slide down the cave wall opposite him.

"First," he says, searching my gaze in the gloom, "it is obvious I have caused you much pain. I want to apologize for that. It is the last thing I ever wanted to do."

I blink, suddenly uncertain. I did not expect an apology. I expected... well, I don't know, exactly. Knowing Eurus, I assumed he would brush aside my hurt, redirect the conversation to calmer waters, the matter resolved, yet... *He hears me.*

"Second," he says in a quieter tone, "I should not have said what I did. My words were hurtful, as I wanted them to be. But it is not for the reason you think, bird." The East Wind shudders, cups his hands around his mouth, blows into them. "I said those things because I didn't want Demi to know how important you are to me."

The chill that has consumed my body subtly abates as my lower belly warms. I hear his sincerity, but what he said before... "Why?"

"On the chance that I did not make it through the third trial. Who would protect you then? If they knew how I cared for you, they might go after you, use you, trap you as a plaything, and I couldn't bear that." He scrubs his hands down his face—drawn, tinged in gray. "You're wrong, bird. I do care for you. I'm sorry for not telling you sooner."

"B-but you and Demi. You looked—" The thought is enough to make me retch. "You looked like you *belonged* together."

For whatever reason, this saddens him, which in turn pulls at my heart.

"I don't want Demi. I haven't wanted her in a long time. We were young. We didn't know who we were or what we wanted. Looking back, I see the ways I used our relationship to distract myself from my father's abuse." He shrugs. "Demi wanted more. I couldn't give it to her. As it was, I could barely care for myself. But over time, I needed things from her, and she could not give that to me. She would not put me first. Ultimately, it drove us apart. And now that I've come to know you, I understand that we were never right for each other."

I shake my head. How desperately I want to believe him. "But you seemed so invested in what she was up to, more so than just for using her to gather information. I thought it was because you still loved her."

"Oh, bird." The East Wind pinches the bridge of his nose, head shaking in sympathy. "That's because Demi is a member of the Council of Gods."

24

"What!" I shriek. Slumped against the opposite wall, Eurus frowns, face pinched into a grid of nerves and fraught trepidation. He shifts position with a wince of pain, the tips of his wings splayed across the ground. "I thought you knew."

"No! I—How was I supposed to know that?"

"She was at the welcome banquet."

"So was every other immortal participating in the tournament." Except—the very first trial. Twelve seats for the Council of Gods, yet two had been empty. When I asked Demi about the two missing council members, she offered an explanation for one of the empty seats, but not the other. And the reason why Eurus wanted nothing to do with her? It could not have been clearer.

"By the Mother," I mutter. *Look with your eyes, Min. See what is right under your very nose.* "Why didn't you tell me?"

"If you knew I was planning to end her life," Eurus says, "I feared you would let slip about my plan."

Maybe I would have. Then again, maybe not.

"At first, I did not want you speaking with her because of her involvement with the council. But as time went on, I saw the advantage in it. Demi knows the competitors, and she devised the trials alongside the other council members. I thought she might let her guard down with you and hint at what lay ahead. Once I saw that you were becoming close . . . well, how could I tell you that I planned to kill her? You would never have given me Eastern Blood. And I didn't want to take that friendship from you, truthfully. You deserve a friend, Min. Even if I wanted nothing to do with her."

I shake my head, turn to glare at the stone underfoot, as if it might provide me guidance. Forgiveness is like the softened body of a clam. To reach it, its armor must be pried back. But he kept this information from me. Information that may have influenced my actions in the goddess' presence. I could have better protected myself against the divine.

"Regardless of your motives, you should have told me," I say.

He nods, then drops his eyes. "I know. I'm sorry."

"Trust requires effort from b-both parties. If you want me to trust you, then you need to be honest with me." As for Demi, she probably assumed I knew of her title.

"I know, bird." He hangs his head. "It is hard for me to trust others, but it is no excuse for the hurt I have caused you. I was wrong. You *are* trustworthy. You have proven your commitment to this task, and for that, I am indebted to you."

His gaze is heartfelt, open. I fear he sees the deception in my heart. *Trustworthy.* What a beautiful lie I have spun.

All this time, I have been in contact with Lady Clarisse, yet he hasn't a clue. That all-consuming rage spurred me to send my most recent message through the Courier. What will happen when I return home? Will her ladyship be lying in wait, a fox in the brush? The notion floods my stomach with an awful dread. The East Wind will die should Lady Clarisse get her hands on him.

Do I confess and risk abandonment? I will not survive this trial without him. If I were to tell him now, it might cause him to lose focus, which could be to both of our detriment. If I tell him after, though . . . What if he returns to St. Laurent and destroys all that I hold dear?

I shiver, my focus shifting to the deepening chill. Soon, night will shed its dusky skin.

Noticing my discomfort, the East Wind climbs to his feet. He sways, and my apprehension threatens to spill from the container in which it is bound. Without the antidote, Gray Snare will continue to weaken him. It has likely crippled his powers, too. "I'm going to gather wood for a fire. Stay here."

"Wait!" I grab his arm. "Won't the light attract the competition?"

"We need to get warm, bird."

"I'll survive." I would rather take my chances against the cold—a peril I understand—than whatever deities lurk beyond sight.

One of his eyebrows arches high. "And what of me? You said this poison would lead to hypothermic shock."

I wince. He is right. A fire will help ward off the imminent chill. "Perhaps it is worth the risk."

He searches my gaze before disentangling himself. "I'll be back shortly."

I watch his form blur, then vanish into the surrounding forest.

Knees drawn against my chest, I shiver, teeth chattering as I await his return. The forest is alive, steeped in darkness. Any subtle crack or rustle draws my body bowstring-tight.

Footsteps. I tense, but it is only Eurus, bearing an armful of sticks. He catches himself against the wall, his body trembling with the ice beginning to eat at his veins.

"Let me," I say, taking some of the load from his arms and gently guiding him toward the ground. As he arranges the sticks in a pile, I point to a small plant resting at his feet. "What is that?"

Eurus cups his hands over his mouth to warm them. "You mean you don't recognize it?" he asks in surprise.

I shake my head. Whatever this pink-budded plant is, it does not grow in the mortal realms.

"I know something about plants that you don't." He seems absurdly pleased with himself. I glare until he laughs and crushes the leaves inside his fist. "I wish I could say I knew the name of this specimen, but I don't. My brother, Zephyrus, told me about it when we were young. If you clamp it inside your palm, the leaves release a flammable oil that can be applied to kindling. Then, I shove my power through my fist so it heats to a spark..." Eurus' expression slides out of focus as an acrid scent uncurls. With a hiss, he drops the leaves—now alight—onto the pile of wood.

The East Wind droops beside me, out of breath. My trepidation grows, threatening the bounds of my skin. Gray Snare works quickly, but I fear he needs rest, as do I. And how are we to navigate the darkened wood?

"Does Demi suspect foul play?" I ask him.

"Doubtful." He dabs at the sweat slipping down his neck. "I've told her nothing about your skillset."

But I did. I wince. "And you still feel certain this is the right choice?" I press him. "Killing the council?"

"I do."

Then he has not changed. And I have wasted precious energy attempting to forge silver into gold. "Can I ask you something?"

"You can. But whether I answer depends on if I like the question or not."

With a gentle nudge, he bids me shift closer, and I do. Our thighs brush. When his eyes slip to my mouth, I press my lips taut, fighting the urge to throw myself into his lap. "Do you think it will have been worth it, to kill the council after all is said and done?"

"You don't understand," he says, and the fire is in his eyes, pooling straight down to the bottom of his black pupils. "The council as an establishment has done too much harm to me, and to others. I have to do this."

"Why? *Why* do you have to do this? You cannot change the fact that you were banished, or neglected. I truly think that if you were to forgive—"

"I won't forgive them," he growls. "I will *never* forgive them."

What Eurus voices is his truth, but he cannot see beyond the boundaries of himself. "Do you feel this?" I capture his hand, place it over his heart. "That is your heart, which beats only for you. You are safe. Your father cannot touch you. The council cannot take you from your home, not truly." I tighten my grip. "You will always carry the scars of your past. But you have the power to decide whether you allow them to hurt, or heal."

There is a snap of dry wood, sharp like a broken bone. Eurus appears moments away from charging out into the darkness. That must mean I have hit a particularly deep wound.

"I only say this because I know what you feel," I tell him. "For so long, I let Lady Clarisse's actions *define* me, hurt me, make me feel worthless—"

"You're not worthless, bird."

"I know that now. And neither are you." I brush the damp strands from his forehead, grazing the area of scarring where his hairline has receded. "What if, when the time comes to poison the council, you decide you will no longer allow your past to hold sway over you? What if," I say, "you could start anew?"

He tosses a stick onto the fire, its warmth having gradually filled the cave to thaw my stiff limbs. "I'm not sure if that's possible for people like me," he says.

"People like you?"

"Irredeemable."

My heart aches for him. How could I have gone so long without truly seeing the depths of the East Wind's self-loathing?

"It is," I assure him. "It absolutely is." Seeing the doubt there, I continue to push. "You have come so far already. I look at you, the god who stole me from my home, but who I have grown to care for—"

His head snaps up. The blacks of his eyes are large enough to fall into, and fall into them I do. As his slow, salt-tinged exhalation mingles with mine, his breath slips into my parted mouth. The scent of his skin once threatened to drag me back under the black waves of memory. Now? I do not think it would be so terrible a thing, to drown.

Softly, the East Wind murmurs, "How would I go about doing that?"

"You give yourself compassion," I whisper. "You acknowledge you did the best that you could. You commit to loving yourself wholeheartedly.

You do not allow those deceitful thoughts to take over. You see yourself as others see you." I swallow, force out the rest. "As *I* see you."

A gentleness blurs the harder lines bracketing his mouth. It becomes a fire-bright warmth, a yearning. "And how do you see me, bird?"

It is too complex a thing, to arrange all that I know about the East Wind like fixings of a brew. For he is forceful and he is hesitant. He is renowned and unknowable. He is wounded, terribly so, yet healing, too. He will not always reach first, but he will capture my hand should I do so instead. He is rigid in his beliefs, but they have softened over time, perhaps even altered shape. He is all-powerful, yet he has not one friend.

The truth, I've found, is not so complex. "You are many things, Eurus," I say. "Just when I believe I've started to understand you, I learn there is yet another facet to uncover." It is something that cannot be described, only experienced and known. The East Wind, whom I fear I have given my heart to. He hasn't the slightest clue.

"You are many things as well, bird." As though handling glass, Eurus cups my face with tender pressure and delicate fingertips. "Kind and gentle, compassionate and generous, practical and bright, and," he adds with a quirked mouth, "beautiful, but especially when angry."

I laugh, and he laughs, and the levity, though brief, brings a much-desired optimism to our temporary shelter. How I long to close the distance, but desire cannot be born from a single individual. It must be shared.

"Bird." His eyes crimp with affection. "Min." Thumb pressed to my chin, he draws it downward, gaze fixated on my mouth. "How long do I have before my strength gives out?"

"A day, maybe two?" Might a different antidote slow the poison? But that would mean leaving him to search for ingredients, and I would almost certainly lose my sense of direction, or stumble across another contender, or both. Our greatest chance of survival is sticking together, working toward a common plan: killing the other competitors before they kill us.

He shivers, his eyelids fluttering shut. "I'm cold."

"I know." And the worst has yet to come.

While I help Eurus settle next to the fire, the low tolling of the bell ripples out over the night-encased forest.

"What does that sound mean?" I ask him as I remove his wet boots and socks and set them near the licking flames. The fabric of my clothes has begun to stiffen with dryness.

"It means that one of the participants has fallen," he mumbles drowsily.

That was the seventh instance of the bell. If we are lucky, it will have claimed one of the Fates. I wonder if Arin is still alive. Part of me hopes that he is not. I certainly do not want to be responsible for his death. We must outplay, out compete, and outlast the four remaining competitors. The Council of Gods will not make it easy. Whoever walks through that door must earn it.

The hours wane. The night deepens. I stack the logs and build the fire high, great, smoky plumes belching toward the cave ceiling. As Eurus continues to quake from the poison moving through his bloodstream, I stare at his shivering form. My mouth goes dry, and a crackling awareness consumes me. Only when skin touches skin might there be relief from the cold.

And so I strip. Buttons undone, nightgown removed and tossed aside, so that my exposed flesh shivers in the brisk air. When I stand in nothing but my undergarments, I crouch at the East Wind's side, fingertips hovering over his shoulder. I do not know why I hesitate. It is worth a try. Anything is worth a try.

"Eurus." Instead of his shoulder, I brush his cheek. It is icy and bloodless. "We need to remove your wet clothes."

Rolling onto his back with a groan, he blinks up at me, brow scrunched as his eyes struggle to focus. "Bird?"

I clear my throat awkwardly before removing his cloak. The strange fabric, something like leather but softer, is almost completely dry, as if it has repelled the water. Beneath it, he wears charcoal trousers and a plain, long-sleeved shirt. I undo four buttons before he stiffens in realization. "What are you doing?" he growls in alarm.

"Undressing you." The steadiness of my voice pleases me. My heart, however, is a different story. "Your cloak is dry. You can put it back on after your clothes are removed."

He grabs my wrist. I shake him off. He is not thinking clearly. That is fine. I've enough faculties to think for the both of us.

As I bare his chest, the breath leaves my lungs so violently I feel faint. The sheer enormity of his torso is a canvas of skin dusted in black hair, marred by a significant scar dripping down the entirety of his left side like a spill of shiny white paint.

I am not a particularly violent person, but I'm certain I could kill Eurus' father in this moment. The sight of Eurus' chest sickens me, for there is scarring, and then there is this: a hot melting of skin that has bubbled and blistered and cooled.

"Boiling oil."

My gaze leaps to his. "Excuse me?"

"My father," Eurus grinds out, "poured boiling oil over me. He wanted to see how high my pain tolerance was and gave me a potion that suppressed my body's ability to heal. This is the aftermath, what I must carry even though he is gone from this world." He studies the scarring in disgust. "It is ugly."

"No, it is beautiful."

He shakes his head, saying nothing.

My throat tightens the longer I stare at his hurt. I shouldn't. It will cross a line, a great, bold line shaded between us. But my body is already in motion as I lean down and gently brush a kiss across the scar.

A soft, pained sound squeezes past his throat. His eyes flick to mine. They are darkest caverns, deep fathoms.

There is an ache in me. It is like thirst or hunger—only through consumption will it be quenched. What do I wish? To press my mouth onto his skin and warm it with slow breaths. To move higher, toward his neck, and lower, toward his abdomen. As I begin untying the East Wind's trousers, he bats at my hands with a strangled, *"What are you doing?"*

"I've already told you. You're losing warmth to your wet clothes. Sharing body heat will help us survive the night." Again, I reach for the ties. Again, he shoves my fingers aside.

I huff out my frustration. "Eurus."

"Bird."

"Either you remove your trousers, or I do it for you. Choose."

In the firelight, his eyes appear glazed. When my tongue darts out to wet my lips, he tracks the motion.

"Turn around," he whispers.

I do, though it feels akin to exposing my back to an apex predator as Eurus sheds his wet clothes. My pulse crests to a shrill hum in my ears. "Are you under the cloak?" I ask.

"Yes."

All right. Well. That is good. Quite good, I think. "Um." I clear my throat, reminding myself that I have lain with men before. Well, one man. Of course, this is not *that*, exactly. This is for survival. "I'm going to s-slip under the cloak with you. I'll wrap myself around your back."

"Can you even reach all the way around?" He sounds as breathless as I do.

"No hurt in trying, right?" My laughter snags, splintering into fragments.

There is a long pause. When he speaks, it is with unusual brittleness. "What if I curled around your back instead? That might make things easier." The click of his swallow sounds. Or maybe that is the snap of the fire, which is alive, as we are, and burns and burns and burns.

Slowly, I turn to face him. The black of his eyes and hair is in striking contrast to the pale of his complexion. After a moment, I nod my compliance. "Let's try that."

Lying curled on his side, wings folded across his back, the East Wind lifts the cloak in offering, watching me all the while. The sight of his calf ensnares me. It is carved from muscle, covered in sparse hair.

I do not allow myself to question my decision as I slide beneath the fabric and carefully seal myself along his front. The unexpected coolness of his skin causes me to flinch. I exhale and sink closer, my spine stamped against his chest, the muscle of his bicep cushioning my head. Our legs overlap. He doesn't attempt to untangle them. I struggle to breathe with some semblance of normalcy.

"All right?" I whisper.

The East Wind clamps his other hand over my hip in a distinctly possessive gesture. "Yes," he rumbles.

Incredibly, the space beneath the cloak warms to a point where I begin to sweat and Eurus' shivering abates. I am both relieved and fraught with nerves. *Rest*, I think. *It will do us both good.* But I am awake, I am aware, I am so, so alive.

My breasts grow heavy, their points tingling against the fabric of my breastband. When I shift against him, the unmistakable shape of his arousal prods me in the lower back.

I stiffen, feeling Eurus' slow breaths growing increasingly erratic. Our legs slot deeper, my feet curled into his large, warm calves.

A terse breath whistles out of me, for the hand on my hip has begun to move, an easy drift up to my shoulder, the callused pads of his fingers an abrasive drag against my skin. I bite back a moan as the East Wind presses closer. What of propriety, decorum? Eurus is a god. I am mortal. But he is alone, as I am. He has suffered, as I have. Regardless of what has come before, we now have only each other. It means something that he trusts me enough to allow my touch at all.

"Bird?" he whispers after a time.

His fingertips continue to glide up my ribs. I squeeze my legs together, as if that might stymie the dull pulsations developing in the secret place between. "Yes?"

"You know the torture I endured in the tower?"

I nod, wondering if it is possible to catch fire from touch alone.

"This is worse."

It is fate. It must be. For who can claim the meeting of two hearts—one of immortal origin, the other of human brevity—would begin in discordance and end harmoniously? We should not fit together. There are countless arguments to support that stance, not least of which is my collusion with the woman who intends to kill him.

But I know now I cannot allow Lady Clarisse to capture the East Wind. He is no caged bird, and I would not clip his wings.

Slowly, I roll onto my side to face him. The fire burns low. It shades the severe angles of his face and mutes the scarring near his hairline. My hand slips lower. The East Wind's abdomen contracts as I brush the trail of hair leading from his navel, skirting the heavy shaft hanging between his powerful thighs. When I trace the crescent of his hip bone, he hisses out a breath.

I snatch my hand away. "S-sorry."

"No." He reaches for me. "Don't stop." His eyes never leave mine as he returns my hand to his abdomen. "You will not hurt me," he murmurs with certainty.

A thread of guilt pulls in my chest. There is still time to repair the mistake I have made. Once the trial is done, I will send a message to Lady Clarisse, claiming Eurus' ax has been destroyed. If she believes it to no longer exist, there will be no need to search for it. He should be safe. "Eurus—"

He catches my chin, forcing me to look at him. "Keep going, bird."

My mouth is dry as old parchment. My tongue has forgotten how to shape itself. But my hand glides low, lower, skating across every subtle peak and vale of his muscled abdomen until it hits dense pubic hair. There my fingertips pause, the soft bristle feathering my knuckles.

Eurus lifts his hips, and as our eyes meet, I circle his shaft in my hand. It is firm, yet there is give beneath the veined skin. A gentle squeeze near the base, then higher, toward the flared head. I give him a torturously slow stroke. A rough, unintelligible sound grinds past his teeth.

Heat flares through my core, and as I peer at him through lowered lashes, I marvel at the power my hand holds. The East Wind's hunger is acute. He stares at me like a man starved. It tells me I am worthy. It tells me I am *more*, that I am *only*.

Again, I squeeze, and all the breath leaves Eurus' body. Already, the musk of his skin has invaded my senses, my world narrowed to the red staining his cheeks. I brush his wide cockhead with my thumb, delighted by the early seed seeping through the slit. He shudders, and that, too, is heady.

"You like that?" I whisper.

His eyes are black, black, black. "You know I do," he growls.

By the Mother. My face feels scorched, the skin all but peeling away from the heat kindling beneath. If I had even a sliver less of willpower, I would have already climbed onto his lap, legs spread, and taken him inside me.

Because in his arms, I am powerful. I am alluring. I am self-assured. And so, catching the translucent bead, I smear it around the crown, beneath the lip where sensitivity lingers, and use it to ease my path down his shaft.

He drops his head, panting. "Fuck." He then gives a slow thrust into my curled fingers. "Your hand feels divine."

The act feels delicious, borderline forbidden. This *should* be wrong. Not only are we caught in the final trial's web, but poison works its way through Eurus' system. But I don't care. Neither does he. And that is powerful in its own right, to know we choose each other.

Catching the back of my neck, the East Wind holds me in place, lowering his mouth to the curve where shoulder and neck join. He bites gently. The sting drags a soft sound of need from me, the flat of his tongue cooling the minor heat.

I continue to work Eurus over, playing with his balls for a time until he catches my hand and moves it back to where he wants. As he swells in my grip, he keeps his hand curled over mine, showing me without words his preferred pressure and pace. Every so often, a low grunt escapes him, and his wings gradually unfurl.

My skin tightens. Without having realized it, my strokes have increased their pace. Fast, faster now. Eurus ruts against my hand, his rhythm faltering as he peaks. With a broken cry, he erupts, coating my fingers in white webs of seed.

The hoarse peal of his desire burrows between my legs. My core pulses, hard. I squeeze my thighs tighter against the ache, trying to ignore it.

The glimmer of his eyes holds mine in thrall, and I ease closer, only half aware of our surroundings. It has grown uncomfortably warm, his flushed skin kissed with the fever of mine.

"Min." It is deep, his voice, my name mere vibration.

I catch his arm as he reaches for me. "Wait."

Eurus searches my face. Fearing that he will sense my betrayal, I drop my gaze. It is one thing to give him this pleasure. It is another to build intimacy based on a trust that does not exist.

"I thought you wanted this," he says, confused.

"I do." But I can't allow this to go further. Not tonight. Not until I have reversed my wrongdoing. "You are unwell. You should save your strength."

He frowns, and a lock of hair falls across his brow. I brush it aside and frame his cheek.

"When?" he whispers, gaze lifting to mine. "I have thought of this, of you and me, together." He appears uncertain, which in turn makes *me* feel uncertain. "We kissed. I assumed that was proof enough of how I felt."

"We did," I concede. "And what if I told you that I also have thoughts of us together?"

Eurus slides his hand along my forearm, elbow to wrist. "Then I would tell you I am here to bring you pleasure, in whatever form you desire, at whatever time you wish." Lifting my hand to his mouth, he bestows a kiss onto my open palm, eyes never leaving mine. My fingers twitch, curling inward against the tickling sensation. "I would take my time with you, bird. This, I promise you."

As his eyelids begin to sink closed, I murmur, "That is all I am asking—that we take our time. Rest, Eurus. Morning will be here soon enough."

After a time, he succumbs to sleep, but I remain awake, lifting his words like pebbles from a creek bed, admiring their smooth texture and eroded curves. The East Wind is not mine. He will never be mine. But for now, I pretend there exists a realm where he and I might belong together, and I quiet my mind, settling against him near the fire that is heat and vitality and light.

25

"Bird."

I startle awake. The room is swathed in darkness, yet a large form looms over me. My heartbeat spikes, and I recoil, hands lifting to protect my face. The voice comes again, breaking through the heavy fog of lingering slumber. "Steady, bird."

That rough, growling resonance pierces the haze. I sag onto the ground, scooped hollow of feeling. Lady Clarisse is not here. She is far from the City of Gods, back in St. Laurent.

Eurus tugs the cloak away from my face, peering down at me in concern. I blink rapidly in the brightness. Daylight. A cave. The third trial.

Slowly, I sit up, my bones creaking in protest. "How long was I asleep for?"

"A few hours. I thought it better to let you rest." He cradles my cheek in one large hand, searching my eyes. He has donned his now-dry shirt and trousers, black hair disheveled. The fire has burned to coals.

Heat climbs my face, and I pull away. "Sorry," I murmur. "I thought y-y-you were someone else."

His eyes are too grave. He knows. Of course he does. We are two sides of a single dented coin, one mortal, the other divine.

"How are you feeling?" I murmur, noticing the tremor in his hand. "Cold?"

The sweep of his thumb along my jawbone speaks of how far he has come, this immortal who once refused touch of any kind. "There is a chill in my bloodstream," he says. "I can feel it moving toward my heart. My legs ... they grow weak."

Deep breath. This is not the end. Not yet, anyway. "What of your power?"

He releases a small sphere of air. It is unable to hold its shape for long. "Still there, but it wanes."

As I expected. "We should keep moving. Seek out higher ground. We'll have a better idea of the arena's layout that way." And hopefully spot some of the remaining competitors, if the Mother of Earth wills it.

I'm moving toward the cave entrance when the East Wind grabs my forearm, faster than I believed was possible. "Wait."

He tilts his head, listening. I am motionless, my awareness of our surroundings coming into sharper focus. The scent of crushed leaves and loam swells inside my nostrils.

"Someone approaches," he murmurs.

A blink, and he scoops me into his arms, darting to the rear of the cave. He pulls me into a tight nook, between his thighs. The dark folds of his wings act as a shield against the shadows collecting at our backs.

"What is it?" I murmur into his ear. This close, I expect the heat of his body to blanket my side, but he shivers, his muscles contracting incessantly in an attempt to pull warmth back into his limbs.

"I can't be sure," he says, the words oddly thick, "but it sounds like ..." He swallows. "Stay here. I'm going to take a look."

"What? No!" I snatch at his cloak with one clawed hand. "It's not safe."

"It won't be for long." He searches my eyes, and in their clouded depths I spot ... something. It is unfamiliar in the way the sea is unfamiliar, wrapped in terror and awe both.

We come together. The kiss is sweet, yet brief. Eurus vanishes in the light beyond, moving far more quickly than I would expect from someone who has been poisoned.

I remain crouched in place, sweat trickling from my underarms. Round and round my thoughts spin. What to do? Should I stay here? Or perhaps I should go after him. But what if I endanger him further? No, best to stay safe. *And small. And do nothing.*

Nothing, I can do. Nothing, I am familiar with. And it is *nothing* that has gotten me into this mess. I have come far, haven't I? Farther than I would have believed. As it is, I no longer wish to be someone who observes from afar.

Beyond the mouth of the cave, the sky is clear, untouched by clouds. The slope toward the river reveals the unbroken wood. Seeing as Eurus is too weak to fly, he would not have gotten far on foot.

As I follow his tracks downhill, an animal's bellow erupts from across the river. Was that Eurus? Or another competitor? His footsteps end at the river bank. He must have crossed onto the other side.

A fallen tree offers a means to traverse the swiftly moving water. Once I reach the opposite bank, I plow through a thicket of bramble. The thorns are many. They draw blood with their pointed fingers, stinging kisses alighting on my cheeks and arms. I break into a clearing and slow, ears straining for sound.

A rustle to my left. I spin, snatching a fallen branch from the ground. Not that it will do any good against these immortals. And now I feel particularly foolish for having abandoned the safety of the cave.

There is a footstep. Another.

I lift the branch with both hands, braced for whatever emerges from the undergrowth.

It's Arin.

The slender, dark-skinned god emerges into the dappled light. He carries his staff with its serpent-carved head. His clothes are torn, and scabs dot his arms and the side of his neck where a deep puncture wound oozes. I lift my pitiful weapon higher as he regards me in shock.

"Min? What—" But he shakes his head, scours the clearing, before his focus returns to me. "Where is he?"

As if I would tell him. "Gone."

Staff raised, he steps forward. My pulse flutters a warning. "He's not dead. The bell didn't ring. So tell me, Min. Where is Eurus?"

"I just told you. Gone. I don't know where he went." And thank the Mother for that.

"You expect me to believe Eurus abandoned you?" Arin shakes his head. Gone are the easy smiles, the flirtatious nature. The sinuous motion of his hands reminds me of a snake. "I have never seen him so protective of anything, much less a woman." Another step forward. "So where would he go?"

Sweat pours down my face as I am forced into retreat. My mind turns to numbers. The miles separating me from Eurus, how far I might be able to run before Arin catches me. If I scream, it will draw Eurus' attention, and I want to avoid placing him in danger when he is weakened.

"Keep your distance," I warn, hefting the branch higher. Leaves crunch beneath my feet, and my back hits a tree.

The curl of Arin's mouth is a poor facsimile of a smile. "I don't want to hurt you, Min, but I will, if you do not tell me where he went. Is he lying in wait? Injured?" I keep my expression neutral. "Tell me!"

I swing. Arin leaps nimbly out of the way. He lifts his staff, and I watch, horrified, as the eyes of the carved serpent begin to glow.

"Do you know what this staff does?" Before I can respond, he presses forward. "It has the ability to draw strength from anyone it touches. For immortals, this means their power. But you? You haven't any powers. So it will draw from you your very essence of life." Round and round the staff twirls, Arin watching me all the while. "Is that what you want?"

What I want is to survive this day.

"Last chance," Arin says.

Again, I swing. He dodges, darts in close, grasping my neck and slamming me back against the trunk. The eyes of the snake capture mine. They glow liquid gold, and as I attempt to lash out, my limbs stiffen, curbed by some repressive force as something like acid pools in my lower belly. It sparks, catches fire. It burns.

A wild shriek cuts the air before I bite my tongue, my scream muffled as the pain gouges into my gut.

"Scream as loud as you wish," he murmurs. "The sooner Eurus hears you, the faster he will come."

The wrenching sensation sharpens. It feels like my ribs are being pried apart, my internal organs rearranged in uncomfortable ways. *Say nothing. This is not the worst you have endured.* My only hope is that Arin will decide to keep me alive as leverage against Eurus.

Another twist of his staff, and my knees buckle. Numbness consumes my fingertips, spreads up my arms. The pain erupts through my chest, and my cry crumbles. *Mother of Earth*, I plead. *Help me.*

"Is this a tea party?" croons an icy voice I don't recognize. "Why did I not receive an invitation? You know I dearly love tea."

Arin releases me. I collapse into a ball, shuddering. My ears are ringing, a high-pitched whistle burrowing straight through my temples like a thousand threads of white lightning. It takes a great effort to lift my head, and every slight motion washes my body in pain.

When the fog finally recedes, revealing who has stepped into the clearing, my stomach drops. One of the Fates.

This sister appears to have fought the forest and lost. Multiple lacerations mar her chest and arms where the fabric of her tunic has torn away.

She limps into the clearing, teeth bared. "Didn't I tell you I would find you, Arin? Didn't I promise your death would hurt?"

The goddess stumbles, but manages to catch herself against a tree, panting. "You think you can kill my sisters and get away with it?"

Her gaze then shifts to me. They are vacant, those eyes, like a hearth gone cold. "And the mortal. Escaped the cave, did you?" As my heart stutters in comprehension, the Fate's lips curl in satisfaction. "My sisters and I thought your participation would be a delightful addition. But where is the East Wind, I wonder? Too focused on protecting his weak mortal to win?"

She sneers before returning her attention to Arin, who trips backward, staff raised. And as the Fate draws a dagger from her belt,

I bolt in the opposite direction, Arin's screams chasing me into the forest's deep.

Miles later, my legs give out. I hit the ground, falling into a pile of damp leaves cloaking the forest floor. Rolling onto my back, I gaze up at the small breaks in the canopy. Sweat slicks my skin, and despite the climbing sun, the shade breeds frost.

I cannot run forever. I cannot *hide* forever. The longer I act as prey, the more I am convinced I will perish as such.

But I deserve no such fate. My next step? Find Eurus. If he returned to the cave and found it empty, would he have assumed the worst? I should return, but I'm hopelessly lost, with neither weapon nor direction to guide me. And what if the East Wind has succumbed to Gray Snare? If he is unable to call for me, the odds of finding him are slim.

After backtracking toward the river, I follow its winding path, the swift, dark waters hurtling downstream. Always, I keep to the shadows, listening. At some point, the bell tolls again, and again. Two more competitors dead. Only three left alive.

As I creep alongside a fallen tree, a subtle crunch alerts me. I freeze. "Eurus?"

Footsteps to my right. Ducking behind a tree, I peer toward a clump of bushes, frowning. It sounds like a hound, nose to the earth, snuffling heavily. When the animal pushes into the open, I recoil in horror.

It is . . . I'm not sure what it is, exactly. It is a bull, it is a man, it is all beast. Though distinctly human in shape, its long, hairy torso is bent forward, its hands—no, *hooves*—planted into the ground. A pair of filthy trousers hangs from its narrow hips. A whip thin tail lashes at its flank. And those eyes . . . yellow, like tepid water choked with grime.

Mother, it is ugly. I'm not sure what shadow realm birthed this creature, but I can't imagine it has ever experienced a warm welcome.

I hold myself still as it searches the area, at one point drawing near enough that I catch a whiff of its stench. I gag and switch to breathing through my mouth.

The beast vanishes, but does not go far. Every so often, I catch sight of its hunched spine through the wood. I'm not sure how long I wait for it to vanish before I decide to risk retreat. Every minute brings Eurus closer to collapse. I simply cannot delay.

But I underestimate the creature's keen hearing. As the leaves stir around my ankles, its head snaps in my direction, snout lifted to scent the air. From its chest emerges a low growl of warning.

I run.

The only direction is this: away. I bolt right, plunging through the shadows, toward a denser area of the forest. With a burst of speed, I manage to pull ahead, but only briefly. By the time I reach the bank, my thighs quiver weakly. But I do not stop. I can't. The predator in pursuit forces me through the river, which is so swollen it has nearly overflowed its banks.

Water drags at my calves, thighs, waist. It rises toward my breasts, its icy touch chilling me to the core. The silty riverbed slinks over my toes as I edge toward the middle of the waterway, doing my best to block out the trilling of alarm bells somewhere in the back of my mind. The current is far stronger than it appears. It continually seeks to upset my balance.

The water has now reached my shoulders. My teeth are chattering, yet I am careful. Too careful, some would say. So I'm not sure how my feet slip from under me. I only know my balance is lost as I fall into the water and am swept downstream.

The rapids break over me. I gasp, spitting water, and go under, spinning forward and backward. The river bends. I'm tossed around its curve. Ahead, a toppled tree dams the water's rush. I kick hard, reaching, the tips of my fingers skimming one of the branches. I manage to catch the bough, the sudden lurch wrenching my shoulder painfully.

The beast, too, has been swept along by the current. It hurtles straight for me.

I scramble up the trunk, managing to haul myself from the water. I have nearly reached the shore when the beast collides with the tree.

Wood crunches beneath me with a horrific splinter. I scream and toss myself forward, landing in a graceless heap half in, half out of the river. On hands and knees, I crawl. Up, up, up the sloped bank, before I bolt into the woods. "Eurus!" By the Mother, where is he?

The sound of hoofbeats signals the creature's pursuit. I dare not look behind me, lest I lose speed. My throat has been scraped raw, each punctuating gasp a knife tip gouging flesh. I haven't the strength to outrun it. Haven't the strength to climb a tree. My legs wobble, and I grit my teeth, push and push and push. Another bellow cracks the air. It is close.

As I leap over a large root, I catch a low-hanging branch, use my momentum to swing myself around the tree. The beast crashes into a bush, having not anticipated my change of direction.

"Bird!"

I glance up with a gasp. Eurus soars over me, one arm outstretched. The span of his wings fully blankets the earth below. Ahead, a fallen tree blocks my path.

"I'll catch you," he calls down.

My foot catches the trunk, and I shove upward with all my might, launching myself as high as I can go. The East Wind catches me midair around the waist, and we veer sharply to the right, whisked between two massive conifers.

Except the edge of his wing catches in one of the branches, and we're jerked sideways. I shield my face from the piercing limbs. One stabs me in the neck, a shallow slice across my collarbone. Leaves scatter with a furious hiss of sound.

"Shit." The East Wind thrashes to and fro, wings flapping in a desperate attempt to regain lost altitude, but then we are falling, down and down and down. My stomach drives into my throat. I clutch Eurus tightly, eyes squeezed shut.

We hit the ground.

The East Wind struggles to roll over. "Bird? Are you hurt?" He grasps my face, peering close. His skin is like ice, tinged blue around the mouth.

I shake my head, wincing as I push to my feet. "I'm all r— Behind you!"

He's up, shoving me aside as the beast appears through the undergrowth. As soon as it sights Eurus, it goes still. Its sallow eyes boil with a wrath that goes beyond simple misunderstanding. It has been exiled, imprisoned, disgraced. A twig snaps beneath its heavy hoof.

Eurus sends a blast of air at the beast. The tendrils shift into thick bands of rope that wrap its bony legs and snout, but sweat pours down Eurus' face from the effort. How long will his power last before it is depleted?

The East Wind is so focused on the bull he does not notice a slim, dark figure emerging from the thicket, staff raised.

"No!"

I ram Arin from behind. His weapon flies from his hand as we hit the ground.

I'm crawling toward it when Arin grabs my ankle, yanking me backward with a muffled curse. Before he's able to grasp the staff, I throw myself onto his back, wrap my arms around his neck. His head snaps back. Agony explodes through my forehead, and I fall to the ground, half-blind with pain.

The East Wind emits an ear-shattering roar. There is a sickening thud somewhere to my right.

My eyes crack open. The world blurs, then settles into place. Arin is crumpled at the base of a tree. Meanwhile, the bull has been contained in a spiraling mass of winds.

Curling his hand around Arin's throat, Eurus lifts the smaller immortal, slams him back into the trunk of the tree, his face so close their noses brush. Even weakened, the East Wind is no mere deity. He towers. He looms.

"You touch Min," he snarls, "you die." A wind-carved blade appears in hand and cuts toward Arin's neck.

"Wait!"

The wind-sword halts a hair's breadth from the smaller deity's throat.

Eurus says, his expression whittled to the finest rage, "He tried to kill you, bird."

My arms shake as I push myself upright. "I know," I whisper. But when I arrived at the City of Gods, I had not one ally. I was a mortal, a stranger in this realm. And Arin ... he was kind to me. It is something I have rarely experienced, that kindness.

"He will kill you if I let him go," Eurus growls as Arin's struggles lessen. "Do you want to live or die, bird? Choose."

My teeth sink into the soft flesh of my cheek. I promised myself I would never treat others as Lady Clarisse treated me. It is not for me to decide that my life is better than, more deserving. But today's decision impacts the morrow's rise. Something folds in me. "I don't want to die," I whisper.

He strikes. By the time I process what has occurred, Arin lies dead, his throat cut.

Shock enfolds me, and I turn away. A scarlet pool slinks across the forest floor, outlining my bare feet in red. As if from a great distance, a low bell tolls.

In the end, only one can walk through the door of the final trial. And yet, I cannot help but mourn Arin.

An explosive howl disturbs the birds from their roosts. The beast, who has been thrashing against the East Wind's bindings, pushes forcefully against the substance. With a last cry of rage, the creature tears through its bindings, charging straight toward the East Wind.

"Run, Min!"

Into the forest's depth I plunge. *Away, away, away.* But—Eurus.

I lurch to a halt, peering through the shadows shivering between the clustered trees. As the East Wind hits the ground, the beast stabs downward with a splintered branch torn from a tree. Its points tear through the membrane of Eurus' wings. He releases an agonized yelp.

"Eurus!" I begin fighting my way back through the bracken, thorns be damned.

Wrenching himself free, the East Wind blasts the beast into a tree with his waning power. Briefly, his eyes meet mine, and in their depths, I see every fragment of his past colliding, a tempestuous meeting of *then* and *now*. "Go! I'll be right behind you."

"But—"

"I promise. Now *go*."

I do as the East Wind says. I go, and I do not stop until my legs threaten to buckle. As I weave through a great mound of roots, however, pain rips through my shoulder. I hit the ground with a shriek and spot a gash in my flesh where an arrow clipped me.

From the shadows, there emerges a blaze of reddish light. My lungs seize. Milk white skin and hair like flame, and a black whip, gleaming.

"Eurus' mortal." The Fate's weapon slithers through the grass at her feet like a dutiful companion. She halts, looming over me with a sharp-toothed grin. "We meet again."

I thought Arin had taken care of the final Fate, but I was wrong. One of her wings hangs lopsided from her back—broken. That must explain why she travels on foot.

I glance around, but she is alone. The last of Eurus' competitors, if I am not mistaken, now that Arin is dead.

I open my mouth, but the goddess snaps her wrist, and the whip coils around my neck, the cool leather an unexpected bite against my skin. "Uh-uh." A firm tug cuts off my air supply. "Not a sound. Understand?"

The pressure migrates to my eyes. It is too much. I nod desperately, relieved when the whip loosens long enough to allow me to draw breath.

"Here is what we're going to do," says the Fate. "Eurus is all that stands between me and victory, and I intend to walk through that door. You're going to call for him. You will mention nothing of my presence." Her eyes sit like holes in her face, full of untold horrors. "If you cooperate, I promise not to kill you. Once Eurus is dead and the door appears, you are free to walk through it. Agreed?"

I cannot deny my heart. It yearns for the East Wind in all ways, but ... I want to live. Is that so bad a thing?

Mutely, I nod. The whip uncoils from my throat.

"Eurus!" It takes every effort to lace my tone with enthusiasm. "Eurus, this way!" My cry ripples out, a joyous declaration.

"Bird?"

"Over here!" My voice cracks.

The Fate cants her head. Clouds drift across her eyes, which blur in confusion. Suddenly, she bolts in the opposite direction. I watch her departure with unease. Something has changed.

"Bird!" Eurus calls.

"I'm here!" I scream. Pushing to my feet, I sway, catching myself against a tree.

Then it comes, a bottomless echo, straight from the belly of the beast.

My pulse crests, for it is a sound most familiar, and it soaks St. Laurent in its ominous roar daily: the surge of a great, powerful wave.

My head snaps in the direction of the low rumble. Birds scatter with shrieks of warning, and the earth trembles underfoot.

The East Wind appears, stumbling through the thicket, eyes ringed white with fear. "Min, climb!"

He catches me around the waist, shoving me up the tree, one hand planted on my backside. It jolts me into motion. My fingers latch around the lowest branch. From there, I scramble up, reaching for the next handhold as a deafening eruption engulfs us.

Curling my fingers around the bark, I glance down. Eurus leans against the trunk, noticeably frail.

"Keep going," he barks. "Don't worry about me."

I haul myself higher into the tree, then higher still. *Don't look down.* If there is one rule of survival, let it be that. Despite his waning strength, Eurus manages to pull himself amongst the boughs.

The ground rocks, and I clutch the trunk with bitten fingertips, whimpering. From this vantage point, I see the whole of the surrounding wood, its leafy crown grazed by a gentle wind. But amidst the tranquility, something stirs. There, in the distance, a great wave breaches the horizon, barreling forward in a gnashing of white foam.

Up to the next branch, a thick creaking of wood. As I scramble higher, my foot slips, the skin of my palms stinging as I clutch the bough above me until I regain my footing.

When I look back down, however, the East Wind remains slumped on the lowest branch, face gray with exhaustion. "Eurus!"

"I'll be all right, bird." He gulps for air, his back pressed against the trunk. Sweat slides down his face.

He's too weak, I realize. Out of the corner of my eye, I see the tree begin to give way. "I'll come help."

"No!" As he inhales shakily, his dulled eyes meet mine. "Keep climbing."

And leave him to drown?

There is no victory without the East Wind, no triumph unless it is he and I, together. The flood nears, yet I will face it, as I have faced each obstacle that came before.

Carefully, I descend to the branch above Eurus. Trees snap and shatter in the wake of the water's force. "Grab my hand."

He stares at my outstretched fingers with kindling fury. "You can't lift me," he argues. "I'm too heavy. Now get back up the tree!"

"I can try." Wildlife flee across the forest floor. A flock of birds explodes skyward, their caws of distress soon muffled by the impending roar. "Hurry!"

"I will not be responsible for your death," he snarls. "Listen to me—"

"No, *you* listen to me," I hiss with a deranged flash of teeth. "I'm not leaving you. You either take my hand, or we stay as we are. Choose." My heart quivers. My legs have all but liquified, each massive tremor draining their strength. Live together, die together, so long as I am not alone.

Whatever emotion clouds the East Wind's expression—horror, fury—it spurs him to grab hold.

By the Mother, he's heavy. I heave, my back screaming in agony. Something pops in my wounded shoulder, and I yelp, my grip loosening.

Eurus leans against the trunk, panting. His wings dangle from his back like pieces of a corpse. And all around, the air is alive, a great roar dousing all thought. "Eurus, you need to climb. *Now.*"

As I tighten my fingers around his hand, the flood breaches the undergrowth. Trees collapse, shatter into a thousand fragments. Then the wave slams into our tree.

I scream. Water slaps my face, demanding I yield. I choke, inhale liquid, yet it passes, and I blink to clear my vision. The tree bends, creaking ominously, as the force of the flood threatens to yank its roots from the soil.

All the while, the current streams over branches, under leaves. It swarms Eurus' waist—higher, to his chest. My eyes widen as the surface creeps upward, nearing his neck. My bone-breaking grip is all that connects me to Eurus.

Another drag of the tide, and my shoulder joint ignites with pain. *Mother, grant me bones of iron.* I bite the inside of my cheek, clinging to the branch with all my strength. Felled trees drift by as though they are mere twigs in a child's pond.

Suddenly, the water slips between our fingers, and his grip loosens. I dig in my nails as the East Wind's eyes meet mine.

"Don't do it," I cry.

"It's all right, bird," he soothes, and I have never heard a more feeble lie. He knows, and I know. If he continues to hold on, we will both be ripped from the tree.

I stare down at his face, all the more beautiful for its imperfections. Why do I only recognize the truth when it is far too late?

"This isn't how it was supposed to be," I choke out. And what *would have been*? In an ideal world, forgiveness, peace, a shared life. But I see what will follow the moment Eurus releases his hold. The weight of his wings will drag him down, hold him beneath the surface until his lungs fill with water. "Hold on. Just for a little while longer."

A shudder runs down his arm and into mine. "I haven't the strength, bird. This isn't your fate, you hear me? Your fate is to live."

"As is yours!" A sob cracks my sternum in two. "Please, just . . ."

He lets go.

"Eurus!"

The swollen waters suck him down. He slams into a tree and is swept downstream.

I scream as the trunk lurches, roots releasing their hold on the earth. *No.* A sharp keen wells behind my clenched teeth. I scan the churning water, my eyes so choked with tears I cannot distinguish his shape from the forest. Eurus will survive. He *must*.

On the flood sweeps, and still on. Though my unstable shelter bows against the rushing water, I keep my eyes open. Now is not the time to collapse. I am alive, which means there is still much to do. Eventually, the flood will move on, and when it does, I will follow its path of destruction. I will not stop until the East Wind is found.

Because he and I were not destined to die. We were destined to live. Not survive—*live*. And maybe . . . maybe our fates are not separate, as I had initially believed. Maybe they are, in fact, intertwined.

After a time, I realize the water level is dropping. Its rush has slowed.

The moment the flood has eased into a trickle, I clamber down the listing tree, feet sinking into the sodden earth. Debris litters the forest floor. The sun punches through countless new breaks in the wood where trees had once stood. My breath stirs the still air.

From afar, there comes a snap, followed by the crash of a collapsing branch. Then this: the low tolling of the bell.

With each discordant clang, my stomach drops lower, hips to knees to feet to ground. The water took my father, but he was mortal. The East Wind would not go quietly. Foolish of me, to think he would not go at all.

I race in the direction I saw Eurus vanish. In addition to the wooden fragments, numerous dead animals litter the ground. Ahead, I spot something. I gasp, quickening my pace, then slow upon recognizing its shape.

The last of the Fates, red hair strewn about like cobwebs, neck broken.

My lips quaver. I seal them tight, eyes stinging. If not for Eurus, I would have met my death in that ferocious water. But I was saved. The day is not yet done.

Less than a mile later, I spot the East Wind slumped against a tree, nursing a broken arm. It is a sight like summer, a brilliant, most vibrant sun.

My breath comes short. I vowed I would not break, not yet. I would wait until we had returned to the privacy of our palace suite.

But he is whole. A bit bruised, perhaps, and shaken, but not broken like those splintered trees. And as his eyes meet mine, a sob fights its way free of my clenched teeth.

Eurus limps toward me, mud-spattered wings trailing behind him. His expression is one of agonized relief. "Bird."

I fall into his arms. How can I not? The brine of the sea fills my nostrils; I inhale it greedily. And his voice, his *voice*. It is a balm as he murmurs reassurances, a promise that I am safe, and he is well, and we are together.

"I thought . . ." Another wavering breath shudders out of me. No matter the years that pass, I will never forget the image of his hand torn from my grip, its disappearance beneath the rising flood. "Eurus—"

His mouth crashes onto mine, eager tongue parting my lips, and I've half a mind to rip off his cloak and finish what was started in the cave. As I press forward, he releases a soft hiss of pain. His arm!

When I attempt to pull away, Eurus growls, "No," and hauls me closer.

The kiss is one of insanity. It is everything, every fraught terror, every broken thread of yearning, every sugar-drenched wish of tomorrow.

By the time we pull apart, I'm panting. "The beast," I manage. "Was that the one everyone's been talking about?"

Grave is his mouth, the narrowing of his black eyes. "Yes, but it is dead. I imagine the council captured it, thinking it would make good sport for the final trial."

Of course they would. "When you were swept downstream, I—"

"Bird." One of his large hands cradles my face. "I'm all right," he whispers, brushing his lips with mine. "We both are."

Thank the Mother of Earth for that.

It is then he takes me into his arms. The dripping fabric of his cloak sticks to my chilled skin, yet I do not feel cold in the slightest. But his trembling gives me pause. The poison!

I pull back in worry, only to find the East Wind laughing. "What is it?" I ask in confusion.

His chuckle tapers off, and he points. "Look."

The door.

Perched on a distant hill, haloed by a red sun, its gold-plated frame is every dream realized. I have never seen a more beautiful sight.

"We did it, bird." Eurus gazes down at me, and in his eyes, I see a depth of emotion I have yearned for, quietly, on those particularly frigid nights in the privacy of my bedroom. "We won."

Biting my quivering lower lip, I nod, throat too tight to speak. So we did.

Together, arms wrapped around each other's waists, we hobble toward salvation. With every step forward, the earth rises, but not once do we lose our footing. Then we are standing before the door, outlined in a ring of light. The East Wind offers his hand. It says, *I am with you* and *You are not alone* and *Together, always.* As I slip my hand into his, Eurus turns the handle, and together, we stumble through.

26

I HAVE NEVER RESTED SO WELL AS I DO IN THE HOURS FOLLOWING the third trial. I am nestled under thick blankets on one of the infirmary cots, a wall of windows overlooking the ivy-covered courtyard. Below, deities mill about, some reading on benches beneath the large shade trees, others congregating near the fountain to discuss the tournament.

Eurus lies unconscious on a neighboring cot. The grime of his clothes sticks to his skin, his every cut a vibrant red against the bruises mottling his face. I would reach for his hand were I not afraid it might wake him. After he was given the antidote to Gray Snare, the healer administered an incredibly strong sleep potion, to allow his body to recover. He will need to stay overnight for further observation.

One hundred and ten contestants entered the tournament, but only one triumphed, in the end. The East Wind claimed victory, but at what cost? Tomorrow, at the victor's banquet, he will poison the Council of Gods with Eastern Blood. It may be his hand doling out the sentence, but what of his silent accomplice—me? Do I not hold some responsibility for the council's demise?

Once my end of the bargain has been fulfilled, Eurus will take me back to St. Laurent, where Lady Clarisse lies in wait. The knowledge wedges a tightness against my ribs. Then again, what did I expect?

The City of Gods is not my home, nor my heart. I will leave and he will stay. This is what was always written.

An hour later, I'm discharged from the infirmary. While Eurus recuperates, I return to our suite, where I pen a final message to her ladyship.

Dear Lady Clarisse,

I hope this letter finds you well. I come bearing unfortunate news. The East Wind's god-touched ax has been destroyed. A tournament took place in the City of Gods, and his weapon was smashed to pieces in the process. I apologize that I was not able to carry out my promise. I know how eager you were to acquire it. If it is a potion of immortality you seek, I am certain we can find another way.

—Min

There. That should stop her scheming.

With the letter and an extra generous helping of Nan's strength tea in hand, I venture down to The Blind Oracle, where the Courier sits at the bar nursing a glass of whiskey. He agrees to deliver the final letter and accepts the tea for payment. I then return to the palace, where I draw myself a bath, scrub the filth from my skin. And when the water is all murk, I dry myself with a towel, don a clean sleeping gown, and tumble into bed, where I think no more.

I wake to the sound of rushing water.

Snapping upright, I gasp, a hand to my chest. Darkness swathes the bedroom. Dried saliva blots my cheek, which I hurriedly scrub clean with the sleeve of my sleeping gown. I blink as my surroundings come into focus.

Is that . . . ? I frown. It sounds like water slopping over the rim of a tub.

Dropping my legs over the edge of the mattress, I push from bed, easing open the door. The main chamber of the suite is empty, though three candles brighten the space. A light splash sounds from within the washroom. Then: a low, tortured groan.

Gooseflesh stipples my arms and legs, and warmth gathers in my pelvis. The East Wind—bathing. But of course, who else would be behind that door? He must have been released from the infirmary.

My eyes squeeze shut as Eurus emits another satisfied groan. Would it be absolutely absurd to enter the washroom? I could help wash his wings, that hard-to-reach area between his shoulder blades. It would be no hardship.

He sighs as though he sinks deeper in the water, and I imagine his wings draped over the sides of the tub. A low, breathless exhalation escapes me before I can call it back.

His sigh cuts off. "Bird?"

I bolt to the opposite side of the room. Just as I throw myself onto the sofa, the East Wind emerges from the washroom, enveloped in a hot cloud of steam, a towel wrapped around his solid waist.

My face flames. I never believed myself capable of envy, but I am incredibly envious of that towel. Water beads like diamonds across his supple skin, stretched taut over thickly muscled arms, shoulders, and thighs. The plane of his abdomen is demarcated by shallow grooves.

Eurus stares at me with dark eyes. My insides quiver beneath his regard.

"How are you feeling?" I ask him.

He hesitates: step forward, or stay put? In the end, he approaches, one hand gripping the towel at his waist. "I should be back at my old strength in a few days."

The scent of his soap—lemon and sage—mists the air. I drink it down. "I'm glad to hear it," I reply.

"Did you worry?" he asks, much knowing in his voice. And perhaps a shred of vulnerability, too.

"I did." The longer he gazes at me, the more I fear I will do something rash, like leap into his arms and wrap my legs around his waist. "You were in good hands, but . . . I did worry," I admit, my words fading to a whisper.

Perhaps that is a sentiment he is not willing to scrutinize too closely, for the East Wind abruptly says, "I need to change."

I nod, swallow. "Of course." My eyes track his retreat into his bedroom. I release a long, *long* exhalation. My skin fizzles with heat.

When the East Wind reemerges, dressed in trousers and a crisp, button-down shirt, he takes a seat on the opposite end of the sofa. I study him, never more aware of his body than I am in this moment. Helplessly, my eyes drop to his mouth.

His nostrils flare, and he murmurs, one arm outstretched, "Come here, bird."

After a slight hesitation, I slide toward him and allow him to tuck me against his side.

"How does it feel?" I ask him. "Victory?"

Shadows carve the corners of his mouth and eyes. It is a long moment before he responds. "I suppose I thought I would feel some sort of relief." He stares out the window for a time. "So why does it feel as though nothing has changed?"

That, I cannot answer. I am not privy to the inner workings of the East Wind's heart.

"You won," I say, but for whatever reason, I find it difficult to dredge up the enthusiasm. "This is what you wanted."

"What I wanted," he murmurs to himself. Before I can fully evaluate that comment, he stands, tugging me to my feet. "I've a gift for you— for tonight's banquet."

"A gift?"

He draws me toward the dining table, where a gift box rests. I study it with an odd sense of fear. The wrapping paper is an iridescent green, the bow so ornate it reminds me of a flower.

"Go on," he says. "Open it."

I slide the top off the box. Pushing aside the delicate tissue paper, I pull out a long, sleek, ruby gown rippling like a wave of boiling lava. My breath catches. "It's beautiful." Gold gemstones stud the curved neckline, leading to two thin shoulder straps. I've never owned anything half as fine.

I lower my arms. "I don't know what to say."

"Generally, a *thank you* will suffice," he says with unexpected affection.

Carefully, I fold the gown back into the box. "Thank you, Eurus."

"Will you try it on?"

"Um." I nibble on my lower lip. "I suppose." He continues to stare at me until I swipe the box and carry it into the washroom, the scent of lemon and sage a perfume against my skin.

After slipping on the slippery red fabric, I brush a hand down the bodice. It fits quite well, though the waist is a tad large. The heels, which I uncover at the bottom of the box, are equally fine, though their added height forces me off-balance. I pray I do not trip.

The gift box holds another surprise: lip rouge and blush, which I use to draw color to my skin. Lastly, a pearl clip to adorn my hair.

The moment I exit the washroom, the East Wind stares at me like . . . I don't have the words. Like I am his sun and his moon. Like the world may end, but I will still be here, a vision sent from the gods.

"You look . . ." He advances toward me, his daze burned away to reveal a depth of longing that frightens me even as I find myself willingly drawn into its folds.

I cross my arms, drop them, cross them again. "Do you think the gown is too immodest?"

He catches my hands in his much broader ones. "It's perfect, as are you."

So many complicated emotions crowding forward. "Thank you," I whisper shyly. I feel beautiful, which is not something I have felt in, well, ever. "You look very handsome as well." And he does. Trim trousers, emerald shirt tucked into his belted waistband, and shining leather shoes, the same polished black as his wings.

Catching the point of my chin, he draws my face gently upward. "You are sad, bird. Do you not like the gown?"

A great cloud hangs over me. What are gowns and trinkets compared to what lies in my heart? Soon, it will be morning, eve having progressed beyond my reach. I am not ready for farewells.

"Eurus." I gaze at him openly, my eyes wet. "When we met, you were an absolute brute. You were angry at yourself, at your father, at the world. You did not trust, and for good reason. I can't imagine the courage it took to return home and face those who hurt you.

"Despite that, you proved change is possible," I continue. "And that sometimes we don't need what we once did to move forward in our lives."

His wings rustle in an endearingly bashful manner. "Min—"

"Please, listen to me." I grasp his hand so he does not feel alone or judged. Once, his touch speared terror through me, for I believed he would treat me as Lady Clarisse had done. But I was wrong. Now, the warmth of his skin brings calmness, security. "I'm not going to plead with you to reconsider poisoning the council. The choice is not mine to make."

His throat dips with emotion, but I go on. I cannot stop. "I know how painful it is to even *consider* granting forgiveness to those we believe do not deserve it," I whisper. "But at tonight's banquet, I hope you think about what forgiveness means for you. And I hope that, when the time comes, you'll forgive, and let go."

Attendees mill about the palace parlor. Its ornate chandeliers emit soft lamplight, and the numerous sofas, armchairs, and chaises have been arranged in intimate groupings throughout the room, where the gods can drink and relax.

Eurus, a dark, winged shadow at my side, rests a hand on my lower spine. With the plunging back of my dress, it is almost inevitable that his hot skin will kiss mine.

Tonight, the East Wind will demand his favor from the Council of Gods. He will be welcomed back to his homeland. Then he will take Eastern Blood, poison every last one of the twelve council members for having banished him. Three weeks later, the entire council will be dead. It is everything he wants.

As though sensing my trepidation, he squeezes my hand. "Everything will be fine," he assures me.

So he claims.

A short, squat deity whose sandaled feet glisten with oil draws Eurus into discussion. Since the East Wind revealed his face in The Blind Oracle the other night, many have begun to acknowledge him, treat him with courtesy.

While Eurus talks, I wander to a table laden with hors d'oeuvres. As I stuff two cheese tarts into my mouth, someone taps my shoulder, and I turn.

"Arin!" I gape at the dark-skinned god. "What are you doing here? I thought..."

He appears uncomfortable beneath my scrutiny. His weight shifts, one leg to the other. "The Council of Gods decided, as a reward for such an *engaging* tournament this year, that they would resurrect those that were killed in the trials. Which is lucky, I guess." He frowns as he says this. "But that's not what I wanted to say to you." He takes a breath. "I wanted to apologize for my behavior in the tournament."

"Don't," I whisper, touching his sleeve. "It's in the past. I don't hold it against you."

"You should."

My time in the City of Gods has not been without its epiphanies. Arin may be a god, but he has family he cares for. He bleeds, as I do. "You sacrificed your life for your sister. It was a selfless thing to do."

"Hello, Min from Marles."

I stiffen. It would be rude to ignore the goddess, who has appeared at Arin's side, so I dip my chin. "Demi."

She studies me intently. "I'm glad to see you made it through the tournament unscathed."

Unscathed? I scoff. "Yes, well, no thanks to you." The Council of Gods so dearly loves their entertainment.

Her gaze is wary. I have been a mouse all my life, but this goddess has suddenly found herself facing a venomous snake. Demi is no fool. She recognizes something has changed. "May we speak privately?" she asks.

I chew on the side of my cheek, considering her request. I do not have to agree if I do not want to. But a part of me dearly wishes this has been a gross misunderstanding. "Very well." I follow her into a small study, moonlight limning the curved wooden desk. Once I pass through, she shuts the door behind me.

At once, Demi seems to deflate. She is a tall woman with great presence, but even she is minimized when distant from the light. "So," she says. "Now you know."

Fury climbs my skin so readily I wrestle with the urge to scratch at her eyes. "That's all you can say?" I spit. "*Now you know?*" I would never expect this lack of consideration from someone I'd believed to care for me. "You lied to me," I hiss. "All this time, you were on the council, and I was too stupid to see past your façade." How deeply do I really know the goddess standing before me? If she is on the council, then she must be one of the most powerful and influential of all the gods. "Who are you? What do mortals call you, I mean?"

"I believe in Marles, you call me the Mother of Earth."

My gut lurches with bitter poison, that Demi would jest in such a manner. "I see. You're making fun of me. Well, I don't appreciate it—"

"Min," she says, sorrow swimming through her eyes. "It is the truth."

My face grows uncomfortably warm, and I realize how crowded the study feels, with its bookshelves and desk and chairs. "You can't be. You—"

You smell of chervil.

I press a hand to my stomach. I had spoken of the Mother of Earth before, at length. Demi had every opportunity to reveal her identity. It feels like further manipulation that she chose not to, taking advantage of the poor mortal. "You should have told me."

"Yes." She looks away, her eyes downcast.

"So why didn't you?"

The goddess wraps her arms around her front. "I'm sorry to say I don't have a good answer for you beyond that I enjoyed what it felt like to live a life of anonymity, however brief."

"I thought we were friends," I whisper, voice warbling.

"We are, Min."

"But you were only using me to get information on Eurus, weren't you."

The Mother of Earth reaches for me. I take a step back, warning her without words to keep her distance.

"That's not it," Demi says. "It was never about getting information on Eurus. As I said before, our relationship was over long ago. Though I do still care for him, I wanted to spend time with you because I enjoyed your company, if you can believe it."

I do not.

"If you still care for him," I say, "why didn't you try to help him? Why did you vote to banish Eurus and his brothers from the City of Gods?"

"Min." She sighs, and at her back, the darkness shifts, thinning around her generous curves. "There is no easy choice. There is only *a* choice. Unfortunately, I am on the Council of Gods. If I want my voice to mean *anything*, that means acting in accordance to what we all believe is best for the realm, whether or not I agree with it."

"So what you're saying is that your word means nothing."

The goddess opens her mouth, closes it. A bell chimes, signaling the start of dinner.

"Excuse me," I mutter, all but tripping in my haste to escape the study.

As guests begin moving toward the dining room, I search for Eurus. Our eyes meet across the parlor. His wings flare slightly, forcing others back.

He is one stream, and I another. We carve our paths, meeting beneath the large, glittering chandelier. As he takes my hand, his wings curve at my back, helping to cloak me from passersby. "What's wrong, bird?"

"I don't want to talk about it," I mutter.

He glares at something over my shoulder. Demi, I assume.

"We should take our seats," I say. "Is everything prepared?"

"Everything is as it should be."

My belly roils at that. *His decision*, I remind myself. In the end, I control nothing. It is his life, not mine. Even if the thought of a world without the divine leaves me drenched in sweat.

The dining room boasts a long table surrounded by no less than one hundred chairs. Each seat is marked with a place card. Eurus and I sit next to each other somewhere near the middle, with a clear view of the lightning god, who sits at the head.

The first course is served. Then: wine, sloshed into jeweled chalices. The divine drain their goblets, signal for more. My eyes flick to the place cards, then to the individuals seated around me. Seeing as Eurus did not warn me against it, I assume it is safe to eat, and to drink.

Throughout the meal, conversation builds and wanes. What does Eurus think as guests gulp glass after glass? Demi is on her third drink, I believe. Not that she deserves my concern.

At some point, the lightning god pushes to his feet, his chalice lifted. "To the victor."

The attendees follow suit. "To the victor!"

He turns to appraise the East Wind, who stares back at him calmly. "Congratulations on your accomplishment," he says. "Of over one hundred competitors, you alone triumphed. It speaks of your diligence, your unflagging perseverance. I cannot think of anymore more deserving." He lifts his glass. "To Eurus."

"To Eurus!"

Glasses clink. Once the commotion has died down, the lightning god continues. "As you know, the reward for winning the tournament is a favor of your choosing from the council. This is not granted lightly. We will do our best to accommodate your request, should it be within our power to do so. Have you considered what favor you would like?"

Demi looks to Eurus, then to me. I glance away, fighting an odd sense of guilt.

"I'd like more time to think about it," the East Wind says, "if you are amenable?"

I wipe my mouth, having already resigned myself to a sad, lonely night. Then I frown, replaying his response. Wait... What does Eurus need to think about, exactly? Reversing the banishment was always the plan.

The lightning god appears intrigued, as does the rest of the council. Asking for an extension is likely unprecedented.

"Very well," the lightning god says. "I will give you until the end of the month, by which time you must decide on your favor."

With that, everyone returns to their meal. Dessert is served. The plates are cleared. People begin to amble back into the parlor for another drink.

Meanwhile, Eurus rises to his feet, and I scramble upright as well, accepting his offered arm as we return to our suite. There is much I might ask of him, but I hold my tongue. An echoing passage is not ideal for private conversation.

Once we've returned to our rooms, I pull away from him. "What was that?" I demand.

"What was what?"

"Why didn't you ask the council to reverse your banishment?"

He strays toward the sofa and settles into its cushions, his back to me. "I need more time to think about it."

More time? "But you've had many hundreds of years to consider this." Possibly more. After all, I do not know how long the East Wind has been exiled from the City of Gods.

His shoulders hunch. I stare, for it is unlike the East Wind to shrink from a challenge. "Things change," he says.

"Like what?"

Only then does he turn, leveling me with those eyes of black fire. "You."

Stupefied, I plop onto the edge of the sofa. The East Wind's hard, heavy thigh presses against mine. My mouth goes dry, and I ball my hands in my lap so I do not curl them around the muscle there. The silence frays.

"Well," I begin slowly, "so long as you get your favor before the poison works its way through the council members' systems, you shouldn't have anything to worry about."

Eurus is up, drifting toward the window. He rubs at his brow, drops his hand with a heavy sigh. "I didn't administer the poison."

The air in the room smells of coastal waters. It does not instill fear in me as it once did. "Why not?"

At last, he turns. His armor is gone, his heart is exposed, and I have never seen anything more magnificent. "You were right."

"About what?"

"Everything. I thought of what my life would look like in a decade, a century, a millennium. Do you know what I saw?" He looks to me, dark eyes solemn. "I saw myself as I am now. I saw myself waking each morning, having struggled to sleep, my mind twisting onto itself in its attempts to turn back time, undo the hurt that has been done. And I asked myself if that is what I wanted. If I wished to live out my days in suffering. And I don't want to live that way anymore, bird. All I want now," he says, "is to live a life of peace."

It is suddenly difficult to swallow, for I, too, desire a life of peace. What does that mean, that we both strive for the same tenuous ideal? "And what does that look like to you?" I whisper.

In three strides, he is across the room, framing my face in his broad hands. "It looks like all the days we have spent in each other's company. It looks like your body against mine, and the ease with which we coexist."

I reach up, curl my fingers around his wrists. *Yes*, I think. But it was not always so. Those initial days and weeks were far from peaceful.

"I feel belonging with you," I murmur to him, a bit of shyness creeping into my voice. "I know it's foolish—"

"No." He shakes his head. "Not foolish. *Right*."

Eurus has always worn intensity as though it is a cloak to be shrugged on, and I have generally shied away from it, but now I embrace it, I fall into it, and I have never in my life felt more free.

"You're going back to Marles," he says, fingers sliding up into my hair. "That was the plan. And yet, I want you, Min. I want everything you're willing to give me. And if we only have tonight, then I'm not going to waste a second denying what I know is true."

"And what is true?" I whisper.

"That whatever time we have left, I wish to spend it with you," he murmurs, and lowers his mouth onto mine.

27

My mouth parts, and salt bites at my tongue, a bright sting. Gently, the East Wind coaxes me into the kiss. His tongue glides against mine, a subtle drag as it withdraws. I follow blindly. He demands, and I give, no questions asked. It has taken many weeks and countless missteps, but I trust him to guide me. After all, he is deliberate, he is thorough, he leaves no part of my mouth untouched, whether teeth or lips or tongue. A soft, thready moan slips out of me as my grasp on reality weakens. Deeper and deeper I sink, into a place of obscure depths.

The East Wind is so tall I'm forced to stand on tiptoes to reach his hair, which I sift through my fingers. It means something, that he accepts my touch freely, no retreat, no flinching, no fear.

He maneuvers me toward an armchair, kissing me all the while, before settling us both into its generous cushions. Our legs tangle. A feverish wave laps at my skin, and it grows sensitive, painfully so.

His fingers dive through my hair and massage behind my ears, down toward my nape. My scalp tingles so unbearably I am convinced it will lift free of my skull and float away.

Catching my hips, Eurus shifts our positions so that he is seated beneath me, reclining against the chair back. And still, we kiss. The muscled strength of his thighs warms my backside, his massive wings draped over the chair arms. Pulling my legs wide so the fabric of my gown pools between them, he drags me forward onto his lap.

As his shaft nestles against my folds, I shudder against him, breaking our kiss momentarily. His girth is considerable, a throbbing heat.

Slowly, eyes locked onto mine, the East Wind grasps my hips and shifts me across his erection, back and forth and back and forth. The zing of pleasure between my thighs is so intense my eyes all but roll into the back of my head.

"Good?" he murmurs, a smile in his voice.

I nod, too dazed to articulate a proper response. "Don't stop."

"Worry not, bird." His voice roughens to a low rasp. "I do not intend on stopping until we have both reached fulfillment."

He then increases the pressure, angling his hips so that the head of his cock continues to brush the small bud concealed at the top of my folds. A hard pulse of pleasure sends a tingling wave branching down my legs. I choke back a softened plea.

"You are," Eurus murmurs in awe, "the most beautiful woman I have ever seen." He tucks a strand of my hair behind my ear. "Your skin is like moonlight. Your hair, black velvet. The opal roundness of your face..." Onto each feature, he bestows a kiss. Right cheek, then the left. Forehead, nose, chin.

Warmth climbs to my ears. His compliments are too dear. I wish to hoard them as diamonds, each a separate yet distinct brightness. "It's the dress," I protest.

"No." He grips the tops of my thighs. "Gown or apron, dress or undergarments, it is you I see, Min." His mouth brushes mine. "Bird."

It frightens me, this emotion. Might there be love woven alongside the affection? "I am no goddess—"

"Stop." He presses a finger to my mouth, silencing me. "I do not want one of the divine. I want you. I want Min and no one else: the ingenious bane weaver, the courageous mortal who pushed me to be a better man. The woman who is as kind as she is giving, who is stronger than she ever believed possible, with a beauty beyond measure. The woman who is good," he murmurs. "Perhaps too good for the likes of me."

I might never understand how a god can look upon a mortal and see no flaws. Or maybe I am wrong and the flaws are what attract. Because the East Wind, as I have learned, is both terribly flawed and mesmerizingly fascinating. He is both. He is all.

My smile is slow growing. Eurus watches it take shape, his eyes softening. I am beautiful not *despite*, but *because*. I am beautiful *because* I suffer. I am beautiful *because* I have hurt. I am beautiful *because* I am sometimes lost, or frightened, or insecure. And I am worthy of good things, regardless of whether I am mortal or divine.

"You, too, are beautiful to me," I tell him, tracing the scar that blots the left side of his face.

To this, his mouth curls, as though he does not share the sentiment. "There are others less unsightly than I."

"And?" I stare at him. "I do not seek perfection, Eurus. I do not want it. Without faults in the earth, there would be no mountains, no canyons, no caves or rivers or cliffs. It is these things that give the realm shape, and I would not trade it, not for anything. Nor would I trade you," I say, sweeping my thumb across his chin, "my beautiful, scarred immortal."

In the darkness of the suite, the East Wind leans forward to capture my mouth. When he nips my lower lip, I angle forward on a gasp, driving my core hard against his stiffened shaft.

Pleasure spirals through me. It demands *more, yes, there*. I widen my legs so my center makes contact with the damp fabric of my undergarments and the hard heat of him beneath his trousers. As his hands return to my waist, I begin to work on the buttons of his silk shirt.

The fabric parts, and there is his chest, its smattering of dark hair, one half scarred, the other unblemished. I blink in stupefaction. It is unfairly chiseled, the plane of his abdomen taut with strength. I told the East Wind I do not seek perfection, but his body is close to it.

"You act like you've never seen a man's chest before." Then his eyes narrow. "Have you?"

I clear my throat. "Once. But it was not as impressive as yours."

He seems ridiculously pleased by this. "Good."

Dipping my head, I press a kiss to the scar knitted across his shoulder. My hands wander down, down toward his erection. But I purposefully skirt the area, the tips of my fingers skimming the rise of one hip bone, his upper thigh, before I free the buttons of his trousers.

His erection springs out into my waiting hands. My mouth goes dry. By the Mother, I might take it into my mouth, but the throbbing between my legs is insistent now. Instead, I shift back onto his lap and press my heated core fully against him. I urge myself onward, welcoming the delicious burn.

A rough grunt sounds from his chest. As I circle my hips, I seek out the slight flare of his cockhead, making sure I deliberately rub against it with my driving motions. I do this until Eurus' breath stutters and he breaks away, gasping.

I smile, peering at him through lowered lashes. His face has slackened. He is spellbound, completely absorbed by the sight of my sensuality.

"Have you deceived me, bird?"

My heart skips a beat, and I grow cold.

But he leans forward, catches the lobe of my ear between his teeth. "Have you desired me all this time?"

The truth is, I *have* deceived him. I sent that message to Lady Clarisse with the Courier, promising I would return home, his god-touched ax in hand. But that was before I realized the mistake I'd made. Now that Lady Clarisse believes Eurus' weapon has been destroyed, she will have no further interest in him. That should be the end of it.

"Bird? What's wrong?" Eurus peers at me in concern.

"N-nothing." I wince, forcing my mouth into an upward curve.

"If you want to stop . . ."

"No!" I lean in, rest my forehead against his. "I don't want to stop," I whisper.

His hot breath tickles the shell of my ear. My nipples harden beneath my dress, and my mind wanders to my dresser, where the jar of honey that Demi purchased for me from the market a few weeks back now rests. "Could you give me a minute?"

Eurus releases me with a slight frown as I dart into my bedroom to grab the jar of honey. Back in the sitting area, I set it on a low table, Eurus regarding me in curiosity.

The East Wind is, without a doubt, every alluring nightmare come to life: his form sprawled in artful repose, shirt and trousers unbuttoned, erection exposed, and the great span of his wings framing his powerful shoulders, a glittering mural of polished ebony.

I have lived my life thinking *maybe not* and *bad idea* and *don't be foolish*. But no ill thoughts cloud my mind as I catch the hem of my gown and begin tugging it over my head. I toss it onto a nearby chair, followed by my undergarments.

His hungry gaze wanders south. It skims the slight rise of my breasts, travels down my stomach to the pink center between my spread legs.

"Bird."

The endearment is ground down by desire. I know what he wants. He need say nothing else.

With the jar of honey in hand, I drop to my knees between his legs.

He straightens in surprise. His mouth parts, his eyes wholly black as he watches me open the lid with a soft *pop*. I dip my pinky into the amber substance, then draw it into my mouth. The East Wind twitches as I suck it dry.

"I wonder what it would taste like on you," I murmur, a question in my voice.

The intensity with which he studies me is like the sun. I am the wick, and he the flame, and look how luminously we burn. "Are you asking for my permission?"

"Yes," I whisper.

He shoves his trousers down to his ankles, where they catch around his boots. The muscles of his calves flex as he plucks the jar from my hand, dips a finger inside, and swipes honey over the swollen head of his cock.

He then inclines his chin, watching me through heavy lids. "Proceed."

Heat scours my face. There is something particularly enticing in having supplicated myself, safe in the knowledge that Eurus would never truly take advantage. He might dictate the when and where, but I hold the reins.

Golden sweetness drips across the slit of his crown. It mixes with a translucent bead, the added weight causing the droplet to quiver as it reaches the lip and hangs there.

My mouth floods with saliva as I reach out to grip him. He is so large my hand cannot circle his girth fully. I'm apprehensive about whether he will be able to fit inside me, but I nudge that concern aside as I flutter the tip of my tongue along the length of his shaft before sucking the head into my mouth, bathing the broad shape in a wet heat.

A prolonged *Ahh* cracks out as the East Wind tosses back his head. The sound is a torment. I suck him deeper.

"Fuck, your mouth will be the end of me." At the next hard suck, he goes rigid. "Oh, gods."

Soft laughter ripples outward from my throat and along his shaft. Eurus digs his heels into the rug, hips lifted. I interpret that as an invitation to add more honey, more sweetness. A slow, enthusiastic lick along the underside of his erection drives Eurus' fingers into my hair. I wince at the sting along my scalp.

"Sorry," he whispers, loosening his grip. He's panting, eyes blurred.

My smile is far too smug. "Don't apologize." It is a heady feeling, having reduced this all-powerful deity to simple grunts.

I return to my sweet yet cruel ministrations. Eurus' body tightens as I lure him to the edge before backing off. Again, I coax him nearer to completion. At one point, I add my hand to the mix so that every inch of his cock is wrapped in warm, delicious pressure.

"Bird." His breath comes short. His hands make claws around the chair arms. "Feels . . . too good."

I peek through my lowered lashes. Give a nice, long suck.

"Fuck!" Hauling me upright, the East Wind flips our positions so that I'm sprawled across the armchair and crushes his mouth onto mine.

The kiss stings, our mouths so fully mated I am convinced I have climbed inside his skin. The scent of his arousal fractures my thoughts, and I moan as he cups my breasts in his massive hands.

A hard pulse of warmth floods between my thighs. His rough palms scrape deliciously across my aching nipples, which he flicks playfully. He then replaces his hands with his tongue, dampening one nipple, pulling back so the cooler air draws it to a painful point.

Eventually, his dark eyes lift to mine. "I'd like to return the favor, bird. That is, if you're up for it."

He must sense my confusion, for he grips the tops of my thighs and tugs them wide so that I am bared indecently before him. His nostrils flare, and he dips his head near the glisten of my aroused flesh.

My heart stops. Just . . . collapses inside my chest.

I nod, and Eurus lifts my legs, draping them over his shoulders so my heels rest between his wings. A beam of moonlight pierces the gloom to bathe the right side of his face. The East Wind, born of shadow and storm and strife. How did we get here? How is it possible that I—a mortal woman—have found myself caught in his arms?

Hot pleasure douses my every thought as he rubs his palms along the outsides of my thighs, settling in. Tracing the edges of my folds, he gently opens me before leaning forward. His mouth parts. I tense in anticipation of the touch.

A hairsbreadth away, he halts.

I shift position in an attempt to lift my sex toward his mouth. "Eurus." My core pulses in demand. It wants the thorough devotion of his tongue, the raw sounds of his pleasure.

Instead, his eyes flutter shut, and he inhales.

The sight scorches me from fingers to toes. When he opens his eyes, I gasp. They are wholly black.

"Do you know what I want most, bird?" the East Wind rumbles.

"N-no?"

"This." Snatching the jar of honey, he dabs some onto my folds. Before I can process what is happening, he sucks them into his mouth.

I cry out, pressing against his fervent tongue. He growls hungrily and laps at the honey, coasting lower. He lingers at my entrance, tickling the outer edges until I relax and open slightly, allowing his tongue to push halfway inside.

The sight of Eurus pleasuring me sends another scorching wave to flood my insides. The burn, the *burn*. I release a string of mangled pleas, my voice growing hoarse. It is everything. Too much, yet not enough.

I dig my heels into his back, forcing my core harder against his mouth as he continues to lick ever deeper. The heat builds. I gasp, hips lifted. "There. Please. Oh—"

At the next hard suck, I shatter.

Ripples shudder outward through my core, and I keen, grabbing fistfuls of his hair as he anchors my hips, continuing to pluck at the raw, open nerves between my legs until the wave dissipates and I sag back into the chair.

"I can't move my legs," I whisper.

The East Wind barks out a laugh. Every crease of his smile, every awkward tug around his scarring, even the glisten of wetness coating his lips from where he tasted me ... I have fallen for this god. There is no way around that truth. And I don't know what to do about it.

We shift positions once more. Eurus draws me back onto his lap, our faces tucked close. My knees dig into the cushion, a soft squeak in the night.

"You're in control," he says, his features drawn sharp with hunger.

After positioning his cock at my entrance, I sink onto Eurus in measured increments, my body gradually adjusting to his girth. I feel every inch of him, from the solid base to the wide head.

"Good?" he murmurs, watching me through hooded eyes.

I nod, rising onto my knees. Then I sink back down.

I delight in the East Wind's shiver, his focus honed to repress his body's urges: to claim, assert, plunder. And that, I think, will simply not do.

Capturing his mouth, I increase my pace, a hard, brief fuck, until I manage to wrench a choked groan from him. Only then do I slow, soothing his throbbing cock with the warm clasp of my body.

"You're teasing me," he manages.

I smile. "Maybe."

"Well, don't stop on my account." When I shift my hips forward a fraction, his cockhead grazes my front wall, and I falter, the waves of pleasure vaulting ever higher, sharpened peaks that shave my desire to the thinnest of blades.

The East Wind rests his head against the back of the chair, eyes hazy as I ride him. Eurus might be a god amongst gods, but here, now, he is a tool used for my own pleasure. And as I feel myself tightening, Eurus urges me onward, praising me with *Good girl,* and *Keep going, bird,* and *I love the way you look when you're fucking me.* And I feel beautiful, empowered, strong, seen.

"Eurus." I choke for air as his hands wander up my front, one settling like a heavy collar around my neck. The pleasure-pain is splintering my mind.

"Tell me how it feels, bird," he grinds out against my mouth. "Tell me how I fill you. Tell me there is no one else."

The chair squeaks in time with his thrusts. Through slitted eyelids, I watch Eurus' expression grow strained, sweat beginning to bead on his brow. He demands the truth? I will give it to him.

"It feels better than anything I've ever experienced," I pant out. "You're the only one who can make me feel this good. There is no one else. There can't be." And I mean it, because in this moment I cannot bear to consider a future without him. Without this. Without *us.*

"Gods, bird, I—" Eurus bites back an oath. "Don't stop."

My core pulses, and I am that much nearer to release. Drawing his touch downward, the East Wind grazes my legs, hips, stomach. Each fingertip, a spark along my skin.

I bite the inside of my cheek, another moan caged behind my teeth. *Yes, there, please, more.* I've the crazed urge to burrow into his chest, wrap myself around his heart and lungs so there is no separation between us.

When he brushes the nub above my drenched sex, I tighten around him. Again, he sweeps the pad of his finger across, tracing the raised edge. Sweat weaves down my face and neck. It spatters Eurus' chest, and I must be out of my mind, because I lean forward to lick him clean.

He groans, watching the place where our bodies join, his shaft glistening with my wetness. At the next thrust, he hits a spot that makes me see stars.

"I'm close," I gasp.

"Come for me, bird," the East Wind croons. "That's it."

I fall forward, sobbing out my pleasure as my core clamps tightly around his shaft and I tumble off the edge into release.

Down, down, down I spiral, the pressure crushing on all sides. The dull pulsation at my center abruptly sharpens and explodes outward. I bite Eurus' neck, my cry muffled. The world blurs, then whites out completely.

Yet still I move. And still he moves. The East Wind fucks me hard, and he fucks me deep, and I take it, because I want to know that I have driven him to insanity. We have no beginning and no end. We are perpetuity, we are the earth and sky, we are the black fathoms of the sea. And I have never felt such belonging, such safety, as I do now in his arms. This god, this wretched divine, my captor. He is more than his past, more than his scars, more than the darkness and grief and isolation. Eurus might not know it, but he is mine.

The world returns to me in pieces. There is sight: the moon's pale touch painting strips across the room. Then sight drifts to sound: the creak of the chair frame beneath our combined weight. And sound drifts, then, to touch: the East Wind's weighted palm dragging up my spine, then down. The sweetest of kisses pressed upon my brow.

Gathering me close, Eurus carries me to his bedroom and settles me amongst the pillows. They smell of him, of Marles. I burrow into the blanket's many pleats while he stretches out alongside me, one hand curved over my hip, the other playing with strands of my hair.

I cup his warm cheek. Might I tell him how I feel? That I do not wish for the sun to rise. That I promise to shield his heart from the world's sharp corners. That I love him wholeheartedly—mind, body, soul—and never wish to be parted from him.

The answer is this: I cannot. Because tomorrow, he will take me back to St. Laurent. I will live out my mortal life, and he will live his days eternal. These are the rules that bind us. There can be no other way.

Eurus skates a thumb across my cheek. In the pools of his dark eyes, I see a thousand shivering stars. "I am," he whispers coarsely, "very glad to have met you, bird."

I cover his hand with mine, finding it suddenly difficult to swallow. How far must I fall before the impact shatters my bones? Sometimes, I envision a world where I could have both Eurus *and* St. Laurent. I could have belonging *and* security. But the image remains unfinished. I am given only glimpses, pieces: the future incomplete.

We have only tonight.

28

I ROUSE SLOWLY, SHEDDING SLEEP AS CLOUDS DO A WARM SUMMER rain. The weight burdening my limbs is profound. They sink deep into the soft mattress, surrounded by blankets and a small mountain of pillows. Through the cracks of my eyelids, dawn makes itself known.

Tendrils of light flutter through the window to paint the floral wallpaper. I watch their elaborate filaments dance across the leaves and vines, my thoughts far away, cocooned in velvet. Last night, I gave the East Wind my heart. I regret nothing.

Memories of Eurus' hands, and his mouth, and the unexpected gentleness of his lovemaking rise up from the depths into which they'd settled. Never before had I felt so prized, like I was both made of glass and tempered steel. He looked at me, and there was no need to quail, flinch, retreat. I was beloved. I was seen.

Shifting onto my back, I freeze. In the corner of my eye, the East Wind's massive form lies sprawled across the bed, wings and all.

Soundly, he sleeps. The airy touch of the budding morn cascades over his slackened face. One side is sculpted with a scrupulous balance, featuring a straight black brow, rounded nose, the cut of a flawless cheek. It is beautiful, exquisitely carved. But I much prefer its scarred reflection.

My attention drifts to the crest of his wings. Sunlight reveals their true depth of color. Not wholly black, as I had believed, but cerulean and jade, even shades of dusky pink.

Reaching out, I trace the long, arched bone extending from his upper back. Eurus shudders, and his wing eases open, stretching like a cat in the sun.

When my attention returns to his face, I find him staring at me.

My mouth goes dry. "Good morning," I whisper.

He smiles sleepily. I dare say it is adorable. "Good morning, bird."

Curving one broad palm around the back of my head, his mouth descends, catching mine with a lazy twining of his tongue. I return the kiss eagerly, wrapping my arms around his neck without hesitation. It is a testament of his trust in me that he does not flinch.

After a time, he breaks away, his eyes hazed. "Did you sleep well?" he rumbles in that smoky tone.

"I did." Only now do I recognize the ease slumber provides when my body perceives no threat. "And you?" I study his expression for subtle signs of nervousness. Often, the mouth speaks one thing, the body another.

"I cannot remember when I last slept so deeply," Eurus admits.

This, I understand. Back at the estate, my sleep was shallow, fitful. Always, I listened: footsteps in the kitchen, on the stairs. Lady Clarisse might interrupt my rest at a moment's notice. The racing heartbeat I once knew, that constant state of heightened vigilance—gone.

The East Wind twists a lock of my hair between thumb and forefinger. All the while, I gently explore the contours of his chest. When his mouth shapes its downward bend, I rub his jaw until it softens.

"I hope I didn't wake you in the night," he says. "Did I . . . ?"

"No night terrors," I reassure him.

Relief draws the tension from his frame, and he settles deeper into the mattress. For a time, all is quiet, and I fear cracking its frail shell. Today is a beginning, but it is also an ending. Am I a fool to desire a life where I am granted not simply one night, but years of them, each morning spent in the East Wind's arms? "Do we have time to grab lunch in the city?"

He gazes out the window for one, two, three heartbeats. I sense he is troubled. "Technically, with the tournament having ended, I am required to depart the city before noon."

I stare at him in confusion. "I thought you were going to ask the council to reverse your banishment?"

"I am still undecided." He frowns. There is something in his expression that I cannot fully decipher. "Can I ask you something?"

There was once a time when Eurus believed change to be impossible. But look how far he has come, to exchange demands for requests, suspicion for faith. He has evolved, as have I. We are both better for it. "You may."

"What are you returning to, in Marles?"

For whatever reason, I feel the need to tug the sheet over my head, a flimsy shield against this probing inquiry. "I have my work, as you know. I have the town. And my memories of Nan."

"But you are not happy. You are not appreciated or treated with care. You are worked like a dog, and were treated as such."

His words sting. That must mean they hold some truth.

"I do recognize Lady Clarisse's mistreatment of m-me," I admit, pulling my knees to my chest. "But with all due respect, Eurus, you are a god. You have the means to build a life that is meaningful to you. Most mortals must accept the circumstances they've been given."

"Maybe I don't know what it means to be mortal," he says, "but I do know you deserve so much more than what that woman gives you."

"I know," I whisper. "That's why I'm leaving her employment."

Eurus rears back. "You are?"

I nod. "I want to continue my grandmother's work. I have some money saved. After Lady Clarisse sells the estate, I'll need to find a place of my own, somewhere I can build my business." I must accept that it might not be in St. Laurent. Lady Clarisse is extremely possessive of her clientele. She would never allow another bane weaver to infringe on her empire.

"Min, that's wonderful." He grasps my hand, holds it to his face. I swipe my thumb across his cheek affectionately. "Why the change of heart?"

"I am not the same woman I was. It's all right to want something different." It is natural to feel that I have changed.

Leaning forward, he brushes a kiss across my brow. "I'm proud of you, bird."

I smile, albeit sadly. "Me too." There is much I will gain. But there is much I will lose, too.

While Eurus begins to dress, I yank on my undergarments, my motions stilted with fresh grief. Is this all there is? One passion-fueled night, then morning, the sun burning away the memory like dew on grass?

"Will you, I mean . . ." I swallow, draw forth my voice. "Will we see each other? After?"

Eurus pauses in dragging his wrinkled shirt over his head. His wings droop, their crenated edges skimming the rugs underfoot. "If my banishment is overturned, I will be expected to return to the City of Gods. It is generally frowned upon for the divine to meddle in mortal affairs."

My heart drops straight down to my toes. "Right. Of course." How quickly things change. Last night, we were twined tightly, our limbs blurred, distinction lost. Yet a gulf has opened between us. It holds this ambiguous future, the knowledge that I could have the East Wind, I could have St. Laurent, but I could not have both.

While Eurus begins packing, I retreat to my bedroom. My tools are cleaned, sorted neatly in their box. What remains of Eastern Blood, I dump out the window. It will be the last poison I ever brew.

The East Wind is folding a pair of trousers when I poke my head into his bedroom. The urge to move closer, flatten my body alongside his, has sharpened in the time since separating. But I maintain my distance.

"I'd like to say farewell to Demi before we leave," I tell him.

He lifts his head. For a moment, all is laid bare across his countenance, every conflicted emotion, the turmoil unrequited questions bring. Then it shutters, and I am left with nothing.

"Very well," he says. "Meet me downstairs when you're done."

I find Demi in the kitchen kneading a ball of dough, flour coating her from wrist to elbow. Last night's exquisite gown has been exchanged for a humble cotton dress. Bare feet poke from beneath the hem, and her dark locks have been secured in a messy tail. No face paint.

"So," she says, shoving the heels of her palms into the dough. "You're leaving us at last."

Upon reaching the kitchen table, I halt. The pain from when we last spoke lingers. "I wanted to say goodbye."

"Goodbye." The goddess gives a near inaudible scoff. "I never liked that word. What is so good about parting?" Lifting the ball, she hurls it against the battered tabletop, and again, again. She punches the dough, hard, before expelling a shuddering breath.

"You're upset that I'm leaving." It is not a question, though I would have phrased it as such, once, unable to trust my intuition for fear of what it meant if I were wrong. But I see now that sadness is sadness, no matter whether it is mortal or divine.

"I understand this is not your home. Of course you would not stay." She stares down at her flour-coated hands. "But I confess I've grown"—she huffs—"*attached* to you."

It should not warm me, to hear her express her fondness toward me, however reluctant. But it does, and my soft, mortal heart lowers its guard. "My presence here was always temporary," I remind her.

"I know," she whispers, head hanging, "but I don't want us to part when things are unfinished."

Then those lambent cat eyes lift to mine, and they shine with unshed tears. The sight roots me in place.

"I'm sorry I was not honest with you. I regret that, Min. I really do."

My airway tightens, for I *feel* her remorse, know it to be genuine. Can that not be enough, I wonder.

"Look," I say, moving around the table. "I understand why you did it."

"It was a lie."

"What?"

"Yesterday, you asked me how I could have deceived you. I told you that if I wanted my voice to have meaning, I needed to act in accordance with what was best for the realm. But it was a lie."

"I see." When her fingers curl claw-like into the dough, I reach out and gently extract them. "Why didn't you tell me the truth?"

"I was afraid," she says, "of what you would think of me if you knew the truth. How your perception of me would change."

She turns to face me. Demi is a goddess, yet she is small in this moment, her back stooped by guilt. "I didn't vote for the Anemoi's banishment. At least, not at first. Originally, I voted *against* their banishment. I did not think it right, considering the Anemoi had helped seat us into power. But I was afraid."

"Of what?"

"That if I was the sole dissenting opinion, the council might question my place amongst them. If they had voted me out, I would have no voice at all. So I changed my vote. I am ... ashamed of that. Ashamed that I chose to remain silent."

I can understand that. However— "If you love someone," I say, "you don't turn your back on them."

The goddess proceeds to separate the dough into four balls. For once, she is unable to meet my eyes, instead of the other way around. "That's the thing, Min." She presses them flat, shaping the edges into shallow shells. "The truth of the matter is, Eurus and I never loved each other. The divine are notoriously selfish when it comes to affection. We demand it but are unwilling to give any ourselves. But you, love?" She sets the first tart onto the sheet pan, then the second, saying, "I have watched you all these weeks learn to love someone who has not been shown love in a very long time."

Does she speak of Eurus, I wonder, or does she speak of me? "Can I be honest?"

She places the next tart onto the pan, then nods, albeit reluctantly.

"When you informed me that you were the Mother of Earth, I didn't believe you. Not initially. I always expected the Mother of Earth to be,

I don't know, modest? Approachable? Not outfitted in expensive gowns and shoes that pinch your feet. Not that there's anything wrong with that," I rush to say. "But it surprised me."

For whatever reason, Demi appears terribly aggrieved. Her words, when they come, are sorrowful, and low. "I suppose I have always been fearful of embracing this side of myself."

"Why?"

"Look around, love. I am surrounded by beautiful goddesses daily. Who would want to follow a frumpy woman in an old dress, who would rather dig in the dirt than sip wine on a garden terrace?"

"I would. You are beautiful in whatever you wear, but I think this suits you better." Reaching out, I rub the worn, olive-colored cotton between two fingers. "You remind me of my grandmother."

Startled laughter bursts from her mouth. She snorts behind her hand. "Sorry. Just . . . that's not exactly what I expected. I mean, I know I'm old, love, but I don't *look* it."

"I wasn't referring to your looks. More so your morals. Nan was humble. She didn't need much. Even though she emigrated from Jinsan, the people of St. Laurent loved her just as she was." As did I. "What I'm saying is . . . feed whatever brings you peace in your life. What is the point of living if we cannot be our true selves?"

Demi swallows, lifts a hand to her throat. Two tears wind down her cheeks. "I will keep that in mind, Min from Marles."

With that, I take my leave. I'm nearly to the hallway when Demi calls, "Don't forget what I taught you."

I turn around to face her. The goddess has taught me much. I'm not sure what, specifically, she refers to.

"Cinnamon," she elaborates.

My lips curve. "I won't forget."

Blueberries and cinnamon: the perfect complements. Rather like Demi and myself, if I do say so.

The East Wind waits for me in the eastern garden, having claimed a bench beneath a patch of laurel trees where the creek runs clear. The morning holds a chill. Soft mounds of orange dot the grounds where fallen leaves have collected. Eurus wears his cloak, though the hood rests against his back, no longer a shield to hide his features. With his elbows braced on his thighs, he sits with his face in his hands, an image of frustration, or defeat, or both.

As grass crunches beneath my loafers, his head snaps up.

"Did you find Demi?" he asks.

I nod, drawing my coat tighter around me, my rucksack slung across my back. "I will miss her." My one friend in this world, bound to the City of Gods.

The East Wind looks elsewhere, briefly. He is sad when he turns back to me. I do not like seeing it, his sadness. "We shouldn't delay. It will take the majority of the day to reach Marles."

I shiver and shove my hands into the pockets of my coat. It is cold enough that my breath makes steam of the air. "Aren't we using the same doorway we entered from?"

"We will fly. We have the time." He considers me in uncertainty, as if expecting a rebuttal, but I've none to give. It will be nice to spend these last hours in the East Wind's company.

He cradles me in his arms with effortless strength, and his immense wings unfold. Muscles engaged, he sinks into a crouch, then explodes skyward.

My teeth begin to chatter as each beat of his wings drives us farther from the city. From this height, I see its cobblestoned roads, its elegant edifices crowned in ivy and wisteria. Farther out sits the massive dome of the arena. Then there is the palace, which shrinks ever smaller, its stained-glass windows blotting to gray until, eventually, a cloud drifts across my sight.

I settle in for the journey. Of course I would be sad to leave. This realm is a wonder. And yet, I am not so sure I would want to live here. Its facade suggests a certain level of perfection, a lack of suffering and darkness. But that cannot be further from the truth. Its unblemished visage shields the pocked interior, the weakened areas where rot has taken root.

We soar over Eurus' homeland for many an hour. A long, mountainous eruption sketches a jagged line to the north. On one such peak, I believe I spot a shining white city overlooking a shadowed valley, but then we are past, rivers sparkling like starlight below. Open plains unfurl, and large herds of hoofed animals gallop along, some with curling horns, others possessing dusky coats interrupted by gray stripes.

But the earth cannot extend forever. It reaches its cessation, and now we soar over open sea.

A nervous tremor shivers along my skin. I do my best to ignore it. They are calm, these waters. Idyllic, even, with their ruffled white collars aptly bound across their necks.

Over time, however, the waves rupture with increasing ferocity, stirred by the churning mass of clouds ahead. And within the storm's impenetrable wall is the rocky island that stands alone.

Eurus fashions a protective dome around us as we fly through the worst of the squall. And there is the manor, her rain-dampened stone piled into turrets and ramparts, balconies and terraces. And there, too, is the tower, a room that was both prison and sanctuary.

Seeing it now, from the outside, I understand a place needs not have a locked door or walls to feel like a cage. It could be a sprawling, ivy-covered estate, or the tiny broom cupboard tucked within.

Angling my face toward Eurus, I shout over the wind, "If you return to the City of Gods, what will happen to the manor?"

His eyes thin against the salt spray. "I haven't decided yet." A particularly strong gust buffets us, and he tightens his arms around me until we level out. "Technically, once I return to my homeland, I am forbidden to live in the mortal realms, but I may keep the manor, just in case. Or I'll let the sea take it."

A thread of sorrow moves through me. It was within the walls of the manor that I learned of the kindness a bowl of stew could bring. "Won't she get lonely?"

He shrugs, yet there is a reluctance in the motion. "I enchanted the manor because I had no staff to tend to the place. Since I won't have need of it, I'll likely remove the enchantment—"

"No!" I cry. Eurus drops his gaze to mine, expression bewildered. "You can't do that. She's alive. She . . . she feels things."

"She's not real, bird."

"Who are you to decide what is real and what is not? You created her, Eurus. You can't just discard her when you no longer have use for her." My voice dies, and I swallow thickly, these words hitting too close for comfort.

"Somehow, I sense this is not about the manor," he says. "Cover your face."

He banks right, forcing us through the storm wall. I cover my head, trusting that Eurus' arms will hold me. One of his large hands shields the back of my skull from any wayward debris. The roar expands, then retreats, the worst of the squall behind us.

"If it's really that important to you that the enchantment remains," he says quietly, "maybe *you* should consider keeping the manor company."

It does not immediately process, this suggestion. "You mean live on the island?"

"You mentioned needing to find someplace to live, now that you intend to build your own business." He frowns at me. "Well?"

But Eurus would not be there. It would feel too empty with him gone. "How would I make a living? Without the town, there would be no one to sell my teas to." And I would be stuck, unable to venture to the mainland for fear of the water. "It seems a bit excessive, asking clients to pick up their teas by sailboat."

"You're right," he replies, sounding a bit put out. "Forget I mentioned it."

Ahead, the horizon lies pressed beneath the jeweled sky. But the line shifts, blurs, hones itself into clarity: the cliffs of Marles.

Soon, the sloping green rooftops interrupt the rolling hills of lavender, which ripple in a seaside breeze. St. Laurent, its perfume of fresh bread and earth, hits me. I blink away tears. Weeks have come and gone, yet it looks exactly as I left it, from the crooked bends of Market Street, to the rolling carts selling pastries outside the bookshop.

A few merchants carting goods into town glance up as we angle toward the estate. From this height, it is clear how severely the structure has fallen into disrepair. The roof sags around the chimney. A portion of the back wall has begun to crumble. And the iron fence, which once shone proudly at the end of the long dirt road, has dulled beneath a thick coating of rust.

We land in the overgrown garden, amongst the vegetable beds and potted herbs. I touch a strand of Eurus' windblown hair, brush it from his forehead.

"Thank you," I say, "for returning me home."

He glances at the back door, eyes watchful. "You'll be all right?"

I smile and nod, because that is what is expected. Yes, I will be fine. It will hurt, our parting, but I will heal, in time. "And . . . you'll be well?"

His lack of immediate response points to uncertainty. But then Eurus says, "Yes," and I am forced to accept his answer, regardless of whether it is what I wish to hear.

I hesitate, fighting the urge to lunge, catch, hold tight. Maybe I am foolish to hope his suggestion that I stay in the manor meant something more.

"Take care of yourself, bird."

"Wait." I am desperate, I am bold, I am driven by impulse as I reach up, grasping his face, my hands twining in the strands of his hair. Tugging his head down, I crush my mouth to his.

My emotions burst their cage. I eat at his lips hungrily. Eurus responds with equal fervor, plundering my mouth's soft depths. I fist the weave of his cloak, telling him with lips and teeth what my voice fails to express. *I love you* and *I need you* and *Don't go.* But he has his life, and I have mine, and our journey ends where it begins.

Gently, the East Wind pulls away. "Bird, I—" Except his attention locks onto something over my shoulder, and he stiffens.

I turn, squinting into the distance where the road vanishes over the hill. A line of what appear to be armed men top the rise, dressed in long, flowing robes the color of old blood, their dark hair and skin suggesting they hail from somewhere to the south. Ammara?

"What is this?" Eurus mutters. He scans the ten, twenty, thirty soldiers marching toward us, swords drawn, their curved edges aglint. At the front, leading the armed men, are Lady Clarisse and Prince Balior.

My mind has frozen. Did Lady Clarisse not receive my most recent letter? I told her the East Wind's ax had been destroyed in the tournament. Is it possible the message was never delivered? Or that she didn't care to read it?

Lady Clarisse waves in the distance. "Hello, Min," she calls. "And you've brought company!"

"What is going on here?" Eurus demands. "Why does she stand with Prince Balior? Why do they approach as though prepared to do battle?"

I stare at him, wide-eyed, unable to speak.

"Tell me!" he roars.

But my words do not come. For woven through every rigid muscle of his face, there is understanding, just as there is heartbreak.

His eyes shutter, and he takes a step back. "You called them here," he says, "to capture me."

"No!" I choke out. "N-no, I mean, I told Lady Clarisse that I would be returning today, yes, b-but I did not th-think . . ." Each word is a stone rolling downhill, tumbling into the next, a great jumble of uselessness. "I s-sent her a note—"

"A note?" The scarring on his face contorts, rippling over bone. "What note?"

I feel close to vomiting, or passing out, or both. What have I done? Something unforgivable. "After you took m-me from St. Laurent," I begin in a tremulous voice, "I found a way to send messages to Lady Clarisse. I wanted to return home. I was trying to r-reach her in hopes that she would s-s-save me."

But I realize how utterly stupid that was. Lady Clarisse was never coming to save me. Why should she reward disobedience with a rescue? Why should she care? She doesn't.

The East Wind continues to stare daggers at me. "That still doesn't explain why she is *here*, with Prince Balior and his army."

"No, you're . . . you're right." I take a breath. "We made a deal. She p-promised to sell the estate to me if—"

"By the gods," he mutters, scrubbing at his face. "You mean this entire time I was falling for you, you were planning to deliver me to that witch?"

I press a shaking hand to my queasy stomach. I'm going to be sick.

"You spoke of belonging," he continues, eyes full of hurt, "and I was beginning to believe you might be right. That maybe we *did* belong together." He shakes his head in disgust. "I'm such a fool."

"No," I whisper, reaching for him. "That's n-not it—"

"You're a liar, Min. Like everyone else." He brushes my hand aside.

"If you would just *listen* to me—"

"Listen to you?" He straightens to his full height, and I flinch away from him. "It's clear that everything you've told me, everything you've done, has been to draw me back here so that woman could recapture me. So no, I will not listen to you. I've already heard enough." He strides off toward the road, his wings half-extended. I scurry after him as the soldiers march steadily nearer, a wreath of darkness coiling between Prince Balior's hands.

"Eurus, you're going the w-w-wrong way."

"No. It's time I end this. Time to kill the witch, once and for all." His eyes cut to mine, and he sneers. "So sorry to ruin your grand plans."

"I didn't mean for this to h-happen!" I cry.

"You were corresponding with her the whole time!"

I open my mouth, snap it closed. "At first, yes. But after the second trial, I began to question wh-what I was doing. I grew to *care* for you. I told myself that I wouldn't h-help her anymore. That I wouldn't betray you. But then I overheard you telling Demi I meant nothing to you, and I w-was hurt and angry, so I sent Lady Clarisse a message, informing her of when you would bring me h-h-home."

A wretched sob overtakes me, but I force out the rest. "Wh-when you told me why you said those things to Demi, I realized my error, and as soon as we returned to the p-p-palace after the tournament, I sent another note to her ladyship, claiming that your ax had been destroyed—"

"My *ax*?" It is frightening how the whites around his eyes thin, how the pupils enlarge, like two blots of ink. "What does she want with my ax?"

Perhaps he already knows. Perhaps nothing matters, in the end. "Immortality," I whisper. "She intends to use your heart's blood to create a potion of immortality. But to d-do that, she would have to k-k-k—" I falter.

"Kill me?" he asks with lethal quiet.

I can't speak. I have already said too much.

"All this time, you've been plotting my death," he spits, peering down his nose at me.

"No! That's not it—"

"You betrayed me," he growls, the words eaten by all the rage and hurt I myself have felt. "And that cannot be undone."

He shoves past me up the garden path. Bolting after him, I scream, "What did you expect me to do? When we first met, you treated me like a prisoner, a servant. I did not owe you a thing! And even after I fell for you, you made it obvious that it could never w-work between us. You told me yourself that once you r-return to the City of Gods, you are barred from living in the mortal realms. When you are gone, this estate, this town, will be all that I have left!"

"You could have come to me!" he roars, whirling around, his winds snapping outward from the motion. "You could have trusted me enough to inform me of these things. You think I don't understand the lengths someone will go to in order to return home? I was willing to die in this stupid tournament so that the council would reverse my sentence."

"*I* could have trusted *you*?" I gape at him. "The god who stole me from my h-home and used me to enact his revenge? Who forced me into a bargain in order to *earn* my freedom?" I glare at this giant of a god in bewilderment. He has completely lost his mind. "My only option was to keep my head d-down and focus on helping you win the tournament, because you never would have let me go otherwise. You wanted me as a tool," I whisper, pained, "but you didn't want *me*."

"That's not true, bird." A quiet admission. "I was going to ask you if you wanted me to stay with you at the estate. I was going to suggest that we could build a home together, if you chose. If you wanted that."

My heart. "I *do* want that—"

"Then why would you do this?" Eurus crowds my space. I drink him in, wishing I were not so weak. "Why go to such lengths to hurt me?"

The world melds into hot streaks of color. Lady Clarisse, Prince Balior, and the soldiers are so much closer now. "You need to leave. They will capture you—"

"I don't give a damn about that," he snarls. "Tell me why you chose that witch, who has never showed you an ounce of kindness, over me. She's nothing to you—"

"No," I grind out. "She's my mother."

29

The East Wind stares at me with eyes like voids. Beyond, storm clouds heap the distant cliffs. "Another lie, is it?"

"It's not a lie." If I could, I would claw my heart from my chest. I would hold it over open flame, watch muscle and tendon recoil, then wither into collapse. What is done cannot be made undone. The price must be paid. "Lady Clarisse really is my mother."

"Your *mother*," Eurus emphasizes. "The same woman who tried to drown you as a child?"

A wad of saliva clogs my throat. I choke it down with a whispered, "Yes."

He shakes his head. "This can't be real. You call her *my lady*."

"Because that is wh-wh-wh—" I swallow, grit my teeth. "That is what she wanted me to call her."

Following Nan's passing, Lady Clarisse inherited the estate after having returned to Marles following many years away. I was her daughter, our shared blood a burden, but I could be put to use, diminished to a set of hands that could slice and stir, press and pour. The first time I called Lady Clarisse *mother* after her return, she threatened to cut out my tongue.

Let me be clear, she'd said. *I am no more your mother than you are my daughter. You cannot imagine what I would give to trade your life for my husband's, but unfortunately, I'm stuck with you. Whatever childish optimism you harbor in thinking we will ever be family, discard it now. From this moment on, you will refer to me as Lady Clarisse.*

"Gods." Eurus regards me in outward horror. "And now you *work* for her? Why, Min? She's horrible. She *tortures* people. She tortured you!" The intensity of his gaze, its furious simmer, pierces me. I am no better than an insect with its wings pinned. I could not fly away even if I wanted to.

"Because she—" I stop, try again. "B-because—"

"Why?" he demands, insistent now. "Why, after everything that she's done to you, her every effort to belittle you, would you want to help her?"

"I don't know!" I scream. "I just . . . I want her to love me." There was never a time I did not crave that. Drowning or not, abuse or not, she was the only maternal figure in my life, following Nan's passing. And maybe a part of me always saw Lady Clarisse as the wounded daughter Nan described her as. Someone who did not fit into this realm, who never felt quite at home. When she met my father, according to Nan, she was changed—for a time. Then he was taken from her, and she was left alone to care for her infant child—all that remained of the man she loved. "She was going to s-sell the estate," I go on. "It is my only tie to my grandmother. If I did this one thing for Lady Clarisse, she promised to sell it to me."

He gazes down at me in disgust. "And you believed her?"

Yes. And then, no. But by then, it was too late. "I wanted to prove I w-was worthy," I say, voice softening. Even to my own ears, it sounds pathetic. "If I gave her what she wanted—"

"She is no mother to you, Min. She doesn't love you. She loves only what you can do for her." He shakes his head, jaw clenched, and turns away.

The sight spurs me forward. "Eurus, please. I'm sorry, it's just—"

"There is no *just*," he barks with a crazed laugh. "Don't you see? You were the first person I trusted in centuries. And now you've proven to me what I already know. People will use you, abuse you, discard you. It is a cycle without end."

My eyes sting. There is truth to his words, for I once believed the same. I have now betrayed the only person who has ever truly cared for me, aside from Nan. "If I can explain," I press, the words garbled, torn to pieces by emotion.

"What is there to explain?" he murmurs. "You have shown your true colors. As far as I'm concerned, there is nothing left to say."

"Please don't do this," I weep. "I love you."

He recoils, hand lifted to thwart a blow as his expression collapses into one of repulsed disbelief. "You *love* me? Did I hear that correctly?" He belts out a crow-like laugh, a vicious caw. "Unbelievable. Is there nothing you will not lie about?"

Distant thunder growls, and I question how much of the approaching storm is natural and how much is connected to the East Wind's fury. The bare trees rattle ominously as, turning on his heel, Eurus heads for the front gate, his gaze locked on Lady Clarisse and her trailing army.

Catching the fabric of his cloak, I try to yank him back, but I have all the strength of a leaf in autumn, and he doesn't falter. He is simply too strong.

"Eurus, please, you have to get out of h-here. They will catch you—"

The East Wind spins, breaking my hold. His eyes boil as he peers down at me. He is every shade of gloom, every facet of the realm's darkest corners. My heart quails in his presence. "Let go," he says.

I shake my head and manage to squeeze out, "They will kill you!"

"I am a god," he rumbles, and a coil of air explodes from his palm, lashing toward Lady Clarisse. A shield erupts between Eurus' power and her ladyship as Prince Balior casts the protective spell.

A flick of his wrist, and Eurus blasts the prince's shield. A band of wind loops around Lady Clarisse's neck, yanking her clear across the grounds. She screams, thrashing like a fish on a line, and my stomach pitches as she's lifted high, legs kicking as they dangle, face blotched a ruddy pink, then violet, then blue.

"Eurus." I am crying too hard to say much else. "Please . . ." Lady Clarisse has never shown me an ounce of kindness, but the thought of her brutally murdered, *gone*, plunges me into a spiral of confusion. "Please, don't kill her."

The East Wind's expression hardens, masked by a rage so profound I can only assume that in this woman, he sees his father, who treated him no better than vermin. But I see it then—a crack running through the marble of his countenance.

His shoulders sag, and Eurus drops her onto the walkway amongst the dying grasses and weeds. Before I'm able to properly thank him, he brushes past me and launches skyward.

I race after him, but Lady Clarisse snags my ankle from where she has fallen. "I don't think so," she spits.

I kick out. She releases me with a snarl.

I sprint down the walkway, past the rusted gate, before lurching to a halt. Prince Balior's soldiers have ceased their forward march, arrows aimed at Eurus, who dives, down, down, down. A ravenous darkness rolls toward the East Wind, who spins to avoid its touch.

"Now!" Prince Balior shouts.

Arrows loose. The East Wind drops to avoid the deadly points. While the men reload, he speeds toward a soldier and blasts a hole clean through the man's stomach.

I lift a hand to my mouth. A second soldier succumbs to the same fate. All the while, Prince Balior's power chases the East Wind through the sky, over the surrounding forest. Another burst of shadow swarms Eurus' torso, but he generates a sphere of air that expands outward, forcing the wisps off his skin. Even I can see that his speed flags. He has yet to recover his strength from the final trial.

There must be a way to help him.

Spinning around, I dash toward the estate, the front door clapping shut as I trip across the threshold. I'm rifling through drawers when I recall *The Practice of Herbal Remedies*, nestled safely against my waistband. I rip the volume free, flip to a section in the back: airborne poisons.

"I'll take that." Lady Clarisse snatches the book before I'm able to consider my options. She tucks it into her apron smugly. "Whatever plans fill that empty head of yours, discard them. Prince Balior will overpower the East Wind easily." Of this, she seems certain. "It is only a matter of time."

My breath comes short. I fight the urge to shrink, as I have done countless times before. Looking at Lady Clarisse, the woman who birthed me, I see how she has aged, fine lines charting the years of her derision toward my existence. An elixir of immortality may protect her from death and the pain of losing a loved one, but it cannot eradicate the poison in her heart.

"Give me the book, Lady Clarisse."

She quirks an eyebrow, gives me a scornful once-over. Her facial scar, usually smoothed over by her beauty teas, is more prominent than ever, an engorged vine crawling across her features. She received the mark when a splintered plank from my father's capsized boat tore open her cheek. According to Nan, Lady Clarisse was able to cling to a large rock until another fisherman rescued her. By then, the sea had already claimed my father's life.

"You are either with me or against me, Min," she murmurs. "Remember who stole you from your home. Remember who *gave* you a home." She reaches for me, and I recoil—yet her hand is gentle as it curves around my upper arm. She guides me to the bay window overlooking the grounds.

"See that man?" She taps a fingertip against the windowpane. "He is not from our realm. He has no interest in your life. I am doing you a favor, understand? One day, he will leave you. And you will be alone."

I watch the East Wind fell four soldiers in less than a heartbeat. He wields no weapons, no arrows or tempered steel. He has only his fists, which find the soft, vulnerable parts of their bodies, and his winds, which act as his blades, slicing into guts or cutting across bared throats.

"Why are you doing this?" I whisper. "Why align y-yourself with this prince? He is dangerous."

"It's business, Min. I want the East Wind's heart, and Prince Balior is all too happy to help me acquire it. When every last god in the mortal realms is dead, none will have the strength to oppose the prince and his growing army. The East Wind is all that stands between him and total control."

"Eurus will give you nothing," I whisper. "He *will* fight. And I already told you that his ax was lost in the tournament."

"As it turns out, there are other ways of getting what I want, with Prince Balior's aid." Gripping my shoulders tightly, she murmurs into my ear, "He is a god. His world is not yours. It never will be."

Maybe. But I would never forgive myself if I did not do everything in my power to save him.

Pulling free of her, I bolt outside, down the garden path. Lightning cleaves the sky, and for a moment, all is bathed white.

The East Wind arrows toward the prince, who launches a swift barrage of blows: small, churning spheres of deepest black. He dodges one, two. The third clips him on the flank, and he veers, slamming into a tree.

My loafers slap the dirt as a writhing mass slinks over him, pressing into his eyes and nose and mouth. "Let him go!" I scream.

Air explodes outward from Eurus' body, but Prince Balior shields himself easily. His soldiers are not so lucky. A handful fall and do not rise.

The shadow returns to coat Eurus head to toe. In seconds, his motions slow, then stop altogether. I've nearly reached the armed men surrounding him when something wraps my ankle, pulling taut. I hit the road with a broken cry.

"Is he bound, Prince Balior?" Lady Clarisse calls from behind me.

I lift my head, blinking back tears of pain. My former employer glances down at me, sniffs, and steps over me as one would a puddle of mud.

"For the time being, yes," replies the prince.

"Excellent." The soldiers part, allowing her entry. "If you could please administer this brew to the East Wind, I would very much appreciate it." She passes over a vial containing a yellow liquid.

The prince regards Lady Clarisse with an indecipherable expression. A loop of shadow lovingly drapes his neck. "What is the purpose of this potion, madam?"

"Nightmare's Blood," she coos. "He won't offer the location of his island otherwise, nor will he tell us how to disable whatever enchantments protect his manor. Once we reach the island, you are free to kill him and take the manor as your stronghold. But I want his heart."

Seemingly in accord with this line of reason, Price Balior gestures one of his men forward. "Hold him down."

The moment those shadows peel away from the East Wind's face, he thrashes wildly, eyes ringed in white. Strands of hair cling to his reddened face, and he snarls as one of the soldiers pries open his clenched jaw.

After dumping the serum into Eurus' mouth, the soldier slams it shut, holding it closed while Eurus sputters, air whistling through his nose. There must be a sedative in the serum, for his limbs slacken, his eyes drift out of focus, his head lolls.

"Eurus!" When he does not respond, I kick away the shadows binding my ankles. I'm up, charging past the wall of soldiers, elbowing them aside.

A force sends me sideways against a tree. The impact rattles my bones, and I drop as Lady Clarisse advances, face pinched with loathing. The toes of her boot hit my thigh. I shrink against the trunk.

"You are *this* close," she whispers, thumb and forefinger pressed before my face, "to being dropped into the sea. Is that what you want, Min? Because I can absolutely make it happen. Do not think you are irreplaceable. Plenty of women would love to assist me, now that the estate is sold and my new shop set to open within the week."

My stomach drops. *Sold?* "You lied to me."

"*I* lied to you?" She cackles. "And what, pray tell, did I lie about?"

"I thought . . ." I swallow, push out the words that burn. "You s-s-said you w-would—"

"What have I told you about the stuttering?" she snaps. "Speak clearly."

I clamp my teeth to muffle their clacking. Only now do I realize how smoothly my speech has flowed these past two months. "I thought you w-were going t-t-to—" I wince, bite down on the next stumble. "Sell the estate to me."

Lady Clarisse blinks, head cocked, an odd gleam in her eye. "Sell the estate—to *you*?"

Has she forgotten so quickly her promise to me? I fist my hands together at my front. "You told me that if I b-brought you the East Wind's god-touched weapon, you w-would sell the estate to me."

She appears curiously stupefied by this information. "I'm not sure why you feel the need to lie. I never said that. Selling the estate to a wealthy buyer was always the plan, if I am to afford a new shop in town. Why I would ever give you the opportunity to ruin that is beyond me."

No. She's lying. She has to be. And yet, my spine hunches forward, as a dog submits to its master. "But—"

"Let me be clear, Min." Lady Clarisse takes two steps closer. The reek of old blood clings to her work apron. "You work for *me*. Your interests are mine. The things you care about are the things I care about. You are lucky to have the position you do."

"But I b-brought you what you wanted," I protest.

I've never heard a sound so derisive as the laughter pelting from her mouth. "If you had not disobeyed my orders to begin with," she says with false sweetness, "we would not be in this mess. Or did you forget that you entered the northern tower against my orders and released the prisoner?"

My eyes drop to the dirt road. Here, it is harmless, it is safe. "I'm sorry for disobeying you. I thought . . . as your daughter . . ."

Pain explodes across my cheek. I fall backward, hand pressed to the spot where Lady Clarisse slapped me. When I at last lift my head, I meet her cold, unfathomable gaze.

We have always shared the same eyes—or so I had believed. Now that I peer deeper, I realize how wrong I have been. Hers are utterly devoid of life. Chilled, broken stone. "You are not my daughter," she spits. "My daughter drowned years ago. You are my assistant. Nothing more."

With that, she rejoins Prince Balior, who creates a dark cloud onto which he and my former employer step. It lifts them into the sky, the East Wind curled at their feet, partially obscured by the vapor. If I'm not mistaken, his eyes open, staring straight through me.

"Lock her in the tower," Lady Clarisse commands.

A soldier wrenches my arm behind my back, forces my knees to the ground. I scream and manage to slip one arm free, but a second soldier pins me against the ground. "*Eurus!*" I scream.

Higher and higher the East Wind rises—east, toward the sea. But no matter my frantic cries, no matter my incensed struggles, he regards me with a blank expression, the withdrawn regard of a stranger, as if he does not know me at all.

30

From the northern tower, there comes a scream.

It erupts from my throat, cracking against the eroded walls of the cell, its pitched ceiling and filth-streaked floor. I slam my fists against the thick steel door, again, again, again, until skin tears and blood slides down my wrists. The sharp, coppery scent cuts the air's brine, and my throat constricts around another budding cry. Lady Clarisse is far from here, likely halfway to Eurus' island by now. She does not care. She will not come.

I slide down the door, limbs crumpling in a useless heap. A sob splits open my sternum. The sound bleeds out, collapsing into a cycle of fitful weeping.

Slow, stupid Min. Lady Clarisse was right. All this time, she was right. Because I did not see what my life had become. I could not separate my desire to belong from the truth of her character. She does not love me. She never will. And now I have sent the East Wind, the god to whom I have given my heart, to certain death.

The fault is mine. My previous life was not ideal, but it was bearable. I knew my place. I knew what to expect, every day a dulled reflection of its predecessor. Then, change: a prisoner in the tower. I could not have known he was one of the divine. I should not have questioned, but I could not help myself.

Now, with power at Prince Balior's fingertips and the East Wind likely dead, what will the treacherous prince do? With no one strong enough to oppose him, who is to stop him from invading Marles and making it his own?

Here, in the burying dark, I allow Lady Clarisse's poisoned words to drip over me.

You are useless, girl.

Not a thought in that empty head of yours.

Go, I don't want to see your face.

I shrink into the corner, become shadow. I make myself as small and insignificant as possible, yet another smear of grime on the floor.

This is what Eurus endured. This stone cage, this icy nothingness. For months, I listened to his agonized cries. It repulses me that I so easily turned a blind eye to his suffering. Yet here I am. *Bird.* It seems I was always meant for a cage.

When Lady Clarisse returns—if she returns—I will beg for her to release me. Then I will leave. There is no home for me here, not anymore. With the estate sold, I will gather my belongings and root elsewhere. As my former employer, she may have refused to promote me, but today, I grant my own title: bane weaver.

Wherever Eurus is, that is where I will go, armed with my poisons, poultices, and teas. I cannot imagine he would fold so easily, truth serum or not. The manor may have enchantments that further protect him. Until then, I must wait.

As I settle against the wall, however, something pokes the back of my thigh. I sit up, running my fingers along the worn stone and its hidden cracks. I tuck the chilled object against my palm, trace its slender shape: a key.

The spare key from Lady Clarisse's stash. I'd accidentally dropped it when Eurus swept me into his arms, preparing to launch through the window all those months ago. It is worth more than gold, more than the promise of immortality. It has but one name: hope.

Cold metal bites my fingertips as I insert the key into the lock. The sound echoes in the black, and I am heaving open the door, leaping across the threshold—

Three large men stand at the top of the stairs, blocking my way forward.

I study them warily, fists raised, not that it will do any good. They are twice the size of me. "Who are you and what are you doing here?" I bark, not in any mood for civility.

First, the tallest man: white skin, coal hair pulled into a low tail. His face looks as though it has been carved from marble. A coat wraps his broad shoulders, silver buttons lined waist to collar.

To his right, a boisterous head of caramel curls. I recognize this man immediately: Eurus' brother, Zephyrus, formerly known as the West Wind. Green tunic and green eyes, the latter of which crinkle at the corners, suggesting amusement.

The shortest man is also the broadest, the most still. His skin is darkest of all, the brown of pinecones, thick eyebrows bridged over a large nose. A violet robe, much like the one Prince Balior was wearing, swathes his muscled frame. It is he who says, "We were looking for our brother when we heard your scream."

My eyes flick to each man: pale, dark, burnished sun. "All right," I say slowly, "but that still doesn't tell me who you are." I lift my fists higher, just in case they suddenly rush me. I've the window at my back, still broken. Every so often, a breeze spirals inside—

I straighten. He said *brother*. Three men, and with Zephyrus present... "You are the Anemoi," I state. "The Four Winds."

The West Wind bows at the waist. "At your service."

The pale-skinned man rubs at his forehead in what I believe to be irritation.

The robed brother opens his mouth to speak, but Zephyrus hurriedly says, "This thing with Prince Balior has gotten out of hand. When we heard a rumor that the prince was returning to Marles, we decided it was time to end this before it reached the City of Gods. So we gathered at Boreas' fortress. It's really quite something. Hundreds of doors leading to alternate realms... Anyway, we pass through one of the doors to Marles. Came out of a woman's closet, if you can believe it—"

"Zephyrus," growls the tall, black-haired man. "We're wasting time."

The robed man steps forward, hand outstretched. "My name is Notus," he says, and his gaze is steady, his demeanor calm. The South Wind, if I'm not mistaken. "These are my brothers, Boreas, the North Wind. And you've already met Zephyrus, it seems." I nod. "Where is Eurus?"

At this, my expression falls. "Probably on his island by now. He's been captured by Prince Balior."

"Captured," Notus murmurs, frowning. He tugs at the apricot-colored head scarf wrapped around his hair.

"I'm sorry, did you say his *island*?" Zephyrus crosses his arms in mock outrage. "Why hasn't he invited us for a visit?"

"Focus," growls Boreas.

"It's my fault," I whisper. "I b-betrayed him, and now Lady Clarisse will kill him and use his heart's blood to create a potion of immortality."

The Anemoi gaze at me in various shades of puzzlement. Though they look nothing alike, I do note a similarity in their mirrored expressions. "Slow down," Boreas says. "Who is this Lady Clarisse?"

I shake my head, throat thickening.

"Min," the West Wind murmurs. "It is Min, right?" He crosses the old, worn floorboards to where I stand. "We can't help you unless you tell us what we need to know."

He's right. It is a blessing that Eurus' brothers are here at all.

Briefly, I describe my relationship with my old employer, why she has aligned herself with Prince Balior, and how they intend to carve out the East Wind's heart.

"Then none will be able to defeat Prince Balior," Boreas murmurs, his aloofness thawing into something resembling apprehension. "At least, no one in the mortal realms." He frowns. "We heard the beast was killed in the tournament. Is this true?"

I nod, glancing between the three men. "What about your powers?"

Once more, Zephyrus, Notus, and Boreas exchange a look of silent communication. It is Boreas who says, "Our powers are no more. We are mortal men."

My stomach sinks. Right. Eurus mentioned this, if I recall. He found the idea of his brothers' mortality downright appalling. "Can you handle weapons? Maybe a sword?" I ask hopefully.

Dark-eyed Notus lifts his chin. The walls of the estate shudder as the storm crawls ever nearer. "I am skilled with a sword. These two—" He gestures to his siblings. "Not so much."

"I would have my bow if *someone* hadn't forgotten to bring it," Zephyrus quips.

The North Wind looks prepared to shove his brother out the window. "How was I supposed to know you wanted the bow?"

"We were gathering to face a prince of darkness. Don't you think I would want some sort of weapon?"

"Not my problem," Boreas snaps.

"Why are you trying to help Eurus after so many years?" I ask them.

The Anemoi glance at one another, then away, each harboring a separate guilt.

"Our father was a hard man," Zephyrus murmurs, "but we could never have imagined the abuse Eurus suffered at his hands. It was our fault, really, for failing to notice sooner. We had our own interests, our own lives. The day he returned with *wings*—" He breaks off, swallows. "Eurus refused to discuss what had happened, or why."

It is not my place to explain the *why*. If the East Wind wants to enlighten his half-siblings on their shared blood, he will do so in his own time.

"It is no excuse," the South Wind interjects fiercely. "We were not there for him then, but we can be there for him now." He then shifts that clear-eyed gaze onto me. "Neither mortal nor god is spared the guilt of betrayal, or of neglect. We have all done immoral things. We have paid too high a cost. The question is, will you let it break you?"

I study the three men before me: the North Wind, the West Wind, and the South Wind. They have traveled far to aid their brother. An opportunity to set things right. A chance to make amends.

"Come," I tell them. "I know where we can acquire blades."

The basement below the estate is a soiled hovel, a hole in the earth. At the bottom of the rickety staircase, I light the wall sconce. The shadows withdraw, but only just.

Here, crammed between chilled walls of dirt, the air reeks of old piss and blood. The stench is so putrid I'm forced to breathe through my mouth. Lines of cells stretch end to end down the long, slanted space. The low ceiling forces Boreas and Zephyrus to crouch, though Notus is short enough that he need not worry about knocking his head.

The imprisoned creatures retreat from the sudden glare. Due to wounding or prolonged emaciation, they do not move quickly. Behind me, Boreas swears softly. I bite the flesh of my cheek as a deep shame rises from the depths of where I'd buried it.

I did not often venture below. Lady Clarisse spent countless hours here, gathering whatever ingredients—hair, tears, fingernails, organs—she required. If I did not witness the atrocities, then I could not be blamed for them.

"What is this place?" The South Wind's tone is low, horrified.

"This is where my m—Lady Clarisse—conducts her experiments on immortals. She uses their ... parts to create poisons and teas, which she then sells to the townsfolk of St. Laurent."

Zephyrus has covered his nose with his tunic. Boreas peers into a nearby cell, saying nothing at all.

It is clear to me now just how perverse her ladyship truly is. And how spineless I have been not to have fought against this injustice.

In the corner of my eye, an immortal slinks toward the cell door. It curls its long, semi-translucent fingers around the iron bars, the eel-like body clothed in tattered rags that may have once been trousers, a tunic. The creature gazes at me with large white eyes set over a slitted nose. In the end, I'm forced to look away.

"Has Lady Clarisse ever captured gods, aside from our brother?" Notus asks.

Zephyrus and Boreas turn to peer at me as well.

"Once," I admit. "A minor goddess, if my memory is correct. After extracting the necessary, um, supplies however, she let the goddess go."

"Does she release the immortals once she no longer has a use for them?" Notus presses.

Has a use for them. It sounds horrible. "Y-yes." I accidentally inhale with my nose, and the reek hits full force. I gag and quickly shift back to breathing through my mouth. "Well. Actually, I'm not sure. Lady Clarisse always claimed she set them free, but I don't think that's true," I mumble, my voice tapering off.

A faint scratching comes from somewhere down the line of cells. I study the men, wondering if they will punish me for my negligence.

"What did she extract?" the North Wind demands.

There is no easy way to say it. The words will hurt. "One of her lungs, I believe."

The men utter a string of curses.

"I can't remember any gods from recent memory though," I hurriedly add. "The majority of Lady Clarisse's tonics use parts from other immortal creatures, as they are easier to come by."

"You mean easier to capture," Boreas spits.

I drop my eyes, shame-faced.

"So," the West Wind murmurs behind the cloth shielding his nose and mouth. "Our list of enemies has now multiplied."

"She must die." Notus' deep rumble shivers across my skin. "She is a threat to all of immortal-kind."

Die. My breath comes short. "That's a bit hasty, don't you think?"

"You would allow her to live?" Zephyrus cuts in. "To continue hurting innocents for her own gain?"

"No! You misunderstand me."

"Zephyrus is right," Boreas says. Somehow, he has closed the distance without me having realized it. "Shall our list of foes extend to three, then?"

My back hits the wall. Dampness seeps into the fabric of my thin, cotton dress. "I'm on your side," I protest.

"Really," he growls. "Because it seems like you have known of this atrocity and have done nothing to prevent it. How long have you been working for this woman?"

"Leave the girl alone, Boreas." The South Wind shoves himself between us, a pillar of strength to break the encroaching wave. "She's doing the best she can. We need to keep our focus."

Nausea slips noose-like around my airway. It tightens subtly. "The weapons are over there." I point half-heartedly to a storage closet, the door partially ajar. A small whimper comes from one of the cells, and I wipe the sweat from my brow. I feel sick.

But I cannot falter now. I must take responsibility, and so I nudge open the closet, hardening myself against the sight before me: every manner of weapon and tool, the majority of which Lady Clarisse has used to draw what she needs from those captured immortals, whether blood or hearts, livers or eyes or teeth. "Take whatever will best serve you," I say.

In silence, they gather their weapons. I, however, turn to look at the long line of cells. I have run, I have evaded, I have denied. But I owe it to myself—and to those suffering—to witness the impact of my neglect.

And so I gaze into the cells. There are broken bones, open wounds, amputated limbs, missing eyes and ears and tails, cracked horns, holes in mouths where teeth had been. One particular creature looks like a bear or wolf, or maybe a large cat, with its arrowed ears. Difficult to say, considering the severity of its emaciation.

I'm sorry, I think. *I should have helped you. But you will suffer no longer. From this moment forward, you will be free.*

Upon reaching the end of the aisle, I remove the key ring from my pocket and return to the very first cell. The Anemoi watch as I begin opening doors, freeing those imprisoned.

One by one, the immortals scurry down the aisle, up the stairs to the estate. Some limp or hobble. Others growl at me in warning, refusing to leave until I retreat from view. I wish them speed and health and hope they are able to return to their homelands soon.

When I enter the cell of the eel-like immortal, it shrinks back. I reassure it in a soft tone that I won't hurt it.

"You're free now," I murmur, my heart breaking all over again.

As I reach out, the creature flinches away, yet I lay my palm on its battered face gently, smoothing away the flaking blood.

"Be well," I say, and follow the Anemoi up the stairs and into the light.

31

We run. Zephyrus dogs my heels, with Boreas and Notus bringing up the rear. Farmland and vineyards frame the dirt road, their grasses rippling in a brute wind. In the distance, St. Laurent pokes through the cover of dense forest. The single spire of its chapel rests as a white scar against the gray. When the lane splits, I veer right, the low growl of thunder warning us away from the coast. By the time the harbor comes into view, the first pelting droplets have begun to fall.

A shout draws my attention toward the town. Through the hazed drizzle, I spot robed figures herding St. Laurent's denizens down the main thoroughfare. Arcs of fine metal ornament their hands: swords.

"The soldiers." I turn toward the brothers in alarm. "They're taking the town."

People flee into shops and homes. Someone falls beneath a blade.

Notus looks to the harbor, the storm, back to me. "What do you want us to do?" he asks, fingers tightening around the hilt of the sword he carries.

They await my decision.

That old voice, the one that casts me as something insignificant and overlooked, makes itself known. It tells me in no uncertain terms that I haven't the right to direct these men. Who am I to dictate our next steps? I am no leader. I have erred, not once, but countless times in a thousand different shades.

It turns out, that voice knows nothing. I shunt it into an abandoned room and promptly shut the door. "Eurus comes first, but I don't want to leave my people vulnerable." We are farmers and bakers, vintners and weavers—unfamiliar with combat. "Is it possible one or two of you could stay behind to defend the town?"

Zephyrus steps primly forward. Two daggers hang from his belt loop. "I will stay. Truth be told, I'm not particularly thrilled with the idea of facing another great evil." He shrugs, suggesting it's a perfectly reasonable explanation. "And someone needs to protect all those delicious baked goods."

"Whoever stays behind needs to be able to *fight*," Boreas snarls, his frustration cutting through the hiss of falling rain. "You're useless with a sword."

"Now *useless* is a harsh word."

The North Wind glowers down his long nose at his brother, having acquired a spear for himself. "You should have asked Brielle to come in your stead. At least she knows one end of a blade from another."

"Funny you should mention it. I *did* ask my wife to accompany me. She refused, told me this was our mess to fix. Well, Eurus' mess." He crosses his arms, blinking droplets of rain from his eyelashes. "It's not like we have many options."

"Enough of this," Notus says, softly but not weakly. "Boreas, you and I will stay here to protect St. Laurent's people. Zephyrus, you go with Min. At the very least, you can swim, right?"

The West Wind wrinkles his nose. "Of course, though I don't know the first thing about sailing. I assume that is how we will reach his island? By boat?"

I glance between the brothers, their expressions fixed into various degrees of vexation. "Yes," I say, "but I don't know how to sail either." The thought hadn't crossed my mind, truthfully. I suppose I thought the vessel would miraculously direct itself through the storm, straight toward Eurus' manor. Stupid.

"See?" Zephyrus waves a hand. "It would be better if someone who has experience with this sort of thing accompanied her. Notus, you have that sailer of yours—"

"But I don't have my winds," he snaps.

"Well, I don't either!"

My attention shifts to the rain-shrouded harbor below. Its waters claw high. The vessels lurch, ramming against the docks.

One brother will not do, I realize. We four must brave the storm, the sea. The sooner we're able to defeat Prince Balior and Lady Clarisse, the sooner we can return to help the townsfolk.

"We will all go," I say. "Notus will man the boat. Zephyrus and I will help with the sails. And Boreas . . ."

The North Wind, who is drenched head to foot, glares at me with all the rancor of an irate kitten. I clear my throat. "Keep watch and have your spear ready."

Moving toward the cliff-side stairs, I carefully pick my way down to the harbor, the Anemoi bringing up the rear. The roaring tide sucks at the slickened docks, and the shutters of the harbormaster's cottage slam open and shut. Every so often, one of the waves manages to breach one of the creaking boats, dousing the contents inside.

As I scan our options for transportation, the North Wind strides to the end of the dock where the salt-encrusted boards sag underfoot. "How far away is this island?"

"Difficult to say," I reply. None of these boats appear capable of withstanding the squall's onslaught. They are too small, too wobbly, too decrepit. "It took Eurus less than an hour to fly there."

"Which means it will take us hours yet," Notus says, scrutinizing a nearby skiff. "And that is without sailing directly into the wind."

"I assume you know where we're going?" Boreas says to me dubiously.

"Of course." Sort of.

Zephyrus paces up and down the docks, rubbing at his arms miserably.

"Over here," the South Wind calls.

The sailboat he has selected boasts two masts and is surprisingly spacious above deck. Elegant script marks the wide stern: *Ma femme*.

After the brothers embark, Zephyrus offers his hand to help me aboard. Despite the racing of my heartbeat, I step onto the deck. While the Anemoi stow their weapons and bicker over who does what, I crouch near one of the masts and grab hold.

And we're off. As soon as we leave the shelter of the harbor, the first roaring wave slaps us sideways. The vessel pitches. I scream, salt dousing my eyes as Notus adjusts the sails and orders Zephyrus to steer us into the wind.

The Bringer of Spring clutches the rudder in borderline hysteria. "I don't know what that means!" Another wave sloshes onto the deck, and he yelps.

"Turn it to your left!" he shouts.

Deeper and deeper we venture into the storm. The sea grows so rough that half the time we are being smacked in some nameless direction. I cling to the mast with both arms, knees drawn to my chest and loafers soaked through. Twice, I nearly spew bile.

And all the while, I pray to the Master of Sea as lightning rends the sky in two and the wind builds to an ear-shattering wail. To our right, a rising wave collapses onto itself. It reforms moments later, having swelled taller than before. Terror cuts my heart clean through.

"Min!"

My head whips around. I blink through the sea spray as the South Wind climbs from below deck and strides toward one of the masts, a coil of rope slung over one shoulder. Of us four, he alone is able to maintain his balance as we're pitched and tossed without end.

"Take hold of the rudder," he orders me. "Zephyrus and I need to patch the holes in the sails."

I glance upward, trying not to vomit. One sail has a large tear near the corner. The other, a few smaller nicks in the canvas.

I swipe at my wet face with frozen fingers. "What about Boreas?" I manage through chattering teeth. "He is stronger than me."

"I need him to keep the sails open while we repair them."

A reasonable request, I suppose.

Despite my wobbling knees, I push into a standing position, clutching the mast while the boat pitches down the valley of an incoming wave. Higher the wave rises. Its black wall seethes before my eyes. I whimper, my airway squeezing so tightly it crushes my scream to dust as the wave breaks over our creaking vessel, soaking us to the bone.

The North Wind, who has snagged one of the ropes attached to the front sail, shifts his weight to the opposite side of the hull to prevent us from capsizing. His arms draw taut, the muscles of his back contracting as he pulls open the slashed canvas.

My arms do not wish to part from the sturdy wood, this pillar of stability. But these men are counting on me.

Unlocking my fingers from around the mast, I begin shuffling toward the stern, clutching the gunwale to maintain balance. The sea-soaked floorboards are treacherous, slick where algae has bloomed. Then the boat dips, launching over the curved shoulder of a great wave. I gasp and seize the closest thing in reach—Boreas.

We are airborne, if only for a moment. We hit the sea in a spray of icy droplets.

Scowling, the North Wind pries my fingers loose and directs me to the rudder. Once I've grabbed hold, Notus and Zephyrus refocus their attention on patching the sails.

The rudder fights me, wanting only to follow the sea's current. I do my best to keep it straight. Meanwhile, I hunt the waves beyond the thick cloud of rain, seeking rocky crags. A brilliant white bolt cuts the sky, followed by an ear-shattering boom. I flinch, stooping closer to the deck.

"Turn the rudder to the right!" the South Wind bellows. Somehow, he has managed to tie himself to the mast with rope and struggles to sew a patch onto the sail. Zephyrus works on the other sail with equal effort.

I shove my weight against the mechanism, each wave heaving higher than the last.

"Your other right," he barks.

The stern rolls. My feet leave the ground, fingers yanked from the rudder. I'm launched skyward, and then I am falling, plunging through the roiling black sea.

All this time, it has been waiting. Its pointed nails grasp at my kicking legs, the tangled strands of my hair, for it remembers me, a child, a sacrifice made so Lady Clarisse could exchange my life for that of my father. Is it fate that brought me here, after all this time?

Another wave bowls me over. I'm spinning, grasping desperately for an anchor. My lungs twinge in warning. A furious kick in some senseless direction, and something grabs my hair and *yanks*. I break the surface, retching sea water.

"Pull her over!" Notus shouts.

I'm hauled onto the boat. My limbs flop in a heap of drenched fabric and pooling water. Rain lashes my skin, and I blink against the sting. Seconds later, Notus heaves himself aboard.

"Give it up, girl," Boreas growls. He swipes at his dripping hair, blue eyes boiling against the gray. "You have no idea where we are or if we are even heading in the right direction."

"We just have to find the eagle-shaped rock," I manage through chattering teeth. "It's close to his island."

His eyes bulge in disbelief. "Eagle-shaped rock? In *this* storm?" He shakes his head at his siblings, who appear equally concerned. "We should turn back."

"No!" I shove myself upright, grab hold of a nearby crate. We spin, lurch, dip in a never-ending tumult. "We're close. We have to be."

"Are you out of your mind?" Boreas roars. "Any longer at sea, and there will be no returning home. We're lucky we haven't capsized yet!"

I scan our surroundings desperately. Rain, rain, and more rain. How long have we been sailing for? The marker should be close, but . . .

"He's right, Min." This from the West Wind. "It's best if we return to St. Laurent and—"

"No!" I bark with a glare. Boreas' blue eyes harden like two chips of frost, but I will not cower, I will not bend. "We're not going back. If you disagree, feel free to jump ship."

With that, I march over to the rudder, tilting the handle to the left so as to ease our passage through two colliding waves. I'm pleased when the brothers take their positions at the sails without argument.

It is a constant battle. I'm not certain how much time passes as we fight our way through the storm, but eventually, a large, dark shape emerges from the dim: the sleek head and hooked beak of an eagle.

"There!" I scream, pointing. "That's the rock!" And beyond: the crowned turrets of the manor.

Notus takes over, steering us toward the beach at the south side of the island. The wind and hail worsen, but only until we manage to break through the wall of the storm. Then, an eerie silence descends. As soon as we hit shore, I fling myself onto the wet sand with a small sob of relief.

Boreas glances away uncomfortably. "Mortals," he mutters.

"Don't forget, you're one too now," Zephyrus reminds him as he gathers their weapons from below deck and passes them to their respective owners.

A small footpath winds its way toward the great, ominous edifice in the distance. Step by step, I lead the Anemoi toward the manor, moving as quickly as the uneven terrain will allow. A side door directs us to one of the expansive corridors. It is a dark stretch, broken only by small wells of light.

"Not bad, not bad," the Bringer of Spring comments, briefly studying one of the oil paintings displayed against the elegant wallpaper. "I have to say, Boreas, Eurus' place is *far* nicer than yours."

"Shut up," snarls the North Wind.

Where would they have taken Eurus? Unfortunately, I never had the opportunity to explore the manor in her entirety. Might there be a dungeon below? What of barred cells?

"Eurus!" I scream, and the cry falls into an echo, carrying my fear down the shadowed passageway.

How soon would Lady Clarisse kill Eurus? Without his god-touched ax, she would not be able to end his life, but what sort of atrocities does Prince Balior hold up his sleeve?

As we pass by a sitting room, I spot a plate of food resting on a side table, the meal having gone cold.

I gasp. *The manor*!

"Can you lead us to Eurus?" I ask the enchanted building.

At the end of the hall, a lamp flares to life.

"This way!" I call.

The Anemoi and I race toward it, barging through the double doors at the end of the hall and emerging into pouring rain. A small paved area gives way to a long, grassy strip that veers off the edge of a cliff.

In the distance, the East Wind kneels, bound by shadow, Prince Balior and Lady Clarisse crowding his back.

Boreas sprints toward them, spear held aloft. Without bothering to turn around, the prince lifts a hand, and a tendril of darkness twines around the North Wind's legs. He hits the ground, the spear tossed from his grip. Zephyrus and Notus approach warily, their own weapons at the ready.

Slowly, Prince Balior turns. Lady Clarisse glances our way as well, but after a murmured word from the prince, she returns her attention to Eurus, shadow gradually eating him from the waist up. It appears to be keeping him immobile. But—alive. He is alive.

"Notus. A pleasure." Prince Balior regards the other siblings calmly. "And you've brought reinforcements. Let me guess." He points. "Boreas, right? And you must be Zephyrus, the annoying one." He smiles at the West Wind, whose expression has shuttered behind a chilling rage. "So glad you could be here to witness your brother's demise."

Notus steps forward. Though he and Prince Balior share a similar manner of dress, the South Wind's robe is soaked with water, caked in dirt. The prince is immaculate in comparison.

"Why are you doing this?" Notus demands. "Eurus has no quarrel with you. The beast is dead because the Council of Gods willed it."

The prince brushes a damp lock of hair from his forehead, where the skin has folded in perplexity. "I believed as much when it did not return from the City of Gods, but I am glad to hear my suspicions confirmed."

Beyond the prince's shoulder, shadow continues to consume the East Wind. His eyes are closed, his face slack. It has now enveloped his chest and reaches skinny tendrils toward his mouth.

Zephyrus must notice as well, for he has begun to inch his way toward Eurus. The North Wind sidles toward the opposite edge of the grassy strip, as though the brothers intend to surround Prince Balior.

"You see," the prince goes on, "a few days ago, something unexpected occurred: I experienced a new wave of strength. When the beast was slaughtered, its power came to me, and would you believe that I now possess the might of an immortal, like you?" His eyes crinkle. "Oh, that's right. You're no longer immortal, are you? I imagine Sarai is happy about that." His smile falls. "Then again, she was promised to *me*."

Notus clutches his sword so tightly I am convinced he will splinter the hilt. "Tell me you're not still angry that she broke your engagement."

"Angry? No. But I have my pride." He looks the South Wind up and down. "Had you not entered the picture, I would have had my power *and* your wife."

"Watch it," Notus growls.

Prince Balior glances at his nails. "I suppose I will settle for power. It may not warm my bed, but at least it can't betray me." He lowers his hand, which is now swathed in spiraling bands of gray, and advances a step.

Notus bares his teeth. "I would have done anything to keep Sarai away from you. Do you really think killing Eurus will aid your endeavor? The divine will not rest until you are dead."

He lifts his sword, extends the point outward, level with the prince's throat. The wind ratchets to a high keen, whipping the robe around his legs. "Stand down."

"The beast wanted Eurus dead for imprisoning him in that labyrinth," the prince replies. "I owe it to the poor creature to see its last wish carried out. I would not be where I am today without it." He extends a shadowed hand. "But you have a choice, too, Notus. Leave now, and I will spare your life, and the lives of your brothers."

"It's four against one," Notus says to the prince. "I will not tell you again. Stand down."

His adversary smiles. "I'm not going anywhere."

The South Wind lunges. Prince Balior stumbles back, unprepared for the speed with which Notus moves. As he hurries to shield himself, Zephyrus darts toward Eurus, with Boreas approaching from the opposite direction.

A wall of black smoke slams them back.

"Uh-uh." Prince Balior smiles at Zephyrus, having tossed Notus across the clearing. "Tricky Bringer of Spring."

Boreas leaps with a snarl. He evades one, two, three spheres of darkness, before one tosses him sideways. Moments later, Notus is locked blade to blade with the prince, who grins at him through their crossed swords. He shoves hard, a wave of shadow shunting back the South Wind, who dives, slashing at Prince Balior's ankles. The man parries the attack, flinging small shadow blades at his opponent in retaliation. Notus drops and rolls, but not before they cut through clothing, into skin.

"Notus!" Zephyrus tosses his brother both daggers he carries. Catching them in midair, the South Wind flings one toward his foe's chest. As Prince Balior dodges the first knife, a second arrows toward his stomach. The blade sinks deep.

The prince stumbles, face draining of color. Blood sops the front of his robe. "Finish it!" he barks at Lady Clarisse, then tosses her a dagger. She catches it with a triumphant smile.

My heart kicks once, then beats still. *No.*

I sprint for the East Wind, who is now entirely encased in shadow. "Let him go!" I scream.

Lady Clarisse whirls around. Her mouth curls in thinly veiled surprise. "And what are you going to do about it, useless girl? Go back to St. Laurent where you belong and await my return."

I stand my ground. "If you're looking for the East Wind's ax, I already told you it was lost during the tournament. You are wasting your time."

"As always, Min, you are continually two steps behind. I don't need the East Wind's ax." She lifts the dagger. "See this blade? A gift from the beast to Prince Balior. It is god-touched."

Lightning erupts overhead. Its flash of brilliance highlights the long hollows beneath her eyes, the cavities in her cheeks. If I'm not mistaken, the wall of the surrounding storm appears to be sinking inward, almost as if the protections around the island are beginning to falter.

"You're bluffing," I growl, though I dare not remove my eyes from the blade.

"Hm, well, I suppose we can't be certain." She peers at me through short, black lashes. "Shall we try?" The dagger spears down.

As the blade kisses Eurus' chest, I ram Lady Clarisse with all my strength. We crash onto the ground, through thick muck and trampled grass. The dagger flies from her grip.

I dive for it. My fingers wrap around the hilt, yet she claws at my face, screaming, "No!" Her nails catch the edge of my eye, and I recoil with a yelp, the weapon slipping from my possession as I hurriedly lift my hand to protect my face. Blood douses my vision, the world hazed crimson.

Lady Clarisse climbs to her feet, the dagger fisted in her hand, and I lunge, plowing into her stomach. We tumble backward, nearer to the cliff's edge.

She kicks out with one heeled boot. A pained *oof* leaves my body, but I grit my teeth, my sight set on that dagger. Never again will I cower. The realization is fuel, which births fire, and from that fire, the rage of a decade's worth of abuse.

I scream. It erupts, deafening, choked with emotion. Lady Clarisse's eyes widen as I yank on her hair, pinning her in place long enough to pry the weapon from her hand.

Pain explodes across my face, my head snapping sideways from the force of Lady Clarisse's fist. I drop, knees slamming into mud. Rain pelts my body. No, not rain—hail.

Through the blurred roar of the storm, I swear a softly uttered *"bird"* flits through the din. I blink at the East Wind. The top of his skull and a portion of his face have pulled free of the sucking substance, but he struggles to open his eyes.

Meanwhile, the Anemoi are locked in battle with Prince Balior. Together, they drive him toward the ledge, dodging his power, pressing their advantage as he bleeds out from the wound in his gut.

Something shoves me onto my back, and I blink, dazed, as Lady Clarisse sneers down at me, one hand locked around my neck.

"You are nothing," she spits at me. "A waste is what you'll always b—"

My fist snaps out, smashing into her nose. She stumbles backward, but the edge of the cliff is closer than I had realized. And as Lady Clarisse's foot slips over the drop, she snags my leg, pulling me with her.

I scream, attempting to twist free, but I'm already falling. My fingers catch the ledge, and a burn rips through my shoulder joint as I'm yanked to a halt, her ladyship dangling from my legs with a screech of terror.

Below, the sea churns. I blink back tears, praying to the Mother of Earth for aid, anything that might help me survive this day.

"*Bird!*"

I gasp. *Eurus*. "I'm here!" I cry, but the storm strips my voice with little effort.

When I attempt to disentangle my legs from Lady Clarisse's grip, she shrieks, grasping tighter, her sobs rising through the ping of hail on stone.

"Let me go!" I kick at her stomach.

She moans, her words a distorted mess of *Sorry* and *Please* and *Don't let me die* and *I'll be better, I swear it*. I grimace, trying to focus on maintaining my grip. Water slicks the rock. Its corners catch against my palms as they begin to slide.

Suddenly, two tendrils of air loop tightly around my wrists. My heart somersaults with hope as the wind tugs me upward, but then shadow lashes down, severing the bond.

My weight returns, heavy as stone. With Lady Clarisse hanging from my legs, I haven't the strength to haul myself to safety. My arms tremble with weakness. I slip lower down the rock.

"Please, Min. Please don't let me die." Her pleas reach me in muted waves. "Don't let your mother die."

I bite back a yelp of disbelief. "Oh, *now* you claim to be my mother? Where were you when I was young? When all I wanted was to be close to you? To lo—" I bite the inside of my cheek. I cannot, will not, say it.

"Everything I did was for you, Min, don't you see? Only through suffering would you become strong."

"You tried to drown me!" I scream, kicking at her. She breaks into another round of garbled weeping, arms wrapped around my knees as we swing, two leaves in the wind.

"And I was w-w-wrong," she blubbers. "I see th-that now."

My lips curl. "Stop stuttering."

She falls quiet.

I dig my fingers harder into the stone, teeth gritted. The East Wind will come. I just need to hold on a little longer. "You're not my mother," I spit. "You never were."

Only then do I look down at Lady Clarisse, the woman who gave me life but little else. I see nothing of Nan in her countenance, nothing of me. Grief warped her heart, and greed pieced it into something cold and unfeeling.

As her tear-filled eyes meet mine, I understand it is for the last time. "Goodbye, Lady Clarisse."

With a final kick, her hands fall away. She drops, her body breaking on the rocks.

I tilt back my head, blinking away tears. Today was not meant for death. Today was meant for life and living. What hurts is not what *was*. It is what *could have been*. For I have often wondered if there might be a life in which I knew my mother, and was loved by her, and known. And now that will never be.

With her ladyship's weight gone, I thought I'd have the strength to claw my way up the ledge, but the pain in my shoulders is unbearable. I hang there, a dead weight twisting in the wind. "Eurus!"

The soles of my water-logged loafers skate downward, losing contact with the rock. I dig deep, *deep* inside myself, dragging up whatever strength remains. But I am tired. My body has reached the threshold of what it can sustain.

I tried, I think. With everything that I am, I tried.

"I'm sorry," I whisper, and let go.

32

A CHILL WIND WHIPS PAST ME AS I FALL, AND I FALL, AND I FALL. The jagged rocks rise up, the dark sea seething below. A wave reaches for me. It curls, collapses into white foam. All this time, it has awaited my return, and yet, fear cannot touch me. I have come far. I have fought and risen and broken the chains that bound me. If this is where I end, so be it.

Something wraps my upper arm, and the abrupt cessation of downward motion nearly wrenches my shoulder from its socket.

An agonized scream peals out of me. Amidst the gusting storm, I swing wildly, rain pelting my face and bare arms. Somehow, I manage to tilt back my head. My throat locks tight around a gasp. "Eurus?"

The East Wind pitches sideways, and a great bellow of pain leaves him.

His wings. The right one is most definitely broken. The left has been stripped down to gray skin, its scales torn away.

A crash of thunder sets my ears to ringing. "We need to land!" I cry, pointing to an overhang below.

A powerful gust blows us toward the cliff face, but Eurus manages to guide us safely onto the ledge. As soon as we touch down, he collapses with a muffled curse.

"Eurus." Crawling to his side, I kneel, taking his face into my palms. "I'm here."

His eyes soften. He looks at me as though I am a light, a brightness in the encroaching dim. "Min." Wrapping one arm around me, the East Wind crushes me to his chest. "Thank the gods."

I bury myself in his warmth, and gradually, my trembling subsides. We are alive. We have each other, each an anchor in this storm. "I thought you would be furious with me," I whisper.

When I try to pull away, he tightens his grip, as if he cannot bear our parting. "I was. But then I saw you fight your own mother in a bid to save me, and I realized how blind I had been. I know you, bird. I know you're sorry, that you have regret. I should not have been surprised that you were acting against me in the beginning. I treated you horribly. I'm sorry I was not able to see past my hurt."

His apology heals some jagged-edged wound in me. "It's all right," I whisper.

"How did you get here?" he asks, voice low in my ear. "Did Boreas use one of the doors from his realm?"

I have no idea what he's talking about. "We did what most people do when forced to cross the sea: we took a boat."

"You . . . took a boat?"

"With your brothers, yes."

Eurus pulls back, hands on my shoulders. He peers into my rain-streaked face, searching. "You sailed across the sea," he reiterates. "Voluntarily."

"I had no choice."

"Of course you h—"

"No," I repeat, with enough force to halt his dispute. "I didn't."

Whatever he sees in my expression sobers him. It is another moment before he speaks. "Why?"

Does he truly not know? I thought I had been transparent with my feelings, but fear is a fickle thing, and I cannot deny my part in hurting this god I love most.

"Because," I say, "you mean more to me than I believed was possible. Because you are wounded, as I am. Because you are healing, as I am. Because I feel belonging with you." And security and tenderness, desire and esteem. "Because you push me to face difficult truths, even when the change is painful, necessary." And oh, is it necessary. But that is not the whole of it. Not even close. "Because I lo—" My throat spasms, and I catch my breath, push forward into the unknown. "Because I love you.

His eyes are deep, they are bright, they are fathoms, newborn stars. The emotion breaking across his features threatens to be my undoing. Is this the first that he has heard these words?

The East Wind is not taciturn as I had long believed. He is wary, he is guarded, he is mistrustful, but there is a gentleness, too, in his affections, once those walls have been brought low. In the silence following my confession, I witness the collapse of whatever shields remain, all that stone reduced to dust.

He says but one word. "Bird."

I bite my lower lip, tears cutting tracks through the chill rain. "When I said that I loved you," I quaver, "it wasn't a lie. It wasn't manipulation. It is how I truly feel. I *see* you, Eurus, more than I have ever seen another and . . ."

I collapse against his chest with a back-breaking sob. "I'm sorry." They are not enough, these words. They cannot reverse the ache I have caused. But I don't know how else to repair the damage I have wrought. "I am so, so sorry for hurting you, betraying you. I was so afraid and—"

"Shh." He rubs the back of my head, the tips of his fingers making small, soothing circles against my scalp. "It's all right, bird. You're safe. Nothing else matters."

"It's not all right," I weep. "I betrayed you. I broke your trust. I *hurt* you." And in hurting him, I hurt myself. "All because of some pitiful attempt to please a woman who has never shown even an ounce of kindness toward me?" I cry harder. It sounds so pathetic when voiced aloud.

But the East Wind gathers me close, as close as two bodies will allow without sharing skin. "I forgive you, Min. I do. And I'm sorry," he suddenly says, "about your mother."

I shake my head. "That woman wasn't my mother. My mother died the day she tried to drown me." No, Nan was more of a mother than Lady Clarisse ever was.

Pulling back, I gaze at Eurus with all the love I possess. Here is a battle-scarred warrior, a tortured soul, a god whose single-minded vengeance has driven him for centuries. But I see none of this now, only a softness in the planes of his face as he considers me.

We do not speak, only lean forward, mouths seeking as our lips soften into pliancy. One kiss becomes two, becomes three, each one venturing continually deeper, sweeter, hungrier.

In the end, I pull away first. "Your brothers," I whisper. "They came all this way to help you."

Eurus is not amused. "They will get themselves killed," he grinds out, then considers his response. "Well, maybe not Notus. Or Boreas. Zephyrus, definitely."

I am inclined to agree with him. "They may be mortal, but they love you and wish to see Prince Balior gone." Our eyes lock and hold, his uncertain in light of my statement. "You are the only one strong enough to destroy him."

Through the salt and grime and blood blighting his face, the East Wind grimaces. "Prince Balior's strength is greater than I believed was possible. I fear my powers may not be enough."

"What will happen if you are unable to defeat Prince Balior?"

"I expect he will continue to amass power until he has taken over the mortal realms. Then, I imagine he will set his sights on the City of Gods."

It is not meant to scare me, but to offer clarity. When all is smoke and shade, what remains? The understanding that inaction is a choice. I cannot afford to stand idly by. "How can I help?"

"You can help by keeping your distance. I don't want anything to happen to you. I want you safe, understand?" When I do not reply, he shakes my arms. "Bird."

"Yes, I understand." Though I am not willing to remain in the background as I was months ago. Perhaps there is something I could do. I may not be able to fight, but I do know poisons.

Mentally, I flick through the pages of *The Practice of Herbal Remedies*.

Before I can properly identify a solution, the East Wind shoves himself upright. Another gust nearly knocks him over, but I grab his arm, steadying him. Slowly, his wings expand. I hear a soft *pop*, like a bone slipping out of place. Eurus winces.

"Are you fit to fly?" I ask.

"It's not far."

That does not exactly answer my question.

He gathers me into his arms. "Hold on tight."

Looping my arms around his neck, I settle against his chest as he launches toward the top of the cliff where his brothers battle Prince Balior. We alight on the grass near the manor. It is still—too still.

I gasp. Boreas, Zephyrus, and Notus are shadow-bound, piled in a heap. The South Wind isn't moving. Boreas struggles feebly, and the Bringer of Spring stares blankly as black oozes across his face, blotting out his eyes, seeping down into his mouth.

"He's suffocating them!" I cry.

Eurus is already halfway across the terrain, releasing a great, bellowing roar that sets the air to trembling. His ax appears in one hand, and he hurls it toward the ground with ruthless force.

Air erupts to blast Prince Balior off his feet. Before he goes over the cliff, a massive pair of shadow hands pluck him from the air and deposit him safely onto solid ground.

The prince gifts Eurus a thin, closed-mouth smile. Blood stains the front of his garment where the dagger impaled him, but he does not appear woozy from blood loss, or even weakened from the injury.

"Your battle technique is efficient, though crude." He retaliates with an explosion of his own.

Eurus ducks, an arm raised over his head to create a full-body shield, a hardened barrier of air that deflects the attack.

And so it goes. A mortal man possessing powers divine. A deity who commands the eastern storms. Eurus reaches out a hand, dragging the tempest nearer to him. Clouds split and collide. A bolt of lightning tears down his arm, the sky flooded white.

As I squint against the brilliance, a large stone drops from the sky, thudding into a pool of muck only steps away.

I stare at it in perplexity before peering over my shoulder. Did the storm somehow blow a boulder from the beach onto the cliff?

Prince Balior leaps, one, two, three spheres punched toward the East Wind's face. Heartbeats later, a second rock slams into the ground, a stone's throw from their skirmish. Except... My gaze thins against the thickening rain. That's no rock. That looks like...

A startled laugh hiccups through me, and I look to the towering stone edifice in disbelief. A gap in the wall reveals where two stones have been pried loose. I suppose this is the manor's island, too. It is her home, and one always protects one's home.

Another rock peels away from the manor's walls. It arrows toward the prince's back, missing him by inches. The next projectile clips his shoulder. He spins, snarling, only to find an empty stretch of grass.

It is the distraction I need. As Eurus engages the prince in another round of vicious cuts, I dart toward his brothers, who lie smothered in shadow. When I attempt to drag the substance away from their motionless bodies, it suddenly *flinches*.

I frown. Nothing has touched the encasing darkness that I am aware of. When the next gust of sea air skates over the grass, however, the shadow again recoils.

Salt—a common ingredient that protects against dark sorcery.

I'm up, racing toward the manor, shouting, "I need salt!"

A bowl appears on the threshold of the doorway. I snatch it up, sprint back to the brothers' sides. Grabbing a fistful of the white crystals, I toss the salt over the piling shadow.

As soon as it makes contact, the darkness recoils with a piercing scream, gradually melting away until the brothers have shed that consuming gloom.

I shake the nearest sibling. "Boreas!"

He startles, fist snapping out. I narrowly avoid a broken nose. He glances around, wild-eyed, before his piercing blue gaze locks onto me. "What happened?"

"Prince Balior trapped you with his power," I say. "Eurus is battling him now, but ..." The East Wind dives to avoid being impaled by a shadow spear. He hits the ground, broken wings crushed beneath him.

The West Wind blinks blearily as he sits up. "Mother? You know I hate when it rains indoors."

Eurus and Prince Balior lock blades, one a bend of tarnished silver, the other a sheet of deepest night. Hail pelts harder, a sting against my skin. I shield my face, watching with mounting horror as the prince draws Eurus toward the ledge.

"He's going to throw Eurus over the cliff!" I cry.

Boreas attempts to stand. Notus groans and rolls onto his side, a hand to his temple. Zephyrus glances around in confusion.

I can't wait for them. Neither can Eurus.

I sprint toward the East Wind with all the strength I possess. Another clap of thunder shakes my bones as shadow explodes outward from Prince Balior and shifts into the configuration of a massive bull. I push my legs harder, throat scraped raw from a scream dragged up from the very depths of my soul.

The bull lowers its head. Eurus attempts to take flight, but he is only able to lift himself a foot off the ground before the pain of his broken wings forces him down. Seconds before the bull bashes him over the ledge, the East Wind tosses out a noose, which slithers under the prince's guard and wraps tight around his neck. The bull dissipates.

Eurus murmurs beneath his breath, one hand outstretched. Bits of shadow ooze from Prince Balior's eyes and nose. Despite his thrashing, he is unable to tear free, unable to block Eurus' wind-carved arrow from impaling his heart straight through.

Prince Balior gasps, body folding forward. With cold regard, the East Wind sends his winds through the now-gaping hole, stuffing air beneath the man's skin. The prince's shriek is so piercing it draws the hair straight up along my body. And as Eurus' power funnels into his black-hearted foe, the ax begins to disintegrate in his hands.

The sight sobers me. If Eurus is to defeat Prince Balior, it will require *all* of his power—power drawn from his ax; power siphoned from the storm that protects his island; power unearthed from his blood, bones, and internal organs.

Legs braced, he shoves his palms against each other, his expression carved from alabaster as the entirety of the storm shifts direction, swelling like a great tumor atop the island of rock. In his eyes, I see the will. I see the acceptance, the resolve. And slowly, slowly the walls of the storm begin to sink inward.

The winds lash with greater intensity. They do not wish to be directed, confined. But Eurus is their master. He crushes their dispute with his remaining strength and, with a final roar, funnels those last remnants into Prince Balior.

The man tosses back his head, mouth open in a soundless scream. His skin begins to dissolve, sloughing off his bones like ash. With a final word of power, the air ignites, tossing me backward with concussive force. My head slams against the ground, and the world goes dark.

33

"Min!" Someone shakes my arm, hard.

My eyes peel open, and I groan. It feels as if a sharp, slender pick repeatedly gouges the back of my skull, carving straight through bone. When I attempt to shift my head, the pain spikes, and I'm forced to close my eyes until the queasiness passes.

The voice comes again, ringing like a bass chapel bell. "Zephyrus, get her some water."

"Me? Why can't Boreas go?"

Another voice, withered by cold, snarls, "Do what Notus says and make yourself useful for a change."

"I don't even know where the kitchen is!"

"Then you best start looking."

The West Wind grumbles something about dictatorial siblings before his footsteps fade.

In the end, it is the sound of absence that drags me fully to consciousness. The sea, its thunderous roar, no longer overwhelmed by thundering skies. Just the feeding of its tides, those mighty fists hammering against eroded stone. The hum of drizzle, the ping of hail—that, too, is gone.

My eyes flutter open. Blue, its ample sweep, fragmented by wisps of white cloud. A feeble breeze nudges my cheek, and I gasp, clutching Notus' arm as he leans over me in concern. "Where's Eurus?"

The South Wind supports my back as I sit up, appearing worse for wear. "Near the cliff's edge."

Along the perimeter of the grass, a figure lies sprawled across the ground, the North Wind kneeling at his side. He doesn't move.

I stare and I stare. My heart falters, wanes, shrivels into collapse. "Help me up," I rasp.

My every limb aches, and my head throbs with excruciating agony. Boreas retreats at our approach, his expression somber, blue eyes dulled to murk.

I gird myself for the sight of Eurus, motionless. Eurus, broken, his wings crushed beneath him, black scales cast about. But the rise and fall of his chest is a ray of sun spearing through an endless fog. It casts all that was once gray in gold.

Relief weakens my knees. They buckle, sink deep into the mud patching the ground. I smooth back the tangle of Eurus' hair with a shaky hand.

"Bird," he mumbles. His eyes crack open, two slivers of darkness glinting beneath lowered eyelids.

And oh, I have never heard a more beautiful sound than his voice, that coarse rasp of two rocks ground together. My chin quivers. "I'm here."

One of his large hands frames my face. My eyes sink closed, and I angle my cheek against the warmth of his palm. I have never been particularly devout, but if the Mother of Earth—Demi—is listening, I wish to thank her for keeping the East Wind safe. For keeping my heart safe.

"How are you alive?" I whisper.

"Yes, actually, we'd all really love to know that as well," Zephyrus quips from behind me. "You destroyed Prince Balior with the entirety of your power. You should be dead."

Slowly, I swivel my head toward the West Wind, glaring all the while. He holds a glass of water in his outstretched hand. "Do you mind giving us a little privacy?"

With a shake of his head, Notus drags his gregarious brother toward the manor, despite the West Wind's protests. Boreas follows at a clipped pace.

I turn back to Eurus, who gazes at me with a depth of emotion I fear to dissect. "He has a point," I whisper.

As the East Wind takes my hand in his, the air wavers around us, a softened swirl of salt and rock dust. It lacks a certain something, this wind. It is gentler, less turbulent, its nature at last tamed.

"The morning we departed from the City of Gods," he murmurs coarsely, "I approached the council about my favor."

I search his eyes questioningly. "What did you ask for?"

"I told them I wanted to live the rest of my days in the mortal realms—with you."

I am warm. The chill of the muck sucking at my knees, the thin stream of sea air, it cannot touch me, cannot dive beneath skin.

I realize then how profoundly I'd hoped for this, but it was buried deep, all but entombed. I have been alone these last ten years, and I wish to be alone no longer. Knowing Eurus wants to share a life with me, it is more than I could have hoped for. It is *everything*.

I swallow once, hard. "You w-want to live with me?"

"Returning you to St. Laurent was always the plan. But falling in love with a mortal woman from Marles . . ." His throat dips, and if I'm not mistaken, color pinkens his cheeks.

"You love me?" I whisper.

Tenderness, I did not expect. Yet it is in his eyes, the tentative bow of his mouth where his scarring breaks the smooth line of his upper lip. And it is in the point where our eyes meet, a seeking of shelter, belonging.

"Is that so unbelievable?"

When I fail to respond, too overcome with emotion to speak, he goes on, "It did not happen swiftly, or easily, or even willingly. I knew what was happening. I did not want to accept it for fear of the power you would have over me."

As he speaks, his fingers graze my chin. Gooseflesh ripples down my arms, and I shiver.

"But I could not ignore my body's reaction to your presence," he continues. "How my heart would calm when your eyes met mine. How your touch did not incite fear for my safety. Over the weeks we spent together, I felt myself... softening." His lips part as he traces my mouth in a hypnotizing graze of skin on skin. "I was your captor, but you treated me with kindness, even when I did not deserve it."

"You did test my patience a time or two," I say pointedly.

He smiles. It completely transforms his face.

"And that is why my thoughts toward you began to change. I saw what I was previously blind to. Mortal or not, you were a woman, and there was fire in you, though you did not see it. I began to notice the fall of your hair, the shape your hands made as they clasped some object—gentle, even then. And your body..."

The tips of my ears tingle with sudden warmth. "Eurus."

"Do you deny that I adore your body? That I wish for nothing more than to mark it with my mouth and hands, so that all will know you are mine?"

After how thoroughly he'd worshipped me... I delicately clear my throat. "I do not."

His eyes crease with gentle amusement. "You cared for me," he murmurs.

"I did," I say. "*Do*."

He continues to trace my facial features, his expression wonderous, as though he has never seen something so unexpectedly exquisite. "No one has ever cared for me, bird. I grew up believing I was not worthy of love. So when you gave those things freely, it was difficult for me to accept that perhaps you truly did love me, as I had grown to love you."

Now it is my turn to frame his face in both hands. "I love you too, Eurus. I love all that you are, and all that you are not."

The East Wind pulls me close, captures my mouth with his own. Our tongues flirt, and he molds the subtle curves of my body beneath my damp clothes. If there were four walls, a bed, a shut door, I would climb onto his lap and allow pleasure to guide us. Never before have I considered a life where I could have a love like this and feel worthy of it.

With a playful nip on his bottom lip, I pull away. "What did the council say? What about returning home? Reversing your banishment?"

He blinks, and his eyes clear. "They agreed to grant me my wish. But if I want to live out my days with you in the mortal realms, then I must become mortal, too."

Surely he is not suggesting . . . but he is, I realize. The East Wind—*mortal*. "But you despise mortals. You think they're weak—"

"Not all of them," he corrects me. "Not you."

"Eurus—"

"Listen to me, bird." He captures my chin, angling my face down so I'm forced to confront every uncomfortable emotion splayed across his features. "You have taught me more in a handful of months than I have learned in the many millennia of my existence. You are full of courage and resolve. You are steadfast in your morals, unfaltering in your beliefs. You fall, yet always you push ahead, no matter the obstacles in your path."

There had once been a time when I would deny such claims. But I have weathered much in my relatively young life. I do not disagree with him.

"I have witnessed the gods struggle with simple tasks," he goes on. "They are given everything: health, riches, influence. Yet at the first sign of adversity, they collapse. But you, bird—" My cheek grows warm beneath his palm. "You are so much more than I expected from a simple bane weaver. You are good. Too good for me, certainly. You have shown me peace when all I have known is suffering. You have provided me refuge when all I have known is threat. And I would be the realm's biggest fool to let you slip through my fingers.

"I want you, bird. I want everything you're willing to give me, for as long as you're willing to give it. For the remainder of my life, and whatever awaits beyond, I will do everything in my power to bring you happiness. You wish for the moon? I will pluck it from the heavens. There will never be a day when you do not know, with complete certainty, that you are safe, and loved."

The sentiment draws tears to my eyes. I yearned for such things. It was always in vain. "If you are truly mortal, what happened to your power?"

"Gone." At my confusion, he explains, "I used every last fragment of my power to destroy Prince Balior. A god's power may be drained, but it can always be revived, so long as a portion is left in reserve. But I used everything I had. There is nothing left. Not even my immortality."

But his wings ... those remain, curiously enough.

"Now that my power is gone," he continues, "you will be happy to know that my hold over Ammara's rains is broken. They will have already returned to the earth, where they belong."

Gladness wells in my chest. Tucking myself against Eurus' side, I rest my head on his shoulder. "What does being mortal feel like to you?" I ask him.

He rubs my upper arm for a time, deep in thought. "It feels fragile."

"Life *is* fragile," I point out.

He acknowledges my argument with a dip of his chin. "I suppose I will grow used to it, in time."

"You do not regret it?"

"No, bird." I expect hesitation. There is none. "I regret nothing."

As for myself? I mourn the god Eurus was, yet I celebrate the possibility of a shared life, something once secreted behind the high walls of immortality. Without his powers, without the divine touch in his blood, is he still the East Wind, or is he merely *Eurus*? Does it even matter, in the end?

As it turns out, it matters not one bit.

"Does this mean you'll stay?" I ask in tentative hope.

The edge of his laughter catches. I dearly wish to hear more of it. "Did I not confess the depths of my heart to you?" He gathers me closer, so that not even a square of parchment could slip between. "Yes, bird. I wish to stay with you. If you'll have me."

As if there was any doubt about that.

I'd once feared the sea as I feared myself. I feared what lurked below, in the blackest murk, the farthest depths. I feared peering into its glassy surface and seeing some unrecognizable shell or cast. Something forged by Lady Clarisse rather than my own two hands. But water has its nature, just as I have mine. A river always seeks. It must know there is something more, something greater, than the narrow banks of which it is bound.

"I love you, Eurus. All I want is to spend my days with you." I clasp his face with both hands, marveling at its variance in texture. "That's all."

We come together as one. Our mouths and our tongues, our stifled groans and our small huffs of need. The kiss is a hunger and a comfort. For a moment, I swear our souls touch, just briefly.

When we part, he tugs me to my feet, and we wander to the edge of the cliff. The grass is damp underfoot. The island's crags have crumbled in the aftermath of the storm.

"What are you thinking about?" I ask, angling toward him. His patched cloak flaps around his shins.

As his thumb skates across my knuckles, his eyes sketch the horizon. The storm is no more. Never again will he call forth the clouds. Never again will he dam himself behind lightning and hail. "When I said I wished to stay with you . . ." And now he hesitates. "I didn't mean temporarily. I meant it in a more permanent sense."

I assumed as much. "As in forever?"

"As in husband and wife."

My throat squeezes to the point of pain. *This is real*, I think, *and so wonderfully, incredibly right.* "If you are asking me to marry you, Eurus," I manage through a watery laugh, "then the answer is yes."

Now it is his turn to gape. "Really?"

I nod. "Really."

Gathering me into his arms, the East Wind swings us in a circle, taking care with his injured wings. My laughter peals out, and my heart trills, sweet as birdsong. I can see it now. A quaint ceremony at the estate, just Eurus and I, his brothers, maybe a few acquaintances from town. I will wear Nan's old wedding dress and weave flowers in my hair. We will promise one another forever.

Hand in hand, we amble toward the manor, where his brothers have gathered in the shadow cast by the towering edifice. Sharp-minded

Boreas with his snowy skin. Devious Zephyrus with his boyish curls. Somber-eyed Notus and his quiet observation. And lastly, Eurus, who is hard yet soft, guarded yet tender. The Four Winds, together again at last.

"So," the West Wind drawls to Eurus. "Seems like you're one of us now." He plucks a speck of dirt from the front of his tunic. Not that it does any good. He, as well as his siblings, are caked head to toe in filth. "How does it feel being . . ." He glances right, then left, voice lowering to a conspiratorial whisper. "*Mortal?*"

Something the East Wind once considered inferior, less than. But Eurus, who has transformed in ways even I could not imagine, gazes down at me with love in his eyes and says, "It feels like home."

The West Wind pouts impressively. "It's not fair. Why do you get to keep your wings? All I got was an inclination for gardening."

"Zephyrus," the North Wind growls. "Please, for the love of the gods, just *shut up*."

The Bringer of Spring doesn't appear entirely put out by Boreas' aggression. I assume he is used to it. "Now that all this is done—thank the gods—I'm looking forward to returning to my wife," he says, smiling wistfully. "I'm sure Brielle has missed me."

"I imagine she's enjoying the quiet," Boreas mutters to no one in particular.

My mouth quirks. I was never gifted the honor of siblings, but I dare say it would never be boring.

"Not to divert from this reunion," Notus says, "but we really should figure out what to do about those soldiers back in town."

Right. The soldiers awaiting Prince Balior's return.

"If you need to get rid of the soldiers, I can help," Boreas offers. "I have an army at my command in the Gray. But I need to return home first. Eurus, can you still access that enchanted doorway I created for you inside?"

"What door?" Zephyrus frowns, trailing after his siblings. "Is this a secret door? How come I don't have a secret door?"

As the brothers disappear inside the manor, I turn to Eurus. "What now?"

"Now," he says, bracing my hips as he peers down at me with soft eyes, "our lives begin."

My lips quirk with gentle amusement. "Just like that?"

"Wherever you are, bird, that's where I'll be. Your happiness is my happiness. Your will is my will." He lowers his forehead to mine with a contented sigh. Seeing as it is impossible to squash the grin threatening to split my face, I let it come. "What is it you wish to do?"

Over many a month, I have considered this. I have shied from my own potential for far too long. "I want to continue Nan's work. I want to build my apothecary the way she always intended. And I want to do it with you by my side."

Eurus smiles. "Then I am ready to walk that road with you."

Never could I have imagined a love like this. It is not perfect. It has been forged in the fires of mistrust and betrayal, it has withstood cracks and broken edges, but I want nothing and no one else. Our love is beautiful. This I know.

Curling my arms around his neck, I draw the East Wind's mouth to mine, bestowing onto him this newfound beginning, where two hearts meet on an island of rock in the middle of the sea.

EPILOGUE

In which the East Wind Hosts a Family Reunion

There were some words Eurus loathed more than anything. The first was *moist*. Whoever conceived of the term should be eradicated—immediately. The grating whine pairing its articulation, the awkward shape it made of one's mouth. Truly, an affront to the lexicon.

The second was *ointment*. As an adolescent, he had used it to coat the burns that had ravaged his body, and to this day, he could not hear the word without returning to the dim, windowless room where his father had tortured him.

But the two words he despised most in the realm, the ones that dried out his throat and sent him dripping in a cold sweat?

Family reunion.

It was the reason why Eurus was seriously—definitely?—considering lighting himself on fire. That, or tossing himself off the nearest cliff, wings be damned. Mortal or not, it would be far less agonizing than sitting through an evening meal with his siblings and their respective families.

But alas, he had invited them all, at his wife's behest. Boreas and Wren, traveling from the Gray. Zephyrus and Brielle, to arrive from Carterhaugh. Notus and Sarai, journeying from Ammara. All four brothers, the former Anemoi and their wives, gathered in one place.

Eurus felt faint. And he never felt faint.

Hour after hour, he'd paced the sitting room, hands balled into fists. He fully expected to wear a trench into the floor. Min wouldn't appreciate that, considering the time they'd spent restoring the estate to its former glory. The grounds, once unkempt, had been properly groomed, hedges clipped and lawn trimmed. They'd patched the roof, refinished the floors, repainted half the rooms, tackling each project as it came.

Following the defeat of Prince Balior six months before, they had agreed to split their time between St. Laurent and his manor. Summer and autumn in Marles for the growing season and subsequent harvest. Winter and spring on their island, where it was restful. It had taken the villagers time to grow used to the sight of a winged man, but Eurus didn't venture into town often, except to wander the market with Min. And that's exactly how he liked it.

His wife, on the other hand, was thriving since having taken over the apothecary full time. Some villagers were disappointed to learn Lady Clarisse's beauty teas had been discontinued, but they were in the minority. *Lady Clarisse's Apothecary*—renamed *Nan's Tinctures & Teas*—was shifting its focus onto healing. As an added bonus, Min had even begun to make friends with a few herbalists in town. It warmed Eurus' heart to watch his bird's wings unfurl. If anyone deserved the world, it was Min.

Which was why, as soon as they'd moved into the estate, he'd destroyed the old broom cupboard where she had slept for so many years. The basement cells, too, were demolished, every square of blood-soaked soil buried in fresh earth. The former he'd replaced with an elegant, hand-carved bookshelf, which housed Min's herbology books. The latter was transformed into a root cellar. After erasing all signs of Lady Clarisse from the property, Eurus had commissioned a painting of Min's grandmother, which now hung over the sitting room fireplace.

As he peered through the window, a knock sounded at the front door.

"Are they here?" Min bounded down the stairs, flushed and bright-eyed.

"Unfortunately, yes." Still, he brushed a kiss across Min's cheek as she rolled her eyes, all too aware of his distaste for, well, everyone.

Today, as with all days, his lovely wife was dressed in flowing trousers and a lacey blouse, her black hair braided back from her face. With a frown, he traced the raised scar beneath her left eye, where her mother had attacked her. It had healed well.

As though sensing where his thoughts had gone, Min's expression softened. "Are you ready?"

"No."

She huffed, crossed her arms. Her irritation was adorable—and alluring.

Gathering her close, Eurus dipped his mouth to the curve of her warm, bare neck. Min squirmed, then drew taut with a soft gasp of air.

"What if we pretend no one is home?" he whispered into her ear. "We'll return to the bedroom, explore each other's bodies . . ." He trailed off suggestively, skimming her backside with the flat of his palm.

Min shivered and pressed closer. "We can't! I mean, we could, theoretically, but . . . no! What am I saying? Your *family* is here. They came all this way." She bit back a moan. "We can't ignore them."

"Sure we can."

"No," she clipped out, pulling away and adjusting her blouse. "We can't." Her cheeks pinkened, and the bob of her throat compelled him.

Once more, he caught his bird, diving into the honeyed pliancy of her lips, pulling from her throat a sweet sound of need before easing back.

Min lifted a hand to his scarred cheek, peering at him with a depth of understanding that frightened him even as it warmed him. "I'm here," she murmured. "And I'm not going anywhere."

A second knock. He didn't move.

"Eurus, you need to open the door."

Why? The reunion was Min's idea. He'd wanted nothing to do with it. Zephyrus, Notus, Boreas—they had their respective realms, their separate lives. He didn't understand why *quality time* with family was so important.

With an internal sigh of woe, he opened the door.

Notus, dressed in an amber robe and black head scarf, dipped his chin in greeting. He was accompanied by a striking woman with equally brown skin, her linen dress humble to all outward appearances, though the exceptional tailoring and exquisite embroidery along the sleeves suggested quality. As it was, Princess Sarai Al-Khatib of Ammara could have made even a sack of grain look fashionable.

Leaning forward, the former South Wind brushed a kiss across his sister-in-law's cheek. "Min. Thank you for inviting us." He then turned toward Eurus, gaze wary. "Brother."

"Notus," Eurus replied gruffly.

They stared at one another awkwardly until Min stepped forward to take Sarai's left hand. It was inked by an ornate tattoo—twin to Notus'. "Lovely to meet you, Sarai," she said, a twinkle in her dark eyes. "Please, come in. How was your journey?"

"It was quite nice, actually," Sarai said as she wiped her feet politely on the welcome mat. Noting the row of shoes near the door, she toed off her slippers, and her husband followed suit. It was thoughtful of them, Eurus admitted with grudging appreciation.

"Oh, my. This is lovely. I assume the decor is your doing," Sarai said to Min while simultaneously tossing Eurus a look of outward scorn. Not that he could blame her. After all, he *had* placed a curse on her. She had every right to be angry.

"Not all of it," Min admitted, teeth worrying her lower lip in shyness. "My grandmother decorated most of what you see."

"Well, your grandmother has excellent taste. I absolute adore vintage." One of the oil paintings hanging in the foyer caught her eye. "We stopped at a quaint town along the border. They had the most delicious bread I've eaten in my life."

A half-turn, and Sarai spotted the large, gleaming piano overwhelming the center of the sunroom. Already, she was moving toward it, fingertips fluttering across the ivory keys. "Do you play?"

A second knock drowned out his wife's response. Eurus' pulse tripped further yet, as if trying to escape his too-tight skin.

As soon as he opened the front door, a curly-haired explosion caught him around the waist and hefted him into the air. "Brother!"

Zephyrus, dressed in simple trousers and an emerald tunic, smelled of sunlight and sweet grass. He buried his face in Eurus' chest with a happy sigh.

"Put me down," Eurus growled.

"Say please."

Eurus yanked at his brother's hair until he was lowered back onto the ground. Brow quirked, Zephyrus arranged his curls into place. "Not one for affection, are you?"

Eurus failed to respond as a cooling, seaside breeze tugged at the hem of his shirt. For a moment, he missed his winds so deeply he ached.

"Behave," the woman at Zephyrus' side snapped. Her cotton dress, belted at the waist, hugged her every solid muscle and generous curve. She had a blacksmith's arms.

His brother ducked his head, properly abashed. "Yes, dear." Yet he gazed at her adoringly. "This is my wife, Brielle."

Min gaped at the ginger-haired woman. "It's you!"

Brielle reared back in confusion, then froze. "It's *you*. What are you doing here? I thought . . ." Her mouth fell open. "The man you were running from. That wasn't . . ."

Min nodded, fighting a smile. "It was."

After toeing off their shoes, Zephyrus and Brielle ambled into the sitting room, where Min offered refreshments. Meanwhile, Eurus loitered in the foyer, watching from a distance as his brothers and their wives surrounded his wife. Something softened in him at the sight. Perhaps this reunion would not be so bad, knowing it filled Min's heart with the joy of togetherness.

Such tender feelings dissipated as, for the third time, there came a knock at the door.

Internally, Eurus groaned. He considered withdrawing to his bedroom and refusing to emerge until sunrise. Knowing how much this meant to Min, however, he went to greet their newest arrivals.

Boreas, previously known as the North Wind, accompanied his family on the stoop. A black coat encased his shoulders, and eyes the fair shade of frost peered out from a narrow, raw-boned face.

His wife, Wren, bounced a toddler on her hip. She wore a sunny dress, her hair pulled into a messy tail. Their son, perhaps a few years older, clung to his father's trouser leg. With his dark features, he bore a similar coloring to his mother. The youngest, a girl, shared the light eyes and skin of her father.

"Eurus," his eldest brother clipped out.

"Boreas," he responded through a stiff upper lip.

They regarded one another with, well, not *outright* hostility, but at the very least, a healthy dose of mistrust.

Wren glanced between them in exasperation. Their toddler picked at her nose. "Are we going to be invited inside, or . . . ?"

Eurus retreated to allow his relatives entry. And that was another word he found particularly vexing: *relatives*. He knew nothing of Wren, or her children. Granted, he didn't know much of Boreas either. It had been an age since they had spent any significant time together. They were boys no longer.

Boreas' son glanced around the foyer before shifting his attention to Eurus. His nose wrinkled. "Why does your face look funny?" he asked.

"Grayson!" Wren crouched at his side, expression stern. "That was rude. Do you think my face looks funny just because it is different from yours?" She gestured to a sizeable scar on her right cheek. "Apologize to your Uncle Eurus."

Uncle? By the gods, he needed a drink, or several.

The boy, Grayson, ducked his head. His small mouth pursed into a pout. "Sorry, Uncle Eurus." Which sounded more like *Sowwy Uncle Yuwus.*

Wren peered up at him. He stared at her blankly. "What?"

"Do you accept his apology?"

"Er . . ." Out of the corner of his eye, Eurus caught Boreas lifting a hand to his mouth, as though masking a smile. "Yes?"

Gripping his sister's chubby hand, the coal-haired boy guided her responsibly around the room. Boreas smiled at his children before catching Wren's eye. She drifted toward him, mouth lifted for a kiss, which he bestowed. Eurus glanced away uncomfortably, seeking his own wife. Where had Min gone off to?

"Wow," Wren murmured. "This place is amazing. Boreas, come look at this." And she drew her husband into the sitting room. "See these windows? I'd like to do something similar. If we set the curtain rods higher, it would give the appearance of a taller space..."

Zephyrus had disappeared, as had Brielle. Sarai occupied herself picking out a tune on the piano.

Unsurprisingly, Notus was the only one of his siblings able to act rationally. He came toward Eurus, offering him a glass of amber liquid.

"You look like you need it," his brother murmured.

"Bless you," Eurus said, and swallowed down the liquor.

Min materialized at his side a moment later.

"Where did you go?" he muttered. "Why did you leave me with these people?"

"I was double checking the table settings," she said. "And *these people* are your family."

He ignored the second comment. "But you already checked earlier."

"Yes, that is the definition of *double* checking, dear." She tapped his cheek in affection and, he suspected, more than a little exasperation. "Dinner is ready."

Thank the gods. The sooner they ate, the sooner everyone would leave.

Slowly, everyone filed into the dining room. Gold cloth draped the table. Ivory plates and forest green napkins presented an impression that was tastefully whimsical, wildflower-studded vases arranged alongside brass candlesticks.

Leaning down, Eurus placed his mouth at his wife's ear. "It looks beautiful, bird."

"Thank you," she replied, a blush painting her cheeks.

Once everyone was seated, dinner was served. Soon, conversation filled the room.

Every so often, Eurus refilled drinks: water for Wren, wine for everyone else. Or rather, water for Wren and Brielle, seeing as the redhead appeared to be ignoring the wine completely. Additionally, he and Notus discussed Ammara's state of affairs, now that the rains had returned. With agriculture thriving, the realm was well on its way to recovery.

Meanwhile, Min was deep in discussion with Wren, Sarai, and Brielle, the latter of whom picked at her meal queasily. Boreas helped cut his children's food, but otherwise appeared to skirt the majority of the discussion. Lucky bastard.

"So, brother." Keen-eyed Zephyrus waved to him from a few seats down. "What do you think of hosting Midwinter this year?"

There were plenty of things Eurus would rather be doing, such as dousing his hands in hot oil. "You speak as though this plan is already in motion."

"But of course! Can you imagine Midwinter at the estate? Garlands on the mantels, wreaths hung from every window and door." He leaned back in his chair with a happy sigh, fingers clamped around the stem of his wineglass. "Does it snow here? We don't get much snow in Carterhaugh, and I've always wanted to experience a white Midwinter. I imagine St. Laurent is quite festive."

"If you want snow, then perhaps you should travel north, toward the Deadlands," Eurus growled. "I'm sure Boreas would *love* to host you."

His curly-haired sibling grimaced, all too aware of how deep Boreas' loathing of him ran.

"Zephyrus." Brielle caught her husband's arm. "You can't just invite yourself to people's homes. It's rude."

"What's rude?" Min asked, her attention momentarily pulled from her conversation with the other wives. She then began slicing into the cake she had set out earlier, passing pieces down the table.

"I was simply suggesting that it might be nice to host Midwinter at the estate," Zephyrus said with a pout.

Min straightened in surprise. "I think that's a splendid idea!"

It took Eurus a heroic effort to restrain himself from lunging across the table and tackling Zephyrus. He had no interest in making these gatherings a common occurrence. As far as he was concerned, once was enough.

"Then it's settled," Zephyrus announced to the table. "We'll gather next Midwinter at the estate!"

He glowered down at his dessert. Wonderful. Absolutely wonderful.

"Eurus."

His wife's voice drew his attention, and he found himself facing the loveliest vision of the most stunning woman seated beside him, her dark eyes shimmering with a love he believed to have been forever out of reach.

"All right?" she whispered, because of course his darling bird would notice his souring mood.

Maybe—certainly—he despised such gatherings, but never had he seen his wife so happy, so enveloped in belonging, his family now hers. It was a stark reminder that his own isolation had been a choice.

Maybe he could cope with his brothers' presence a few times a year. It was a small price to pay for Min's happiness.

Capturing her hand, he brought it to his mouth, skimmed a kiss across her knuckles. Later, when their family vacated the premises, he would draw her upstairs to their bedroom and show her with hands and lips and tongue all the ways he found her beautiful.

As if sensing the direction of his thoughts, Min's eyes darkened. "I love you," she whispered.

Eurus would never tire of it. Not the words, nor the woman who voiced them: his wife, who held his heart. He would have this—have *them*—for days and weeks and years to come. "I love you, too, bird, in all the ways one can love another." They would build their home. They would stitch their lives with shared thread. And his life would know peace.

"Boreas," Wren called from across the table. "Could you pass the cake?"

AUTHOR'S NOTE

Dear Reader,

Looking back on the Four Winds series, I understand that while these books are, indeed, fantasy romance, they contain a lot of emotional depth in terms of character development. I did not know it at the time, but I wanted to explore trauma. Specifically, I wanted to explore the ways it showed up in one's life, and I wanted to show that the things we carry do not necessarily need to be carried alone.

In this series, you will meet women from all backgrounds and walks of life. There is Wren, who struggles with alcoholism and feels that she does not deserve to claim space for herself. There is Brielle, who has begun to question her faith and place in the world. There is Sarai, who is haunted by grief and deep abandonment wounds. And lastly, there is Min, who has been physically, emotionally, and verbally abused from a young age and embarks on a journey to rebuild her self-worth.

These women are not me, but as with everything that I write, pieces of myself show up in their stories. I've learned a lot through writing this series, and I've had the great pleasure of hearing from readers who have connected with these women, readers who have felt seen. In this final installment, it is my hope that you will cheer on Min as she comes to know herself and her own inherent worth.

Thank you for traveling with me on this journey. It has been the honor of a lifetime.

Alexandria

ACKNOWLEDGMENTS

We've done it. We've reached *the end*, as they say. The Four Winds series has spanned over five years of my life (crazy!) and I did my very best to give our characters a happy ending worthy of a song. Now that we've come to a close, it's time to move forward, time to move on to the next adventure.

But before we can explore what lies ahead, I absolutely want to properly thank those who contributed to this series, because it really does take a village. I did my best to list everyone, but if your name slipped, I sincerely apologize for that and it wasn't my intention to forget you!

A massive thank-you to the Simon & Schuster Australia team: Anthea, Lizzie, Kelly, and Bella.

A tremendous thank-you to the Simon & Schuster UK team: Charlotte, Mel, Kate, and Sarah.

An enormous thank-you to the Saga Press team: Jéla, Caroline, Camryn, Karintha, and Shauneice.

A boundless thank-you to the rest of the Simon & Schuster team: Katherine, Desiree, Michael, Amy, and Ben, amongst others.

An immense thank-you to Story Wrappers and Demi for your amazing covers for the series.

A stupendous thank-you to Carlotta Brentan and Travis Tonn for bringing the characters to life in the audiobooks.

A gigantic thank-you to Robert Lazzaretti for your insanely beautiful maps (this one is my absolute favorite).

A gracious thank-you to my family for their support, especially my parents.

An eternal thank-you to my husband, Jon. You are the true MVP of this journey. It has been a long road and sometimes I did not think I would reach the end. Thank you for your unwavering support and understanding. Thank you for your belief in me. Thank you for loving me through the difficult days. You are my best friend, the absolute love of my life. I could not have done this without you. I love you eternally.

Lastly, an epic thank-you to my readers. I cannot express the gratitude I feel knowing you love these fickle heroes and strong heroines as much as I do. Thank you for every share, every review, every comment, every work of art. Now? On to the next adventure. I sincerely hope you'll join me.

A lush and enchanting fantasy romance, inspired by *Beauty and the Beast* and the myth of Hades and Persephone.

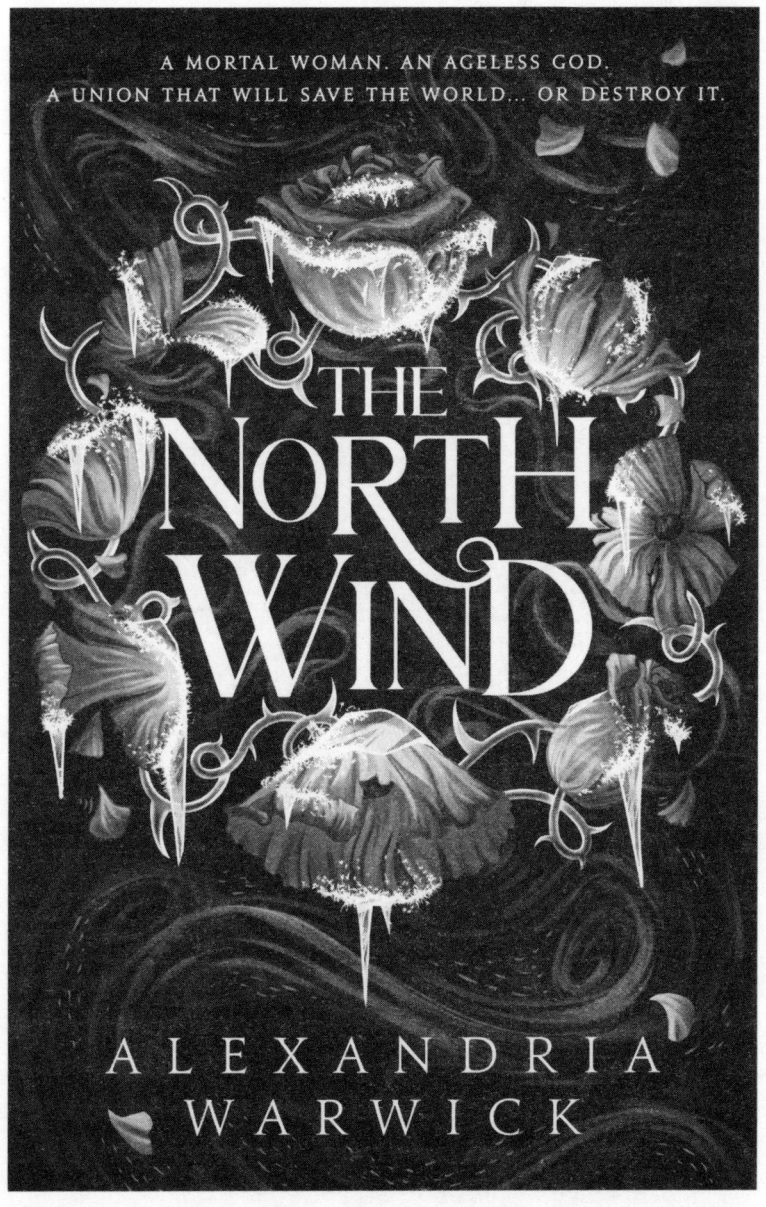

Part of the Four Winds series. Available now.

A darkly imagined tale of forbidden love, inspired by the Greek myth of Hero and Leander and the Scottish ballad *Tam Lin*.

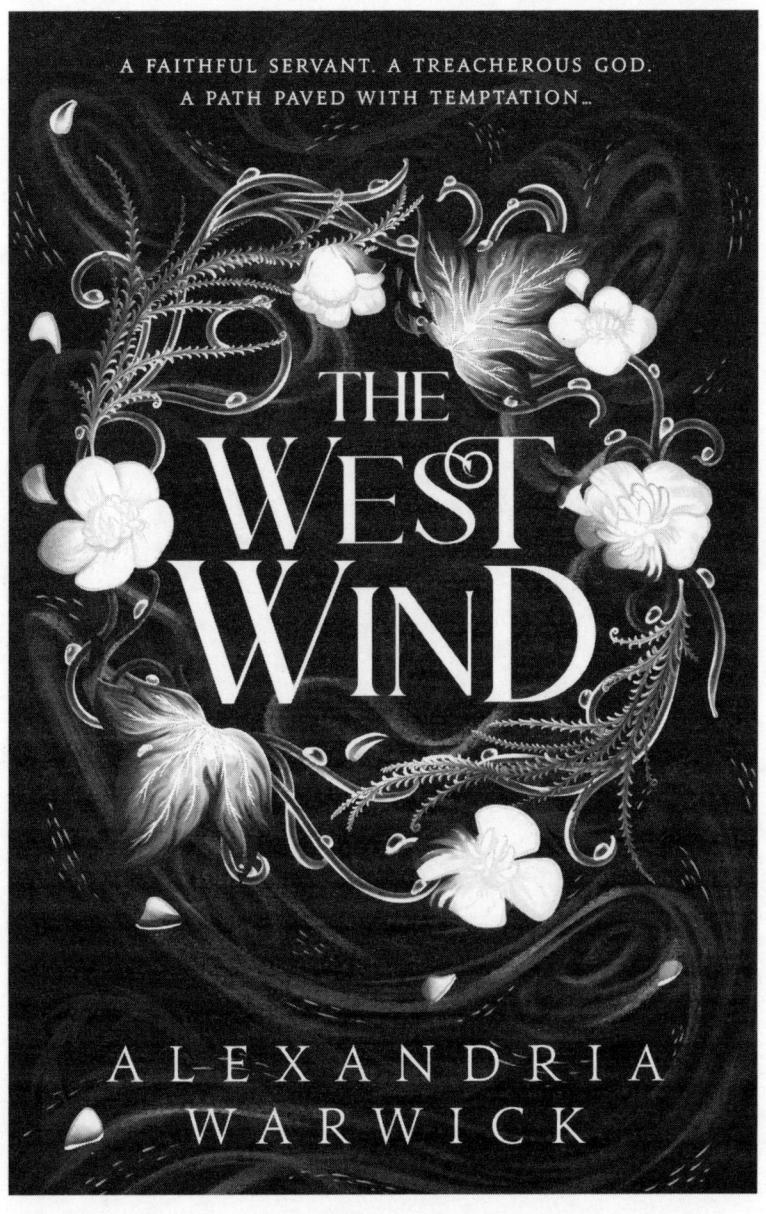

Part of the Four Winds series. Available now.